Cherokee: Left Behind A Saga of the Trail of Tears

Cherokee, Volume 1

Linda Rynell Kristof

Published by Proverbs Publishing, 2024.

This is a work of fiction. Similarities to real people, places, or events are entirely coincidental.

CHEROKEE: LEFT BEHIND A SAGA OF THE TRAIL OF TEARS

Dedicated to:

My Five Little Blessings. Zay, Brey, Nomi, Kay and Belle

I wrote this book with each of you in mind. God Bless you, and be with you throughout your lives.

With all of my love, Haama-Nana

Trust in the Lord with all thine heart.

And lean not unto thine own understanding.

In all thy ways acknowledge Him.

And He shall direct thy paths. Proverbs 3:5-6 KJV

Chapter 1
<u>**LEFT BEHIND**</u>

"Aw-right! I admit it! I'm skeered!" Never did like this big ole hidey-hole of Grammas. Seemed like ever since I were a wee one, I'd hated this big ole black maw, that opened up in the middle of her cabin floor. She kept it covered over with planks, with a bright turkey-red rag rug over it. Yet, in my mind, I could see clean through to the black beneath.

Reason ain't something I was plumb full of there's nothing to be scared about. Gramma's dried food and other fixings were sittin' on planks along the walls. The kettle of coal oil, and the odds and ends, and trappings of life filled out the rest of the space. I'd been down there with her but I never stayed down there by myself before. Gramma wouldn't allow rats, snakes, spiders, or crawly things in her cellar, but that ain't no comfort for this young'un.

"Why you so skeered?" I scolded myself aloud, *"you, the daughter of Ashbill, a member of the tribal council."*

I couldn't stop rememberin' what went on that mornin.' The day started right enough. Since today's my birthday, Gramma let me stay the night for a special treat. Good thing I did since my brother Hiram woke up the day before with speckles on his face, and they were afeared of the pox. It turned out to be poison ivy again. The little dickens ran into things in the darndest places, and always told us a wild tale about where he'd got to.

Gramma said he's a lot like Pa when he was a young'un. A mind of his own, that one. She could recollect Pa as a boy, and his Pa and Ma. Her girl, Elizabeth, was my own Ma. She'd known Pa from the time she was a wee one herself with blond braids down past her waist. Ma let her hair grow her whole life, and never cut it once.

Early, right after breakfast, Gramma gave me the birthday present she'd made for me. It's the prettiest dress I ever did see. She made it from bright blue calico with a scattering of little yellow flowers all over it. She'd tatted a bit of lacework and sewed it on the neck, and the edges of the long sleeves. The colors reminded me of springtime.

I put it on right away, it fit me fine. I laughed, swirled, and twirled, showing it off for Gramma. She told me to hold still as she unbraided my long auburn hair, she said it was the same color as Grandpa's hair as a boy.

She wet my hair, and brushed it, and brushed it until it shone like fire. It curled around my face, and all down my back. She gave me a hug and a kiss, and told me how purty I looked. I couldn't wait to show Grandpa, Ma, and my brothers. The new dress and my pretty hair made me feel proud.

I hated to put on the new gray pinafore to cover up the brightness of my dress, but Gramma told me to be sensible, so I minded her. Before I left, she tied a bright blue ribbon around my neck, and made a big bow on my left shoulder. Then she sent me out for kindling wood to start the fire.

Instead of bringing in the kindling wood, I ran down to Sugar Creek to look at myself in the clear water of the pool by the big rock. I turned this way, and that tryin' to get a good look at my new finery.

I gave up after a while, and went to say hello to all the pretty speckled trout resting in the water under the wide-spreading branches of the old oak tree. I loved this giant tree, and knew it saw a heap of living. It was thick around as a barrel stave. I nearly fell over backward a-looking up to God's heaven to see the tip-top most branches, it stretched up jest that tall.

Every day since spring, I went out to count the leaves as they came out on the tree. It was full now. I enjoyed seeing jest how big the new leaves would grow. Soon, before I knew it, summer would come quick-like. I wasn't much looking forward to summer with all the muggy heat, the bugs, and such.

Yet, today was my tenth birthday, and such a happy, pretty day, that I didn't want to think about nothin' else but how glad Gramma made me feel.

Just then, I heard some noises I didn't understand. I turned and saw a funny thing show up in the sky off to the east, close onto the horizon. A little finger of a dark cloud rose straight into the air from the direction of Mister Ned Storm's farm, my friend Lily's farm.

I climbed atop the big rock. As I watched, the cloud became darker and I smelled burning on the wind. A faint call in the distance, brought my head around. I saw another plume of smoke rise, then another, and another, one about each quarter mile.

I reckoned I didn't know what I was seeing, so I climbed up higher, to the top of the ridge overlooking the creek. The road which ran in front of Gramma's cabin had filled with wailing and sobbing people. They were my Cherokee people coming west down the road toward Gramma's farm, making loud noises. As they got closer, I could hear moaning, crying, and carryings on.

There were soldiers on horseback yelling at them to move faster. They hollered, shook their long rifles, and prodded our people to hurry up. I don't know why the soldiers forced them to leave their fine homes, nice farms and businesses.

In the distance, I saw my own folks, and our neighbors huddling together as they marched. My Pa led a portion of the tribe as was fitting for a member of the tribal council. Ma hurried along beside him, her head high, tears running down her cheeks, her hand held tight against her mouth to stifle her sobs. My brothers, Hiram, and baby Earl, marched along with other boys from the neighborhood as if it were a fun game.

Then it come to me, everyone I knew and loved was out there marching away from me.

"Ma! Ma!" I cried out, with tears running down my cheeks! *Don't leave me! I want to go too!"*

Gramma ran toward me, and frantically called out. *"Caroline! Caroline! Come down now. We must run! Run and hide! I won't let them take you! We need to run and hide, Child!"*

I stood stock still, as stiff as the old dead coon our hound Thumper drug home last week. What did Gramma mean run and hide? Was this a game? What's it all about?

As Gramma ran and searched for me, her blond hair came loose from its pins and whipped across her face. Her blue eyes held a terror I'd never seen before in the eyes of my sweet Gramma.

From off to the east came the sound of more gunshots. Scared now, I climbed down, and Gramma reached out and drug me beneath the low branches of the towering oak. I saw all the mud there from last night's rain. I didn't want to spoil my new dress, but Gramma made me go under the tree just the same.

I strained hard against her. I needed to go find Ma to see what hurt her, but Gramma held me so tight I couldn't move. It felt like her life depended on me staying right there by her side.

Later, Gramma snuck me in the house and into the cellar. I cried and cried. She left me alone, shivering, wet, cold, and muddy while she went back upstairs.

She brought down a lantern, and a basin of water for me to wash in. Then she asked me to change into dry clothes. I wanted to put on my new dress, but I saw by the lantern light, the dress was all muddy. I cried harder, and Gramma cried too.

Later she brought me food and water, but she refused to leave me a candle to light the surrounding darkness. I ate, wrapped my quilt close around me, and laid down to snooze on a little pallet she made for me on the floor. Like I said before, I was scared but Gramma told me I'd got to be brave.

TWO DAYS, WENT BY BEFORE Gramma let me out of the cellar for a bit. She told me as best as she could, that the government of the United States decided my tribe, the Cherokees, held no rights to their big farms, nice houses, and their own businesses. They forced the people from their homes and marched them away to a reservation.

She told how Grandpa traveled to the state capitol in Nashville, to ask the government to change its mind, and bring our folks back home. Gramma didn't hold out much hope though.

The more I thought about it, the more that put me in mind of the stories Ma read me from the Good Book. I remembered the story about the long trek the Israelites first took to Egypt. God traveled with the Israelites. I have to trust that He traveled with my folks too, as they walked to their new promised land on a reservation in the west.

After Gramma told me the news, I turned into her big white apron, and blubbered like a little baby child, instead of a big girl jest turned ten years old. I felt my innards burstin' with the grief I'd held back. When I finished cryin', I felt some better, but I cain't see what the future held fer me.

FULL SPRING COME TO us late in the year. The days of sullen, rainy weather matched my feelings as if all of nature mourned too. By the beginning of July, I'd come to grips with my situation.

My folks were gone and likely I'd never see them again. What hurt me most was not getting to say goodbye to Ma. Even now tears come up in my eyes every time I thought of her sobbing her way down the road. I'd never seen Ma cry!

Gramma's been real good to me. She told me I'd be her girl now since her own girl was away off across the country. I knew I'm not alone in my grief, Gramma lost folks she loved too. She lost my

Mama, who was her own little girl, her two grandsons, my Pa, and all her friends and neighbors.

When Grandpa returned from the state capitol in Nashville, he didn't march as proud as I remembered. He looked and acted different somehow.

He pulled open the latchstring and stood in the cabin doorway. It seemed like he'd shrunk, his face hollowed out like he hadn't eaten a meal in a good long time. His eyes bothered me the most, like the eyes of the hurt little fawn that I come across out in the woods one day last summer. Grandpa seemed about worn out as if he wanted to lie right down and never get up again.

Well, that only lasted a second, for when he got an eyeful of me, he let out a whoop that only came in second to my brother Hiram's best war-whoop. Grandpa grabbed me up and held me to his chest, his eyes filled with tears and he cried like a baby.

"Thank you, God! Thank you, Lord Jesus! Thank you for sparing one of my young'uns!" He cried out between his sobs. Then he slumped down on the floor and held me to him for a spell, until Gramma told me to skedaddle down to the creek, and bring back a bucket full of water for Grandpa to wash up in.

When I lugged the water back to the house, they were together in their partitioned-off room, where Gramma helped Grandpa off with his boots. I set the water down on the table, and tiptoed back outside shivering a bit in the cold rain, it seemed like they wanted to be alone together.

Our dog Thumper ran over to me, and licked my face to satisfy himself that I was still there. I don't want nothin' to do with him, and his slobbery, muddy kisses. That ole coonhound still runs over to our cabin looking for my brothers. When he can't find them, he looks for me to pet him. I humor him because he's all I got left of my own, exceptin' for Gramma and Grandpa.

As I ran out to my favorite spot next to Sugar Creek, the rain slacked up some, and I climbed up on the high ledge overlooking the big rock with the road in the distance. I sat and watched the creek water run away toward the west, and thought about what had gone on with me lately.

Selfish I know, but things are different now since Gramma won't let me out of her sight. If anyone comes to the house, I quick-like hide under her bed in the partitioned-off room. If she knew they's coming to stay for a while, she quick pries open the hidey-hole, and down I go again, into the dark. I'm getting used to the dark now, and I have my things down there all spread out as if I owned the place.

I lost my doll, Sarah. I felt bad because I named her for a girl I knew, and liked from school. So, Gramma made me a new doll from a gourd, with a round wooden head made from a large bead. She covered her head with hair she used from Thumper's tail. She combed it straight, braided it, and wound it around her head. We painted her features with ink, and I made her clothes from the scrap bag. She's a colorful friend. I named her Sarah number two.

We heard rumors that some of our Indian families ran away from the soldiers and lived in the woods, some by Cove Knob, and others near Calf Killer River. We don't know for sure though, as no one's seen them.

Wish't my Pa had run my family away, too, but you have to understand Pa to see how he thought. He believed in the Good Book, and he always said we had to respect those in authority.

Well, when the United States Government, and the Cherokee Council couldn't reach an agreement, he knew it could come to the government taking us away from our land. He right out said we'd go. He didn't want any of our tribe hurt. If the tribe had sworn allegiance to the government of the United States, and become citizens, they could have stayed home, but they wouldn't. They believed in a sovereign Cherokee Nation.

Gramma told me, "It was the Grace of God that spared you, Caroline," from what she called the removal. I think God wanted me here to look after Grandpa and Gramma. I don't know how I'd do it, but I believe he'd tell me in time.

Grandpa's real quiet these days, not like him at all, beings as he's a preacher man borned in Virginia. He and Gramma were friends out there when they were young. He attended college, and met several young Cherokee Indian men at the college. They told him of the need for God in Tennessee. After his schooling, Grandpa heard God calling him to minister to the Cherokee Indians in Tennessee.

Grandpa said he felt peace about the members of his church taken away by the soldiers. He knew they marched with God by their side. He didn't know why God allowed the removal to happen to the Cherokee, Creeks, Seminoles, and the other tribes, but he thought it's because of the greed of the white men.

He's ashamed of his people, and he believed God needed him here to work with the rest of our tribe. He rode out every day searching for them in the hills. There might be three hundred people hidin' out there.

Grandpa told me word came that my Pa's group reached a town a month after they left here. I think he said that to comfort me. Yet later, I heard Grandpa tell Gramma that the soldiers penned our people behind wire at a fort. The people still shed many tears. I cried too, when I heard the bad news. I don't want my family penned up like animals.

Grandpa said storms followed upon each other leaving the people cold, damp, and sorrowful. They caught pleurisy and the ague. He said many of them got sick, and some died. He don't know how much longer my family would be locked up in the fort before the soldiers would march them west. I prayed to God to save my family.

Last week when Gramma come back from town, she told us about the many new white faces at the general store. She said it took all her Christian fortitude to be civil to the other women. She looked angry when she said the name of the family who took over Ma and Pa's farm.

The greed of the white people, and their lust for gold led to the loss of my family, and our beautiful farm. The government said the Cherokee were not allowed to own gold, or dig for it on their own land.

"Caroline! Caroline? You daydreaming out there again, Gal? We've got the chores to do. Come quickly now," Gramma called to me from the doorway, of the cabin.

I looked back toward the house from my spot high on the ledge overlooking Sugar Creek. It's hard to pull myself away. I spend a lot of my time up here thinking of all the bad that's happened to us. I should stop and jest think about the pretty life I used to live with my folks.

Remembering the good don't seem to help me much. It jest made me sad. I needed some good new memories inside my head to erase all the bad ones there now.

The cold rain began beating down on me. I knew I'd been shivering for quite a while. "Here I am! I'm comin' right now, Gramma!"

The memories continued as I walked back to the house, dodging raindrops and puddles, and even later while I worked at my chores. I finally decided it helped me some to remember the good life I lived with my folks.

Chapter 2
<u>TRAPPED</u>

The year I turned seven years old, Pa moved us north to our new home to live near Grandpa and Gramma. There were four of us in our family, then a year after we moved Ma had another baby. I was eight, and my brother Hiram was four years old. The new baby, my brother Earl, became special to me. I cared for him as if he was my own, so much better playing with a real baby, than playing with my doll.

Before we moved, we lived in Georgia, south of the border with Tennessee. Things heated up with politics, and such, so Pa thought we'd be safer in middle Tennessee. Many of our tribe moved then, too. Before long, our neighbors lived around us again.

Pa built us a big cabin, as befits a member of the Cherokee Tribal Council, or even a white man. Our home, built of logs dabbed with mud, was jest like the old cabin that came with the land, but made like two houses one atop another. We stayed in the old cabin while Pa built our new home, later he used it to lodge the men he hired to help harvest the crops.

The top floor of the new cabin was big enough to hold a barn dance. Pa split it up into rooms. My own room was there, snugged right up against the chimney for warmth. I loved my room with its glass window a-looking out over the woods. The window became a link to the world outside, and that world was a big part of me.

Sometimes birds flew onto the sill and peeked in at me. I watched the sunrise in the mornings from my bed in the corner, and I watched the clouds as much as I liked. In the evening, the sunset, the moon and stars rose in the sky just for me. The wind and rain sometimes beat against the windowpane, and it often thundered, yet I never got scared.

My brother Hiram slept in the room next door. He was loud, and his antics made me less lonesome up there away from Ma and Pa. I was snug, comforted, warm, and protected. There was also a small room upstairs where Ma sewed. She brought up a small rocker, and odds and ends of a table and chairs.

Sometimes in the evenings, she'd come upstairs, and gather us around as she rocked in her chair. She told us tales of the Cherokees and other stories that Gramma told of her own family, where she grew up in Norfolk, Virginia, near the sea. We liked the stories of our Cherokee people better than the ones of big city life. Those were harder for us to understand.

Now, mind you, Ma wasn't even a little Cherokee, she had long blond hair and beautiful blue eyes. She grew up here with our people living close around her. She later married up with Pa, and took to the tribe like a pureblood.

Pa claims to be Cherokee clean through, but I suspect otherwise, his bright blue eyes give him away. He told me of a tribe of white men who lived in the south for many years. He never knew who they were, or where they come from, or where they disappeared to. He said the Indian tribes intermarried with these mysterious people. Maybe that's where Pa's blue eyes come from, but I don't really know.

Pa's, pa, and his ma died during an epidemic twelve years before Ma birthed me. Pa was a young man then. After he lost his folks, he began living with a family in our tribe, and they raised him to manhood. Pa told me that much, and I never thought to ask him anymore.

I missed my old home, so one day I took the bull by the horns, as Gramma was apt to say, and sneaked away to our farm instead of fetching water for our dinner. It wasn't my fault though. When I was on my way to the stream, our dog Thumper come up to me, and run off toward our farm over the next hill.

The notion come over me, that I should visit our farm one more time. Gramma would skin me if she ever found out, but I thought she'd never know. I'd run fast and it would only take a minute. Turned out, I ended up having an adventure I'm not proud of.

As many times as we ran over to visit Gramma and Grandpa from our home place, we wore a deep rut through the undergrowth. The bushes parted naturally to let me pass. I felt at home there in the midst of the lush landscape.

A little shiver of anticipation ran along my spine as I passed my play party tree. I stopped for a minute to see how things stood. I still remembered the day last spring before the removal, when my best friend Lily Storm left in a huff, and kicked aside my carefully arranged luncheon of dandelion greens.

I searched around in the dirt, and come up with two thimble-sized acorn cups that we'd used for our dolls' tea. I dropped them in my pocket, and ran off after Thumper, crossing over the creek where Hiram and Earl liked to fish for striped bass.

Next, I come to the big white sycamore tree marking the edge of our land. It did my heart good to see the fields where Pa toiled raising wheat and corn. I always loved the smell of the earth after Pa turned over the raw soil with the plow.

In my mind, I could still see Pa plowing with our horses. I thought about the warm summer days when Ma would let me carry the big wicker basket, full of good food, for Pa and his workers to eat in the fields at dinnertime.

A shivering chill come over me. It was cold for July, but my shivering was from more than the cold. Since I was seeing our farm for the first time since the removal, it felt like death, my old life died and my family seemed dead too, dead and gone.

Pa never put in a crop last spring, and the new owner hadn't farmed the land. He wouldn't have anything to harvest in September. Was he a rich man with no need to work? I'd never heard of anyone rich in our neighborhood. The empty fields made me feel sad. It was too quiet out here with not even a bird singing.

Gettin' near the house and barn, I sunk under the cover of some bushes. A small boy, and a girl around my own age ran after our chickens, scaring them until they scattered. I wanted to shout in indignation. Hadn't anyone ever told these silly creatures if you shake up a hen, she won't lay? They didn't seem to care much.

My home had suffered too, the window curtains hung askew, the porch rocking chairs were overturned and broken, and the front door of the cabin stood ajar. It hurt me to see how they'd destroyed my home.

Those people also trampled Ma's pride and joy, the wild rose bushes and such, that she transplanted from the woods. It looked like a herd of black bears run them right into the ground.

I stood, and made a grab for Thumper as he rushed forward and made a wild leap at the young boy who pulled Earl's little wheelbarrow around the barn lot. I couldn't stop him! The horror flowed right through me.

It was my fault! I shouldn't have run off from Gramma's farm or this wouldn't have happened. I can't lose Thumper, he's all I got! I'd already lost too much.

I whistled, and called for him, but he refused to come. Finally, I chanced those people seeing me, and ran into the open. I whispered to Thumper to mind, and pulled on the loose skin of his neck. He refused to budge.

"Thumper!" I cried out in dismay. "Come home with me, boy!" Tears ran down my cheeks, and terror filled my heart as the girl ran over and began hitting Thumper with a stick. Thumper never even hurt a bug in his whole life. His size and the fierceness of his bark kept anyone from messin' with him.

He growled, and I guess that scared those kids. They ran screaming for the house. The white woman stood at the door with a gun pointed right at me.

"You're one of them redskins, I know," she said in a loud voice. "Your skin color gives you away. I thought we'd got rid of the lot of you."

"No, Ma'am," I told her politely. "I jest come after my dog when your boy set him to barkin'."

"I know that worthless hound," she said. "He comes around here all the time. We've been missin' chickens lately, and he's the one that's a-thievin' 'em."

"No, Ma'am, Thumper never killed one of our chickens in his whole life." I began edging back from the woman. I grabbed a hold of Thumper by the back of his neck and tried to pry him away, but he stood there stubborn and stiff-legged, a-barking and a-carrying on. Finally, I ran for my life.

A huge, flabby white man rushed out of the barn. He caught ahold of me, twisted my arm hard, and bent it up behind my back.

"Stay still or you'll get hurt!" He growled at me.

I grew quiet under his abuse, and shut my eyes real tight. Grandpa taught me to call out to Jesus whenever trouble found me. *Help me, Jesus! I'm sorry, God, that I didn't mind Gramma. I deserve what I get. Tell the man to let me go! Please Father God! I won't never be bad for Gramma again!*

The man growled some more at me, then he hollered. "We'll turn this one in for the bounty, Hilda. The soldiers'll be glad to have one more thievin' redskin behind bars."

He dragged me across the yard toward the toolshed. Thumper made a run at him, but the man kicked him away. Then the woman let loose with a load of buckshot, and Thumper ran howling and whining for the woods.

"Thumper!" I screamed! "You hurt my dog, you good for nothin' polecat," I bellowed, still struggling to get away from the man's hard hold on me.

"Hush up now, or I'll give you what for," the man said as he thrust me inside a dank little shed. I heard a bar slide on the outside of the door. As soon as he locked me up, I heard the white man tell his wife he'd ride for the soldiers.

"BOY! I DONE IT NOW," I said, looking around my dark, dusty prison. I hoped and prayed Thumper knew enough to run home to find Gramma.

I searched along the edge of the building looking for some way out, but my Pa built that shed to last, like he'd built everything on our farm. He had set the logs solidly, and except for where some chinking worked loose, there was no way out. I was trapped!

I found some dusty sacking, and wrapped it around myself. I perched high on an old wooden washtub to get off the cold earthen floor.

For a while, the two young ones catcalled, and poked sticks under the door of the shed to taunt me, but I sat there quiet like talked some to Jesus, and then fell asleep.

I woke in the dark. It was evening, and had brought the cold with it. It couldn't be more than 5 o'clock, but the cold crept in on me like it were midnight. I watched the sun setting through the tiny chinks in the logs. As the night noises began, ripples of fear come back to haunt me.

I know there was time to escape, the man's twenty-mile ride to the fort to bring the soldiers would take many hours going and coming. Once they caught me, I don't doubt for a minute they'd put me in the stockade behind wire like they did my folks.

I don't know where my folks got to either. The soldiers might take me where I didn't know anyone. I heard Grandpa say when they rounded up enough people, they marched 'em off toward the west.

Was this God's plan for me? I wondered. Then I wouldn't have to hide out anymore.

The thought of Gramma and Grandpa left alone with no family put some resolve in my heart. I searched around me on the dirt floor. It was dark, but I come up with a large tin cup, the kind we used every day in the kitchen. This cup was old and worn out, so not much good. I'd try to tunnel with it through the hard-packed dirt under the sidewall to the outside. If I dug deep enough, I might wiggle out, and flee before the man come back with the soldiers.

Digging at the back wall away from the barn, I skinned my knuckles, over and over on rocks hidden in the hard mountain soil. After

a long while I saw a little peek of light come through under the wall. Not light exactly, since the sun already went to bed, but lighter compared to the inky blackness of my prison.

I dug harder and harder, and soon the hole became big enough to stick my hand through. The air outside was cold and wet, the rain began falling again. The hole soon filled with water. It rained harder and harder. I heard the pounding of it on the tin roof of the shed.

"Thank you, Lord Jesus," I shouted as the ground softened and gave way where I dug. "Thank you, Jesus!" I sang to myself of God's goodness, digging faster and faster.

Soon the hole was deep enough, and I began to widen it out to the side. I hurried even more, and my breath come in gasps. I'd never worked so hard in my whole life.

Clearing away the last of the dirt, I laid full length, and got my head out. The cold rain cooled my face. I wiggled my arms and shoulders through, and struggled to get the rest of me out in the open. Good thing I was a skinny girl!

I stayed low, and pulled in tight next to the back wall of the shed. I listened, and heard nothin' from the house. The evening rain continued, and the chickens settled down for the night in the tops of the nearby trees.

The old owl sat high up a pine tree, and hoot-hooted in the night air. I come to my feet, and ran for the protection of the piney woods, hoping the falling rain would hide me.

What should I do now, I asked myself. If I returned to Gramma's they'd arrest her for hidin' a Cherokee, Gramma's, was the first place they'd look! I didn't care if they caught me, but I didn't want nothin' to happen to Gramma and Grandpa. I never thought they would get into trouble for hiding me!

At once, desolation rose up from inside me, and I knew I needed Gramma. I ran home lickety-split. I yearned for her, I wanted to sit by the warmth of the cabin fire, with a bowl of her fragrant stew in my lap. My body quaked hard, I shivered plumb to nothing from fear, and the cold rain pounded down on me.

On the way home, I come across Thumper sitting in the path a-licking and a-licking at a sore leg where the buckshot hit.

"Good for nothing hound," I said, cuffing him on the ear. "Why didn't you run home and get Grandpa for me?" He slobbered his welcome over my face.

As I come near to the cabin I saw lights in the two windows. A whiff of Gramma's cooking hung in the rain-filled air. Wagon tracks told of comings and goings, but everything seemed quiet.

I slipped up to the window and peered inside. Gramma bent her back over the fireplace stirring something in the black kettle. She stood, and rubbed her forehead with the back of her hand holding the big wooden spoon. She turned toward the window as if she'd heard a noise, yet I'd come up to the door on silent feet.

I saw her look uneasily around the cabin then began stirring again. I crept to the door, and pulled the latchstring. The door creaked open, and I stood dripping wet in the doorway.

She turned to me and said, "Caroline!" Before thrusting her hand over her mouth in despair. "Land sakes, Child, you gave me a start. Where have you got to? You look a sight come in, and we'll get you into some dry clothin.'"

"I can't, Gramma," those soldiers are comin' for me. They want to take me away to jail jest like they did Ma and Pa!" I saw the hurt filling Gramma's face. It was as if I'd said I'd killed the President of the United States, Martin Van Buren.

"What you talkin' 'bout, Child?" she said, pulling my dripping self into the room. I filled her clean puncheon floor with a small river of mud and water.

I told her about the man taking me, locking me away in the shed, and going for the soldiers. Gramma began making plans to get me away from the cabin.

"I figured something weren't right when you and that hound didn't come home right away. Your Grandpa would go to the hills just the same and search for our friends. You and I would have to think of some way to keep you safe.

"Here Child, shuck off those wet things by the fire, and wrap up in your quilt. I'll get you some wash water and dry clothes to put on. Then I'll fill your belly with some of this good venison stew. We'll pray and ask the Father to guide us and keep you safe. It'll be alright Child, don't cry, everything'll be alright."

FROM THAT DAY ON MY life changed, no longer was I a ten-year-old girl from middle Tennessee. I'd become a fugitive from the law, and the United States Government.

Gramma was right, God showed us his plan. She got me cleaned up, warmed, and filled with her good venison stew. Then we sat down together in her rocker with me wrapped in a patchwork quilt. She held her big black Bible, and together we read the story of the plight of the Israelites as told in the book of Ezekiel. I'd heard the story many times, for it was a favorite of Grandpa's.

Grandpa tried to compare the plight of our Cherokees with the plight of the Israelites. The difference he maintained was that the Cherokees were mostly an innocent people, many of them knew God, and believed on His word, and in His word. The Israelites worshipped false gods, and God allowed other tribes to capture the Israelites and take them away from the Promised Land.

He tore himself apart trying to figure out how God would allow our people to go through such a terrible ordeal. The Israelites sinned against God by worshipping idols, and turning away from Him. God punished them by allowing King Nebuchadnezzar to take them away to Babylon. Then later, Assyria come in and took more of them away.

I wanted to remind Grandpa that the Cherokee were a stiff-necked people, too. They belonged to the Cherokee nation, and refused to give up their sovereignty, and their land to take the oath of allegiance and become citizens of the United States Government. Yet, I don't think I should tell him that.

As Gramma continued reading to me, she come to a part I don't remember ever hearing in Ezekiel, chapter eleven, verse sixteen. She told me that many years later God smiled on the Israelites, and brought them back to the promised land.

Therefore, thus saith the Lord God, although I have cast them far off among the heathen, and I have scattered them among the countries, yet will I be to them as a little sanctuary in the countries where they shall come.

I prayed God would make these verses come true for the Cherokee. That the tribe would arrive off in the west, God would be with them, and become a sanctuary to them forevermore, just as he was with the Israelites.

After all they went through, God gave the Israelites peaceful lives in their new homes. I decided I would hold to this promise and pray for my tribe.

Gramma in her wisdom gave me what I needed most, God's comfort, her warmth and caring, and a chance for me to begin a new life.

The nearness of my own sweet Gramma soon lulled me to sleep. Later, voices woke me where I lay on Gramma's bed in the partitioned-off room.

Grandpa turned up under the cover of darkness, he brought two of our Cherokee neighbor men, Charley Hawk, and Jed Hicks, to the cabin. He found them at Horse Mountain, and they come back with him to the settlement when they learned that I'd disappeared.

Grandpa sounded grim as he questioned Gramma about what happened to me. "We need to get her away from here, Polly. We can't let them take her!"

"But where could we go?" Gramma asked her voice thick with tears. "We can't leave our home, Amos. Oh, why would God allow this to happen?"

"Polly, we won't question the Almighty," I heard Grandpa say. "Why does anything ever happen? We must obey. I've decided to let Charlie and Jed take her with them to the cave at Horse Mountain. It's not too far away, and it's still safe there. She'll feel right at home with Miz Storm and Lily."

"That's right, Ma'am," Charlie promised. "We'll keep her safe. Those soldiers are a laugh for us Cherokee. They flap around the woods, scaring off the game with their big noisy mounts, and jiggling harnesses."

"They'll never find us. We grew up in these mountains. They get lost five hundred yards off the trail," Jed said with a big laugh.

Gramma quickly bundled me up in buckskins and a jacket my brother Hiram left the last time he visited. They were short and tight, but they'd have to do. She packed a bundle for me, with my quilt, doll, a dress, shimmy, some under clothes, socks and a few other things.

She took shears to my auburn braids, and pulled a snug cap over my head. She cried as she cut my hair. The tears flowed down her cheeks and dripped off her chin.

I cried too, when I saw Gramma's tears, and I cried even harder when I felt my head where my braids used to be. I must look some like Hiram, now. Would I ever be myself again?

Gramma carefully wrapped my braids in a piece of clean linen and tucked them away in a basket on the shelf.

"I'll save your braids for you, Honey. Once you're grown, you can use them to make a fashionable hair switch for yourself, and wear it for formal occasions."

THE RAIN STOPPED BY the time we left the clearing of Grandpa's farm. It started up again as we walked along. The moon shrouded in clouds, hung low on the horizon preparing to set. It wouldn't be long until daybreak.

We walked single file down a faint trail north through the piney woods. Jed carried my small bundle, and told me we'd head to Horse Mountain by a zigzag path to keep us safe. I'd heard stories of Horse Mountain, and knew there was a long walk ahead of us.

Jed kidded with me, and then he became serious. "Don't worry about the man who owns your farm. He won't bring the soldiers for many days. The soldiers are all out on patrol chasing shadows."

Charlie laughed out loud in the still air at the idea. I jumped and cowered beneath a low-growing tree, then asked if we shouldn't be quiet. They looked at each other, and laughed again. I saw their leathery faces split into big grins. I began to grin, too!

These good friends wouldn't let anything happen to me. Yet now they knew Ashbill's daughter was a scared rabbit. I had shamed my father, and I must try to do better.

We walked on through the night, first to the east, then north, then west, and then north again. The rain let up, and the clouds moved away. As I watched, the sun rose, and lightened the sky.

At last, we reached the top of Horse Mountain, and a cave where the remnants of my tribe camped. When we entered the cave several women enveloped me in big hugs, a great peace filled and comforted me.

They brought me to the back of the cave where they gave me some dry clothing, water, and a pone of cornbread to eat. They opened my bundle, spread my quilt, gave me my doll, and urged me to sleep. I praised God, "He was good and worthy to be praised." He had rescued me again.

Chapter 3
<u>SUMMER</u>

After I joined the tribe, they moved us east to Meadow Hill, and a bigger cave. The tribe kept moving east every week or so, farther away from the soldiers.

In the spring of 1839, we moved to Dome Mountain, where we lived in a vast cave. The tribal leaders said we'd stay there.

By the middle of my second summer, I felt settled, and looked at Dome Mountain as my home. Early in the mornings, I'd jump up from the pallet of my crazy quilt, shake it out, fluff up my cotton-covered moss pillow, then I'd set my doll on top kind of nice like. I'd shuck off my shimmy, don my buckskins, and help my friend Lily's ma, Miz Storm.

For breakfast, Miz Storm cooked bannock made from ground acorn flour, dried berries, and herbs, she fried it in rendered fat.

She would simmer a kettle of parched corn through the morning, and add venison, squirrel, or whatever kind of meat she had. Later, we gathered vegetables, or roots, and dried herbs to add to the mixture. It made a fine meal for the middle of the day. Supper, we often roasted meat over the fire if the men were successful at hunting.

Sometimes we had a mess of fish, and a kettle of boiled pokeweed, dandelion greens, or the like to round out our meal. The food was good, we never hungered, and I learned to cook meals without the bounty of the white man's store.

Lily's mom told us stories about how her grandmother lived in the time before the white man come to our land. My folks raised me mostly like a white girl, but I thanked God for showing me how my native blood heritage lived.

My Pa gave up many of the old ways. He set great store by the ironed calico shirts, and the breeches Ma sewed for him. Yet, I have learned the comfort of buckskin shirts, leggings, and moccasins.

I pined for my folks, but not like before. I missed Gramma the most, and imagined how it felt to climb up on her lap for a story, wrapped in my old crazy quilt, like the last night before I left home.

I smelled her lilac water in the folds of my quilt, if I used my mind. Yet, I knew the flavor of wood smoke had chased it out long ago. I'd always remember the comfort of her lap, and her loving voice calling me, honey and child.

I wasn't alone, Miz Storm and the other women saw to me, and my needs, but I worked along with everyone else so we would survive. I'd become more independent, yet every now and again I missed my Gramma's loving.

Grandpa still come to visit me, though not as often, since we lived further east on Dome Mountain. One time, he come to bring supplies, to pray and talk with the men. They'd told him talks with the white officials in Nashville had broken off with nothing gained.

Whenever Grandpa come to visit, he spent time alone with me. We took some line and some hooks, cut us some tree limbs, walked down to the stream and fished to our heart's content. Grandpa's a good fisherman, he's never come home without a mess of trout, bluegill, or bass.

Grandpa told me about God, and about how to pray and stay close to Jesus. When he talked to me in *Tsalagi*, the language of the Cherokee people, I could understand him fine. Yet, more and more he only wanted to speak English. Then, I didn't understand what he said to me.

He seemed to tell me we would be together again, like a family, but he also said I needed to stay with my tribe, and my friend Lily until Bedford County was safe for me to come home.

He said God put me there for protection from the white men who still hunted for members of my tribe. If they caught me, they'd send me out west away from him and Gramma.

I told Grandpa I couldn't understand what he said, so he spoke to me in *Tsalagi.*

"In a little while," he said, when your exile is over, you'll move to a new place, and you'll never let on that you are Indian. You can pass for a white girl with your red hair, and you'll need to do that for all your life. You also need to speak English every day Honey, so you can become fluent again.

"It's well and good you speak *Tsalagi,* the Cherokee language, with the band, Caroline, but you're forgetting your English, and one day when you become a white girl again, you'll need to speak English all the time."

I didn't know how I could mind Grandpa, the tribe didn't speak English anymore, and I never again wanted to speak the language of the white people who took my family away. I'd tried hard to forget English, and I believed I'd forgotten much of it.

I felt more confused after Grandpa's visits, and I couldn't understand when he spoke to me in English. Yet the memories we made together became most important to me. When Grandpa come to see me, I sat on his lap, I could hug him up, and he would hug me right back.

When he left, I missed his whiskery kisses, his joking with me and calling me, "Darlin.'" My life filled me with joy when I was with Grandpa, but once he left, I always wanted more time with him.

One day, after we'd been in Dome Mountain for many months, shots rang out through the dawn. The sentries rushed into the cave roused our sleeping people, and forced them to grab possessions and flee. The soldiers had come to round up our tribe.

I grabbed up my doll and quilt then lit out in the direction the others took. Lily ran behind me, dragging too much, she tried to take all her precious books. I wanted to shout at her to leave them behind, but I knew she never would. Books were as scarce as teeth on a frog, and she treasured hers.

I tripped on the trailing edge of my quilt, and went down plumb at the edge of a bog. I lay there covered in mud. Swift Fox lifted me up and set me once again on my feet. I wiped at the mud, and began to cry.

Shots filled the air behind us, urging me to run. My heart beat like a hammer. Pound, pound, pound, I heard blood racing in my ears. I'd never felt this kind of terrible fear. I didn't want to die. I didn't know why I was here running as fast as my feet could go up, up, high up the mountain to another hideout; high enough so the men could defend us.

When I turned, I saw a flash of blue uniforms through the trees. The soldiers were trying to run us down with their horses! They were gonna get me! I wanted to scream out my fright, instead I ran, and ran, and ran.

Soon, I left the sound and smell of gunpowder behind me. I entered a part of the forest I'd never seen before. The trees stood high, close to the sky, blotting out the sun. Sunlight filtered through the green leaves of the great trees sending down rays of hazy sunlight.

I stopped in one bright patch of light, looked up straight toward God and prayed for my tribe. I felt God's peace, he calmed the quaking inside of me. I spread my quilt, lay down, and rested at the base of one of the giant friendly trees.

Butterflies flitted near me, and one landed on my hand. I sat bemused, and watched it flex its orange and black velvet wings. I'd never had one land on me before, its tiny feet tickled my hand. The butterfly glided away, and left me filled with wonder. More butterflies flew closer, I held still, not wanting to disturb them, yet before long they flew away one by one to find their brothers. I laughed aloud, and thanked Jesus for this precious gift!

What a wonder that God created a perfect creature like the butterfly, and asked it to live amidst the cruelty of the men I saw chasing my tribe today.

I closed my eyes and soon fell asleep. I dreamt of heaven, where the Son of God sat on a throne surrounded by millions of gleaming butterflies.

The late afternoon sun slanted down, and filled me with warmth. Mosquitoes and flies buzzed around me. I felt uncomfortable, so I sat up. I didn't know this place, but decided I should retrace my steps a bit, and see where I'd wandered off the path. Walking along, the trees soon looked alike to me, and I faced the fact that I was lost, and alone in the forest. Still, the beautiful dream filled me with hope.

I come upon the remains of a violent storm, huge trees thrown earthward like a giant's building blocks, heaped to a great height off the ground. I climbed up there to spend the night. It was high enough so the varmints couldn't reach me.

I looked around for something to eat, and found some blackberries entwined with wild roses and bramble bushes. I set to picking enough berries for my dinner. The nearby stream gave me water to drink.

"Thank you, Jesus! Thank you for supplying my needs," I said, praising Him. I pulled the quilt load of my things, and enough berries to last me several meals up to the topmost log in the pile. I stretched out and prepared for my first night alone.

I remained in my hideout that night, and all the next day. I climbed down once for a drink from the stream, and for a nature call, then climbed right back up to my nest. I think I needed time up there, listening to God's birds, and looking up at the patch of blue spread out between the leaves of the tall trees around me.

My bed felt tolerable, leaves filled the crevices of the thrown-together trunks, they made me a fine mattress. I wrapped my quilt around me, and hugged my doll tight. I felt safe away from all the confusion and commotion, just me and God, my doll, and my quilt, alone and at peace.

The dawn of the second day seemed different. It began to mist early on, and it soon turned into a downpour. It wasn't cold, as summer was still full upon us. Yet, I could see that I needed to get out and away from my nest, and on with business. I knew, I needed to get to where I was getting to. I couldn't lie around anymore when there was important things to do.

I wrapped up the rest of my berries, took a good drink from the stream, and set out in a different direction. As I walked, the trees seemed smaller and farther apart. Before long the rain stopped, the sun come out, steamed the land, and dried my clothes.

The day turned hotter, and I needed to get my bearings some, but couldn't find anything familiar to me. At noon, I come to another stream backed up to a rocky cliff, where a little waterfall played down to its base. At the bottom of the cliff, a deep pool shimmered in the hot sun.

I laughed in delight, shucked off my clothes, and hid them and my quilt in a dead tree away from varmints. I dove deep into the clear, cold water.

I giggled and swam back and forth beneath the little waterfall, dove down, grabbed handful after handful of fine sand, and rubbed it through my hair and on my skin to get them clean. I felt trout tickle my toes, and one big catfish took a nibble at my outstretched hand.

I heard a rustling in the brush and ducked down behind a deadfall, hoping whatever kind of animal hid there would run away and leave me be.

Bushes close to the pool parted, and revealed something to me I ain't never seen before. Not a stone's throw away, I saw a boy about my age, but taller and slender as a willow wand. His bright blond hair shimmered in the sun. He slid off his gray mule, and tied it under a tree; shucked off his breeches, and jumped into the water not fifty feet from where I hid.

The boy swam back and forth, but didn't look in my direction. Soon, he took off downstream.

I stole quick-like from the water, grabbed up my clothes and quilt from the tree. The sun felt hot and dried my skin as I dressed. I snuck away and went on with my journey.

The white boy must have lived in a settlement close by. Grandpa told me to stay away from the white men, so I turned away in another direction. I continued on as before, looking for berries to eat, and water to drink and wash in.

The image of the boy stayed with me through the day. I remembered the beautiful image of his shining blond hair and bright blue eyes.

Someday, I promised myself I wanted one like him for my very own. Of course, he ain't Cherokee, so it was jest wishful thinkin' on my part. I should find me a Cherokee man to marry up with someday, to carry on our heritage.

The wild creatures left me alone for the most part. I would climb up high at night, but I could often hear animals prowling below me.

One night, a great horned owl swooped low, and pounced on an unsuspecting mouse, the mouse squeaked and then nothing.

Skunks I worried about the most. I didn't want to tangle with one of those. Likely, I would die from the stench alone.

On the seventh day of trudging through the woods, I chanced upon some familiar landmarks. I stood hidden in a thicket, and peered between branches of a hickory tree. I spied our old cave, but it looked cold and alone, with no familiar people, no cheerful fire, or happy laughter echoing through the cave. It looked as dank and empty as I felt.

As I crept cautiously upward, I saw the remnants from my tribe. I picked up pots, pans, and parfleches of dried food. At least I would eat. I was getting a mite tired of berries, and I couldn't catch fish without hooks. I gathered up what I could, and once again followed the trail up to the top of the mountain where I knew I might find my tribe.

I found more discarded goods, and food on the trail. I also found one of Lily's books, damp now after the rain. I stuck it inside a pack thinking to return it to her. As the trail wove up the side of the mountain, I heard nothing, no birds singing, or squirrels chattering.

What if I couldn't find my tribe? What would I do? I'd been alone long enough to realize I needed people, Grandpa and Gramma, or Lily and Miz and Mister Storm.

What if the bluecoats took them all away? My tears come in a torrent after realizing I was lost, even though I'd partly found my way back. I stiffened my backbone, thrust up my chin, and let God decide what he wanted to happen to me.

Come evening, I slept high up in a small cave on the side of the mountain. When I found it, I poked in sticks and threw rocks inside first, and when nothing run out, I moved right in. It felt cold and damp in the cave. I dug around in one of the packs for warmer clothes, and then wrapped up in my quilt. I wished for a fire, but I knew for my safety I couldn't have one. I cried again, and prayed to my Father in Heaven to keep me in His care.

A brilliant pink dawn snuck inside the cave, waking me. I got up and looked out over the valley below. God fashioned another miracle it seemed jest for me, birds flew black against the rosy sky, and called out to each other, a joyful sound to this lonely girl.

I watched until the sun broke white-hot through the fluffy clouds. Then, I got ready to set out once again, but this time I felt filled with hope that I would find my tribe that day.

The closer I climbed, the more excited I got. I saw moccasin prints here in the sand, a lot of them, climbing up higher and higher. I couldn't say when I would join them, yet I knew God went before me leading me home.

I ARRIVED AT THE NEW encampment called Echo Cave, before sundown. I had come across Jim Two Crows, and his brown mare a few miles back, and he rode me in holding on to his waist. The camp seemed too quiet, but I didn't care. I was just glad to be here with my people again.

In the escape, no one missed me. Yet, when I rode up to the camp, they welcomed me as one come back from the dead.

During the soldier's raid, many of the people couldn't get away in time. One of the tribal council members walked out to parlay with the white soldiers. He said he would give himself up if they would let the others go. He tried to buy time for the people to get away. The soldiers seemed satisfied, and took him, and a few other men off down to the fort where they held a mock trial. They found him guilty, shot him dead, and jailed the others.

On my first night back, I cried hard when they told me the awful news, and who it was the soldiers killed. There was no one to console me. The long faces of the people, and Lily's shorn hair and torn clothing, showed me the harsh reality of mourning her father, Mr. Storm's tragic death. Our tribe had suffered another great loss.

Our tribal leaders told the people to prepare to march many days southeast to Grundy County. The tribe had visited that area for many generations. We would winter there close to a great cave with an abundance of game, and many streams and waterfalls.

We would trap, fish, hunt, and prepare food for the long trek east next spring, to the Great Smoky Mountains, in North Carolina. There we would meet up with other tribal brothers. The deep woods would keep us safe from the white soldiers.

I couldn't sleep, and the next morning, I didn't want to get up from my bed. I was plumb tore up over the loss of our Chief Ned

Storm, and the sacrifice he made to save us from the soldiers. It also brought back to me the loss of my folks all over again!

Grandpa come to our campground soon after sunrise. I cried hard when he entered the cave, and found me still in my little bed. He took me out a ways where we could be alone.

He wept in relief that he found me safe. He'd heard what happened at our camp, and then rode to the cave at Dome Mountain, where we'd lived. He found it empty with our belongings scattered. He continued to search, and a few days later, he chanced on a few stragglers who told him of this encampment further to the east.

He wanted me to understand everything he said, so he sat me down and told me the story in the Cherokee language of our people. He said after this, he would only speak to me in English, so I would become fluent again.

"The blue-coated soldiers surprised our people at the cave on Dome Mountain where you lived for the last six months. The sentries warned your people, then rode back to block the soldiers' advance. Big Ned Storm, and some other men walked out to talk to the soldiers, to stall them, to give the people time to escape. The soldiers took them away, quickly tried Ned in a court, and he lost his life. The other men are still in jail.

"I aim to take you away, Darlin.'" He seemed appalled at my condition. I knew I ain't the prettiest thing, to set foot on God's green earth. I'd been tramping the woods by myself for a week. My clothes looked worn, torn, and bedraggled despite my best efforts to the contrary, and I did emit a faint smell of skunk about my person.

Later in the afternoon, I said goodbye to our friends. The goodbye to Lily and Miz Storm was terrible hard for me, as they were like my family. We cried together for a long while. After Grandpa took me up behind his saddle, Lily offered me her hand.

"Be at peace, Red Bird," she said. "God meant for us to be together. He will see to it." I didn't quite believe her. I thought I would never see her again, so tears tracked down my cheeks for a long while after we left the camp on our new adventure.

"FIRST OFF, CAROLINE," Grandpa spoke slowly to me in English, as we set up camp that first night at the fork of a stream a good ten miles below Echo Cave.

"I've got some pretties for you. Your Gramma's been sewing up a storm, and made you some nice new clothes, and there's a new pair of boots, too. These pretties might be big on you, but in time, you will grow into them. I'd been carrying these things with me for a while, wasn't sure when I'd find you.

"We decided all along for you to only stay with the tribe until we could make plans for you to get away to a safe place where no one would recognize you, or your heritage.

With the council leading the tribe, we thought no harm could come to you. I see now, that was jest foolish thinking. I never expected we'd lose Ned.

"The tribe will take good care of Lily and Miz Storm, so you don't need to worry about them. We will say a prayer for God's peace and comfort for them this evening.

"Your half-birthday's coming up. You'll soon be eleven years and six months old. You've gotten taller, and before long, you'll grow into a fine woman. It would have killed the life out of me if anything happened to you.

"I brought you a package from myself, too. It may not keep you safe, but it would give you shelter from any storm this old life can ever throw at you."

He thrust a small, brown, paper-wrapped parcel into my outstretched hand. I tore the paper, and gasped in delight to see a small Bible, my very own copy of the great words of God.

I threw my arms around Grandpa, kissed his whiskery cheek, and told him in the language of our people that I would cherish the little book like my life depended on it.

He was firm though. He made me tell him the same thing again in English. As I thought about it later, I believed my life would depend on the little book, not for my safety, as much as for my sanity and salvation in the days ahead.

Grandpa showed me scriptures in the little Bible that I could hold onto. I took to Psalm 91, verse 11, as my favorite . "He shall give his angels charge over thee to keep thee in all of thy ways." I memorized it in case I would ever need it.

After a while, he tossed me a bar of lye soap infused with lavender, made with my gramma's own hands. I took along one of my new dresses, and trotted downstream a ways to wash my hair, and rub and scrub my skin as never before. I also washed out my quilt, and the clothing I'd worn and hung them on bushes to dry. Before long, I returned wearing the new dress with the split skirt for riding. Yes, Gramma outdid herself. I stood proud in my new dress.

Grandpa also gave me a new sunbonnet to hide my face, and then something I didn't expect. He strapped a pistol in a holster around my waist. He said tomorrow I'd learn to use it. The pistol brought home to me the seriousness of our decision to ride away from Tennessee.

The government still wanted me, they would hunt for me for having Injun blood in my veins. Even though I was not a full-blooded Cherokee, it didn't matter. I was still an Injun in the eyes of the army.

I couldn't understand what Grandpa said, but he talked to me with his voice and his hands at the same time. He hoped my first language, English, would come back to me more and more.

I hated the white men for what they'd done to my tribe. That hatred led me to want to forget my natural language. I still felt more comfortable speaking the language of my people.

We hunkered down by the fire and ate the good rabbit stew Grandpa made for our supper. Sleep come early for me, since I slept little the night before.

I resolved to be up and about early to fix Grandpa's breakfast, but I didn't realize how tired and worn out I'd become. I slept until the sun rose in the sky. Then, we ate a quick meal of bannock, and made our way on the horse, toward the north and the east.

I don't know why we traveled in that direction, but I didn't care. I just loved to ride along behind Grandpa with my skinny arms wrapped around his thick waist. I enjoyed the mild, sunny day and the way we traveled. That sure beat walking.

Grandpa seemed to know right where we rode. From time to time, he pulled out his compass and took a sighting on the sun as it peeked through the tall trees, and then he would change our direction a trifle. We traveled along a faint path on the forest floor. He called it an old Indian trail.

About noon, we come near a cabin. I wondered why people built a cabin here so far from any settlement, but Grandpa told me the settlements weren't over one day's ride, about twenty miles away.

I spied a man outside chopping wood, and several children playing close to a creek. Grandpa turned the horse away before they saw us, and we rode on in a different direction through the woods. A few miles farther on, he pulled the mare up next to a stream, there we ate our dinner and rested before continuing our journey.

Chapter 4
<u>THE OCEAN</u>

"Caroline, I enjoy traveling in September," Grandpa told me as we rode toward the east along the faint path in the woods.

I agreed with Grandpa, the woods felt cool and the branches of the big trees stretched high above our heads, looking like a bright green canopy.

I listened to the songs of the birds and the buzz of insects and bees. I rode holding on to him, and often nodded off to sleep along with the gait of his mare, Phoebe.

The horse forded creek after creek. Soon the woods all looked the same to me. An uneasy feeling stole over me I marveled to think that Grandpa could find his way through the maze of thickets, green branches, and tree trunks.

At noon, we made camp near a bramble of blackberry bushes. I helped Grandpa pick a considerable number of berries, and stored them in a parfleche slung behind me over the withers of the mare.

Later, Grandpa made us the best meal I'd eaten since I left Gramma, Johnnycake laced through with blackberries. He mashed the berries and sprinkled them over the top of the cake along with a tad of the maple sugar he carried.

After we ate, he took me further out in the woods for another lesson on shooting the gun. He'd given me lessons right along most every day.

The first day, I'd felt awkward holding the heavy pistol but each day I got better and better. Grandpa thought I cottoned to the pistol well, and now could almost hit anything I aimed at. One day I bagged a rabbit, shot its head right off. He seemed pleased. He said we'd have rabbit for supper.

Each day, we traveled until right before sundown. We unloaded the horse, and I took her to a stream to drink, while Grandpa made our supper. He used the fresh herbs and wild onions I gathered along the trail during the day. After supper we sat around the fire, with me right up close to him where he could put his arm around my waist.

"Grandpa, I miss Gramma. When can I see her?" I said in the language of my people. He just ignored me until I tried to ask him in English. It felt funny to be talkin' like that, but he smiled his approval whenever I tried.

"Caroline, one day we'll all be together again, but first I want to make sure you're raised right. You jest got to mind me, and trust everything will come about at the proper time."

I didn't understand what Grandpa meant. Maybe once my English returned, I would understand more. In the meantime, I didn't question the wisdom of the ones greater than me, both God and Grandpa knew I needed Gramma. I don't know why we traveled farther and farther away from her every day. Maybe if I was jest patient like Grandpa said, God would answer my prayers.

As the horse walked along, I thought about the stories my people liked to tell. My Indian name is Redbird, and once again I told myself the tale of "Redbird" that my friend Lily once told me. I'd always thought my name came from the color of my hair, but Lily said, "No!"

"Here's the story the old men told me about you when we were small girls. A raccoon passed a wolf one day, and made insulting remarks to him. The wolf grew angry and chased the raccoon. The raccoon ran fast and reached a tree by the river. He climbed the tree, and lay on a branch overlooking the stream. The wolf saw the raccoon's reflection in the river and jumped in to eat it. The wolf almost drowned. He jumped out all wet and tired, and lay on the bank to sleep.

"The raccoon climbed from the tree, and smeared mud over the wolf's eyes. When the wolf awoke, he found he couldn't see, so he whined. A little brown bird heard the wolf crying. The wolf told the bird that the raccoon plastered his eyes shut with mud. 'If you will help get my eyes open, I will lead you to a place where you can find red paint, to paint yourself.'

"Brown bird pecked at the wolf's eyes until he got off the dried mud. Then the wolf took the brown bird to a rock that showed streaks of bright red paint running through it. The little bird painted himself with it and ever since he became a redbird."

I like to think of the story of the brown bird that became a red bird through a kindness to someone else. Ma said when she bore me, I come with brown hair, later it turned blond, and soon became red, making me a brown bird for a while. I only wished I'd become a redbird through being kind, and helping others, instead of through the kindness of God.

OUR DAYS BEGAN TO RUN together a bit in my mind, as we traveled on toward the east. My leg muscles felt stiff and sore from the scrunched-up position I held on the back of the horse. Once in a while, Grandpa let me get down to walk out the kinks a little.

I didn't know how long we'd traveled. I knew we'd left Tennessee behind, and Grandpa said we were in Virginia, and headed toward a town called Danville. He also said there might be a few smaller towns on the way. I thought Grandpa wanted us to stay well away from the towns, just like the others we'd skirted, yet this time he surprised me.

He led us a couple of miles out into the deep woods. We camped in a clearing close to a fishpond. Grandpa fished, and I set to picking some leftover berries in a bramble of branches eight feet high.

He made us a fine meal of fish, and a nice Johnnycake piled high with ripe berries.

"Caroline," he told me the next morning. "I've used the last of the supplies I'd brought with me. I'll walk to the town to buy food, and talk to the local folk. They know the best trail to take to the east. The town's not over three miles from here.

"While I'm gone, I want you and the horse to wait here for me. Shouldn't take longer than a few hours, at the most. Jest don't fret, you'll be fine, and don't stray from the camp. Make sure you keep the gun belt strapped to your waist. If anyone comes near, the horse will let you know, watch his ears.

Hide in the thicket downstream from the pond, and above all Honey, defend yourself or the horse if it comes to it. You know how to use the gun.

"While I'm gone, make yourself useful. Wash clothes if you're a mind to, and catch us a few fish for our dinner. I'll bring back cornmeal, flour, salt, coffee, potatoes, onions, maybe an egg or two, and a tin of milk if I can find it. I doubt you've drunk milk since you left our home place. Grandpa said goodbye, and walked off. He turned after a bit and waved his hat to me.

A little while later, the quietness crept in on me. I continued to sit on the log where we ate our meals, and chewed some more on the remains of my breakfast. It wasn't that long since I last stayed alone in the woods, and I'm not ready to be by myself again.

Finally, I determined to stiffen up my backbone, get busy, and not think about being there by myself. I took our tin dishes to the pond to rinse. Then I picked as many berries as I could find.

I unhobbled the horse and moved her closer to the pond where she could reach water.

Wish't, I had me a dog. At the camp where I'd lived for so long, there were a few watchdogs to bark a warning. He told me to watch the horse's ears and they'd tell me if anyone came.

After an hour of fishing, eight large fish lay next to me. I cleaned them, and snugged them down with wet leaves. Once I'd finished, I walked the horse to where I could watch her easier, then stoked the fire and added green leaves to make a smudge.

I strung the fish on sticks, and laid them on some big rocks close to the fire. At noon, while I watched the fish, I ate the last leftover cake and piled it high with the tasty berries, and drank a large cup of water.

After a while, it began to rain. The rain caused clouds of smoke to rise from the fire. I hoped no one would see the smoke, or smell the smoking fish, and come to investigate. I was getting wet with no way to stay dry out here in the open, so I moved our packs and supplies under a thick stand of trees. The fish I left on the smoky fire. I went back and forth to turn them.

Grandpa, true to his word, returned after three and a half hours. I sighed in relief when I saw him. He came loaded with provisions. He was cold and wet from the steady rain, and more tired than I'd seen him in a good long while.

I didn't tell him, the lonesomes crept in on me. I just gave him a hug and pretended I'd been fine.

"Well now, Caroline," he said, putting the parcels down under the stand of trees where I'd piled our belongings. He shook the water from his hat and removed his jacket.

"Looks like I should leave more often. Glad to see you've been busy. Smoked fish? Well, we can surely use that in the days ahead."

After supper, Grandpa said we'd reach Danville on the Dan River by the next evening. The day after that, we'd veer to the northeast side of North Carolina, where I'd find a nice surprise for me, there. He told me to turn in, and we'd get an early start. I didn't relish sleeping in a wet bed, and hoped the rain would turn off soon.

DANVILLE WAS A WONDER for me. It was a large, well-established town along the banks of the Dan River. Grandpa told me Danville was four or five times bigger than our town in Bedford County.

He said the Dan River flowed back and forth along the North Carolina and Virginia borders and met up with the Roanoke River a little way to the northwest of here.

We could hear the roar of the river before we come up to it. We followed the path along the river and saw large boulders throwing out swirls of gurgling water that ran in the opposite direction ending in small whirlpools.

Further on, we watched the power of the whitewater swift rapids, as they churned, bubbled, and lifted waves to beat against the exposed rocks. The rapids shot spray in a thick mist above the river, turning the Dan into a sparkling, lively, powerful energy, not muddy and sluggish as the smaller streams and creeks we'd crossed during our ride.

I wanted to try my luck fishing, but Grandpa said the fish wouldn't bite as the heavy rains filled the river with enough food.

We skirted the town, keeping to the back roads and back streets. Once out of town, the woods cleared, and soon we passed tobacco farms. I gawked at the gigantic barns where they hung the tobacco leaves to cure. We hastened through the countryside and finally come to some woods where we'd camp about four miles east of the town.

WE CONTINUED ON AS before, following seldom-used paths and trails. After another five days of travel, I noticed the woods thinned out, and marshy, boggy places loomed up without warning.

One afternoon, Grandpa pulled the mare to a stop. He pointed with his riding crop. "You beware of the salt marsh Caroline, it's quicksand. It would suck you down quicker than a frog with a fly!"

That's all the warning I needed. The morass sat off to the right side of us. I eyed that marsh hard, as we skirted its rim, and breathed a loud sigh of relief once we left it behind.

Grandpa chuckled at my sigh. "You, ain't afraid of any little ole marsh, are you Gal, as much as you been through on your own?"

"I ain't been through nothin', Grandpa," I said after finally getting my words out, puzzled at what he meant. "I'd jest been living with our friends for a while, and one time I took a long walk in the woods by myself for about seven days."

"Don't you know most people don't hide out in caves, Honey? Or men bigger than you have gotten theirselves lost forever in those same woods you passed through that time?"

Grandpa gave me something to think on. I enjoyed being with my tribe, and learned a lot about how to live in the woods, how to trap small animals for food, where to find herbs, and the names and locations of plants we used for cooking and healing. It was fun helping my friend Lily every day, we cooked food, washed clothes, and tanned hides.

We laughed together, and played tricks on each other. I usually bested her in a foot race, and caught the most fish, but Lily bested me in reading, telling stories, and sewing moccasins and leggings. I loved Lily like a sister.

As for my tramp in the woods, I only walked and walked until I found the tribe. In thinking back, God must have led me, for no critter, neither snake nor even a mosquito, come nigh to me during the whole of that long week.

I didn't feel scared, except when that pretty boy dove into the pool. Then I felt scared he would find me in the altogether. God brought Grandpa to me, and he led me away from danger, and now we rode toward the northeast together.

Grandpa continued talking to me in English. I understood him better, and answered back some in English. He said he was proud of me.

In the morning, he told me farther south palm trees, and smaller bushes called palmettos grew. I'd never seen a palm tree, and I don't know if I ever would.

The soil beneath our feet turned sandy now. Without warning, a huge white bird landed ahead of us on the trail. Grandpa called it a seagull. I caught my breath in the wonder of such a large bird. When I looked up in the sky, there were more and more white birds. They screamed as they quick-like dove downward, looking for food. Sea-gull. I liked the sound of its name the sea was jest like ocean. I'd always heard tell of the ocean.

My pa told me about the time he and his friends traveled to the ocean before he married Ma. They camped out on a beach, and launched an abandoned boat through the waves, catching some huge fish. They cooked the fish right there on the beach. Pa always wanted to go back again, and take the rest of us, but we never went, and now we won't ever have the chance to go.

The very air around us felt soft. It smelled fresh and salty at the same time. I heard a roaring in the distance. "What's that sound, Grandpa?" I asked, trying to puzzle it out.

"That's the sound of the ocean waves, Child."

We broke through the trees and bushes, and there sat a vast expense of blue, just a-sparkling in the noontime sun! The ocean!

I felt a thrill clear to my soul, as I slid off the back of the mare and ran right into the ocean surf. A big wave rolled in, and knocked me down flat, then it drug me around and around. I fought to get free, and loved it!

I climbed to my feet, took off my moccasins, and flung them behind me. The sand squished right up between my toes, and the water lapped at my ankles.

Then something invisible drug me toward the water. My feet and legs moved along without me doing any of the moving. I shrieked in shocked pleasure seeing the path I'd created behind me.

Grandpa appeared next to me shoeless, and with his trousers rolled up to his knees. "That's the undertow that's got you, Gal," he said laughing.

I felt hard, little things wiggle in the sand beneath my feet. They seemed lodged in the watery sand. I shrieked and giggled again and again, as they tickled the bottoms of my feet.

He reached his hand below him in the surf, and come up with a handful of some small white and tan creatures. He turned them over with his thumb. "They's sand crabs, Gal! The gulls like to eat 'em."

"Oh, Grandpa," I shouted out. "It's wonderful, Grandpa! Just like heaven! I never want to leave! I'll swim in the sea every day, and chase the birds, and have fun in the sunshine! Thank you, Grandpa! Thank you for bringing me here!" I stopped jumping up and down for a minute and reached up to give him a big wet hug.

He smiled and said, "I knew you'd like it, Caroline! We can camp here for a few days, and rest up before going on to Norfolk."

"Thank you, Grandpa! Thank you!"

I'LL ALWAYS REMEMBER our stay at the ocean. Yet, the days went by too quick-like. On the morning of our fourth day, Grandpa told me to pack up we were leaving.

I never wanted to leave! I wasn't finished yet. I'd learned how to swim out to sea, and float back in on the waves, over and over again. I enjoyed piling up sea shells, digging in the sand, and watching the waves come in and claim what I'd built.

I loved chasing seagulls and the other sea birds, and watching them fly away from me. I needed to dig more sand crabs, and fancied turning some of them into pets. Above all, the few days there weren't enough. I wanted more! I knew I'd never see the ocean again!

Grandpa told me again to get ready to go. I told him, "NO!" He scolded me.

Yet I dug in my heels and refused. He packed the horse, mounted and began to ride. He left me standing there for a minute before I realized he intended to ride off, and leave me alone. I ran after him, he let me run alongside the horse for a long while before he finally stopped, and let me crawl onto the back of the mare.

"Grandpa!" I screamed at him. "I want us to stay here forever. We can send for Gramma! We can live here for the rest of our lives. I love it, Grandpa!" He didn't say a word jest kept us riding north. I shed tears, lots of tears, yet he acted like he never heard me, and that hurt even worse!

LATER, GRANDPA STOPPED by a stream, where we bathed and washed our clothing. I was surprised how much sand I had collected about my person from all my ocean frolicking. I rubbed and scrubbed my salt-dried skin until it returned to a healthy glow. The next morning, I donned a fresh dress, and after breakfast we resumed our journey.

Five weeks to the day, we left Echo Cave, Tennessee, we reached the outskirts of Norfolk, Warwick County, Virginia. That was the first time I'd been in a town of any size since before the soldiers took my folks away, almost a year and seven months ago.

Grandpa said the town of Norfolk, and the surrounding countryside held close to 10,000 folks, more than I'd ever seen together at one time.

We trotted on for a while, then Grandpa turned his horse into the town, and a short time later, we rode onto brick-paved Main Street and the horse ambled along.

I bowed my head away from the curious onlookers, and pretended interest in the storefronts, trying to ignore the rude stares of the townsfolk. They made me feel unsettled.

Maybe they don't see many girls riding astride behind a horse, or maybe they recognized me for who I am, an Injun. I felt myself shake from my head to my gizzard. What if they discovered my secret? Would they haul me away as they did my family?

Grandpa must have felt me shaking. He said, "Steady now, Caroline, you'll be just fine!" He reassured me the night before beside the stream.

"We're going to a place far away from all that went on with your people, Caroline. Folks there won't even think to ask if you're a white girl, or not."

Now, I don't know or care about any of that. I only want those staring eyes to go away. We come to the middle of the town, to the market square, where we saw all colors and sizes of horses tied to the railings of a platform, maybe some kind of a sale going on. Dark-skinned men stood next to the horses holding their bridles, talking to the horses to keep them calm.

I watched a huge crowd of well-dressed men, all shouting and putting up their hands, maybe bidding on the horses, I couldn't tell, and didn't understand what they said.

We continued down an unpaved back street. I noticed names on the top of the large buildings, Paul & Pegram, Thomas Toy, and Franklin Barlowe. He nodded toward them and said, "cotton brokers."

We turned again, and continued to the end of Main Street, and saw a river in the distance.

"That's The Elizabeth River, Child. It runs between Norfolk and Portsmouth. This town's a big shipping center. They export tobacco, corn, cotton, and timber from Virginia and North Carolina, to Britain and other countries.

"The ships return carrying manufactured goods from England. They also import goods like rum and sugar from the West Indies, and send these goods out from Norfolk to other states.

Slave labor produces much of the West Indies, and American products, which come through the harbor. It's the way of life here."

I saw a boat tied up to the dock with many dark-skinned men unloading. It must have jest landed. I guess, maybe the black men were slaves. I knew a little about slaves, as I heard some more affluent families in our tribe kept slaves. I'd never been close to one before, though. I didn't know I'd see slaves here, but maybe so.

Then I remembered seeing dark-skinned men holding the horses at the market. *More slaves*, I thought.

We followed the road fronting the big busy river. It seemed wider across from shore to shore than the rivers I knew in Tennessee.

Large ships, and many small boats sailed to and fro on the river, while many other boats sat idle, and tied up at the quays.

Grandpa continued riding us along the road for several blocks before turning in at a street going off to the west, then pulled the mare up in front of a large house a few blocks from the river.

A sign hanging from a post in front of the house, said, "Hale's Boarding House." Grandpa tied the mare to the hitching post and we dismounted.

"Caroline, this is a fine establishment, you'll like it," he said. "It's big and comfortable. The Widow Hale runs it as a guesthouse. She's a good friend of ours, and I've stayed here many times, whenever I visited, or passed through Norfolk. Her clientele includes many ships' captains and dignitaries who travel to Norfolk on business."

It seemed like a fancy place to me, with a whitewashed clapboard front, real glass windows, and white painted wooden boxes below each window. Someone planted flowers there. I stared in wonder when I saw those, I'd never thought of growing pretty flowers in a box.

Grandpa said they were geraniums. The red flowers looked nice, with the white flower boxes, and the white building. We knocked at the door and Widow Hale answered. She welcomed us, called Grandpa, Amos, and invited us to come in.

Inside the house, the bare wood floors shimmered. When I bent over, I could almost see my face in them, they were that shiny. The widow covered her floors here and there with red carpet strip rugs. She draped the windows with bright curtains made of flowered white muslin. They let in the sunshine, and made the room look big. I saw a long stairway, which reached up to the second floor of the house.

Widow Hale spoke to us with a slow accent, and I could understand her. Upstairs, she told us her guests filled four of the eight bedrooms. She gave us a large room with a fine view of the back terrace of the house, and the woods in the distance. She thought it would accommodate us well. We saw a large, draped four-poster bed in the main room, and a smaller bed in the dressing room.

I went right to the window. Off in the distance, I saw a vegetable garden, big ain't the right word to describe that garden. It covered over an acre stretching down to a stream running in back of the property.

The garden seemed about finished for the season, hay and mulch covered much of the surface. I spied a few pumpkins and gourds about ready to pick, and late-blooming flowers grew along the edges.

Grandpa didn't say why we come here, but I resolved to enjoy the comfy bed, and the hot bath they brought up to my room. This was living, and I had no complaints.

Chapter 5
<u>THE CITY</u>

I awoke early the next morning, and stretched high toward the draperies hanging around the little bed where I'd slept. I felt good and rested, got up dressed and went exploring.

Grandpa slept in the large bed in the main room. I peeked in and saw him snoring the sleep of the just. He said he'd felt about done in last night. I could tell, so thought I'd jest let him sleep. I'd like to look around at the big town of Norfolk. I'd never seen the likes of it before.

Pa would have us travel to New Echota, Georgia, for the tribal council meetings every year. On the way, we'd pass through Chattanooga, a big town to be sure, but Norfolk, Virginia seemed larger and fancier to me.

I tiptoed over to the stairs, and on the way down, stopped to look at all the nicely framed pictures that hung there. Most of the people looked straight-faced. The men seemed like a hard lot. They all wore black suits, some wore white wigs, with not a smile amongst the lot of 'em.

The women too seemed less than easy on the eye, wearing dark dresses trimmed with white laces, and other fripperies. Some women wore a kind of lace cloth over their curls, not really a hat.

By the bottom step though, I found a more recent picture of a young man. The picture made me stop and catch my breath, for this young man seemed near the spittin' image of what I remembered the boy at the waterfall to look like, with bright blond curls, and clear eyes. Yet he looked much older, at least twenty years old, I'd say. Again, I reaffirmed my vow to find me one like him someday, and just as handsome.

I walked over to the front of the house, opened the door, and looked up and down the street. No one moved about so early in the morning. I went through the door, and stepped down to the sidewalk. I walked the length of the block and turned right back again.

I felt eyes on me, and it made me uncomfortable. I looked back and forth along the street, and saw lace curtains pulled aside in various houses. I rushed back to the boarding house, and quick went inside. I'd better wait for Grandpa before I do any more exploring.

Once back at the house, I followed my nose, and looked for some breakfast. I'm not by nature bashful, and it often landed me in a mess of trouble. What harm could it do for me to walk down the hall and look for the kitchen?

I turned into a door on the right where the best smells come from. The warm, yeasty smell of fresh-baked bread made my stomach growl. The cook waved her spoon at me, and told me to seat myself in the dining room and she would serve breakfast in a quarter hour.

The dining room? What's wrong with the kitchen? I put off my plans to have an early breakfast. I felt a little like the brown trout that leaped out of the pond and lay gasping on the bank of the creek.

I retraced my steps back up to my room, passing all the dour looks from the ancestors. Inside, I sat still on the bed clutching my Bible.

"Looks like I'm in over my head again, Lord," I whispered, as I flipped through pages to another favorite part of my Bible, Philippians, 4:6, *"Be anxious for nothing, but in everything by prayer and supplication, with Thanksgiving, let your requests be known unto God."*

AFTER HE DRESSED, GRANDPA found me sitting on the edge of my bed reading my Bible. He looked surprised.

Wash your face and hands, put on your finest new dress and bonnet Caroline, while I clean your muddy boots, and pack." He stuffed my extra clothes, my quilt, doll, and skinning knife into a sack, which he carried.

"You won't need to wear your knife. I put it in the sack for you, and I'm taking the gun belt with me. I'll likely need it more than you will in the city."

We ate a stiff breakfast, with too much food, dishes too pretty to eat from, and too many utensils to eat with. I didn't know what to do, but I managed by watching the others.

I fell in love with the white rolls of bread. I wanted to make a pig of myself, but Grandpa, gave me a warning look. I slipped two of them into each pocket of my dress for later. I finished eating my eggs, scrapple, grits, berries, and drank down the big glass of milk.

Grandpa picked up my sack, took me by the hand, and led me out of the elegant boarding house, away from the table full of well-dressed strangers, and down the street where he said there was an aunt he wanted me to meet.

"You're a lady now, Caroline, and I expect you to act the part. You come from good stock, never let anyone tell you different. A young lady you are, and a young lady you'll be. We'll not raise a young heathen any longer. It's time you learned your true calling in life, being a lady in every sense of the word."

The ultimatum from Grandpa set me back some in my thinking. What did he mean heathen? I'm a believer, some of my friends ain't, but he made sure I knew God.

Me, a lady? I thought. It was hard to hold all the laughter inside of me. I could feel it rolling around my innards, and I wanted to let it explode loud and long.

"It's not funny, Caroline! Your Gramma and I come from quality folk and good breeding. Your ma and pa, your gramma, and me too, all got a little sidetracked in your raising, but no longer. I don't know what got into your ma raising you like a wild Injun."

"But Grandpa, I am Injun, Ma always wanted me to learn about my heritage."

"That's God's truth Child, and the Good Lord knows I'll be the last to deny you your heritage. However, you have other heritage and it's time you get acquainted with it, too. It's dangerous for you to claim to be Cherokee any longer. Nothing good will ever come of it.

"There's a lot to be said for the Cherokee, Honey. They's a fine people. If not, we wouldn't ever have let our girl marry into the tribe. You can remember your family, and the stories of your people, and their ways, yet now it's important that you never let on you are anything more than a white girl.

"Your complexion is browner now since you've been living outdoors for the last year and a half. They don't consider that fashionable, but there's a thousand other ladies here with darker skin. They've come up from New Orleans, or from Spain, or Italy. You'll remain indoors much of the time, and your skin will lighten after a little while. Most people won't notice the difference in you. Now I don't aim to say any more on the matter."

"Yes, Grandpa, if you say so," I ducked my head and continued walking down the sidewalk at his side. I felt more confused than I'd ever felt before in all my borned days. I don't know why he brought all my belongings if we was only going to visit an aunt.

WE ARRIVED AT THE DOOR of a large three-storied, red-brick house. "Caroline, this is the home of my sister, Lady Ashley. This is her Academy for Young Ladies of Genteel Quality."

A woman of color greeted us at the door, and ushered us through the foyer, and into the parlor. She wore a black silk dress, with a fancy white organdy apron. An organdy mobcap covered her dark curls.

Mischief lurked behind her dark brown eyes. She looked about sixteen years old, not too much older than me. Before closing the door, she winked at me, startling me into a wide grin.

Grandpa glared at me, and told me to behave myself. I still didn't understand what we were doing there. I began looking around the room and felt my jaw drop at what I saw. I thought the boarding house was fancy, but this big house looked like a castle. I expected a king or queen to come through the door at any minute. A beautiful thick, blue and red patterned carpet covered most of the polished wood floor. I hated to walk on it, it was so pretty. When I carefully put my feet there, it felt like walking on moss.

Grandpa said we should sit down on a fancy red and white striped settee made of silk or satin, and shot through with shimmery threads. I liked running my hands over the silky surface. A sweet little table sat next to the settee, it held a vase of colorful fresh flowers, and a white stone statue of young girls playing together in a circle.

A great fireplace stood at one end of the room. Above it hung a large picture of a fine gentleman. His bright green suit seemed made of shiny cloth, with a lot of lace at his neck and the wrists of his sleeves. He wore a long white wig on his head.

I saw fancy pictures on the walls. I admired one picture of pretty young girls carrying parasols and walking next to a blue pond under weeping willow trees. They wore fancy dresses, like I ain't never seen before. I wanted to look at the picture closer, but Grandpa cleared his throat and shook his head when he saw me getting up.

"Caroline, I want you to jest sit up straight, put your feet flat on the floor, and keep your hands folded in your lap. I don't want you to open your mouth for any reason unless someone speaks directly to you."

I sat as Grandpa told me, not understanding what this was all about. Finally, I ducked my head and resolved to be good.

"I think you should know that this is the home where I grew up, Caroline. My father worked hard, and became a successful solicitor. He built the house for his new bride, who was my dear mother.

"We entered the house on the second story, the main level of this house. The rooms branch off from the foyer. This is the parlor, a large morning room where Violet teaches classes is there to the left. Further along the hall, you will see a formal dining room, and a substantially sized ballroom with a separate gallery for the orchestra. There are ten sizeable bedrooms upstairs on the third level. The kitchen, pantry, laundry, and servant's quarters are downstairs on the lower level.

"The house sits on a small hill, with a verdant lawn growing down to a stand of woods. A small rushing stream flows at the rear of the estate. I used to do a lot of fishing in that stream when I was a boy," Grandpa said, with an odd look in his eyes.

Maybe Grandpa was remembering, I don't know, but seemed like it made him sad, I thought.

After what seemed like a long wait, the door to the parlor slid open. A tiny, plump lady of fine quality entered. She tiptoed forward, and embraced Grandpa in a tight little hug before settling herself upright on a matching settee amid her layers of shiny blue taffeta skirts. The lady's tiny feet could not even reach the carpet when she sat down.

She rang a little bell, and the same Negro woman brought in a shiny silver tea service, and placed it on a small dark wooden table in front of her mistress.

"Now Amos, whom do we have here?" She asked politely, looking me up and down, from head to toe.

I got the impression a wisp of the skunk smell still remained about my person. I didn't seem to measure up in her eyes.

"Why Violet," Grandpa began a little huffily, "I wrote to you about Caroline, she is my granddaughter. You know they took

Elizabeth away with Ashbill, and the boys. Caroline here is all we have left. Your letter said you'd take her into your school."

"But Amos, I didn't expect her to be a . . . well a woodsy. Polly was always a woman of culture, taste, and tranquility. She could never have such a granddaughter. Then too, this girl seems very young, younger than the others in the academy."

"Things change Violet, as you can see. Now, will you help me out, or do I have to take her to someone else?"

"Oh Amos, you know what a tease I am," she said prettily, reaching over and putting her small white hand on Grandpa's arm. "Of course, Amos, I would adore to show...Caroline, is it? How to become a young lady of genteel quality."

"Oh brother!" I said, without the least thought of how my exclamation would affect this aunt.

"Caroline," she said, with acidic sweetness. "Young ladies are to be seen, and not heard!"

"Amos, I can tell we have our work cut out for us," she said, looking hard at Grandpa.

"I knew you should have stayed here in Norfolk with your church. You can see this young girl has proven me right.

"I am sorry you went away to that college where they filled your head with the notion to go out, and convert the heathen Indians.

Through the goodness of my heart, I have supported your ministry throughout the years, otherwise I believe you and Polly would have starved."

"That is neither here nor there Violet, need I remind you father left this house to you and me in equal shares?"

"And what do you have to show for your ministry to the heathen, Amos? You allowed your precious Elizabeth to marry one. I still shudder to think of that misfortunate alliance. She could have married a professional man, or a man of industry or commerce and enjoyed a comfortable life. She made her bed, and now she is lying in it, as the adage goes.

I pray God keeps her safe. I can't imagine her traipsing across the country with the Indians to some God-forsaken place in the west."

I watched, as Aunt Violet seemed to shudder to emphasize her discomfort at the notion. After a few minutes of her tirade, I realized tears were slipping down my cheeks. I turned my head away, and looked around the beautiful room, seeking a distraction, anything to get my mind off the plight of my lovely mother, and the rest of my family. I was sorry this woman brought that up. I knew I was in over my head, so right then I resolved to talk Grandpa into taking me home. I didn't like his uppity sister one bit.

He looked glum, took the delicate cup of English tea from her extended hand, and gulped it down. Then he seemed to rouse himself.

"We appreciate your support of our ministry Violet, and it is only right you have done so. Now, there's no reason to rehash old family history, particularly in front of Caroline.

You've upset her, and she's been through enough in the last year and a half. I thought you two would take to each other, and she could stay with you and learn what she needs to learn to get along in the world, and maybe, God willing to make a good marriage."

I felt a shock go through my body. What's Grandpa talking about, leaving me here with this fancy woman? She might be a sister to him, but she's nothing to me. She don't even like me. I sensed that right off.

"You may leave Caroline here with me, Amos. I'll do my best for her. As for a fortuitous marriage, I believe we should leave her future in God's hands. He knows best!"

AS I KISSED GRANDPA goodbye, I clung to him, but he set me back down on the settee and left me there. I tried hard not to cry, but the tears kept creeping down my cheeks despite my resolve.

The lady told me to stay seated while she showed Grandpa to the door. I clutched my hands together in my lap, and sent up prayers to God to rescue me, but of course he didn't. It just seemed like maybe he wanted me living here with this woman.

"Caroline," she told me when she returned. "You may call me Lady Ashley, you must never address me as Aunt Violet, or Aunt Ashley. It would not do for the young ladies, who reside here, to learn we have a close relationship."

I vowed to call her Aunt Violet, to myself, just to be stubborn.

Before supper, I saw a few of the young ladies as they walked to another room. A piano began playing, and someone sang. Aunt Violet didn't introduce me. She didn't want to claim a relationship with me. I could see right off that I was an embarrassment to her. I resolved to pack my things, and leave as soon as possible.

She asked me to pick up my bag, she then took me down the back stairs and gave me a tiny room of my own, off the kitchen. It was away from the young ladies for which I was thankful. I'd seen enough of them with their beautiful hair, fine dresses, and lovely manners to match.

The first night I cried myself to sleep, but I woke early refreshed, and eager to explore my new room, and my new home. For breakfast, I ate soft white biscuits, fruit, and a big glass of milk.

After the breakfast dishes, the maid Tezrah gave me a tour of the back of the house and the grounds, as she called them. As we walked along, I asked her about this place since it looked like I was going to live here for a while.

"Miss Caroline, since you come here with Reverend Frost, I will tell you what I know about Miz Ashley's academy.

"My family's worked for the Frosts since Miz Ashley's Pa first built this place. Miz Ashley and Reverend Frost grew up right here in this house. My granny was the first in my family to work here. When granny couldn't work no more, my auntie come for a long spell. Then five years ago, my brother Frank started work here, and two years ago, when my auntie couldn't work no more, I come to work for Miz Ashley. I was just 14 years old, then.

Miz Ashley met Lord Ashley about twenty years ago when

he come from England to stay with his Ashley cousins. Lord Ashley's related to Captain John Ashley, who was a signer of the charter of the state of Virginia. Captain Ashley's family lived in Norfolk ever since 1606.

They got married, and she moved with him back to England. They lived there about ten years. After he got sick, they come back here. The house needed a lot of work, so Lord Thomas Ashley used his family's money to fix up this place the way you see it.

He knew he was pretty sick, and he wanted Miz Ashley to have a nice place to live once he passed on. After he passed, Miz Ashley started this school for the young ladies."

I was glad Tezrah told me the story. It was more than Grandpa told me, and it helped me to see how Aunt Violet established the academy.

Yet, I still did not know why I needed the academy, or why I was here in Virginia at the academy, rather than with Grandpa and Gramma.

I felt like Tezrah gossiped when she told me the story. Maybe she's proud of this place where she and her family worked for so many years?

We walked down a few stairs to a path, which wound through a few big trees, colorful roses, and yellow and red fall flowers. I asked Tezrah their names. She showed me yellow jasmine, forsythia, red flowering quince, and bushes with small white flowers that she called Christmas roses. They didn't look like roses to me.

We walked next to some greenery, and flowering bushes that she couldn't name. The gardens looked beautiful, stiff and formal, not like the wildflowers I knew in the woods and forests. She told me that come spring, many different varieties of flowers would appear.

On the way, we passed small tables and chairs, and a few graceful benches set close to the flowerbeds. I watched a few of the young women walking the paths arm in arm visiting with each other.

We continued east on the path next to the lawn toward the river, and finally come to the woods, there a stream rushed along next to some big rocks. I felt right at ho me, we left so quickly. I promised myself I would be back.

I turned to look at the house, the windows of the two upper stories shone in the morning sun, and bright draperies lined the inside of each window.

Tezrah pointed out the terrace that ran all along the second story of the house. Ten heavy, carved stone columns sat underneath to prop up the terrace. Climbing roses grew up the white columns and covered the side railings of the terrace, beautiful to my way of thinking.

"Oh my!" I said out loud. I'd heard of castles, and I figured I must live in one now.

"I knew you'd like the terrace, Miss Caroline. Miz Ashley often entertains there."

She showed me the large kitchen garden on the side of the house. It was about finished for the season. Next, we come to the pump at the back of the house that supplied water for the kitchen. She told me one of my duties was to pump water into the kitchen buckets and bring them inside. We walked a short distance to the woodshed, where they stored wood for the house fireplaces. I would also need to bring in logs and kindling for the kitchen fireplace, when Cook needed it.

We visited the stables last. I met Tezrah's brother, Mister Frank, and saw the four pretty horses that lived there.

"Miss Caroline" Mister Frank bobbed his head to me.

He seemed nice, and I liked him.

I wanted to visit the stables, and get to know the pretty horses, as soon as they let me. I liked horses, and Grandpa saw to it that I learned to ride.

Later in the morning, Aunt Violet come to the kitchen, and gave me work to do, maybe to earn my keep, she didn't say. She also brought me a dark plaid dress for work, a dark-colored sunbonnet that covered most of my whole face, and a pair of white cotton gloves. The clothing was not new, I could see that right away, but I loved the dress on sight.

"Caroline," she said in a harsh voice. "Your complexion is an abomination, much too dark to be fashionable. I do not know how you lived in your previous life, but beginning today, you will wear a sunbonnet and gloves whenever you venture outside. Perhaps in time, your hideous brown coloring will fade.

"Then every evening prior to retiring, I want you to apply this powder to your face and hands. In time, it should lighten your complexion to a more acceptable hue."

I looked at Aunt Violet, and noticed the milky color of her skin. To my way of thinking, she looked pale and sickly. Hard to believe she tolerated it.

I took the jar of powder from her hand, but vowed never to use it. If God wanted me to have a pale skin, he would have given me one.

When Aunt Violet left, the cook called me over to her. She seemed like a motherly woman. She wore a mobcap, and ringlets from her bright-white hair escaped, and curled prettily around her face. She wore the kindest look in her light brown eyes, and her pink cheeks glowed with health, not the washed-out whiteness of Aunt Violet's skin.

"I am Mrs. Fleming, Child, but you can call me Cook, everybody does. What she give you there?"

"A jar of powder to whiten my skin, Ma'am," I said, curtsying to her.

"How old are you, Child?"

"I'll be twelve years old in April, Ma'am."

"Umm! Umm, and not even twelve years old, yet! Give me the jar, Child. That ain't nothin' a pretty girl like you need concern herself with."

She took the jar from my hand and emptied the contents into the dustbin. Then she washed and dried the jar, and filled it with fine white flour.

"Miz Ashley won't be none the wiser unless you let on. Now put the jar in your room, and every now and again pat some of this good flour on your face and hands. It will look like you're doing what she wants."

I helped in the kitchen, hauling wood and water for Cook. I understood that kind of work. It ain't no different from what I did for my gramma at the cabin, and at the encampment with my tribe. I felt comfortable in the big warm kitchen.

Cook kept a fire going in the fireplace day and night. Each day, she cooked a variety of meats on a spit turned by her twin nephews, each taking turns. The first day there, my stomach got the best of me, and I could feel the spit filling my mouth at all the delicious smells.

I took my meals with the kitchen help that day, and for the next months. Aunt Violet told me she wanted me to get civilized before letting me meet any of the young ladies who lived upstairs in the house.

On my second and third nights in the house, I didn't sleep well. I woke up tired, but held up my end of the work. If Aunt Violet turned me out, where would I go?

I thought about Grandpa riding farther and farther away from me. I thought about my friend Lily too, and talked to her a little in the language of our people. I knew I shouldn't, Grandpa wanted me to forget being Cherokee. He said I needed to become a white girl. English seemed a mite easier for me, but I don't want to forget my other heritage.

The fourth night, I dreamt I walked down to the Elizabeth River, after supper. There, I watched the reflected glow from the sunset transform the river into waves of brilliantly moving colors.

A little off the path, a small boat secured to the shoreline waited for me. I untied the rope painter attached to the bow, and climbed into the boat wanting to take a little ride, enjoy the sunset, and maybe catch a fish or two.

I pushed off from the shore, and sailed, on the river. The current caught the boat, and drove me farther out into the slipstream of the fast-moving river. I threw the sea anchor over the side to slow my progress, but the rope followed the anchor into the river, I couldn't grab it in time! I looked for oars, but there were none.

I was lost and alone, more alone than I'd ever felt in my life. I saw no other boats, or ships on the river, only the great current.

The flow pulled me to a little sandbar out in the middle, it looked empty. I struggled to get out of the boat, but took too long. Again, the powerful stream caught the boat, and rushed me faster and faster south, away from the town.

I woke up to great wracking sobs. I lay there quivering in every muscle. I cried! "Help me, Grandpa, help me! I'm all alone, Grandpa! Where are you, Grandpa?"

Then I realized no one slept near me in the house, I was truly alone. Cook and Tezrah left after supper, once they finished work for the day. Aunt Violet and the young ladies all slept upstairs, two floors above me.

The dreams came again for several nights. I thought about the dreams during the days working in the kitchen. I didn't know the meaning. A message? I hoped I would be bright enough to figure it out.

I was on a boat, floating in the middle of the river, the current flowing fast around me. No one helped me, or cared enough to save me. I was all alone!

After a few days of this, I realized those dreams echoed my new life. I was here alone. I shivered when I thought of that horrible word, *ALONE*!

I was drowning! I didn't know what to do, or where to go. Then it come to me. Grandpa gave me away to Aunt Violet, I knew that, but I knew too, I was not alone, Jesus was there with me!

I prayed, *"Jesus you're all I have, help me see you're all I need!"*

By Friday of the second week, I felt some better. Cook took to me right away, and let me help some with the food in the kitchen. She called me her poor little honey child. She put her arm around me when no one was looking, and slipped me sweetmeats to eat on the sly.

At night when I read my little Bible and prayed, I thanked God for His goodness in giving me such a kind woman to befriend me, a lost little girl.

I GLIMPSED A FEW OF the young ladies who resided at the academy from time to time. They reminded me of the fluff of dandelion flowers, all white and pretty, with little substance. I heard them twittering to each other. I was not sure what they twittered about.

They wore pretty, light-colored morning dresses trimmed with lace and ribbons. Later in the day, they changed to darker-hued afternoon dresses, and they wore beautiful elegant dresses for supper. They seemed to always be changing clothes.

The laundress was forever complaining about all the morning gowns, afternoon gowns, and evening gowns, and their accompanying chemises, pantaloons, and layers and layers of underskirts that she needed to wash, starch, and iron each day.

If that's what makes a lady of quality, I thought to myself one day, *then I'm just as glad I won't ever become one.*

Aunt Violet tried to get me to give up some of my wild ways. She'd regular-like, have me come into the morning room, where she worked with me on my reading and ciphering.

When it comes to what she called diction lessons, well now, I just didn't see no sense in it at all. What's the difference how a body says something? I didn't want to open my mouth around her. I was wary of her always telling me,

"No Caroline! We do not use the word, 'ain't.' We say am not. I am not, you are not, he, she, it is not."

I mimicked her English accent with all my might, but it come out sounding almost as bad as our hound Thumper whining at the moon.

To be fair to her, she warmed up to me a mite. She brought me some dresses and undergarments, which weren't much different from what I saw the other young ladies wearing. Tezrah told me Aunt Violet kept a closet stuffed full of clothes the young ladies outgrew.

Besides my three work dresses, there was a blue gingham morning gown that I loved to death. I wore it to my classes. I'd never owned nothin' that pretty before.

Then there was also a pink one with figures running all over it, a dark blue afternoon gown, and another one a kind of piney green in color. Since I didn't eat with the young ladies, I didn't have to dress for dinner.

Aunt Violet told me to change dresses every day. I couldn't get the hang of that. I didn't get dirty, not like I used to at home. She promised me when I grew more ladylike there was a green silk, she wanted the dressmaker to sew up for me. She said it would complement my coloring, whatever that was.

I guess I'm getting along. I missed Grandpa, though, I was mad at the way he lit out of there so fast. I hoped guilt rode his back at leaving me alone with strangers. I knew it wasn't the Christian way to think, but that's how I felt. He promised me he'd be back soon with Gramma, but three months passed by, and I ain't seen hide nor hair of him.

I packed away my thoughts of striking out on my own. I didn't know where I'd go, and I'd have nothing to hunt with as Grandpa took the gun belt with him.

My skinning knife, I prized above everything else I owned, except for my Bible. Mister Ned Storm made the knife his own self. He always wore it in the sheath on his belt. When I first arrived at our tribe's camp, he took the knife and the sheath off his belt, and handed them to me. He cautioned me to take good care of them, to keep them safe, to oil the knife, keep it sharp, and it would serve me throughout my life!

I liked to take my knife out at night and remember the time living with our friends in the wilderness, and the big friendly man who lost his life saving our tribe. I hid the knife back behind a drawer in my dresser. I never wanted Aunt Violet to know. She wouldn't understand!

Grandpa wrote me a short note. It arrived during my 4th month of captivity at Aunt Violets. He said our friends from Tennessee planned to move, and eventually join The Eastern Cherokee, a settled tribe in North Carolina. In 1819, they signed a treaty with the government, received land, and were not taken away during the removal.

My biggest friend turned out to be the little Bible Grandpa gave me. I could open it up anytime I got lonesome, felt sad, or blue, and God's word was right there to cheer me up. When I felt bad, I read from Proverbs. I liked the verse, *"A merry heart maketh a cheerful countenance: but by sorrow of the heart the spirit is broken. Proverbs 15:13."*

The verse told me to be happy, and not worry about the bad things I was facing. It was like a message from God and it made me feel better! I went around telling myself, *"A merry heart! A merry heart,"* whenever I needed a little cheering up.

I MADE FRIENDS WITH Tezrah, the kitchen maid. Aunt Violet don't like it, but I needed to talk to somebody. Tezrah asked me to call her Tezzie. She told me herself, that she was born a free Negro. She lived in the town with her father and mother.

I also got to know Tezzie's brother, Mister Frank, a little. He's a free Negro, too. He hired on to work for Aunt Violet as the handyman five years earlier. He lived in town by himself.

His job was to care for the horses, the barn, the paddock, and he oversaw the men who looked after the lawn and gardens. He also worked as the butler when Aunt Violet entertained.

Mister Frank a funny man, called himself a Jack-Of-All-Trades. I liked him. He took special care to lift my spirits from time to time by whistling a merry tune, or telling me a funny joke, or a story about his growing-up years. He's older than Tezzie, at least four years older.

Tezzie told me stories about Mister Frank, and his new girlfriend, Labella. She said they talked about gettin' hitched. Tezzie liked to talk about men and gettin' hitched a lot. She told me she kept her eye on a man who worked as a clerk in the mercantile. She said he worked at a respectable job. I agreed with her, but I didn't see why she couldn't find something else to chatter about. Men didn't interest me, except maybe the pretty boy, I saw that one time when I was alone in the woods. I'd have liked to see how much he knew about fishing.

One day as I helped Cook at dinnertime, she asked me to take baskets of food out to some Negro workers who sat under a tree close to the barn.

They'd worked all morning in the gardens, and looked quite tired. I saw them shake their heads, and mutter to each other. I did not know why. They seemed mad about something. Then, one of them smiled as I walked closer. The others stood removed their hats, and nodded their thanks when I sat down the food baskets.

They reminded me of my great loss. I could mutter and shake my head too, because the government took my family away. Instead, I prayed every day that God went before my folks, and protected them. I couldn't imagine marching all the way west through the winter snow, and cold. I prayed they survived.

In my heart, I still cried out for my ma, pa, and my brothers. I can almost feel their spirits around me if I closed my eyes tight, and looked inside me deep enough. Someday, God willing, I was going out to Indian Territory, and I would see my folks again. I trusted God, my folks still lived by then.

Chapter 6
<u>NEWS OF THE REMOVAL</u>

February arrived, and each day the robins and wrens sang their cheerful songs from the apple trees in the lower garden. When I could I liked to walk outside along the paths, and through the gardens after a storm to enjoy the freshened spring air.

Thank you, God, I prayed, *I'm alive here, and not living up north, where a blizzard raged for the past three days.*

It'd been five weeks, since the last time I went outside on my own. Then, Aunt Violet dressed nicely, and with three of the older girls in tow, drove in the surrey to the parsonage where the vicar's wife invited them for a musical afternoon, and refreshments.

The constant stormy weather kept me indoors more than I liked, and I felt long overdue for a day to myself. Again today, Aunt Violet drove away for the afternoon, with three more of the young ladies with her in the surrey.

I slipped outside, happy to be by myself for a change. The other young ladies, seemed content to just stay inside and sew, play piano, or visit with each other.

Once out of the house, I walked to the stable to pet the beautiful brown horse called Chocolate. I wanted her to get to know me, so I could begin riding her.

Aunt Violet believed I was still unsocialized, so she often excluded me from various entertainments, I was happy to say. I couldn't see myself sitting still for the whole afternoon, a cup of tea in one hand, and a plate of dainty cakes in the other, while some woman with a wobbly voice gave out with the latest arias from England.

I tried my best to be demure, and to learn all the proper graces as Aunt Violet called them but so far, I was still clumsy and gauche, her words not mine.

The gardens beckoned to me. I walked down to the rushing stream to see if I could do some fishing. I returned to the house with a nice string of fish for supper.

When I come into the kitchen, Cook smiled, and told me, "Madame has arranged for a gala ball. Today, I am planning the menus and the decorations."

Later, Tezzie said she enjoyed Aunt Violet's galas. She loved to dress up in her party costume, and serve at the dinners. She said it was exciting.

"I have a secret to tell you Miss Caroline, but you can't tell a soul." That got my attention. No one had ever trusted me with a secret.

"If you want to have some fun, the night of the gala, go to bed early as your aunt will tell you to. Then, when you hear the music begin, you can sneak upstairs. There's a small room next to the minstrel's galley. It has a fine view of all the doings."

I would go and watch the gala ball, I thought. *I needed some fun.* The idea lit a bubble of joy in my heart!

I spent most of my free time in the kitchen helping Cook prepare for the gala ball. I enjoyed cooking more than watching the young ladies as they primped, dressed themselves, and filled their hours with giggled conversations comparing the attributes of the various young men. Not my cup of tea as the saying goes.

The day of the big event finally arrived. Aunt Violet asked me to retire to my room at 5 p.m., and not leave for the rest of the evening.

I heard the orchestra warm up their instruments about 8 p.m.

I loved music, and a full orchestra made a big difference in the sound and quality of the songs they played. I opened my door to listen.

A little while later, I snuck out of my basement room, and up the back stairway. I pressed my body next to the wall and held my breath not wanting to be discovered. Finally, I reached the minstrel's galley and the little room next to it.

I went inside and crouched down. I was there a good long while before the orchestra once again tuned up their instruments. Then, all at once there was a big crash of drums, and the music began.

I kneeled and looked through the opening to watch what went on downstairs. I could hardly believe what I saw.

Beautifully dressed young ladies walked slowly down the stairs to the foyer. A line of young gentlemen stood beside the last newel post on the stairway. As each lady reached the foot of the stairs, a young gentleman crooked his arm, the young lady placed her gloved hand there, and together they slowly walked to the ballroom.

The ladies in their beautiful dresses, reminded me of bouquets of flowers. The young gentlemen wore fancy black suits. It touched my heart to see so much beauty.

The orchestra played a waltz, and the young couples began to dance. I clamped a tight hand over my mouth to keep from laughing out loud.

I decided then and there I would never dress up fancy, or dance with a young gentleman like that. I wondered if that's what it's like to be a young lady of quality? If so, that's not for me!

I RUSHED INTO THE MORNING room a trifle late for classes one morning, earning a frown from Aunt Violet.

"Young ladies pay attention, please! We are not here to chat," she said, clapping her hands sharply together, bringing quiet to the group of five.

"I want to impart to you a little of the history of our fair city of Norfolk. Since you now reside in this fine city, you must learn to converse and reply intelligently about our city's illustrious history, if a young man happens to comment on it to you."

I heard a series of sighs from the young ladies, causing Aunt's frown to deepen. Me, on the other hand, I was excited to learn the history of Norfolk.

"In our history lesson today," she continued, "we will learn about the brutal attack on our fair city by the British, on January 1, 1776.

Our city suffered severe destruction when four British ships leveled the entire waterfront, many fine homes, and over 50 thriving businesses with cannon fire. The brutal attack led to the Revolutionary War.

"Fortunately, my father, still a young man at that time, did not endeavor to build this treasured home until many years later. Therefore, it did not suffer during the onslaught.

"By 1820, our city fathers completed the rebuilding of our illustrious city. The quick rebuilding shows the fine mettle of the citizenry of Norfolk. They rose above the devastation to restore, improve, and beautify, which enabled Norfolk to become a rare jewel in the crown of our great state of Virginia.

"Today, our city has become a substantial municipality of commercial, philanthropic, and enterprising achievements. I am proud to be a citizen of Norfolk, and I trust you young ladies are too."

ONE WEEK, WE STUDIED the soldier statesman Andrew Jackson, and our existing president, Martin Van Buren. Aunt Violet called President Jackson, "that beloved man." I understood that to mean Aunt Violet honored Andrew Jackson. She went on to say, "Martin Van Buren was a far cry from our country's beloved soldier-statesman Andrew Jackson." I tended to agree, but I believed both men equally bad.

She continued, "I shall never forget the day that I personally served refreshments to President Jackson at a reception held in his honor at our church. He graciously stood, clasped my hand in both of his, bowed to me, and addressed me as Lady Ashley." I watched Aunt's face blush with pleasure at the memory.

As for me, I could never cotton to the man who first wrote the order to remove my Cherokee family from our home in middle Tennessee, but I couldn't tell that to Aunt Violet, she would never have understood.

Our current president, Martin Van Buren, another politician I disliked just as much, or more than Andrew Jackson, enforced Jackson's edicts. I remembered word for word what the newspapers wrote about Martin Van Buren.

In his first message to Congress, in December 1837, Van Buren called the Indian Removal, *The settled policy of the country*. He also said, *The decrease in numbers of the tribes within the limits of the states and territories has been most rapid. If they are removed, they can be protected from those associations, and evil practices, which exert so pernicious and destructive an influence over their destinies.*

Aunt Violet looked at the Democratic Martin Van Buren as uncouth. She told us that during his campaign for the presidency he coined a new phrase, "O.K." It stood for "Old Kinderhook." Kinderhook, New York, was where Van Buren was born.

Aunt Violet said she would never use that disgusting phrase, "O.K." it was just another example of the boorishness of the man. She also called him the little Dutchman, because his family immigrated from Holland in the 1600's.

Aunt Violet touched lightly on politics, but it sparked my interest. One time when I was in the stables, I saw Mister Frank reading a newspaper, and I asked him what it said.

"Here, read for yourself, Miss Caroline. I'm finished with it."

I took the paper back to my room, and learned the country blamed Van Buren for the panic of 1837, when economic conditions in our country took a downturn resulting in a depression, loss of jobs, and the closing of banks and businesses. Yet Van Buren vowed that he inherited much of the turmoil from Andrew Jackson's policies, something else I would never tell Aunt Violet.

A few days later, Aunt Violet taught that from October to December in that year of 1840, we would see the election of a new president. She went on to say, that Van Buren's opponent from the Whig Party, the honorable William Henry Harrison, would himself, never repeat anything as vile as O.K.

Sounded to me like she had changed political parties, she must have abandoned the Democratic Party, and now favored the Whig Party, and as such she endorsed General Harrison, a former governor of Virginia, and an old hero from the War of 1812!

The newspaper presented Harrison's slogan, "Tippecanoe and Tyler too" that phrase captured the attention of the voters. Thereafter they called General Harrison, "Tippecanoe."

I also learned to make small talk, like comments about the weather, the fineness of the repast, if we were dining, the latest song, or a popular new book, most of that seemed mindless to me.

For the time being, learning to be a pampered lady of quality, made me feel content. I'd see just how long I would put up with it!

Before bed, I read Proverbs 1:7, *"The fear of the Lord is the beginning of knowledge: but fools despise wisdom and instruction."*

That was me all right, a fool. I needed to thank God that I gained wisdom and instruction, and not gripe and complain about it. God in his time would get me to where he wanted me to go. When I got there, maybe he'd equip me with enough knowledge so that I'd no longer be a simpleton. At least, that's what I prayed.

THE YEAR SCURRIED BY for me, April 22, my thirteenth birthday, the church bells rang loudly as I finished dressing for the early service. Aunt Violet made church one of her instructive periods.

All the young ladies departed the day before to enjoy the Sabbath with their respective families. Me, I only had Aunt Violet. Tezzie too went home to worship at her own church with other people of color.

That morning, I wore my new green silk. The first dress, ever made for me by a dressmaker. It complemented my coloring, as my aunt liked to say. It also lent rich, red highlights to my auburn hair, and a pretty sparkle to my green eyes. Aunt Violet taught me to notice those things when selecting a costume to wear.

The skirt was still short, fitting for someone of my age. It brushed the tops of my fashionable black boots, Aunt also bought for me. The dressmaker left a deep hem on the gown, so when I was old enough, it could be let down. A long skirt would be mine in three years, on my sixteenth birthday, if I still lived with Aunt Violet, and if the fashion of the dress still pleased me.

A bit of white lace petticoat peeked underneath the hem when I raised my dress, to carefully ascend the stairs, rather than run up as I usually liked to do. That showed I was more ladylike in my deportment. Another of Aunt Violet's words, not mine.

Aunt Violet seemed pleased with my progress in becoming a lady. Right after breakfast, she carefully tied a black velvet choker around my neck. It matched the black velvet ribbon trim of my dress. She also handed me a new deep green bonnet, with matching black velvet trim. It was large for me, so I'd wear it for several years. When I put it on, I lifted my chin a trifle, and the green feathers from the bonnet swayed in front of my eyes. I giggled with pleasure.

On the way to the door, I paused at the mirror in the entryway. I told myself. *Well Caroline, you are purtier than a speckled pup. No, that ain't right, I mean, that isn't right.* I should say, *"You are lovely my dear, in a low-voiced English-Virginian accent,"* as I imagined my dream lad would speak.

"Caroline! Don't dawdle!" Aunt Violet said sharply! "We must get on!"

In the great State of Virginia, the church we attended was a monstrous building. It sat at the end of the street where we resided. Aunt Violet called it a granite edifice. She told me it was fifty years old. The first time I attended there, I almost fell over when I craned my neck to see to the top of the golden cross, that sat upon the main spire.

The church located atop a small knoll gave us a view of the Elizabeth River. Aunt Violet always took my arm as we walked down the street to the church, and climbed the seven steps to the front door.

Once there, I always tried to linger and look around, since we had climbed up pretty high. I found it interesting to watch the boats going back and forth along the river.

Aunt Violet hardly noticed the view. "Do not be a simpleton, Caroline," she always told me, as she impatiently took my elbow in her hand to direct me the way I really did not want to go.

Once inside, we passed through a big room that Aunt called the vestibule. The ceiling went up as high as the roof. Inside the church, we walked on a thick red carpet down to the family pew.

Each family occupied their own box seating, with doors on each end of the pew, maybe to ensure no one sat with any other family. A brass plaque fastened in the middle of the door to Aunt's pew, said, "Lady Violet Ashley."

The first time I went to church with Aunt Violet, I felt scared I would make a mistake, and embarrass her. I sat like a wooden statue, only kneeling when she knelt, standing when she stood, and sitting when she sat. I didn't open my mouth to sing, not wanting my accent and backwoods diction to come forth and humiliate her.

After that, I grew more familiar with the opulence of this huge church, another of Aunt Violet's words. Rainbow-hued sunlight beamed through the stained-glass windows, golden candle sconces lined the walls, and lighted candles surrounded the carved golden cross, which stood in the center of the ornate altar.

There was a kind of little hut on the right-hand side of the church close to the seating area, not exactly a hut, but a small wooden stand open on the sides and covered over with a carved roof. The reverend climbed the curved stairway, and stood inside this shelter to deliver his message. I don't know why.

The church services there were like nothing I'd ever seen at home. When Grandpa preached, an assortment of neighbors filled the backless, wooden church benches. Before the removal, Indian families, the white men who married up with the Indian women, as well as white families who lived in the town came to hear Grandpa speak.

I tended to shy away from some of them, but Grandpa accepted everyone, as was fitting. Lately, he wrote that now, mostly white families attended his church services

The people in this church dressed elegantly, and seemed like a quiet lot. They sang and bowed in prayer, sat, stood, or knelt. The service consisted of songs, the readings of the daily office, the Psalms of the day from the Bible, a short sermon from the reverend, and the closing prayer. No one could fall asleep in this church service the congregation were always getting up and down from their seats.

After the reverend's benediction, Aunt Violet opened the door from our pew, and once again we walked the deeply carpeted aisle to the front door. Aunt took her time, she did not speak to anyone, but smiled and nodded her head deeply to other women of her age. No one spoke to me, and I felt grateful to Aunt Violet for the dark bonnet, which partially hid my face.

Aunt was kind, in a cold distant way, yet how my humble and lovable Grandpa could have such a sister only God in His heaven would know. I'm sure she saw it as fulfilling her Christian duty to civilize and educate me to the best of her ability.

I prayed at the service for God to help me do right by Aunt Violet, she tolerated me, kept me safe under her wing, and tried to knock the wildness and backwoods out of me. I prayed God would bestow his special blessings on my family, on Grandpa, Gramma, and Aunt Violet, as well.

IN THE FALL OF THE year 1841, I was thirteen and a half years old. Aunt believed I was more responsible, so she allowed me to walk alone to the mercantile. There, I asked the clerk for Lady Violet Ashley's mail, paid out the required number of coins, then walked slowly back to the house as if I collected the mail every day of my life.

I didn't stop to see what the pack of dogs chased after down the center of Main Street, and I didn't stop to poke the bundle leaning against the side of the mercantile to see what it contained.

Caroline, I told myself. *You are growing up. You have more important things on your mind these days, leave the running and poking to mere boys.*

I sounded like Aunt Violet. Could it be that I was becoming a lady? If so, I resolved never to lose my nerve, my heritage, or myself. Upon returning to the house, I presented the mail to Aunt Violet, and she handed me a letter.

I ran, and bragged to Tezzie, then rushed out back to the privacy of the sheltering garden, and a graceful stone bench. I hurriedly broke the seal, and read the words before me on the page:

Dear Granddaughter, I arrived safely home from my travels to the east in October, after my latest journey. As you know, I have the concerns of our friends heavy on my heart. I met with several of the tribal chiefs, and prayed with them. I believe in time they will rebuild themselves a rich, new life in North Carolina. Keep our friends, and those important matters in your prayers. I know in my heart that God will do his utmost to help our friends establish themselves in the new land.

I still feel much sorrow, I realize I failed in my efforts to keep your own dear parents safe from the removal. I pray word would arrive of their condition, I understand, the journeys west should be completed by now.

Many perished during the incarceration in the stockades, but I felt our folks survived. They traveled with Reverend Jesse Bushyhead, and through the grace of God, many more in his contingent would be spared than others who traveled without God in their midst.

I trust God cared for our family. I believe he would have kept them safe and secure during these last months, I know he'll have his hand on them in the future.

I am holding to the promises as told in Isaiah 51:11, "Therefore the redeemed of the Lord shall return, and come with singing unto Zion; and everlasting joy shall be upon their head: they shall obtain gladness and joy, sorrow and mourning shall flee away."

God is also watching over you, and keeping you safe. Be a good girl, and mind Lady Ashley, Caroline. When you met her, she seemed like a lot of fuss and feathers, but she has a heart of gold beneath her underpinnings. I wouldn't have left you with her if I'd thought different!

The following are my thoughts for you, from Colossians 2:1-2. Caroline:

For I would that ye knew the great conflict I have for you and for them at Laodicea, (our friends). And for as many as have not seen my face in the flesh, that their hearts might be comforted, being knit together in love, and unto all riches of the full assurance of understanding, to the acknowledgment of the mystery of God, and of the Father, and Christ. In whom, are hid all the treasures of wisdom and knowledge.

I say lest any man should beguile you with enticing words. For though I am absent in the flesh, yet am I with you in the spirit, joying, and beholding your order, and the steadfastness of your faith in Christ. As ye have therefore received Christ Jesus the Lord, so walk ye in Him, rooted and built up in Him, and stablished in the faith, as ye have been taught, with thanksgiving.

Your Grandfather,

THAT WAS SOME LETTER my grandpa wrote me. His ending was so high sounding as if he were preaching a sermon, or something, not at all like he talked to me in person.

What did he mean to be good and mind Aunt Violet? How long would I have to stay here? When will Grandpa and Gramma come to take me home? Would I have to go all the way through, and become a young lady of quality before they come and get me?

I held the letter to my chest, and sobbed my heart out. And why didn't Gramma write to me? Didn't she miss me as much as I missed her?

I re-read the parts of the letter which concerned my folks.

"Thank you, God, for keeping them safe," I prayed. Again, I vowed I would join them in the new land the first chance I got. I didn't care if they lived in a cave, and we hunted for our dinner. It would be better for us to be together.

The tears continued, and I cried for my old life in what Aunt Violet called the wilderness. I missed it all, the piney woods, every familiar tree, stump, and rock, Sugar Creek, and the brown trout who rested there in the shade of the old oak tree. I even missed that ole bag of fleas Thumper. I needed him to come, knock me flat, and lick my face until I felt quivery all over with his joy.

I put my letter from Grandpa away in the bottom of my trunk. I would read it again another day when I didn't feel so sorry for myself.

I couldn't write to let Grandpa know I got his letter. He sent no return address, and I knew about the danger if people found out where I'd gotten to. I would have to trust in God and Grandpa.

Now, I needed to go fetch wood for Cook, and help prepare the noon dinner.

I CHANGED INTO MY WORK dress, and ran out the back door to the woodshed, forgetting my sunbonnet in my haste. I made a pile of sticks and found a nice log to take in for the fireplace.

On the way out, I spied a pile of old newspapers stuck in one corner of the shed. I saw right away the dates of the newspapers were from several years ago. I leafed through many of them, and felt thunderstruck when I saw articles on the Indian removal.

I hid the pile of papers beneath some pieces of cast-off furniture. I'd retrieve them later, and take my time reading through them to look for information on my folks.

Grandpa tried to tell me some of the whys and wherefores of our people, rounded up, shackled, imprisoned, and then made to walk for months to the west, but I can't remember much of what he said. I was still shaken by what went on with my tribe.

It was little enough I knew, they never talked about it when I lived with our people. We were busy living life, trying to stay alive, and not get captured. Now, maybe I'd learn more.

"Indian Removal Accomplished!"

. . . declared the headline from the first newspaper in the pile. My body quivered, and I gasped for breath, to think that these people in the state of Virginia, so far from my Tennessee home, could have heard about what went on with my people. I can't imagine they would care other than to say good riddance. I read every word of the article, and then looked for more in the other newspapers.

The articles were all there, as if the good Lord put them aside for me, so I could follow in my mind where my folks went, and why. I hid the newspapers under the paper lining at the bottom of the trunk Aunt Violet gave me, and smuggled them to my room, over a week, one newspaper at a time down the front of my dress. I read them late at night after Aunt Violet made sure I was fast asleep.

Someday, I aimed to show them to Grandpa, as soon as he came back for me. I wanted to keep them my lifelong to show my children and grandchildren, if I ever bore children of my own, and if I ever told them the truth about myself.

Now, I could see how shameful it was to have Injun blood in my veins. The government, white citizens, and even the white neighbors I grew up with and went to school with all hated my people.

Reading those papers told how much Ma, and the family went through. The soldiers forced them away in the spring of 1838. Grandpa said the military incarcerated them in a stockade all summer with very little food, and no shelter from the heat and bugs.

One paper said, "The journey to the west began in October, and they traveled through the winter. It took six months of the worst kind of hardship before they reached reservation land set aside for the Cherokee Nation in the west."

I could not imagine six months of travel, most people walked, even when they were ill. It resulted in 4,000 death, the old, the young, and the very young, those who couldn't cope with the hardships forced upon them. I believed they should be in the West by now. I hoped, and prayed that my family had settled well after their ordeal.

I was blessed I didn't have to witness all they suffered. I knew they walked through a powerful cold winter. The soldiers removed our families from their homes with little more than a blanket bundle of things thrown together. Many left their homes without shoes, or any of their possessions.

The soldiers allowed other families an hour to gather what they could take. I guess it depended on which soldiers rounded them up. Many of the wealthier families were allowed to fill wagons with clothing, food, and possessions. I was sure they fared much better on the journey.

I remembered seeing Pa with a big pack on his back. Ma carried a large bundle, and both of my brothers carried smaller bundles over their shoulders. I hoped they carried enough food, blankets, and warm clothing to see them through to the new reservation.

How would they have known what to bring when the soldiers forced them to get right out of their homes? How could they know how long it would take before they would see the new land? Would they have foreseen what kind of clothing to take, and how much food they would need? The weather felt warm when they left their homes. Would they have thought to bring heavy quilts, blankets, and winter clothing?

In the newspapers, it said they marched in every kind of weather. Once their shoes and moccasins wore out, they walked barefooted and left behind bloody footprints. My people called their march, "The Trail Where We Cried."

Many of my people believed in what they called the white man's God, Jehovah. Others followed medicine men, and believed as our people have always believed, in the spirits, which surrounded the Tsalagi, the mountain people.

I prayed that through their tragedy many of our people converted to the one true God, who loved everyone with his everlasting love. He is not only the God of the white man.

Reading about what our tribe went through distressed me. I wanted to wear my heart on my sleeve, but I could not go through my days with a spirit of grief and despondency, or Aunt Violet would question me.

I tried to get through each day as if my heart were whole, and not broken inside of me. In some ways, I was sorry that I found those newspapers, but in another way, it made me glad to know how much my family suffered. My grief I offered to God on their behalf. I prayed every night to our great, and good God to take revenge for the Cherokee, my innocent people, to make the white man suffer as my people had suffered.

Chapter 7
<u>MIRIAM</u>

It was a warm day for April, lessons over, I sat outside on the carved stone bench, feeling sorry for myself. Aunt Violet still thought I was too uncivilized to mingle with the other young ladies, her words, not mine.

I watched the flight of a robin redbreast, then chanced to see one of the young ladies come sneaking around the backside of the house. I was surprised to see her outside during their rest time.

She couldn't see me, the bench where I sat was sheltered by a great weeping willow tree. I liked to sit there under that big leafy umbrella, and peek out through the fronds and imagine all sorts of things.

That must be the new girl, I told myself, being familiar with the look of the other 16 young ladies by that time.

They took daily naps, so their cheeks would remain pink for the evening. Aunt Violet required the girls to get all rigged out in their finery, so she could hold court with them in the dining room. They must look their best and prettiest, as those evenings were the times the young ladies learned their social graces for dining and dinner conversations.

From time to time, Aunt Violet invited eligible young men from many of the finest Norfolk and Hampton, Virginia families to dine with the young ladies, all strictly proper, and it gave them young gentlemen to flirt with, and practice their wiles upon.

As soon as the girl was a little way from the house, she picked up her wide skirts and began to run like the devil himself was after her. She ran clear past me, and before I knew it, she climbed the fence and took off through the woods.

Well! I thought to myself, she doesn't act like a lady of quality, that was something I would have done.

I decided to follow her to see where she headed. I walked on cat's feet, came to the fence, and went over it. I looked ahead through the woods and saw a bit of dark blue traveling swiftly in the distance.

I kept still and went from one tree trunk to another, just walking and pausing to study the situation, then walking on again further into the woods. If Aunt Violet found out, she would skin me.

My excuse? I wanted to see that the young lady wasn't hurt. Sounded good to me, but I was jest that plumb curious.

As I followed the faint path through the trees, come close to the Elizabeth River, a big river with a lot of underbrush along the bank, where I could hide if I needed to.

The blue plaid dress came into view right away, and what I saw made me throw good intentions out the window. The young lady had flung herself down on her side on a patch of grass, there, she sobbed for all she was worth.

I cautiously crept within hailing distance of her. When I come closer, I saw a very pretty girl, with her dark brown hair curled prettily in ringlets all down her back. Her white, white complexion, was shot through with red as tears scalded their way down her cheeks.

Abruptly she sat up, and spying me frantically rubbed her fists into her eyes, brushing away tears. She tilted her chin and took on a stubborn pose.

"I suppose they sent you to bring me back to the house," she said in low-voiced rage.

"No, Lady Violet, didn't ask me to come for you," I answered the girl.

"Then why are you here?"

"Well," I began, and then ran out of words not wanting to tell her I was spying on her. "I was just out walking when I saw you. I thought maybe you were in some kind of trouble." I prayed God would forgive me for the lie.

"Well, I am not in any kind of trouble," she replied frostily.

"Sorry to have bothered you," I told the girl and turned to go back the way I came, not anxious for Aunt Violet to find me missing too.

"Don't-don't go," she beseeched me. "I am sorry I was rude . . . it is just so hard here. I didn't know it would be this hard to make friends with the other girls. My mother and father left me in Lady Violet's care while they traveled to Philadelphia where my father must conduct some lengthy business."

"That's O.K," I told her, using the new word for the first time. "I don't know anyone either. Lady Violet won't let me chat with the other girls until I am older," I lied again. "My folks are gone, too."

"Oh, and where have your folks gone?" She asked getting to her feet and brushing off imaginary pieces of dust from her immaculate gown.

"Oh," I said, like a simpleton, "they are journeying to the west. Why, look at that boat just a steaming to beat the band down the old Elizabeth River," I told her pointing at a flatboat loaded up with all manner of building supplies. I sought to distract her from where in the west my folks could possibly be traveling.

"I guess we best be getting back," I told her reaching out to clasp her hand. "We can come again another day. Lady Violet would be annoyed if she learned you weren't resting for the evening's doings."

101"You are right, of course, I don't know what got into me, I rarely let myself go in such a fashion," she apologized to me.

"My name is Caroline Ashbill," I said, giving her a polite little curtsy as Aunt Violet had taught me to do.

"Miriam Saunders," she told me. "I believe you and I are going to be friends, Caroline Ashbill. In fact, I am certain of it." "Shall we meet again tomorrow?"

"That's fine with me, Miriam." I felt warm all over. I had a new friend, a real friend! Tezzie was my friend, but Miriam was different.

She was a lady, older than me, yet she still wanted to be my friend. Maybe I was not such a woodsy as I thought.

I HAVE NOW LIVED WITH Aunt Violet for two years and six months. Yet, it now seemed like my days rushed along like the current in the middle of the Elizabeth River, for my friend Miriam made all the difference.

Miriam seemed so full of fun and not at all proper like the other young ladies of quality. When I was with Miriam, joy bubbled up inside of me. I thanked God every day for my new friend.

My life changed in more ways than just having a new friend. I became a young lady. My body grew, and almost burst forth from my new clothing.

Since my menses began, Aunt Violet said I was now a woman. I could do without that, but Aunt Violet told me I had recently embarked upon a beautiful new part of my life, since I could now bear children. I needed to trust God with that, bearing children were the last things on my mind these days.

Miriam and I shared many things in common. Once out of sight of the house, we both felt contented enough to just plunk ourselves down on the bank of the rushing stream running through the back of Aunt Violet's property.

Mariam like me, raised her petticoats to her knees and squished her bare toes in the good soft mud while we fished late afternoons after our lessons. There were other things in common too, since our folks thrust us both off on Aunt Violet, while they traveled.

She bared her soul to me telling of her big home with its twelve white columns, and six house servants. Her Pa, a famous doctor and humanitarian, traveled often.

Miriam's Ma doted on him and traveled with him all she could. They used to take Miriam and her Negro mammy with them to care for her, but Miriam had missed too much schooling while she traveled.

They also felt she should have young ladies to keep her company, thus there she sat next to me while we enjoyed the afternoons together at the creek.

I was a good listener, and I scooted by her questions about me, as slick as skating on an icy pond. I would not tell her about my people, nor that I was Injun. It just wouldn't set right.

Instead, I told her I was the daughter of a king who lived in a faraway country. Now I was not telling fibs, for I knew Jesus and God were my kin. Since my folks and Grandpa and Gramma were all away somewhere off to the west, God was all I got. He was all I needed, so I'd discovered!

I was glad Miriam didn't show much curiosity about my folks. I would have loved to tell her about Grandpa and his ministry to the Cherokee, and I would have welcomed the opportunity to share my faith with her, but I thought it best not to. I didn't want to answer questions about my former life, and I hesitated to get in over my head with Bible discussions.

Miriam often went to church with Aunt Violet, and me. She didn't seem to get into the singing and such. She sat there like a bump on a log, and wouldn't do much more than stare straight ahead, daydreaming like.

Aunt Violet tried and tried to get Miriam to stand, kneel, and sit as we did. A stubborn one, she would not comply.

"I worship in my own way," she told us one Sunday. I wondered what she meant.

My happy life continued for the next four or five weeks into spring. Then Aunt Violet decided I could accompany her to the tea parties, socials, and Christian Endeavor meetings. That meant I was socially acceptable. I chafed at all the sitting around wasting time in the afternoons.

"You are furthering your education, Caroline," Aunt Violet told me with impatience when I complained.

Why would I need to learn tea pouring, and fine stitching? I aimed to be the first lady frontiersman in history. I wanted to go through life with my skinning knife, a gun, or a fish pole at my side. A horse of my own would have fulfilled my dreams, and made everything even better!

Aunt Violet informed me I needed to learn how to attract an exceptional young man. That floored me. I'm not aiming to attract me no young man, except maybe to see if I could best him in the fine art of fishing!

Of late, Miriam seemed very interested in some of the new ideas Aunt Violet presented. She began taking better care of her hair, and filed her fingernails to smooth ovals. One day, I asked her to go fishing with me, and she told me that fishing was for children.

I knew I stood there with my mouth hanging open. Why just the week before last, she and I were trying to see who could pull the most bass from the stream, looked like I was gonna be on my own again.

THE YEAR PASSED QUICKLY, and Aunt kept us constantly engaged, as she called it. She taught us many new lessons. There were our studies, of course, but Aunt also introduced us to the niceties of how to entertain in our future homes.

We examined menus. Aunt told us which meat, poultry, or fish we would serve for each kind of dinner party, or festive occasion. Along with the menus, Aunt asked us to write in our journals bills of fare to guide us in the selection of dishes for the daily table. She gave us an example: We would mainly use chicken in the summer. Potatoes or rice must accompany most every meal, and dessert was typically a pudding, or something more elaborate on special occasions.

When we entertained, we must serve fish with a savory sauce, or filet of beef with mushrooms in January. Roast turkey or cold roast beef, was always served in February. Veal cutlets or roast leg of pork in March. Roast leg of mutton in April. She continued through the year ending with Christmas, boiled turkey with oyster sauce, roast goose with applesauce, boiled ham, turnips, winter squash, hot coleslaw, and for dessert, mince pie, plum pudding, lemon pudding, and cranberry tart.

Much of this I found useless, but I wrote it down just the same. Maybe someday I would need to prepare a meal for Grandpa, and this way I would have an idea of what to serve.

April 22, 1843, my 15th birthday, Aunt allowed me a small party of celebration. The younger girls joined me in the parlor at 2 o'clock. There we ate small dainty sandwiches, sweet cakes, and drank tea and fruit juices.

The girls filled this time with happy and excited conversation. I laughed until my sides ached. They gave me many wishes, predicting a gallant suitor in my immediate future.

They complimented me on the choice of my costume, and they told me I was pretty! I blushed as red as my hair, happy and pleased at their attention, I truly felt like one of them, and a young lady of quality for the first time, entertaining my friends, just as Aunt Violet taught us.

MAY 15, AUNT VIOLET announced that since the warm weather returned, we would begin serving low tea in the afternoons, and we would dine later in the evenings. She told us how very much she enjoyed her tea times in England, while married to Lord Ashley. She said we must learn the proper way to prepare tea, as we would serve a great many teas in our future homes.

"The tea ceremony," she instructed, "is a grace we must cultivate as an important part of our gracious entertaining of guests." She described to us the differences between low tea, and high tea. She taught us the many different varieties of tea, and the proper way to brew, and steep the tea.

"Above all," she said, "you must use your creativity in planning the menu, decorating and arranging the tea table, brewing and pouring the tea."

Aunt Violet gave each of the young ladies a date and time to hostess a tea. We would have three each week. The other two days of the week, Cook and Tezrah would serve us in the parlor.

My turn to arrange the tea, came on Thursday, June 27. Picked to go last, I was not surprised, and this filled me with glee. That gave me the opportunity to see how the other girls prepared their teas, and I hoped I might learn from their mistakes.

The first tea was presented by a petite young lady, named Audra Lehigh, who had descended from a prominent family of Virginia. Her grandfather, a patriot officer of the Revolutionary War, brought fame and renown to her family through the high circles of the Washington legislature he frequented. I was excited to see how a true blue-blooded lady of the realm would present her table.

I remembered her tea as a dismal failure. Her linens, and table arrangements looked atrocious they did not suit. The tea tasted bitter, and she shook so hard when she poured, the tea spilled all over the floral cloth.

She would not allow Cook to help, so her crumpets were soggy and the toasted bread scorched. I liked the sweetened strawberries and clotted cream she presented for dessert.

After the tea, Audra stamped her little foot, and declared in a loud voice, "I do not know why you forced me to take part in a tea ceremony, Lady Ashley. I shall have servants to prepare my tea. I shall preside at the tea table as the maids fill the cups, and serve the repast, that is most fitting for one in my position."

No one blamed her for her failure, of course. She never set foot in a kitchen in her life. She was Aunt Violet's darling, and popular with the other young ladies. Everyone commiserated with her, and praised her to the skies despite her poor attempt.

I enjoyed seeing what each young lady offered when it became her turn. Most served plain tea, with toasted, buttered bread, and jam. Frequently, they would serve a thin slice of dry cake with fruit. I relished the fruits as, most used strawberries since they were in season.

My friend Miriam's tea table seemed more elaborate, she used the best dishes in the cabinet, Wedgewood blue, and sat them on a bright, blue tablecloth, but it lacked a central theme.

Miriam, another girl to eschew help in the kitchen, presented us with individual flat sweet cakes, which declined to rise. The tea tasted quite strong. I laced mine with a lot of sugar and cream. Miriam held her head high, and despite the poor showing, she earned smiles and nods from Aunt Violet and the other young ladies. She prepared the best tea so far.

MY TURN CAME AFTER several weeks. I determined to show the others a proper low-tea experience. I was used to helping in the kitchen, and unlike many of the young ladies, I knew a little about cooking, and this gave me a slight advantage.

Thursday June 27, dawned bright, and sunny. Excitement raced through me as I thought about the tea. I rose early, went out to the garden and woods, and gathered tall stems of the red trumpet creeper vine, branches of the small, white fragrant flowering boneset, and complemented the arrangement with branches of southern lady fern. I arranged those in a pretty vase.

For each place at the smaller tables, I made corsages of sweet bay magnolia blossoms, and delicate blue violets, then added native grasses to each, and tied them with ribbon. I left them in a moss-lined basket in the springhouse to stay fresh until the afternoon.

I finished my lessons, and went to the kitchen. I did not appear for the noon dinner. Instead, I helped Cook with dinner preparations, so she would have time to help, me. I was determined my tea would be the very best. Tezzie assisted me, as my friend, and because Tezzie wanted to see me do well for the young ladies.

Since the weather was pleasant, Aunt Violet gave me permission to arrange my low tea on the second-story terrace. Tezzie showed me pure white tablecloths in the linen closet. We ironed the cloths together. She smiled, and laughed when I became distracted and almost forgot about the hot iron. She saved the cloth before it scorched. Such fun!

We joked together as we laid the cloths over the five tables where the young ladies would take their tea. I chose the pretty rose and white luncheon service, banded in silver. It would lend an air of elegance to the tables. I wanted the very best for the young ladies.

We covered the largest table with an intricate tatted, lace-edged white cloth. The elegant flower arrangement sat at the back, giving a festive air to the table setting. I placed a tray with small plates, and berry bowls on the right side of the large draped table.

Cook was excited too. She helped me prepare a silver tureen of mixed stewed fruit. I brought it to the table, and set it next to the tray with a large spoon. Tezzie would place berry bowls in the center of the small plates, and then serve the fruit with a heap of fine, white sugar in the center of each dish. The rosy goodness of the fruit gave the table a pretty appearance.

On one side of the table were large platters of pinwheeled fruit bread, buttered, sugared, and sprinkled with cinnamon. I prepared a dish of tea biscuits, and a tray of freshly baked white bread, sliced to 1/8-inch thickness, a leaf pattern mold of butter, and a knife sat alongside.

Across from the breads, I set small platters of thin sliced cold meats: beef, ham, and tongue, sliced cheeses, and a pot of fresh, soft cheese. Nearby, a silver plate held sliced cucumbers and tomatoes, and both sweet and dill pickles.

Yesterday, Cook gave me an encouraging hug as we baked my crowning glory, a three-layer brown sugar cake covered with walnuts, and a sprinkle of cinnamon on top. It looked luscious, and sat in the center of the table. I could not wait to try a slice.

On a small table, I set three ornate white and rose porcelain teapots, a large carafe of boiling water, and three kinds of loose tea. A silver tray held bowls of sugar, and cream.

A white wicker basket contained the cups, saucers, and spoons. At the proper time, I measured the tea and poured water into the teapots. The tea would steep in the boiling water for six minutes before I poured it into the porcelain cups.

The young ladies filed onto the veranda, led as usual by Miss Lehigh since she enjoyed a higher station in life. I was excited and fluttery, and glad to have Tezzie standing by to give me courage.

I couldn't have asked for nicer weather, or a prettier day. Yet I felt a sudden urge to bolt, I wanted to lift my skirts, and run for the shelter of the woods and the stream.

My red and white striped costume, more elaborate than warranted for this occasion, matched the table. I knew I overdressed compared to the other young ladies. I usually saved this costume for church and special occasions. I dressed as a red bird that day.

The young ladies wore their spring cottons and dimities in pretty pastels. They reminded me of flowers themselves. I noticed several of the young ladies glancing over my table preparations and my state of overdressing.

Others picked up the small corsages from the tables and commented on my floral arrangements. I couldn't imagine them out in the woods, so they may not have enjoyed seeing the trees and wildflowers in bud and bloom.

Miss Lehigh and Miss Atwater, who were bosom friends, both looked down their elegant noses at my table arrangements.

"I doubt if I could eat a thing," I heard Miss Lehigh say to Miss Atwater. "I imagine she must believe us to work in the fields, there is too much food for a simple tea." Miss Atwater nodded in agreement.

They took their seats. All the young ladies looked with expectation at Aunt Violet, whom they called Lady Ashley. Aunt Violet lent her critical eye to the table arrangements, and my food presentation. She looked up at me and gave a slight nod.

Phew! I thought to myself. I passed one hurdle.

Aunt Violet welcomed us, and began addressing the young ladies.

"I am very proud of how you each have comported yourselves in the manner of your low teas. The teas were gracious and very enjoyable. Each of you arranged and presented your teas in a different fashion, thereby giving us glimpses of distinct varieties of graciousness, many of which you may want to follow when entertaining in your future homes.

We have learned distinct ways to arrange a table, and the choicest varieties of foods to serve our guests. I thank you for your efforts.

"Everyone followed the traditional example established for a low tea, with the exception of Miss Ashbill. Her table arrangements are delightful, and I am sure the repast is delicious, but Miss Ashbill did not follow my directions.

"Today, she is serving high tea. If Miss Ashbill invited us to high tea, we would have dressed ourselves according to custom. As you can see, Miss Ashbill has costumed herself in the correct manner. Without further ado, let us partake of Miss Ashbill's offerings."

After Aunt Violet's observations, my face flushed as red as the stripes in my dress. Perhaps I didn't pay close enough attention when Aunt Violet explained about low tea, and high tea, my presentation being much more elaborate than the tea of the other young ladies. Yet that was what I decided to serve, and I hoped they would receive it well.

While Tezzie served the fruit, I took my seat and poured the prepared tea into the delicate cups and saucers without spilling a drop. I noticed many of the young ladies glanced over at me, turned to their friends, and snickered behind their hands as they rose from the table.

I noticed too, that they heaped their plates. I held my head high and smiled at everyone. I was glad to see I made a good impression with my food. Aunt Violet filled her plate higher than was acceptable for a lady.

The young ladies returned to the tables with their plates, seated themselves, and engaged in laughter and friendly conversation. They seemed to have forgotten me. I saw a few surprised nods and glances come my way as they consumed the food, and sipped their afternoon cup of tea. They seemed to enjoy the repast, the dining outside, and of course, each other's company and conversation.

I filled my plate, but stood along the side of the veranda, and watched the peaceful view of the woods in bloom. I could have sat next to Miriam and the other girls I knew. Yet, I did not know many of the older girls, and I would not become the butt end of their jokes. Aunt Violet never claimed a relationship with me.

Too nervous to eat, I took a few bites of everything. The food seemed very good. I felt peaceful about my first attempt at entertaining, despite failing in my endeavors according to Aunt Violet. I believe I passed some of the test. They voiced no complaints, and the food disappeared – every crumb.

As the afternoon progressed, my hands shook ,grew moist with fatigue, and the embarrassment of the day. I rubbed them against my dress, but stopped when I saw Aunt Violet eyeing me. I wanted nothing more than for the teatime to end. Then I could run upstairs, dress in my work clothes, and go out to sit by the stream and relax.

Tezzie stood nearby to help where she was needed. She caught my eye, and gave me a wink when she thought no one else looked on. A laugh filled me, and a huge grin filled my face, but I hid it with my hand so Aunt Violet wouldn't see.

God gave me the gift of hospitality, but I never knew. I loved preparing tea for the young ladies. I did my very best, and made it as gracious as possible. I could have prepared a less elaborate tea, like the others, but it did not seem nice enough somehow.

Thank you, Jesus. I sent up a silent prayer. *Thank you for going before me.*

SUMMER ARRIVED FULL upon us with heat, humidity, and bugs without number. The thirtieth day of June, many of the young ladies returned to their homes until the fall. A few of the younger girls remained, Miriam among them.

I felt let down after the elation of my high tea presentation, as Aunt Violet called it. I guess it raised me up a notch in the eyes of some of the girls.

They invited me to the morning room a few days later. They quizzed me about corsage making, and asked for the recipe of my brown sugar, cinnamon, walnut cake. We laughed together at nothing, and I went away feeling more content, somehow.

Grandpa hasn't written lately from the Tennessee home front. In the past, I received a few letters every month, other times it would be two or three months between letters, depended on how often he traveled. He wrote about his visits to pray with the Cherokee councils.

One time, he wrote, that Gramma, went along with him to visit the tribes and to help the women. In Grandpa's last letter, Gramma sent me her love, and apologized for not writing. They both felt danger continued to exist making it impossible for me to return home.

As for my folks in the west, Grandpa wrote nothing about them. When I looked at how I lived before the removal in our cabin on the farmstead near the piney woods, it seemed dreamlike. The faces of Ma, Pa, and my two brothers mostly slipped away from my memory.

I remembered Ma's yellow hair, her smile, her blue eyes and the way she smelled after she washed her hair, and rinsed it with lavender water infused with herbs.

Yet, I couldn't put it together in my head to form Ma. I still missed the way Ma held me close, with my head resting on her shoulder while she patted my back.

Pa's big frame filled my mind. I remembered his black hair, deep-set blue eyes, high cheekbones, and his prominent nose, but that was a figure with no animation. I could see him as he searched the sky to check the weather, sighted along the barrel of his musket to bring down a deer, or followed along behind the plow.

As a tiny girl, in the evenings before bed, Pa would take me on his lap and read to me from the "Cherokee Phoenix" newspaper written in the language of our tribe. I treasured those memories. Yet, my favorite was Pa dressed in his formal ceremonial robes his turbaned head lifted high like a king.

The memories seemed disjointed and fractured, not the actual flesh and bone that I yearned to see. More than anything, I wanted to reach back just once to touch my family, and have my family touch me. Yet, I knew in my heart that may never happen.

I wished with my entire being that the government hadn't taken away my folks. The Good Book said not to hate, yet hate I did. I hated the greedy white men, grasping for things, more and more things with no thought or care for whom they hurt. They strived hard to prosper, and climbed their way up in the world on the backs of those they cheated.

It's the Gold! Gold, they discovered on Cherokee lands, which drove the white man to unspeakable crimes against our people. Depression filled my mind, making me think and overthink, too much, but that's because I had nothing better to do.

MY LIFE CONTINUED WITH the daily lessons and helping Cook and Tezzie in the kitchen, where we laughed at my obvious cooking mistakes. I changed clothing four times a day, and always looked for an opportunity to escape the house for the woods, and the lively stream.

I relished being outdoors in the sunshine, reading my Bible, fishing, and watching colorful birds and small animals. On the days, Aunt Violet took herself to Christian Endeavor meetings, or teas without me, I saddled up the little mare Chocolate and rode around the property.

The first of July, Aunt decided I was ready to mingle with the other young women. She asked me to move from the coolness of my small room off the kitchen to a smaller hot, seldom-used room on the third floor. So, I might cultivate a few friendships, which might help in my quest to find an affluent husband. I must have passed the test as a "young lady of genteel quality."

Miriam and three or four of the other girls seemed to find me interesting, and we chatted and drank tea together upon occasion. I learned finger games from the girls.

I was awkward with the string and button. They chuckled with me at my gaucheness. I vowed to practice until my fingers became just as nimble as theirs. They also taught me different ways to wear my hair, and dress myself to become a true young lady of quality.

Since summer, our daily lessons turned into a week's worth of lessons. We studied diction, etiquette, deportment, and Aunt Violet added the study of art, knitting, crochet, needlework, and such.

She taught me to sew a fine seam, as she called fancy needlework. It easily filled my hands, and left my mind free to skitter hither and yon. I needed more to fill my mind and distract my thoughts, which dwelled over much on my situation here, and my folks there, maybe still marching farther and farther away from me.

Grandpa and Gramma seemed lost to me, even though they wrote promises of visits, and my release from the structured societal prison where I existed. Yet nothing happened. I wondered if it ever would!

Someday, I told myself, I would shuck off my finery, and take up the good dresses Gramma made for me, hidden down at the bottom of the trunk in my room. I would remove my skinning knife from back behind the drawer of the chest. I would pull on my boots, run to the stables, saddle up the little mare, Chocolate, and ride away from Virginia. She liked me better than the other young ladies, or so I told myself. I spent more time with her, and rode her every chance I got! I thought of her as mine.

Besides, if I rode off on the mare, Aunt Violet could store my things for other young ladies to wear in the future, or sell all the finery and fripperies stuffed into my wardrobe. They should bring in enough money to cover the cost of raising me to become a lady. I won't need those things in the woods. What would I do there with silks and taffetas?

I might keep one, my dark green silk gown for memory's sake. The seamstress used large seams, and made a deep hemline. When the need arose, I could lengthen the hem, and let out the side seams.

Maybe someday I could marry up in the dress, or an even lovelier one. I would need to find a pretty man first, one who maybe looked like the blond boy by the creek.

"Caroline! Pay attention to your needlework! You are wool-gathering!" Aunt Violet told me with a frown, bringing me back to the present.

"Yes, Lady Ashley," I replied, looking at the misshapen stitches along the edge of the dainty scarf I hemmed.

AUGUST, MY LEAST FAVORITE month of the year, never seemed to end. Today dawned even hotter than usual. The dressmaker arrived to measure us for ball gowns. She began with Miriam, and then me. She would take the measurements of the other young ladies once they returned for the new school year in another week.

Aunt Violet planned a ball for the third Saturday in September to welcome the young ladies back to school. My first ball, I could not imagine me at a dance, let alone a formal ball. In the past, Aunt Violet excluded me from such doings, as I was first too young, and then too gauche and naïve.

After my first visit to the minstrel's gallery, I visited there as often as I could on other festive occasions, through the years. I would sneak upstairs from my little room next to the kitchen, and hide next to the minstrel's gallery. I would listen to the music and sneak peeks of the older girls dancing, and flirting with the young men of the city. I would silently laugh at what I saw, yet I kept still, so as not to get caught and banished to my room.

And now, all of a sudden, it seemed to be my turn to dance at a gala ball. When I thought about that, I got quite flustered. I would not know how to act, or what to do. I could not see myself dancing with a young gentleman. I was just not interested.

Then it come to me, I would know what to do. Aunt Violet tried to beat those niceties into my reluctant brain for almost four years.

Aunt told us that we would dance in the grand salon. She sent invitations to many of the young gentlemen of Norfolk and the surrounding areas.

While I waited for the seamstress to call me upstairs to the sewing room, I began every now and then to stick my needle in and out of a new sampler:

"The Lord is in His Holy Kingdom.
Let the Whole Earth Stand in Awe of Him."

When the seamstress called my name, I laid aside my sewing, straightened up my back, and rose delicately to my feet, since Aunt Violet watched. Then I moved with grace to the staircase, and ascended to the sewing room.

It was still a puzzle to me why I needed to learn to embroider a sampler, and do needlepoint. How would this help me live in the woods? There ain't, were not, any fine parlors there. I could see that sewing and mending, knitting, and crochet, were another matter. I would need those skills in making clothing and linens for my future home.

I met Miriam on my way up. She sniffed, laughed in an unpleasant tone, and gave me a wink that about floored me. I wondered what she knew.

"You'll find out!" she said, descending to the floor below.

I knocked on the door and Mrs. Sally Preston bid me enter. She seated herself at a table piled high with bolts and bolts, of the loveliest silks and satins I'd ever laid my eyes on. She asked me to remove my costume, and I stood there in my petticoats whilst she took my measurements.

Then she took up a light, green silk, sprigged with tiny pink roses and darker green leaves, and held it up to my front. When I saw the dress goods, I held my breath until I felt about ready to burst.

The fabric reminded me of the woods in the spring, the green of new leaves, and the delicate blooms of the wild rose just beginning to burst forth. From then on, I vowed to become a young lady of quality if it meant wearing such lovely dresses for formal social occasions.

My brain whirled making me a little faint with excitement. I stood straight as a stick, and extended my arms out to the sides, while Mrs. Preston draped the cool fabric about my person.

"That will do dear," she said through a mouth of pins. "I will stitch the dress, and we will have a fitting one week from today at the same time."

"Yes, Ma'am," I said, bobbing a curtsy. I knew I should leave, but I couldn't stop fingering the lovely silk fabric.

"Lady Ashley suggested you may have your dress a trifle longer this once. Next spring, if I am not mistaken, you will be sixteen years old, and then we could lengthen the skirts down properly.

When I fashion your dress, shall I use larger seams and add a deeper hem, so you could alter it in the future." She looked up at me, with a small smile, from where she sat. "Yes, I could do that for you," she decided, patting my hand.

I was surprised at the leniency of Aunt Violet in the matter of my skirt length, and I was grateful too for the kindness and understanding of this good woman.

I almost shouted my thanks. "Yes! Ma'am! Thank you, Ma'am! I would love that. I want to keep the dress for always." Then I skedaddled down the back stairs, across the lawn, beyond the stream and into the woods, where I let out a good, loud, Injun war-whoop.

Chapter 8
<u>THE BALL</u>

That loud whoop made me feel better. It released the built-up excitement from inside me. I walked farther on until I reached the Elizabeth River. It flowed along the border of the town.

Standing in the woods alongside the shoreline, where no one could see me, I watched the busy river rush by on its way to the ocean. I liked the old river, and the little stream running back through Aunt Violet's land. The stream put me in mind of our big oak tree, and the creek flowing around it near our cabin in the woods back home.

I remembered the speckled brown trout. I would lie on the bank of Sugar Creek, and reach down into the water, scratch a little on their backs before they would dart off to wherever trout darted off to.

That memory, and many others made me a little teary-eyed whenever I thought of my life before the removal, so I tried hard to keep my mind on the here and now.

My former life, I thought of as my pretty life with my beautiful mother, and my strong and kind father. I'd have given up my new green ball gown with the tiny pink roses, and green leaves for one glimpse of my little brothers. Never thought I would miss the likes of them two, yet I did.

After a while, I returned to the stream, sat on my favorite rock, and watched the mayflies skitter along the top of the flowing water.

"There you are, Caroline, I thought I might find you here." Miriam walked over, and occupied a rock close beside mine. She held her delicately shaped nose high in the air, and her silky, dark brown hair flowed softly down her back. She carried a book, and looked at me with disdain where I sat next to the river, feet bare, and petticoats up to my knees.

"I heard some kind of yell a while ago. I realize the difficulties you have in becoming a lady, but one must try harder, the rewards are well worth the effort." She sniffed like a lady and applied her handkerchief to her nose as if she smelled something foul.

"I'd never noticed the stench of the stream before. Smells like something died down there," she said, pointing with her book.

"What do you think of our dressmaker?" She continued.

"I liked her, she is making me the most beautiful gown in the world," I said.

Mariam just sniffed, and then went on. "I wonder where Violet found her. I would have preferred to use my own dressmaker, but she lives too far away, and your aunt would not consent to bringing her here. I guess that one would have to do, but I don't care for her, at all."

Her mention of my relationship with Aunt Violet gave me a start. I felt upset. If she knew, the others knew too. I never let on. Did Aunt Violet let it slip?

She looked out at the clear day, and the flowing stream before turning back to me. "I selected a yellow watered silk. The fabric will have to do, as she seemed limited in her selections. I would have chosen to wear red. It would have complemented my complexion and dark hair much better than yellow.

"I told her to lower the décolleté. I want my charms to be visible, she will do as I say, or I will tell Lady Ashley. If she does not comply, she may soon be out of a job, I must look enticing on this important occasion."

"Enticing?" I responded. "What's that?"

"Why Caroline, I must be attractive to appeal to the eligible men. The only way I could ever leave here is to marry."

"Marry?" I queried like a simpleton. "Why would you want to do that, when there's so much to see and do yet? Why would you want to drag a boy around with you? They only get in the way, always wanting to best you at hunting and fishing."

"Oh, Caroline! Caroline!" Miriam said, laughing aloud. "You are so quaint and unsophisticated. I don't want a boy. I want a man, a handsome man of means and property. He must be someone who will worship and cherish me. One who will make me the crown of his life," she said dreamily.

"Well!" I said, "I don't want any truck with the likes of that. I am not a piece of fine China to put on display. I would keep my neckline at a modest level, and if I ever felt the need to get hitched up, I want a man I can partner with, like my ma and pa. They work together, help and support each other. They laugh, dance, and sing together. I want someone like that, but I don't want him until I see the entire world, and try everything for myself first."

EXCITEMENT BECAME A tangible part of our lives. Aunt Violet filled our days with plans for the ball, discussions of the menus, the entertainment, the fittings of our ball gowns, shopping trips for shoes, and decorations for our hair. All the fine frivolity and frippery as Grandpa would call it, only gave me a headache. I saw no need for it.

Whenever I could, I snuck outside to get away by myself. I walked to the Elizabeth River, and watched the current, and the boats run by. It calmed me somehow. After my walk, I always ended up by the little stream, doffing my shoes and stockings, and sticking my feet in the water, which seemed a mite cooler each September day.

One afternoon, Miriam rushed over to me all a-twitter. "Your aunt is in a fine rage," she shrilled. "She could not find you! She searched the house first. Then she sent me to see if you were in the garden. The dance master has arrived, and we must not keep him waiting. All the young ladies are there in the ballroom ready to begin the dance lessons. You are delaying everyone again."

"Fiddlesticks! I'm not goin' to do no dancin'," I explained to her, my native diction showing. I stood, and faced her with my arms crossed tightly across my chest, "so I don't need no lessons!"

She grasped my wrist, and pulled me toward the house. "Do you want me punished?" she hissed.

"No," I said, hesitating, "but I ain't a-going to do no dancin'!"

"All well and good, Caroline," she told me as she pointed to my shoes and stockings. "You put those on, and return with me. You can take up the matter of dancing or not with Lady Ashley, enough of your stubbornness!"

"You do not know when you are well off, Caroline. Come along now, your aunt is in a fury. I told her you went out to pick flowers for the table. She can never find you anymore. You spend too much time here away from the house," she lectured me in a stern voice.

"Now, I will help you gather a few flowers. Then, we need to get back, before she punishes me on account of you!" she said, flouncing away toward the house.

I followed along, dragging my feet. I reached down and plucked a daisy or two from time to time. I realized again she called Aunt Violet, my aunt. I thought the relationship secret. The secret must have slipped out somehow.

"There!" Miriam exclaimed when her arms were full of flowers. "Now, let us hurry to the house."

When we reached the house, we entered through the kitchen door, and gave the flowers to Tezzie. I ran upstairs to change my gown and make myself presentable.

"Caroline Dear," my aunt trilled in a high falsetto voice as I reached the ballroom. "Where ever have you been? Herr Baer has arrived for the dance lesson."

I could hear the strains of a waltz in the background. I peeked inside the doorway to see all the young ladies lined up following the steps of a tall, militarily erect, blond gentleman. I watched a beam of sunlight from the long window light on top of his golden head, as he swayed and dipped to the music.

He turned and beckoned to me. His bright eyes pierced me to my soul. I quivered. I did not know myself anymore. He told the musicians to stop playing, then he turned and smiled at me as I walked through the doorway. He bowed to me, extended his arm, and asked in a deep musical baritone, *"Darf ich diesen Tanz Fraulein haben."*

Oh! My! I 'bout fell through the floor, as I realized he just asked me to dance. All the young ladies began to twitter and cover their mouths with their hands. I knew I blushed a deep cardinal red. I had just lived up to my secret Injun name, Red Bird.

After a little hesitation, I stepped right up to the dance master. I took his arm, and walked at his side, my head up, and a smirk in my eye.

The rest of the lesson seemed a blur in my mind. All I remembered was the bright, blond head, and the clear blue gaze of the man bending down to clasp me around the waist as we danced.

Before I knew it, the lesson was over, and the young ladies departed the ballroom. I was alone with the dance master. He smiled, offered his arm, then escorted me to the staircase, made a deep bow, turned, and walked away to converse with Aunt Violet, leaving me stunned and looking after him.

SATURDAY, THE THIRD one in September, arrived before I knew it. I was busy with dancing lessons, the fittings of my ball gown, shopping, and discussions with the young ladies about how to fix my hair, and what to wear around my neckline for ornamentation.

All this constant busyness was enough to give a coon dog the hives, and chatter? I felt plumb wore out with it all, the day before the ball. On Saturday, though, I got up before dawn all a-twitter just like the other young ladies. None of us could sleep.

Later, the afternoon, Cook would give us a small meal like a low tea. Then they made us take a nap at 4 o'clock, so we would be fresh, and have sunshine in our cheeks, as Aunt Violet was wont to say.

I don't know how the day passed so fast. I think I spent most of it standing in front of my ball gown staring at it in slack-jawed bemusement. It was the prettiest thing I ever saw on God's green earth, 'ceptin' the morning a couple of springs ago when I saw God's wonderment in the woods in the form of a tiny green rosebush, full of miniature pink roses, kissed with dew, and shimmering with jewel-laced spider webs.

Then, like today, I felt a queer awareness, as if my throat clogged with tears, yet I was elated, and at peace for the first time since they tore my ma and pa away from me.

THE DELICATE REFRAINS of violins reached us upstairs where we stood in our finery, putting last-minute pats to our hair and costumes. I felt hollow inside, excited yet nervous all the same. Hard to believe I was this pretty creature, with ringlets of auburn curls all down my back, and crowned like a queen with a lace and feathered tiara.

From the delicate rose tinted cameo, fastened around my neck with a green velvet ribbon, to my rose-colored slippers, I looked like someone else, yet I saw a hint of the familiar, too. The shape of Ma's eyes and her smile looked back at me, and I recognized Pa's aquiline nose and high cheekbones. There they both were, looking right back at me as if they blended to become me.

I felt a great peace from God. I finally believed Ma and Pa were fine and safe, as if the Holy Spirit gave me that knowledge. I knew, too, the evening would go well for me. I could put my jitters to bed, and enjoy myself, at least I hoped to.

I thanked and praised God for his goodness in keeping me safe these four years with Aunt Violet. Then, with a lighter spirit, I picked up my fan, and swept my way down the stairway, a trifle late, but all right by me.

I peered into the doorway of the ballroom, watching the whirling figures of the young ladies held at arm's length in the arms of the young gentlemen.

Miriam floated by in her sea of yellow-watered silk. I saw she lost the battle of the lowered neckline, but she made up for it by batting her eyes at a tremendous rate, at an old gentleman of at least twenty-five years. He looked settled, and unfit, with a wispy brown top-knot, and a rounded stomach.

"Vernon Falcon, the heir to the Falcon fortune," I heard one of the several matron chaperones say, as they whispered and pointed with their fans. They sat to the left of me, in front of a decorative potted palm.

"She would be a lucky young woman to snare that one," her friend returned in a loud stage whisper.

"She looks glorious, she should have no trouble there," said the first matron.

I knew my opinion did not count, yet to my way of thinking, I'd rather dance with the pretty dance master, Herr Baer, than that jackanapes Vernon Falcon, fortune or not.

When the music ended, the young ladies allowed the young gentlemen to lead them to the refreshment table, their fans fluttering to beat the band. I stifled my laughter. That was the most work I believe I'd ever seen them engage in since I came to live with Aunt Violet.

The young ladies returned to their seats with their escorts. and sipped from delicate punch cups.

The maestro announced the next dance. A mad scramble began among the young men to claim the prettiest girls for the dance. I stayed there by the stairs, watching from the doorway. No one seemed aware of my presence, just the way I liked it.

Then I felt someone walk up behind me. I turned a little and there he stood, the dance master, suited up prettier than I ever saw him; resplendent from his elegant swallow-tailed coat to his shimmering silver and black brocade weskit, and black satin cravat. His blond hair gleamed in the light from the candelabra. He wore a mischievous gleam in his clear blue eyes.

"Ich Bitte um dieses Tanz Fräulein Ashbill?" he asked, giving me a courtly bow.

Again, I felt prickers run down my spine. I stood there a second then smiled, and placed my hand on his arm, I lifted my gown, and walked tall beside him to the dance floor, where I too whirled to the music in my green silk ball gown alongside the other young ladies.

After the dance, Aunt Violet hurried up to me. She thrust a dance card into my hand, and whispered to me, "You were to dance with Mister David Blankenship, not the master, Herr Baer. Read your card, Caroline. Your next partner is Mister Abbot Parmenter." She pointed to him with her fan.

I saw an older man tottering toward me, large in the hindquarters. He bowed, and asked for my hand. I fluttered my fan at him a bit, then leaned in. and asked with courtesy, "Please excuse me, sir? I am not feeling well." I just couldn't bring myself to dance with the likes of him.

Aunt Violet stood with her back to me, so I scooted out of the ballroom, and left as gracefully as I could. I lingered in the foyer and peered around.

When no one was looking, I made for the back terrace. There I gulped down huge draughts of fresh air in relief. I knew I didn't belong back there in the ballroom. I could see that ballroom etiquette would become a good part of my education if I lived a life as the pampered wife of an important man. Yet I have a far better future in mind for myself.

I looked with longing at the lantern-lit walkway below. I would make a run for the stream, and my favorite place, but I knew in my heart Aunt Violet would have a conniption if she did not find me close by since she went to so much trouble on behalf of me, and the other young ladies.

Seated in comfort in a dark corner of the terrace next to the last of the cascading roses, their pleasant fragrance enveloped me. I felt better, thankful I left the ballroom.

A gentle breeze stirred the air. I shivered a little, but decided to stay. Before long, a man walked out onto the terrace, seeming to look for someone.

"Der you are, Fraulein Ashbill, I was seeking you. I have brought you a cup of die punch."

"So very gracious of you, Herr Baer, I needed the air after the closeness of the ballroom," I replied, fluttering my fan.

"I agree Fraulein, dis ist much more pleasant. Ballrooms can be very varm," he replied with a chuckle, taking a seat on my left.

Now what do I do? I thought to myself. Here I am alone, in the dark with this kind, and handsome man. Bad enough I'd snuck away, but if Aunt Violet found me here with the dance master, it would muddy my name and reputation. I could hear her now!

"For shame, Caroline!"

We chatted for a few minutes, and I sipped at my cup of punch. When the orchestra quit playing, I knew, I should return. The dinner would begin soon.

"Shall we return, Fraulein?" Herr Baer asked. He proffered his arm to me, and we walked to the fashionable dining room.

Aunt Violet met me at the terrace door and hissed, "Wherever have you been, Caroline? Well, never mind, go in now and find your seat. You will dine with Mister Abbott Parmenter. He is a well-established young man in the community."

As I appeared at the entrance of the dining hall, Mister Parmenter bowed low, then tucked my hand into his arm, and led me to the table. He pulled out my seat, and I sat ladylike as Aunt Violet taught me. I smiled and thanked him with a pretty speech. I tried not to think, not wanting to bolt outside again.

Tezzie appeared along with other servants bringing in the many platters of elegant cuisine. We began with fruit compote in cut crystal dishes. I knew which of the many spoons to select.

The second course, a pecan-encrusted filet of trout nestled with vegetables on delicate ribbons of crisp lettuce. That afternoon I watched as the fish seller delivered the trout to the kitchen.

Next, Tezzie served platters of the meats, filet of beouf, and deboned and roasted wild duck. She appeared at each gentleman's elbow. The gentleman then selected delicacies to fill each young lady's plate from the silver serving trays.

I waved my fan, and pretended to eat. I smiled and conversed about nothing at all, as far as I could tell. Yet, I played the game as Aunt Violet had taught me. The prize being an eligible young man to court me, and after a while to marry me, and finally put the disgrace of my heritage behind me, or so I decided.

I wanted none of it, but Grandpa told me to mind, and mind I would. I felt bribed with lovely dresses, adornments, and a longer length to my gown, since Aunt Violet broke with convention, I was almost sixteen years old.

Mister Parmenter attended to my every need. Still, I was not used to a young man fawning over me. The gentleman on my right told me his name, Daniel Courtman. He escorted Miss Sadie Halle. Mister Courtman did not appear much taken with the pert little blond, but vied for my attention with Mister Parmenter.

Miss Sadie seemed upset that I received the attention of her young man. She sent me evil glances every time Mister Courtman turned in my direction. I did not know why two gentlemen attended to me.

Miss Sadie was a small, exquisite blond with big blue eyes and a dimple, which winked in and out of her chin whenever she smiled. She smiled very little right then.

Elegant course followed elegant course, until after an hour, Tezzie presented a luscious Charlotte Russe for dessert. My favorite, made with ladyfingers, and topped with Bavarian cream, garnished with cherries and a sprinkle of cinnamon. I could only manage a bite or two. I felt very flustered and weary of it all.

Aunt Violet tapped her crystal glass for attention and announced that the young ladies would retire to the parlor, while the gentlemen stayed to enjoy their brandy and cigars.

I followed the others to the parlor, and decided instead to sit in the morning room where it was dark and still.

After a quarter of an hour passed, the strings of the orchestra began. The young ladies returned, and the young gentlemen met them with arms crooked. Mister Abbot Parmenter bowed to me. I curtsied to him, fluttered my lashes, and grimaced to myself. I hoped I could find an excuse to disappear, enough of this enforced gaiety.

As the orchestra completed the selection, I thanked Mister Parmenter, curtsied, and he escorted me to the tranquility of the foyer. There a bevy of young gentlemen met us outside the door leading to the ballroom.

Each requested the honor of dancing with me. Then I knew, I was standing in a thick pot of trouble. What was the matter with those young men? Lovely young ladies stood close by waiting for their escorts, while the escorts tried to engage me in conversation.

The orchestra prelude began for the next waltz. I heard the young ladies twittering together, they sent mean looks my way. I needed to leave at once so the young men would return to their senses, and seek their partners for the next waltz. I could not understand what they were doing.

Aunt Violet appeared in an instant. "Caroline!" she whispered to me.

I felt my face flush, and the nervousness arose from within me. She believed I was to blame, and that I encouraged these young men. I turned, curtsied to the assemblage, and made my way to the stairs, twittering laughter followed my withdrawal.

I heard someone say, "Who does she think she is?"

The music resumed, and with my leaving-taking, I felt sure everything became peaceful once more.

I sat upstairs on the edge of my bed in the hot little room, fanning myself. I still did not know what happened, or why the young men surrounded me when a bevy of beauties stood not a stone's throw away from them.

I was uncommon ugly, I knew that. Maybe they sought to make fun of me. I was sorry Aunt Violet felt the need to teach me to find a rich husband.

After a while, I slipped out of my ball gown, and the breath-catching undergarments, and put on my everyday dress. The music continued to play. I knew the ball would go on into the wee hours of the morning.

I snuck down the back stairs to the rear of the house. I wanted to go out and sit by the stream, but if Aunt Violet heard about it, she would be livid. "Young ladies do not go outside unaccompanied, at night." Silly rule, in fact most of her rules were silly.

As I walked out into the lantern-lit garden, I could see a man in the distance, striding along and smoking a pipe. I couldn't make out his identity until a glimmer of lantern light reflected on his blond hair. I recognized Herr Baer, the dance master. I could not allow him to see me the way I was dressed. I turned to go back inside only to stop at the sound of his voice.

"Fräulein Ashbill!"

I did not wish to speak to him.

"Ist any zing de matter, Fräulein?" he said with a concerned look in his eyes.

"No, Herr Baer, I am fine. I felt a little tired, so went up to my room. It was stifling there, and the lawn looked inviting."

"Der ist no blame, Fräulein, des affairs could be quite tedious," he said with a laugh. "However, I am glad Zie are here. I vant to tell you, how you say? Auf Wiedersehen."

"Goodbye?" I repeated like a ninny.

"Ja, Ja, gut-bye! Ich vill sail to mein country, in die morgen, Fräulein. I must rejoin the army."

"Oh, must you go Herr Baer? I am sorry you are leaving." Yes, I was sorry, and the thought amazed me that I could care for this older man.

"Ja! Ja, Fräulein!" Ich vill take a turn around die Garten vonce more, before saying gut-bye to Frau Ashley.

Das ist a beautiful house. Ich will miss this, und your fine land. Gut evening and Auf Wiedersehen, Fräulein Ashbill, Ich vill not forget you." He bowed low over my hand, and brushed it with his mustache in a kiss.

"A good evening to you, Herr Baer . . . go with God." I blushed and stammered.

He quickly left. I watched him take the steps to the terrace two at a time as if he couldn't get away from me fast enough.

There you, see? I told myself, *now you know. Men run to get away from you, the handsome ones, in particular. All you can attract are the ones the fleas on a dog would not want to live with, like Mister Abbot Parmenter.*

I laughed at the thought, long and loud, before putting a hand over my mouth. It would not do to have Aunt Violet hear my laughter, and find me in the garden.

I BELIEVE THE DANCE changed me. It helped me toward a new beginning. That evening, I felt grown-up, womanly and attractive. Then the next thing I knew, my kid feelings came over me again, like when Herr Baer couldn't get away from me fast enough. I still felt embarrassed.

Yet, I thought about things differently, a kind of daydreaming. Like, what if I found a young gentleman? Then just as quick, I thrust the thought away from me as unworthy.

The day after the ball, flowers began arriving at the house for the young ladies. I received a tiny spray of violets from that Abbot Parmenter. Most likely, he sent them from a sense of duty, rather than any affection for me. After all, I ran out on him. I laughed when I remembered the look on his face as I mounted the stairs at a run.

When my small flowers arrived, Aunt Violet held them to her nose in delight, and inhaled their fragrance.

"My name flower," she said, "how appropriate for your first nosegay, Caroline. You made a good impression on the young man. He knew the proper flowers to send to you, not too ostentatious. You could do much worse than an alliance with Mister Parmenter. True, his family is in trade, but they own a fine home, and he drives the latest phaeton with matching grays."

I stifled my laughter, until she turned away called by another young lady holding a similar bunch of violets. Aunt Violet only saw what she wanted to see.

At dinner, I heard whispers going around the room that the dance master had departed, sailing home to his own country, Germany. The knowledge gave me a little chill, realizing I would never see him again.

Late in the afternoon, before supper, I received a large bouquet of a variety of colorful roses delivered to the door by a young boy. The bouquet, larger than that of any other young lady, caused even more twittering in my direction.

The note was written first in German, and then translated by a different hand into English:

"Liebe, Fräulein Ashbill, Diese Blumen, sind Blaß im Vergleich zu Ihrer Anmut und Charme. Eines Tages werdet ihr die Herzen vieler junger Männer berühren, so wie ihr sie berührt habt, meine."

"These flowers pale in comparison to your grace and charm. One day you will touch the hearts of many young men, just as you have touched mine."

Auf Wiedersehen,

Herr Albrecht Baer

I read the note several times. Herr Baer must have been sipping spirits to say such nice things about me. His words caused a warm glow in my heart, and I knew my name would now be mud with the young ladies, since I received the biggest, and most colorful bouquet.

Then I realized I would miss him. I did not know him, yet I felt my heart flutter at his memory. I guess God blessed me, or maybe afflicted me to have strong feelings for handsome, blond young men, with pretty blue eyes.

Chapter 9
<u>**A NEW DIRECTION**</u>

"We enjoyed a very successful ball," Aunt Violet told us the following Monday morning, prior to our lessons. The young ladies nodded to each other, and smiled in anticipation.

Me, I sniffed, I felt like saying it was just a lot of trouble to fetch a husband for each of these girls. I guess that meant I was cynical.

"Now, we must put our past successes behind us, and proceed while the young gentlemen are still available. Our pleasant fall weather works well for us to plan sailing parties, and picnics on Saturday afternoons in October.

"At the beginning of November, we will arrange a few evening socials with Miss Lehigh, Miss Adkins, and Miss Thorndike performing on the piano, singing solos and duets. Ladies, I especially request that you work together on a rendition of, "I Know a Bank Where the Wild Thyme *Blows*." The song is especially suited to your exquisite voices. As you may know, the words of the song come from William Shakespeare's, A Midsummer Night's Dream.

I know a bank where the wild thyme blows, where oxlips grow and violets nod their heads, canopied with luscious honeysuckle interspersed with sweet-smelling ramblers and wild roses. Titania sometimes sleeps there at night, lulled to sleep among the flowers after her dancing.

Aunt Violet paused to dab at her eyes after reciting those words, she cleared her throat, and then continued.

"I desire that each of you young ladies would contribute to our evenings with songs, recitations of poetry, or essays. At the close of the recitals, our staff will serve unusual, and delightful refreshments to crown the evening's entertainments.

"November the 29th, I have arranged for a night at the Portsmouth Playhouse, where together with the young gentlemen, we will enjoy a renowned production, featuring a celebrated theatrical company from New York City.

"December 17, prior to the conclusion of the school term, I will invite select young gentlemen of Norfolk, and their parents to a Christmas cotillion open house, buffet dinner, and social.

"I expect each of the young ladies here to send an invitation to their parents, or close relatives, and to plan and present some form of special Christmas entertainment. I am sure everyone will be well received."

The young ladies squealed in delight. They began chatting about what they planned to wear, and how they could show themselves to the best advantage during the various entertainments. They finished their discussions by comparing the individual merits of some of the young gentlemen. Several of the young ladies showed interest in the same man. I wondered if they would vie with each other for the man's attention.

I hoped I would not have to attend any of Aunt Violet's soirees, or even worse, have to perform at them. Fortunately, God gave me no fine arts talents to share, unless of course, they wanted me to speak on the fine art of hunting and fishing, or show them the many pairs of stockings I knitted to give to the poor at Christmas. I laughed to myself!

"That will be all ladies," Aunt Violet said, clapping her hands for attention. "We will directly proceed with our philosophy lesson for today."

WEEK FOLLOWED WEEK, entertainments, parties, socials, the evening at the theatre, and the elegant Christmas open house were over at last. I patiently rebuffed the attentions of Mister Abbott Parmenter, and other young men until they turned their attentions elsewhere, to my extreme relief.

My blessing of the season arrived early in November when Aunt Violet overlooked inviting me to provide entertainment at the various socials. I watched with enjoyment as the other young ladies performed. I thanked God I was in the audience, and not up there embarrassing myself.

The young gentlemen, as well as the many socials, left me cold, except for the night at the theatre. I enjoyed it much more than I expected. We dressed elegantly, and drove to the theatre in hired carriages. The young gentlemen met us at the door of the theatre, and we proceeded inside, two by two. The Portsmouth Playhouse glittered with crystal chandeliers, and plush velvet seating. The love story and the beautiful music touched my heart, and I floated home as if in a dream.

Christmas came as a bright spot in my black-and-white world, yet the weather remained rainy, damp and foggy, no snow or ice. No chance for a white Christmas. Hard for me to get in the Christmas spirit as I could still recall the cold, crisp, and frosty days of my Tennessee childhood Christmases.

This year, three days after the final social and dance, on December 17, I drew a big sigh of relief as Miriam and the other young ladies departed for their homes for a two-week vacation. I would have to pretend no longer, and I could be myself again, at least away from Aunt Violet.

Aunt also seemed to enjoy this time away from the young ladies. She attended many festive socials, parties, and service projects with her friends. Fortunately, she did not ask me to accompany her.

I could not remember many of the Christmases since begun to live with Aunt Violet. When I first arrived, it took me a long while to get used to living here, and the constant pining for my folks kept me from enjoying the celebrations. I stayed away from everyone in the house and frequented the kitchen. I helped Cook and Tezzie whenever I could. I felt more comfortable there.

During the next few years, Cook always asked me to catch fish for our Christmas dinner. I usually brought in enough fish, so she would have enough to salt or dry, and put away for dinners after Christmas.

I looked forward to helping prepare the many food baskets to take to the poor, and accompanied Aunt Violet on some of these outings a few days before Christmas. I enjoyed meeting the families, and played with the children while Aunt Violet visited with their parents.

Again, this year, Cook invited me into the kitchen to help with Christmas preparations. She knew how I dearly loved to assist in preparing the many dishes.

The kettles full of simmering spices emitted a delicious smell that permeated the large house. We made fruitcakes, compotes, rich custards, and puddings. We released the hazelnut cakes from their wrappings where they laid soaking in rum for the past two weeks.

The house felt quieter without the young ladies. They were home enjoying family celebrations of their own. Yet Aunt Violet would still entertain. She invited friends to high tea at noon, on December 23, and planned an elaborate Christmas Eve supper for forty guests.

A day before the celebrations, I spent an afternoon at the stream, and caught a large assortment of fish. Cook cleaned and seasoned them and would use them as one of the appetizers at the Christmas Eve supper, and the first course of Christmas Day dinner that I would enjoy with Aunt Violet in the large dining room.

December 23, came and went. I attended the high tea, and curtsied as Aunt Violet taught me. She introduced me as her niece to her many friends for the first time. I sampled the finger sandwiches, ate a bit of cake, and sipped daintily from my cup of tea, before edging away to my room and my Bible. Aunt Violet did not miss me. She enjoyed a high old time with her friends.

I spent much of Christmas Eve helping Cook and Tezzie with preparations for the elaborate Christmas Eve supper before retiring early to my room, with a full plate filled with many of the delicacies we'd prepared.

Christmas Day, I attended services with Aunt Violet, and we returned home to a bountiful feast, of baked fish, glazed turkey cutlets, corn, sweet potatoes, okra, soft white rolls, persimmon jelly, pickles, and for dessert, sago pudding, rum-soaked hazelnut cake, and a fruitcake with clotted cream.

A very satisfying luncheon for me, with Aunt Violet sitting at the opposite end of the long table in the dining room, she did not break the silence except to compliment Cook on the delicious repast!

After the meal, I brought over a little gift for Aunt Violet. I hand carved a rose from some soft wood I found in the woods. I honed my skinning knife to a fine edge, drew a rose on the piece of wood, and began carving the outline, then I carved in the petals. I left two edges attached to the rose those turned into leaves.

I painted the rose a bright pinkish-red color, and used a variation of greens for the leaves. Once it dried, I buffed it until it shimmered, then I wrapped it in a bit of silk I found in my sewing basket, and tied it with a velvet ribbon.

I did not have much experience in carving. It took me several months of trial and error to complete the rose. I remembered watching Pa, his friends, and Grandpa carving from time to time. Now knew a little more about carving, and thought I would like to pursue this new interest at another time.

I did not know what Aunt Violet would do with the rose, not the usual gift the other young ladies bestowed on her. I figured she would have drawers filled with lace-edged hankies, pen wipes, pincushions, sweetmeats, and candies. I wanted to give her something unique.

When I presented the gift to her, she seemed surprised. I watched her catch her breath as she lifted the rose from its nest of silk, and turned it around and around. I thought I saw a mist of tears in her eyes before she became herself once again. Of course, I was not sure, and could have imagined it.

"This is quite pretty, Caroline, and I thank you. Please extend my gratitude to the gentleman who carved this rose for me."

I thought about nodding and telling her that I would give the gentleman her thanks, but my old stubborn streak came up from somewhere inside, and I said, "I made the rose for you, Lady Ashley, in gratitude for all you have done for me." I guess I floored her because she couldn't say a thing for a full minute.

"Again, I thank you, Caroline. I will find a safe place to keep this rose, but please do not let the other young ladies know that you ply a knife, that would never do."

After dinner, Aunt Violet went for a ride to the country, in the chaise with some of her friends. Since the weather turned mild, I took my Bible and fishing pole and walked out by myself to the stream. I played the scene over in my mind. I couldn't tell if I offended Aunt Violet with my carved rose, or if it pleased her. Perhaps it would not do for her to encourage me. I offered the gift of the carved rose to God. I knew he appreciated my efforts.

When I returned to the kitchen, I found the house quiet, Tezzie and Cook left to spend Christmas with their families. I cleaned the few fish I caught, and put them to soak in milk and spices. Cook would return in time for supper.

I dressed in my riding habit, and walked quickly to the stables, saddled Chocolate with the side saddle, and took a little ride along the Elizabeth River. I have never ventured forth so far alone. I enjoyed myself, and I hoped Aunt Violet would be none the wiser. "Young Ladies are not to ride unaccompanied," so she tells us!

DECEMBER 29, A BELL rang in a distant part of the house. Tezzie answered the door. A neighbor brought Aunt Violet's mail after returning from the mercantile.

"Letter for you, Child," Aunt Violet said from the entrance to the morning room.

"Thank you, Lady Ashley," I answered reaching for the dirty, water-splotched letter, heavy with sealing wax, and the stamps of passage. I turned it over to reveal my Gramma's fine spidery handwriting. Without asking permission, I dropped my sewing, and ran from the house to my favorite spot by the stream.

"Caroline!" Aunt Violet called out, but I ignored her.

"Gramma!" I could not believe what I saw, I wondered why she wrote now and never before. I received many letters from Grandpa, he wrote me short, terse notes to the point, and not much else.

I held Gramma's letter to my heart, feeling the thick missive. I knew her small, close penmanship, covered both sides of the pages. My hand trembled a little before I got up the courage to read her greetings to me.

Fifteenth of December, 1843,

My Darling Caroline,

You may receive this message from me after Christmas. Today, your grandfather and I are thinking of you, as we prepare to celebrate the birth of our Lord and Savior Jesus. We wish you a Happy Christmas there in Virginia.

My heart is full as I take pen in hand to write you our good news. Word came today that your parents are safe. They left the removal group soon after reaching Kentucky. They found a secret place to live in a small town in the state, and have been there for the past two and a half years.

They sent no more information of their whereabouts. They are still in great danger of discovery. Many people there turn in escapees for the bounty.

During their march through Kentucky, your brother Hiram disappeared one night. Over the next several nights, your parents and brother Earl slipped away to search for him. White Christian families hid them from the soldiers. They want to stay in seclusion for a longer time before making future plans.

Your grandfather left home this morning, riding to Kentucky, to search for your family, and be reunited. Please do not get your hopes up. He might not find them, but he would try. They included no information of where they were living.

Amos did not want me to tell you, but I felt you should know, then you could pray for both your grandfather's safety, and the continued safety of your family.

Before he rode out, your grandfather asked me to write you this message:

Caroline, remain there in Virginia, and become a lady, like Lady Ashley, and marry well. You see, Child, that's your chance for a secure future. Lady Ashley is a good woman. She will teach you everything you need to prepare for your new life.

Remember us, but do not risk yourself by trying to return home. No good would come of it if they took you away. God saved your life when the soldiers removed your family from us. Let's not risk the blessing.

You are now, 15 and a half, it is time you thought of beginning a life of your own. Your grandmother, was only a few years older, when she left all, she held dear, to marry me and move here to Tennessee to live. It is fitting for you to begin a new life there in Virginia.

I know the sorrow you feel in being away from us, but in time you will adjust. With Violet, you have the chance for a good new life away from the strife and sadness we still face here. We wish you all of life's best. We pray nightly for God's continued blessings to remain with you.

Take the enclosed money draft, and letter, to the bank there in town. Your father left this money with us. He knew there was a risk that the government would take him and your family away. He did not want the soldiers to confiscate the money. We know he would want you to have it. You should have enough to live on until you meet a fine young gentleman of your own to care for you.

We will always love you, and remember you, Granddaughter. You are continuously in our prayers.

Your loving, Grandparents

I squished up the letter, and held it close. I felt anguish worse than the day the government tore my family from me. I had pinned all my hopes on Grandpa coming back for me. It hurt to read that Grandpa and Gramma didn't want me anymore.

They wanted me to stay here, and marry up with some young gentleman, most likely one Aunt Violet would pick out for me. That's all I could think of that Grandpa would never come back for me. Glad my family was safe, but if I stayed here, I would never see my folks, or Grandpa and Gramma, or the piney woods again.

What in God's sweet name, would I ever do my whole life long being the wife of a rich man? These hands were the hands of a practical woman, a woman who could wrench a living from the soil, shoulder to shoulder with a frontiersman.

"God in heaven," I cried out, "save me from this fate!"

IN JANUARY, THE YOUNG ladies returned to the academy, and we resumed our lessons. My respite ended, and time stretched out to infinity in front of me, my days plodded along with sameness one rainy, dreary damp, day after another.

I was quieter in my spirit, and I minded everything Aunt Violet told me to do. It was not worth the effort to be stubborn any longer. I finished reading my Bible all the way through, and began reading at Genesis again. I had that single comfort. On the first day of March, winter seemed to turn into spring, and it made me feel a trifle better.

For some time, I'd noticed Aunt Violet regarding me oddly. Finally, one day she confronted me. "Caroline, you have sulked long enough," she began after I seated myself in the morning room.

"I have tried my best to take the place of your unfortunate parents. I know this life seemed somewhat foreign to you after the way your parents undertook to raise you.

"Whatever possessed my brother, your grandfather, and his lovely wife to leave their fine, comfortable life here for the wilderness, I will never know. You are the sad result.

"I could honestly say when you first came to me, I doubted you would ever become much more than a wild girl, but you have shaped up admirably. Someday, you will be an asset to a fine young gentleman. You must put your past behind you, and think of your future as the wife of a successful man of business, or commerce.

"As you must know, I too received a letter from your grandparents. They wish you to remain indefinitely with me in Virginia. In view of this, you must take an interest in your life. You have sulked in your room long enough. I want you to join the other young ladies in the socials, and the charity work with enthusiasm, and a willing spirit.

"You have lived here several years, long enough to acclimate yourself to your situation. Therefore, I no longer want to see a long face presented to me. If you cannot be happy, you must learn to hide your feelings. A young lady of quality never wears her heart on her sleeve.

"Before too long you will celebrate your sixteenth birthday. You must look to your future. As my niece, the young gentlemen who are the cream of society, will seek you.

"I will not have your dour face filling these young gentlemen, or the young ladies with despair. Several of the young ladies have sought me to ask if you were ill. I no longer want your despondency to distract them from their own future endeavors.

"And, regarding the young gentlemen, you are to be gracious. You will accept their kind invitations, and follow my instructions on how to make them feel comfortable and at home, while they are our guests.

"You are not to excuse yourself, and remove your person from the ballroom, to the garden, the terrace, or upstairs to your room. You are to remain, and graciously accept all invitations to dine, or to dance with these young gentlemen.

"Then to the best of your abilities, you must strive to show interest in their conversations, and follow the social graces I have taught you. This is the only way you will attract, and interest a fine young man. You must allow yourself to be friendly and sociable.

"Men are not interested in marrying a wild girl. They want someone who is sweet, refined, and demure. I will not have it, if you behave oddly, as you did last fall with the dance master. I still shudder to think how brazen and bold you were with that inestimable young man.

Never again, will you overstep yourself in such a fashion. If it happens, I have ways to curb your wild spirit. Do we understand each other, Caroline?"

"Yes Lady Ashley, I will try to be good," I said, hardly knowing what she asked of me.

"Now on to other things," she continued. "As a special celebration, I have arranged a ball for Ann Marie's eighteenth birthday, on Saturday, May 5. Ann Marie will leave us in June, and some think she may soon become engaged to the successful young man who visits her upon occasion.

"That is my fondest hope for you, too, Caroline. You now have the education, and the graces to bring social success to the home of your future husband.

"Thanks to my training, you would be an asset to a professional man. You would make his home an oasis of peace and serenity, where daily he returns to rest after tremendous efforts in his business dealings.

A very important duty of a wife to her husband is to see to his needs, train the servants, and ensure a peaceful life free of strife, where he feels secure, loved and contented. I know you would meet these obligations admirably.

"My new seamstress, Mrs. Brewer, is fashioning a ball gown for you of white, flounced tulle, with a single peach rose at the waist. The white will set off the highlights in your hair.

All the young ladies will appear in white, each with a different style gown, and a different colored rose. Mrs. Brewer has your measurements, and she will begin your fittings this week.

"Now dear, you need not thank me, do as I say and recover your spirits. Go along now, and resume your lessons."

Aunt Violet dismissed me from her presence with the news that once again, she would manipulate me into an elegant, ball gown, and I must face yet another long, boring, evening of smiling demurely from behind my fan, fluttering my lashes, and chatting inanely to some homely or pompous young man.

One thing stood out boldly to me in her long harangue, Aunt Violet wanted me married, out of her hair, and off her hands as quickly as she could find a young man who would take me. The matter of my future was not up to me. I now have a lot more for me to think on, and ask God about.

As I walked to my room, I could hear the excited twittering of the other young ladies as they discussed the upcoming birthday ball.

I wondered how I missed this harbinger of preparation. I felt like my mind existed in a murky wilderness for weeks since Gramma's letter arrived. I wondered how I could escape Aunt Violet's latest threat to my freedom, and my future.

Chapter 10
I AM AN ADVENTURER

The next day, after my morning lessons, I walked the two and a half blocks to the mercantile on Main Street. I haunted the mail office every few days, looking for a letter, and hoping for a reprieve from my exile.

I received a few letters from Grandpa, since Gramma had written to me, but he only wrote weather reports, and the happenings around town and Bedford County.

He mentioned nothing about my future. He also said nothing more about my folks, other than he could not find them when he traveled to Kentucky, and he had committed them to God's hands.

Approaching the store, I saw people congregated around a Conestoga wagon parked in the front. There were young single men, farmers, some with their wives, and the usual old men who gathered daily outside the store to gossip, smoke, spit, and spin fantastic yarns for each other.

They surrounded a tall, sandy-haired man wearing frontier buckskins. The man looked to be past middle age, but seemed fit enough. His dark, furrowed complexion, and faded blue eyes held a look of competence and experience.

The old men put out opinions of their own, as the stranger spoke to the crowd about the wagon train, he planned to lead out west.

"Won't catch me going out west," one old fellow spat in the street then nudged his gray-haired companion. "My hair'll stay put right where it's been these sixty years," he guffawed at his own cleverness.

"Durn right," his compatriot concurred.

The frontiersman smiled, and shook his head at the pair.

"I'll lead the train to Louisville, Kentucky. From there we'll meet up with Captain Ira Harper, and his wagons. He'll take the train on to Independence, Missouri. Then next spring, he'll pick up more wagons at Independence, and lead 'em all to California and Oregon.

"Come with me, and I'll answer all your questions," he told the gathered crowd. "Let's go to the tavern, have a pint of ale, and talk it over. There's already eight wagons in my train camped right outside of town.

"Those folks are ready to cross the continent to a new life, why not join 'em? Last year in 1843, over a thousand people emigrated to the West Coast. Are you going to let other emigrants get ahead of you in claiming the best land out in Oregon, or California?"

I stood there on the wooden walkway, and watched the crowd follow the wagon captain to the tavern. For weeks ever since I received Gramma's letter, I searched my bible for a message from God about what I should do.

One verse kept jumping out at me, from Proverbs 3:5 and 6:

Trust in the Lord with all thine heart, and lean not on thine own understanding. In all thy ways acknowledge him, and he shall direct thy path.

It seemed like God wanted me to stay put, be patient, and when the time came, he would tell me what to do. Yet, how can I be patient when my heart was hurting?

I could not understand patience, when I wanted with every part of me to find my family. I wanted Ma and Pa, Grandpa, Gramma, and my two brothers, I needed to belong to someone again.

Aunt Violet, barely tolerated me. In her eyes, I was a calf of a different color, as the saying goes. I knew she couldn't wait to have the responsibility of me off her hands.

I stood on the sidewalk, and watched the men until they disappeared inside the tavern. When I turned to enter the store, I stood stock-still reading the notice posted on the door:

"WANTED ADVENTURERS TO
Wagon Train Forming! Departure June 8, 1844!
See Captain Benjamin Johnson

What a good idea, I thought. *I could go too.* I wanted to leave Aunt Violet, and go look for my folks. I won't marry some bottom-heavy young man like that Abbott Parmenter, he was ever in my way at the socials.

Or the new fellow, Sidney Snodgrass, who called on me the last couple of weeks, with his balding pate, and his pronounced lisp.

I do not care how much money either of them has. *"Ugh!"* I think to myself whenever I must accept their attentions.

I am an adventurer, and I want to travel west. I cannot go alone, but I could safely travel with a wagon train. *Thank you, God*! I whispered walking inside the store to check on the mail.

I SPENT A CONSIDERABLE amount of time in the store, looking at hats and scarves, threads and thimbles, anything to pass the time until the captain returned. I looked at items I could use if, and when, I made the break from Aunt Violet, and began my travels.

Mister Porter, the owner of the store, gave me concerned looks when an hour went by and I made no purchases. I gave him a pretty smile and took up some dark, serviceable fabrics, that might come in handy.

I chatted a little with Mrs. Porter, and spying the men coming back from across the street, made my way out the door, almost forgetting the mail and my paper-wrapped package.

"Now you men remember we're meetin' this evenin' at the schoolhouse just outside of town. Be there if you want to travel with me! Make up your minds, May the 8th, is fast a-comin'!"

The men left talking among themselves, arousing even more caustic remarks from the oldsters who always populated the front of the store.

The wagon master watched them go, then prepared to mount his wagon. I gulped down my nervousness, straightened my bonnet, and pulled down the jacket to my costume, I stalled a bit before I approached him.

"Pardon me, sir." I smiled my prettiest at him.

"Why, how do you do, little lady, and how can I help you this fine day?" He turned to me and graciously tipped his hat.

"Why, sir, I am an adventurer and I would like to join your wagon train. I want to travel to Kentucky to join my parents and family." You would have thought I asked him to suck a raw egg. His expression turned just that sour.

"You have no idea what you're asking, young woman!" He spat out. "No! That's impossible! I won't allow no lone women in my train. Now if there's nothin' else, I'll say a good day to you, miss."

"But you do not understand, sir." I detained him with a hand on his sleeve. "I can take care of myself. I can ride and shoot. I can bring in meat for the camp cook pot."

"Ha! Ha! Ha!" he replied, throwing back his head to laugh. The old men on the porch joined him in hearty laughter, pointing their dirty fingers at me, hooting, and hollering, to beat the band.

"But sir, I grew up on the Tennessee frontier!"

"A likely story," he said, grabbing my hand and turning it over. "This hand never did a lick of work in its life." With that said, he mounted his wagon, cracked his whip over the team, and skedaddled out of town as if there was a hornet at his tail.

The old men laughed hard at my expense, I left feeling defeated and angry. I would show him, I vowed. He'd be sorry!

PREPARATIONS FOR THE ball went on unabated. The young ladies whispered all morning during our lessons. That set my teeth on edge, and jangled my nerves. I kept thinking about the notice posted in the mercantile.

ADVENTURERS WANTED!

It was hard to contain my excitement. My heart raced whenever I thought about leaving Virginia, and joining the wagon train, for that's what I decided to do.

Aunt Violet, and the young ladies contributed to my nervous animation over the upcoming ball. My ball gown arrived on Thursday, two days before the event.

The seamstress took my measurements six weeks before. When I tried the gown, it required tucking in at the waist and bosom. I had almost quit eating, and had lost weight. The constant turmoil of wanting to join the wagon train drove me to distraction, so I only picked at my food.

I loved my beautiful white dress with the peach-colored rose at the waist, lovely the way all these elaborate gowns are lovely. It boasted a deep neckline topped with a fragile, beaded, handmade lace bodice. My shoulders were covered with delicate beaded lace, embroidered with tiny white flowers that extended down to my elbows.

The dipped-in waistline flared out to complement the three flounces cascading down the skirt, and accented the seven yards of tulle around the bottom of the full-length skirt. Eight silken petticoats belled out, and rustled sweetly as I walked regally, with my head erect as Aunt Violet had taught me.

Since I celebrated my sixteenth birthday two weeks before, I could now wear a full-length dress, and fashion my hair in an elaborate coiffeur on the top of my head, for I was now a woman of marriageable age.

Aunt Violet dabbed at her eyes, turned her head away, and coughed when she first saw me in the dress. If I not known better, I would have thought she felt touched by my genteel image. However, I am sure she must have a touch of her allergies.

Anne Marie, still unmarried at eighteen, provided Aunt Violet with a reason for the ball. More's the pity, poor girl, appealing, yet "getting long in the tooth," and the ball might be her last chance to snag a successful husband.

You are unkind, and cynical Caroline, I chastised myself in the mirror. I smiled, winked at my reflection, and decided not to marry, ever. I wanted an adventurous life. And that did not include being at the beck and call of some oaf of a man who cared more about making money than he cared about me.

Food preparations filled the house with delicious smells. I wanted to run headlong down to the kitchen when I smelled the apples and cinnamon wafting from below. I needed to be there with Cook, up to my elbows in flour, paring apples, and sprinkling cinnamon and sugar.

Once the altered gown hung in my wardrobe, I put myself to the more practical task of unearthing the lovely dresses Gramma sewed for me four and a half years ago.

I shook out the folds of the skirts, and held them up to me only to cry out in despair, for the dresses no longer fit. The hemline, which brushed my boot tops at eleven and a half, instead struck me at the knee. I gazed at the rough, calico cloth, and cried hard. I could not believe I ever thought these dresses were fine and stylish. They were unsuitable, a word I'd often heard Aunt Violet use.

You are not wearing them to a ball, I reminded myself. *You could let out the tops and waists and add to the hems with the fabric you bought at the mercantile, Gramma always sewed a garment to last, so one could wear it longer.*

I turned a dress inside out, and saw plenty of dress goods left at the seams and hemline. In my mending bag, I found some fabric scraps that I could also use to lengthen the dresses. I shuddered inside when my now delicate hands caught on the rough fabric.

"You don't have to leave," I said aloud. "You could forget your family, and remain here as Grandpa planned."

"No!" I answered back. "I want to be an adventurer not a coddled egg like the delicate flowers who populate this house. They are useless in my eyes."

Thankful to Aunt Violet, that I knew how to sew. If I stayed up late the next few nights, it should not take long to fix the dresses. They would be fine for the trail. The dress with the split skirt would be perfect for riding. I planned to ride astride, not sidesaddle. That fact would cause Aunt Violet to have a case of the vapors if she knew.

On the floor, I spread out a groundsheet, and a small tent that I found in the stables. Next, I brought out my blanket bundle of quilts, a ragged one Gramma made for me, and two other thick quilts. I rolled them tightly together.

I needed to face the fact that I would likely travel through spring rainstorms. I remembered riding miserably in the rain with Grandpa on our way to Virginia. I felt more prepared now, since I had found a large slicker in the stable that might ward off the rain. I packed my riding boots, gloves, and a hat, relieved I would not have to go out to buy supplies. That might have attracted attention to what I planned to do.

After the others were abed, I tiptoed down to the kitchen each night for a few food supplies. I sequestered them in the bottom of my trunk.

When I arrived at Aunt Violet's house, Grandpa took away my gun. I could not venture out with only my knife for defense. I decided to look in the stable and see if Mister Frank still kept his handgun there. I'd watched him handle it many times.

One day he showed me how to load it. He added powder and a cap to each chamber in the cylinder. I knew it held five shots. I hoped I could find where he had hidden the gun, caps, and gunpowder in the stables.

Grandpa taught me how to shoot, and I became good at it during our five weeks travel to Norfolk. I prayed I still remembered what he'd taught me, four and a half years ago.

I would need my skinning knife, another knife to eat and cook with, flint to make a fire, a few candles, and a small box of Lucifer matches, easier to make a fire with matches than flint. Also, a plates, a cup, utensils, and two canteens for water, bars of the good soap they made downstairs in the kitchen, a towel, and a facecloth.

The food supplies that I brought up from the kitchen, the last few days, I spread out on the floor. There was cornmeal, flour, salt, some sugar, a pound of slab bacon, some side meat, beans, an onion, a potato, and a small bag of dried apples that Aunt Violet bought from the local farmer.

It would help if Cook had left some biscuits, cornbread, or white rolls in the warming oven of the fireplace. That should be enough provisions to last a while.

With the food decided, I threw open the doors to the armoire where I kept my clothing. I felt overwhelmed anew when I saw all that I possessed. How could I choose which dresses to take? I pulled out one lovely dress after another, wiping away tears as I laid them on the bed.

I admonished myself. *Caroline, when will you have occasion to wear these elaborate taffetas and silks in the piney woods? Even if there were dances, or taffy pulls, others would think you uppity to come dressed in such a fashion.*

Tears tracked down my cheeks as I set aside the dresses. I decided I would pack two of my cotton morning gowns, the blue dimity, and the green lawn with the white lace trim, two work dresses, stockings, and undergarments.

I would take my dark blue serge suit dress for church, my shawl, a cloak, handkerchiefs, and gloves. I added a gold brooch, I fancied, a reticule filled with all the letters from Grandpa and Gramma, my fan, and a bonnet. Too many things, yet I wanted them all.

My eyes kept straying toward my pale green ball gown with the pink flowers and green leaves, my favorite of all the others. How could I leave that behind? I cried again, then I thought about the delicate rose cameo necklace on the green velvet ribbon, and the matching rose-colored slippers that I had worn with the gown.

It came to me that someday I might need a wedding gown. This gown reminded me of the woods in spring. I could not take the petticoats, or the delicate undergarments I had worn with this creation, but perhaps if that time came, I could make others. I was thankful once again to Aunt Violet for teaching me to sew.

The beautiful gown lay on my bed. I draped it in muslin for protection, then folded it to cause the least number of wrinkles, and added the slippers and the lovely, cameo necklace in its case. It all fit nicely in the pouch with my suit. The other dresses I packed elsewhere. I gave a deep sigh of relief, as I replaced the other charming dresses into the cupboard, and shut the doors.

Some of the money Gramma sent me, I stored in a chest in my room. The next time I walked down for Aunt Violet's mail, I would stroll across the street to the bank, and withdraw the majority of the remaining funds, leaving a little money in the account, so they would not notify Aunt Violet of my total withdrawal. With the funds in hand, I could further equip myself at a distant outpost, where no one knew me.

I would leave after the ball with the little horse Chocolate. Most everyone in the house would most likely, sleep until noon the next morning. They would not miss me until the noontime dinner.

Chocolate and I would be fine traveling alone for a few days. I planned to take her saddle, saddle bags, all my bundles, parfleches, and pouches. She seemed strong enough to carry me, and the provisions. I felt like an adventurer headed west. Thank you, God! Thank you, Jesus! I prayed!

THE UPSTAIRS BELL RANG, summoning the young ladies to gather on the landing before descending the stairs to the drawing room. A violin, pianoforte, and cello played sweet, delicate, refrains from the minstrel's gallery.

I felt all aflutter inside, both from the excitement going on around me, and from my secret plans. I forgot my fan and gloves, and ran back down the carpeted hall to my room for them, which meant I descended the stairs last.

The young ladies made a delightful picture in their demure gowns. I caught my breath in surprise as I watched them descend in a cloud of white, each with colorful floral accents. Everyone looked their best, curled, powdered, and scented. The illusion of a beautiful flower garden.

The young gentlemen waited downstairs ready to offer an arm to escort each young lady into the birthday supper. Imagine my surprise when I observed the tall, blond wagon captain there in line. He looked distinguished in a well-cut formal black suit, different from the buckskins he wore when I last saw him. He crooked his arm and escorted Aunt Violet.

I gaped like a fool, not even looking to my left at my escort. I heard a gruff, "Ahem" come from the young gentleman. That brought my head around, and brought me back to my escort, and my lack of manners.

I turned to see Wilfred Addison standing there, his narrow face a brilliant red in embarrassment. I smiled my prettiest at him, fluttered my lashes, and ventured a wink in his direction, causing him to flush yet again.

Wilfred, a fine man, brown of hair and eye, yet a little too tall and bony for my taste, and not exciting by any means, a good steady fella, he clerks at his father's bank. I am sure Aunt Violet paired me with him.

I felt myself fidget through the interminable dinner. I pecked at my food, too excited to do much more, I knew I should eat my fill because of the long night ahead of me.

I think I spent more time straining to hear the tales of the west that the captain regaled Aunt Violet. Than to the dull banter put out by the newest young gentleman assigned to me, Mister Wilfred Addison, sitting by my side at the table.

It seemed the captain traveled everywhere in our big country, and met everyone, of any importance from General Winfield Scott, former president, Andrew Jackson, to our beloved Cherokee principal chief, John Ross, The Ridge, a man of equal importance in the tribe, and other members of the tribal councils.

He said, he'd hunted and trapped with Davy Crockett, and Daniel Boone. He had met with Sam Houston, politicians, and other trappers that I knew of by reputation only. I could tell he embellished his tales some, as several of those famous names were before his time. That made me laugh!

I know I spoiled the evening for poor Mister Addison. I fanned myself from time to time smiled, and fluttered my lashes, as I watched the other young ladies do. I answered his questions with terse one-sentence answers, sure he thought me a ninny, but I did not much care.

The gentleman on my other side, a Mister Sidney Upton, with his snapping black eyes, long black hair, and curling mustaches, tried to get my attention. When I would not turn my head in his direction, irritated he turned back to his own dinner partner, to regale her with his inane conversation.

I looked across the table from him, and observed Katherine Mitchell looking up at Sidney Snodgrass as if she were seeing God himself. There was no accounting for tastes. I wanted to laugh in relief. Mister Snodgrass had at last found himself a young lady, who thought the sun rose and set on him.

The long meal finally ended with Anne Marie, and her escort leading us off to the ballroom. They bowed and danced the first dance of honor since she was "belle of the ball," and the birthday girl.

I danced one waltz with Mister Addison. Then I made my excuses, and almost ran from the room, mumbling something about a headache to the poor man. I hated to leave him high and dry, but I still needed to get ready for my departure. I knew I could not stay away long, but I prayed Mister Addison would soon find himself a new partner.

A little while later, I returned downstairs feeling better. My sewing completed, my traveling dress ready, and the packing finished, including the few things I planned to take, including the silver candlesticks from my bedroom. They would remind me of my years in Virginia, and would fancy up a table wherever I lived. Or, I could sell them if I ever needed money.

A quiver of guilt ran through me, yet I felt the candlesticks were mine for all the long hours I worked in the kitchen alongside Cook and Tezzie, while the other young ladies dawdled in their rooms.

I found a chair in the ballroom, in an out-of-the-way place, and hid my face behind my fan, not wishing to make eye contact with anyone.

I had torn up my dance card, so I did not know who would seek me for the next dance. Relief coursed through me when no young gentlemen came to claim me.

Mister Addison was not in the ballroom, I hoped he had left for the evening. I found I did not care. If Aunt Violet knew that, I would be in even more trouble. I wanted to be on my way. Living here four and a half years was long enough!

The handsome captain went whirling by with Aunt Violet. He was a good ten years her junior, yet he seemed mighty attentive to her. I wondered if he looked for capital to invest in his venture.

In addition to the travelers, I knew he was taking three wagons of supplies northwest to trade with the Indians for furs. I made sure the captain did not see me, as I would not have him telling Aunt Violet, I asked him about passage west on his wagon train.

The evening ended with Anne Marie smiling, and raining moist kisses on everyone. I guess the birthday gala proved a success, Portly Osgood Trevelyan clasped her hand throughout the evening.

Yes, Auntie proved as good as her word. She trained up young ladies, educated them, and started them on the road to proper matrimony. Fine for them, but not for me.

After the ball, I followed the other young ladies upstairs, and readied myself for bed. The servants extinguished the candles downstairs one by one. Aunt Violet stopped by each room to say goodnight to the young ladies. Her best gray silk rustled as she opened my door, and moved into the room.

"Well Caroline," she began. "I hope you enjoyed yourself this evening. Your Grandparents would be proud of the young lady you have become. You would do well to cultivate the affections of young Mister Addison. His father mentored him, and arranged a brilliant future for him in the bank."

"Thank you for all you have done for me, Lady Ashley," I replied. I surprised myself by getting a little misty-eyed when I thought of leaving this good woman, and everything familiar to me over the years.

"Tut, tut, Caroline! It was nothing more than my Christian duty to raise you as a lady, I would certainly help you again. Your grandfather and I were always close. Now, rest dear. The day will shortly dawn, and we have many more lessons for you to learn.

"You are of marriageable age, and need to work on your trousseau. You must complete the twelve quilts, and the various fine linens for your new home when you marry. Goodnight, niece."

With that said, she stooped to brush my cheek with her lips in a show of affection, the first she ever gave me. She left my room to make her way downstairs, extinguish the remaining lights, and close and lock the doors for the night. Her fragrance lingered in the room.

I do not know what to think about Aunt Violet. All these years, I pictured myself as a burden to her. I put my hand up to my cheek, touched by her sentiment. In thinking back, I seemed to recall a bit of moisture in her eye, but couldn't be sure.

My preparations finished, I decided to make one more check of my room, the armoire, under the bed, behind the drawers, and under the lining of the trunk.

It was then I found the small sewn pouch of newspapers that I had saved about the removal. They were tightly folded, thrust in the pouch, and hidden deep inside the trunk.

I gasped, and felt my heart race. I realized I had almost left them behind. I wanted to keep them my lifelong to show Grandpa, and my family if I ever I have a family of my own.

I found a place for the pouch inside a bag where it would remain safe and dry while I traveled.

After a little while, the third floor quieted, except for some whispered tittering from several rooms farther down the hall. I made my toilet, and lay in bed in my traveling dress. Once the house stilled, I threw back the covers, straightened my bed, and tucked my boots into one end of the blanket roll. I would don them downstairs. I slung the two bundles over my shoulders.

The night felt warm, so I would not need my cloak. My hat hung around my neck by its laces, and I strapped the gun I borrowed from Mister Frank, under my garments.

I felt bad borrowing Mister Frank's gun and bullets. I hoped he would not need them. I left him an envelope with a short note, and four gold half-eagles in payment. I hoped it was enough.

I made my way downstairs to a small seldom-used closet near the kitchen. There I pulled out the pair of rawhide parfleches I arrived with four and a half years ago. I had filled them with the food and supplies I needed for the trail.

It made quite a load for me to lug. With my boots on my feet, I crept out the back door, down the stairs, and across the yard to the stables. I dumped my bundles outside, and searched in the dark for the blanket, saddle, saddlebags, and bridle that I hide together in a haystack last evening.

The little mare's soft nicker met me. I fed her a filched apple. Then I saddled and bridled her as Mister Frank, the groom, taught me when I'd first begun to ride. I slung my two parfleche, and the saddlebags behind the saddle, and tied the other bundles on either side of the saddle horn. I led Chocolate outside, closed and barred the stable door, and mounted up.

"Sorry for the heavy load, little girl," I whispered. "Wish I could have borrowed a pack horse, taking you was bad enough. I hoped Aunt Violet would not put out a hue and cry to bring me back."

The moon waned, but I could see well enough to ride. I kicked Chocolate into a slow walk across the yard, and along one side of the house to the path leading to Main Street. Instead, I wanted to tear off down the road to put the academy, and the town behind me, as fast as I could.

I was a poor planner, I just trusted God to take care of me, and see that I got to my folks. I felt a twinge of guilt from time to time when I thought of Aunt Violet. I marveled at the revelation that perhaps she cared a mite for me. She bore no children of her own.

She and Lord Ashley married late in life, and then about ten years ago, he succumbed to an illness leaving her to make her own way in the world. She cared for me in her own way, but she never accepted me. Her ambitions were not my ambitions.

I thought about the letter I left for her on the little desk in my room, not well written, and longer than I wanted. I prayed she would forgive my impulsiveness in leaving her.

Dear Lady Ashley, I am sorry to leave you in this fashion, yet I feel I must make my way west to join my family. I am grateful to you for accepting me into the academy, seeing to my needs, and for your faithful teaching over the years.

I thank you for the fine education, and for your diligence in teaching me to become a young lady of quality. I cannot express my gratitude enough. If I am successful in my future endeavors, it was because of your teaching and guidance.

There are funds in the drawer of this desk to reimburse you to some extent, for the horse and saddle, the candlesticks, and the other supplies I have taken. I am sorry to cause you so much concern.

I thank you sincerely from the bottom of my heart for your goodness to me. When I arrive at my destination, I will write and let you know how I fared.

With my best regards to you and the young ladies,
Miss Caroline Linda Ashbill

It was hard for me to decide how many gold coins to leave Aunt Violet. I asked Mister Frank what it would cost to buy a horse, and he said, if I were to buy a horse, it could cost me around four gold eagles. The saddle and accessories would cost another four half-eagles. I left seven gold eagles, which is about 70 dollars. It should be sufficient, but it did not reimburse my aunt for the inconvenience I caused her to replace the horse and saddle.

I did not say goodbye to my friend Miriam. I could not confide in anyone. I did not want them to bring me back. The thought of a future with Wilfred Addison, or another of his ilk caused me to feel ill. I could not accept that. I was riding away to a new life, with God going before me.

The mare stumbled, and almost fell. I pulled her to a walk not wanting to tire her. I figured I could ride ten miles before Aunt Violet discovered me missing.

With the lateness of the hour when the ball ended, I hoped no one would rise before noon the next day. That would give me time to get further away.

WHEN WE HAD TRAVELED about five hours, I pulled off the main road and trotted a quarter mile along a little side trail. I dismounted in a thick copse of small trees, drank from my canteen, and unsaddled the little mare. I hobbled her a short distance away near a patch of good grass, close to a small bubbling stream.

Plumb worn out, I spread my blankets for a rest. I hoped I could sleep a little, but I still felt the excitement coursing through me. As soon as I lay my head down, I discovered how soft I'd become in the last four and a half years. I felt every rock, and branch beneath me. Finally, the sleep of exhaustion claimed me. I dreamt of the pretty, yellow-haired boy I saw in the woods, so many years ago. This time, he wore the face of the dance master.

Chapter 11
<u>ON THE ROAD</u>

A nicker from the mare brought me upright, and reaching for the revolver I had stuffed beneath the blanket. A deer stood head up, sniffing the air. He smelled me sensed no danger, and bounded away with a flick of his tail across the creek and into the thick woods.

Pulling the pack over to me, I rustled through it looking for the package of ham and biscuits. I took a long drink from my canteen, and ate every crumb of my little meal. I caught the mare, saddled her, piled on my bundles and mounted.

Past noon, I needed to put more distance between me and Norfolk. I prayed Aunt Violet would not send out searchers for me. I reined about, and headed toward the west hoping to throw them off. By traveling on a zigzag course west, then north, and then west again, it would take me over a week and a half to reach Roanoke. I hoped my trail would confuse anyone coming after me. The wagon train leaves Norfolk tomorrow, so likely I would arrive in Roanoke ahead of them.

My days ran together, I rode by night and camped by day. I knew how to find the right roads. Grandpa taught me to take a sighting on the sun and stars on our trip east when I first traveled to Virginia. Each morning, I sighted, and plotted my course before making camp. By traveling at night, I avoided people. So far, I saw no one.

Sometimes I passed isolated cabins, and dogs roused to give me chase when I ventured too close to their homesteads. My food was holding out well. I would replenish some of my supplies in Roanoke if I arrived before the train. Perhaps I could find some place to stay there.

Night travel became lonely. I wished with all my might that Grandpa might appear along the trail, and ride alongside me. Remembering our trip to Virginia gave me courage. I recalled most everything about our time together, how we rode, where we camped, the country we covered, and the things we discussed. Four years, a long time ago, yet my mind was strong and agile. I was blessed with a good memory.

Early on the morning of the fifth day, a rider moved toward me on the road. I ambled along with the sun bright in my eyes wanting to get a little farther along before I camped. I'd slackened up some on my watchfulness feeling secure on the quiet roads, or the man would never have seen me. With no time to pull off the road or seek cover, I touched up the mare and tried to ride past him looking straight ahead.

A ruffian rather than a gentleman, he did not nod and tip his hat to me as was proper. That man moved his horse across my path and blocked me from going through. Then he grabbed for the reins to jerk the mare close to his mount.

I pulled the gun from the band of my dress where I wore it.

"Hold it, stranger!" I demanded cocking and pointing my gun right between his eyes. "Move aside and allow me to pass!"

Emotions flickered in his tiny close-set, black eyes. He licked his lips and began to pull aside his mount before lunging over to make a grab for my gun. I fired knocking the hat from his head.

"You were lucky this time, Mister. I can place a shot wherever I aim!" I said steady enough. "Now, move aside and let me pass!"

A snarl filled his face. He looked again at the big Colt Patterson Revolver I held level with his face. "Yes, missy," he said as he cowered a little in his saddle.

I got the best of him, and I knew I'd made an enemy. He might follow along behind me. I kicked up the mare, tore off down the road and away from the ruffian as if from the devil himself.

I turned to see if he followed, and breathed a prayer of thanksgiving when the road behind me remained empty. Now I knew there were rogues in the area. I'd heard the stories, but like a ninny I learned the hard way and rode right up to one.

We galloped on until Chocolate seemed to slow. I pulled up to give her a breather and spotted what seemed like a little-used path next to a stream.

I followed it as it weaved back and forth through the woods fording the little stream and re-fording it again several times, until I came to a farmstead smoke rising from a chimney on one end of the house.

I pulled the mare back into the shelter of the trees then looked over the farm, before seeking a place to make my camp.

Later, I would approach the farmstead and see if I could buy a few supplies. I wanted people close by in case that fella trailed behind and tried to catch me.

Chocolate hobbled and staked out began pulling at the fresh grass, and drinking from the quick running stream. She looked tired her head drooping. I brought out a nosebag with a little grain to give her strength. We needed to hole up somewhere for a few days, both Chocolate and I needed rest.

I made my bed in a deadfall scooping leaves together for a mattress and spread out my quilts. The whispers of the pines overhead comforted me. They smelled fresh and reminded me of home. I found a few pinecones on the ground. For a snack, I picked out the pine nuts missed by a squirrel.

When I lay down sleep refused to come. I was nervous, I couldn't stop thinking about that terrible man. What would have happened to me if I did not have the gun handy? I knew my rescue came from God. Yet, I do not remember praying, or calling out to Him. He just went ahead and saved me!

A verse came to me: Proverbs 18:10, *The name of the Lord is a strong tower: the righteous runneth into it and is safe.*

Thank you, Jesus! I whispered. *I am in awe of how you led me out of danger!*

Late in the afternoon, I pulled out my best traveling dress and headed to the creek for a wash in the icy cold water, and a change of clothing. I took the mare in with me and gave her a good washing. She blew, snorted and frolicked a little with me. Her dark brown sides glistened wet in the warm spring sun. I rubbed her down with a handful of dry grass. Afterwards, she seemed perkier and ready for the trail.

I donned the fresh dress, and re-braided my clean hair, packed, mounted the mare, and turned her back toward the farm we passed earlier in the day. We trotted to the rock wall surrounding the farm, opened and closed the gate, and walked the horse toward the house.

The chimney on top of the house blew smoke, and a line of wash flapped in the gentle breeze in the side yard. As I drew near, young children played near the barn, and a dog barked and barked in excitement.

I dismounted and tied Chocolate to an upright support on the front of the house. Two towheaded youngsters ran toward me from the pole barn. A hound bayed and followed behind them.

The cabin door opened, and the woman of the house stood gun in hand. She stared for a good minute before she motioned for me to come inside. The woman seemed about ten years older.

She appeared bright and curious, yet a woman of few words. She did not ask about me. I knew it would not be proper, so I set about telling her what she needed to know.

I had prepared my story during the long hours of riding. "My name is Carol Ashe. I lost my folks a while back," I did not say how. "Since, I am alone now, I am riding to join my grand folks out west."

While not a lie, it seemed to satisfy her curiosity about why I traveled alone.

"I'm Louise Davis," she said, laying aside her gun, and reaching out to shake my hand. "I own this farm with my husband, Thomas. These are my two boys, Thom and Ray, and we have a baby girl, Lucille. She is there sleeping in the cradle. Thomas is away out on a hunt with neighbor men, so we are here by ourselves for now."

I told her about meeting up with the man on the road, and she invited me to stay. She said she would welcome the company. I agreed and thanked her, but only if I could help. I took over the choring for her. What a pleasure for me to milk a cow, and feed pigs and chickens again.

The baby snuggled closely in my arms while Louise prepared our supper. The boys washed, and sat at the table ready to eat. She read a passage from the Bible aloud, and we ate with good appetites. I felt at peace for the first time since setting out on the road by myself.

That evening, I stretched out my bedding in front of the fireplace and slept my first good sleep in five days. Morning, a repeat of the night before; I milked, fed the stock, and returned to the cabin with a bucket of milk and a basket of eggs.

Louise fried the eggs, and a pot of gruel bubbled on the hook in the fireplace. She took up the eggs on a platter, and added corn cakes from the iron spider sitting in the ashes of the fireplace.

I filled cups with milk for the boys, and poured the hot fragrant coffee into tin mugs for us. My second solid meal in days filled me with satisfying goodness.

The day passed quickly. I separated the cream through cheesecloth, churned butter, and turned the leavings into a cloth to become smearcase, a kind of cheese curds.

Holding the sweet baby girl filled me with peace. Her cornflower blue eyes fringed with long dark lashes, looked a lot like little spiders on her cheeks when she slept. Almost two months old, she could already roll to her back in the cradle.

I wanted to get myself a precious little child like her one day, I vowed, as soon as I find a pretty young man to marry. *Caroline,* I told myself, *you missed your chance to have a man, and a baby back there in Norfolk. You threw it away.* I grinned despite myself. "We'll see," I said aloud.

The morning of the fourth day at the farm, I determined I should leave. Forty more miles, and I would reach Roanoke. I felt better as I nudged Chocolate to a trot, waved goodbye to Louise, and later galloped down the deserted road toward Roanoke, Virginia.

Roanoke, a historic town, sounded interesting. I heard it called the Great Salt Lick. For generations, salt marshes, or licks, were gathering places for buffalo, elk, and deer, and for the Indians for hunting. I was a mite curious to see it.

Two days later, on the outskirts of the town, I found a well-run trading post. There were four horses tied in front of the store. A few older women were inside buying supplies. A loud bunch of men congregated in the back sitting on nail kegs near the stove, doing a lot of bragging.

Looking around the store, I enjoyed seeing what might strike my fancy. I knew I needed to conserve my funds, so I just settled for a large wedge of cheese, raisins, a paper of lard, a package of cornmeal, some sugar cubes, a few apples, and a small bag of grain for Chocolate. Then, I indulged myself with three eggs, and a tin of milk.

I fingered the fine cotton fabrics displayed at the front of the store *No, Caroline,* I told myself. *Be practical. You need to save your money. You can buy new dress goods in Kentucky once you arrive.*

The young clerk tallied up my purchases, and added a double handful of crackers, and three dill pickles to my order.

I blushed in appreciation, and batted my lashes at him. Didn't hurt to use my wiles every now and then.

Close to sundown, it began to rain. I packed my provisions onto Chocolate, pulled on the slicker, and walked her through the back streets of the town, to escape notice of the townspeople. They didn't need to get a gander at me, a single female riding astride, and alone.

I saw a sign showing the way to a livery stable on Pine Street. The livery man named a fair price to stable Chocolate for a few nights. I did not tell him I wanted to camp in the stall with her, yet I could not stay at the inn in case Aunt Violet sent men to pursue me.

A little distance into the woods, I found a secure place to camp. I made a tiny fire under the trees, and ate a simple meal of cheese, crackers, pickles, an apple, and water from my canteen.

It rained off and on steady-like. It was cold and miserable, and I was thankful for the slicker I wore. After full dark, I sneaked inside the stable, and made a bed in the stall next to Chocolate. I changed into dry clothing, and felt some better. It was rough, but at least I was inside and away from the weather.

I prayed my dear Lord would keep me safe, allow me to find the wagon train, and that they would welcome me to travel west with them. I ended my prayer by asking God to bless, Ma, Pa, my brothers, Grandpa, and Gramma, to keep them all safe, and to bring me home to them before too long.

As an afterthought, I asked Jesus to bless Aunt Violet, Miriam, Tezzie, Cook, and the young ladies. I prayed in Jesus' name and recited

Matthew 21:22, as Grandpa taught me. *And all things whatsoever, ye shall ask in prayer, believing, ye shall receive.*

Chapter 12

<u>THE WAGON TRAIN</u>

Before sunup I gathered a few supplies, and walked out to the woods, where I'd camped the night before. I made a batter of cornmeal, lard, egg, raisins and a little of the milk. I mixed it in my tin plate, made a tiny fire, and baked 6 cakes in batches on a flat rock. I ate a few, and left the rest for my dinner, and supper.

After breakfast, I would walk around the town to see if I could find any news of the wagon train. They must be traveling slowly because it seemed like I'd beaten them to Roanoke. So far, I heard no word of wagons being seen approaching the town.

Maybe it was better they didn't come for a while. A tremor ran down my spine, thinking of what the wagon master might say when he saw me. Likely, he would be angry. Would he turn me away?

I must join the wagon train. They could not turn me away it was too dangerous for a woman traveling alone. I turned my care and safety over to God, and whispered a quick prayer for help.

The day passed slowly, but finally the sun went down. Late that night, I again made my bed inside the stable close to Chocolate.

During the night, men swore and argued vulgarly outside the stable. They pounded loudly, banging repeatedly on the door to open up and let them in. The stable master abed upstairs, hollered at the men to shut up, and go away.

I cringed back into the corner of the stall, and piled hay all around me. I was hidden unless someone walked right into the stall. My hands trembled, and I could not stop thinking what would happen if those rude men found me there by myself.

I did not sleep well, but knew I should leave early before anyone found me. Close to daybreak, I snuck out the back door of the livery and walked farther out in the woods behind the town. I felt safer there somehow. I laid the ground cloth down under a low hanging

155

tree and spread my quilts. I thought it would not hurt a bit if I took
a little nap.

Later, I would fix my breakfast eat, and make the rounds of the
stores seeking word of the wagon train.

AROUND ELEVEN A.M., some men rode into town saying a
wagon train had pulled in beside the trading post. I saddled
Chocolate, paid the stable hand for two nights boarding of my horse,
and rode to the meadow where I heard the train camped close to a
spring.

I slowly walked my mare into their campground. The travelers
were busy unhitching their horses and mules, fetching water,
collecting firewood, and beginning preparations for their noon
dinner.

The captain seemed to recognize me when I rode into the camp,
his eyes narrowed, and his jaw clenched. I knew I would receive a
tongue-lashing.

"What do you want?" he growled impolitely, not even letting me
speak first. He acted disrespectful, and I was a lady.

"I told you single females ain't welcome on my train," he
continued angrily. "Now get yourself back off to Roanoke, before
you cause us trouble."

"I kin take care of myself!" I flared, my accent thickening. "I
only need to travel for a few weeks with the wagons. I won't be no
trouble." He made me mad, seeing his face flushed red with his anger.

Then it came to me. I should not handle the man with
belligerence. I paused, looked at his furious face, and then
remembered my upbringing with Aunt Violet. The captain did not
want a helpless female on his hands, but perhaps I could sway him
with gentility.

Dismounted, I removed my hat, and hung it from the saddle horn, shook my long wavy, auburn hair out of its chignon until it flowed down my back then walked over to the captain, my eyelashes a flutter.

"We haven't been properly introduced sir," I said, extending my gloved hand in a gracious manner. "I am Miss Caroline Ashbill. I am traveling west to live with my grandparents. I would count it as a favor if I may travel along with your train. I can pay my way, and would cause you no trouble."

The captain's eyes widened at the change in me. I went from a wildcat to a young lady of quality in the space of a few moments.

"I heered what she said, Cap'n," A tall, large-boned woman thrust herself forward before he could react. "She kin travel with me, and my man. You cain't turn her away, the varmints might get her. You know, Cap'n, both the four-legged kind, and the two-legged ones abound in these here woods," she said with a loud laugh.

Calls of "Hear! Hear!" And other murmurs of agreement echoed the woman's suggestion throughout the crowd that gathered around us.

"All right, all right, enough!" He sputtered. "According to the charter of my wagon train, we can't take unattached females. They cause trouble." He glared at the assembled travelers and prepared to stalk off to his fire.

"Well then, Cap'n, we'll jest change the rules. We can't turn away a pretty young lady like this one here. All in favor of Miss Ashbill joining the train say right out, Aye or Nay," the big woman, took control of the issue. Many calls of "Aye" echoed through the camp.

"You people don't know what you're asking," the captain sputtered again. "You mark my words you're askin' for a heap of misery!"

"Well, I think the Good Lord knows best, Cap'n," the woman said with a smile.

After the vote, I found myself a member of the Johnson Wagon Train, headed west toward Kentucky, and my people.

EXCITEMENT COURSED through me at the thought of traveling west with these folks. I'd left Norfolk over ten days before, and except for the lady at the farm, Louise Davis, I missed seeing people. The lonesomes had become my constant companion as I traveled.

Living at the academy, I was never alone. Tears of relief pricked my eyes. The kindness of this big woman made me want to sob. She seemed motherly.

I followed her to the wagon where she introduced herself as Miz Waller, and her husband as Mister Waller. The Wallers traveled with four blue tick hounds. The largest dog, the mother of the three half-grown pups, she called Queenie.

Miz Waller told me she planned to keep the mother dog, and give the two male pups to her son. She did not know what she wanted to do with the third pup, a female.

Those dogs took to me like butter to a stack of Johnnycakes. I received a thorough licking from all four of them. That tickled me no end, Queenie-dog about knocked me over in her exuberance.

Miz Waller told me there was no room for me inside. When we peeked in the back of the wagon the first day of my travel, she pointed out the barrels of flour, and wooden boxes of supplies, cornmeal, sugar, beans, rice, and other things. In the middle, The Wallers had piled two big trunks full of household goods and clothes, one atop the other.

She made their bed upon two large chiffoniers at the back of the wagon. They also shared the area with a box of cooking pots, pans, and utensils. Their belongings filled the wagon up to the staves, with no room to spare.

The first night, I shared my "bedchamber," under the wagon with the dogs. Fine with me, they would keep me warm. I laughed at the thought, imagining Aunt Violet's horror if she knew.

Miz Waller and her Mister, as she called him, were mid-along fifty years of age. They had birthed twelve children. The children were scattered throughout the east. She and Mister Waller tired of trying to wrest a living from bare rocky Virginia soil, sold their farm, and joined the train to Kentucky.

The Wallers planned to live with their oldest son and his family near the Ohio River. She missed her son and his wife, their daughter-in-law, who was her favorite of them all. She birthed the Wallers eight grandchildren, aged from one to fourteen, four boys, and four girls.

"Eight young'uns air more than enough for a body to care for," she declared. "I'll want to help Susie out much as I can. Just cain't wait to get there to see the new baby, and see how much the other young'uns have growed. It's been two years since they went to Kaintucky, 'bout broke my heart when they left Virginny!"

"Mister Waller hopes we can quick get along down the road," she continued. "He's most anxious to help our son break that rich, new soil to the plow. Course there'll be a big garden for me to tend to. I jest love gettin' my hands dirty.

It's a mystery to me how once we put these dried up, little ole seeds in the ground, before you know it, little plants sprout up and grow. I'd say God had his hand in all of it!"

I learned a lot while I rode next to Miz Waller on the wagon seat. The second day, she told me, "I like your company, Caroline, you don't have to ride your mare, it passes the time for me to talk to another woman while I drive these cantankerous mules."

Miz Waller liked to talk, and talk she did. I never got a word in. Even when she asked me a direct question, she always seemed to answer for me, too.

Miz Waller decided I was eighteen years old, and running home to my folks from a bad marriage. I do not know how she decided I was a married lady, since I wore no ring. A romantic at heart, I decided.

No amount of nay saying from me would change her mind. She thought my plight too hurtful for me to speak. So, I accepted her story for me. I knew I would only be with her a few weeks, at most.

When Captain Johnson halted the wagons each night, he chose a place with a good rill, or stream, and plenty of forage for the animals. He seemed like a good experienced captain. He'd led trains through here for the past four seasons.

Old Daniel Boone forged a path through the Appalachian Mountains. The government widened the path to accommodate wagons, and now we traveled on that very road. I felt like a modern-day pioneer.

As I rode along, I enjoyed seeing the sights. I could not wait for us to travel high in the mountains. I wondered if we could see where Gramma and Grandpa lived in Tennessee from high on the Cumberland Gap.

The folks here were not yet into the routine of travel. Wagons broke down, and oxen and mules kicked out of their traces unaccustomed to the heavy loads. Dogs fought each other, and horses loosened their tied hobbles at night and ran off. At daybreak, the children went out to round them up. Cows lowed for familiar mangers, and chickens refused to lay eggs. Pigs squealed, and young children seemed to be everywhere underfoot. It was a wonder to me we made any time at all, but we climbed the mountains higher and higher each day.

The fourth day out of Roanoke, the sun rose on a tranquil scene: wagons circled, good coffee smells hung above the smoky campfires, children munched on biscuits and bacon as they herded the animals back to camp, and horses, mules, and oxen cooperated in the harnessing.

That morning, I felt better. My bottom was not as sore from riding the rough board on the high wagon since I'd padded the seat with my quilts.

After breakfast, I decided I would ride my mare. Miz Waller nodded her assent, but she kept an eagle eye on me as I mounted up.

It was still dark as I rode along, with the female pup following me. I could see a little rosy glow on the eastern horizon.

Several young men rode through camp, and approached me, but the little dog barked frantically at them. They tipped their hats, smirked, and grinned broadly, winking at each other. No manners, I decided.

I nodded to them, and pulled the mare aside to let them pass, then galloped on to the front of the train, where Captain Johnson sat by the fire and clutched a fresh cup of hot coffee.

As I dismounted, all the men turned and looked in my direction. The captain glared at me, then continued his talk about the history of the route we traveled.

I stood nearby, and held Chocolate's reins in my gloved hand. The dog circled around the men, sniffed at them, barked and got in their way. Captain still bore me a grudge, since I bested him in the matter of traveling with the train. I ignored his rudeness, and listened while he talked about the history of the Cumberland Gap, which we were about to embark upon.

"We're setting out on the famous Wilderness Road that Dan'l Boone first helped build," the captain said, as he took a sip of his coffee.

"It started as a pack trail, before the govermint hired men to widen it. In the early 1800's after I was borned, 300,000 pilgrims set out, and traveled along the Wilderness Road."

He also told us of the more traveled National Road, which ran from Cumberland, Maryland, to Illinois. He wanted to embark upon that road, but due to the lateness in the year, he figured the Gap would be the best road, as we would find an abundance of game, and active streams along it.

I quivered with excitement as I thought of putting my feet, or my mare's hoofs along the trail of Ole Dan'l Boone.

The men returned to their wagons, and we broke camp as the sun peeked over the top of the highest mountain. My breath caught in my throat at the glory of sunrise in those high places. I thanked God for his goodness to me.

After I mounted, and pulled the mare around, I galloped back to the wagon, and Miz Waller. I needed no more young bucks smirking at me, a supposed runaway bride. I giggled to think of that. Still, Miz Waller's assumption sounded like a good cover story, and I would ride the wagon for sure that day for my safety.

"Well, I'll swan, Caroline. I was thinkin' you was goin' to ride your mare this morning. Well, never mind dear, you jest sit yourself right up here beside Ma. Not a thing can bother you here."

After supper each night, I trotted Chocolate outside the wagon circle to graze with the other livestock. I hobbled, and staked her out on a long tether rope.

Then I washed up at a creek, laid out my quilts, and crawled under the wagon with the four dogs, I quickly dropped to sleep, as wagon travel wore me down.

For the first four nights, everything went well. Then the fifth morning I could not find Chocolate. I had left her just a few paces outside the camp close to the stream.

I searched throughout the camp, but could not find her anywhere. I reported her theft to the captain. He got red in the face, and muttered to himself about durn females.

I did not know what else to do, so I climbed to the wagon seat next to Miz Waller, and tears tracked down my cheeks for quite a while.

The men of the train decided Indians stole her in the night and stole her. I did not believe that. If Indians came to steal, they would have run off more than one little mare.

Later, I spread my quilts under the wagon, just like the past five nights. Queenie and her two male pups ran off after a pack of other dogs. They barked, and yelped as they chased through the undergrowth and looked for the coyotes, we heard howling for most of the evening.

The little girl pup seemed content to snuggle up with me, and soon she snored.

Along about midnight, I woke to a shuffling sound, like feet trying to walk quiet-like. The little dog lifted her head, and her ears perked up. She growled deep in her chest. "No, pup! Quiet, pup!" I said as I listened for a little while, but heard no more. So, I went back to sleep.

A little later, I heard a twig crack as if someone stepped on it. I rose up and felt someone put their hand over my face and thrust an evil smelling rag in my mouth.

I reached under the pillow for my gun, but I could not reach it fast enough. Someone else grabbed it from me. Then they lifted me up and slung me over their shoulder. I fought them hard, but it did no good.

The little pup put up a howl, grabbed the pant leg of one man, and bit clean through into his calf. The man hollered, and swore before he kicked the dog away.

I spat out the evil tasting rag, screamed long and loud, and woke the camp. The man who carried me began to run, banging me hard against his back, I struggled and struggled.

Soon, I heard the loud crash of several guns. The wind of a bullet came close, followed by a loud boom. The man who carried me stopped. He turned to face the men of the camp with me still over his shoulder.

Mister Waller, the captain, and several other men ran up carrying their guns. They took me from him, and set me down on my feet. One man carried a lit torch, and I turned to face my kidnappers.

They were the three men who followed me ever since I joined the train. I lunged at them, and spat in the face of the one who carried me. "If I had my skinning knife, I'd have slit your throat!"

The man laughed in my face, as did the rest of the men who stood there. I was mad, mad clean through. What's the matter with those men not taking me serious?

Miz Waller ran up, put her arm around me, and tried to lead me back to the wagon, but I fought her off. I screeched at the three men and lunged at them. I wanted to do them harm.

Captain caught my arm, and thrust me toward Miz Waller. "Go back to camp, Miss Ashbill. I'll deal with these three."

I began to shake as I walked back to the wagon with Miz Waller. "OOOOHHHH! I sobbed. Those three varmints tried to take me away in the middle of the night for only God knows what!" I screamed out.

A thought niggled at the back of my mind. I turned and hollered to the captain. "Captain, those varmints took my revolver, and see if they know what happened to my mare. They might have her hidden somewhere close by to take me away from the camp."

"Now, now, Caroline, let the men handle it. You're not hurt, jest a little ruffled. You can sleep inside the rest of the night. Mister Waller will sleep under the wagon from now on.

"Glad little pup warned us. God was with you Darlin,' I should'a knowed better then to have a beauty like you sleeping alone under the wagon. It's my fault, Caroline, but these seemed like nice folks in this here train." Miz Waller continued to speak to me in soothing tones until I felt myself relax.

"Thank you, Miz Waller," I said between sobs. "I am sorry I made you worry so much about me! Do not blame yourself. The decision to join this train with no protection was my own. I should have slept under the wagon with the gun in my hand. I knew if I slept elsewhere than under the wagon, those men would have found some other way to get to me! They showed no respect!"

Reaching down, I ruffled the fur of the little pup, thankful she rescued me. I grabbed up my quilt, and other things from under the wagon and followed Miz Waller inside for the rest of the night.

THE DISTRESSING EVENTS replayed in my mind, keeping me awake. My hands shook, and I could not relax. I planned revenge on those three no-good varmints who tried to take me against my will. They had followed me whenever I rode Chocolate along the trail. I could not see any danger they seemed like nice, good-looking young men.

Once I got up the next morning, I helped Miz Waller make our breakfast. Before we ate, I saw a bunch of men coming toward the wagon with the captain in the lead. He pushed one of those young men along. I saw with surprise that the man wore two black eyes, a bloody mouth, and I saw bruises on his face and neck. I did not know the men would take matters in their own hands. He limped up to me with a surly smile on his once handsome face.

"There she is, Henry, now say your piece, 'fore you feel my fist again," Captain Johnson told the man.

"Sorry, Miss Ashbill, we was only funning, thought we'd take you out a ways from camp, and get to know each other better."

"Get to know each other?" I quizzed the man. "I can imagine what you wanted with me. I am a lady, and I do not go unchaperoned with any man." I let him see my anger! "Sides, you no account, with my skinning knife in my hand, you would never walk upright again."

Another man walked up then. I turned my head and saw Chocolate ready to nuzzle me. She looked as good as new. I wrapped my arms around her, and began to cry, darn it!

"Those three led us to her after we persuaded 'em," the captain bragged. "They tethered her about a mile behind camp, I don't know what they'd planned, but it looked like they wanted to ride you away with them."

"We took care of the other two, Miss Ashbill," the man with Chocolate, said. "They won't bother you no more. They're hoofing it back to Roanoke, no boots, no guns, and no britches."

"Now it's up to you what we do with this 'un. Shall we lynch him?" Captain Johnson asked me.

"Lynch him, Captain? Did I hear you right? Yes, he deserves lynching, but no, I think not. Give him what you gave the others. That should teach him a good lesson!"

"Not so fast, Cap'n," Miz Waller thrust herself forward. "You better post a guard, and make sure these three hellions don't try to come back, and steal from the wagon train. If what you say is true, they ain't got no clothes, or food, or horses."

"Rest assured, Ma'am. We rode 'em out many miles behind us. We'll take this one, too. They ain't coming back anytime soon. Jest in case, we'll post a guard, day and night. Now, you know, Miss Ashbill, why I didn't want unattached females on this train.

"You've delayed us long enough, and these good men from the train have missed a night's sleep because of you! Mount up everyone, head west. I'll catch up with you once I dispose of the likes of this one!"

Chapter 13
MARTIN'S STATION

Thank you, Ma'am," I said as I climbed up to the wagon seat, heaved a sigh of relief, and wiggled into a more comfortable position. "Thank you for speaking up for me. I didn't ask for trouble and Captain Johnson acted as if it were my fault, as if I encouraged those men."

"Don't worry your head about it, Caroline. Shows a pretty one like you attracts bees wherever she goes. Those ones weren't gentlemen, in my opinion, and they got what they deserved!" As we moved miles away from those three terrible men, my spirits lifted. I vowed I would not think about them anymore.

Miz Waller reached for the reins, and cracked the whip over the backs of the six mules. "Kaintucky here we come!" She hollered, as she did every morning.

"Kaintuck! Kaintuck!" I repeated to myself. I liked the sound of the name, but not the meaning that I heard whispered among the men.

Captain told us the Indians called the area "Kan-Tuck-Hee," meaning dark and bloody ground, because of the many Indian battles fought there among the tribes. I shivered when I thought of that.

I remembered what the Cap'n told us about Daniel Boone, and the Wilderness Road. I also remembered hearing stories from my people that the Cherokee Nation sold land to an explorer, Richard Henderson to establish a colony. He hired Daniel Boone to go ahead of him, and blaze a trail, and the trail became the Wilderness Road.

Other men followed along behind Daniel, and cut out brush and trees. The trail stretched two hundred miles and went through the Cumberland Gap.

The Cumberland Gap was the doorway through the southern Appalachian Mountains and into the great wilderness of Kentucky. Early settlers in search of land, traveled in groups for safety, and

struggled to survive by living off the land. They each hankered to breach the vast Kentucky wilderness, and build new lives for themselves.

IN GRAMMA'S LETTER, she said there was a possibility my folks now lived in Kentucky. Yet, they could live anywhere in Kentucky. I prayed they found a permanent place, and secure shelter, and someday I would find them.

Then I offered another prayer that I would find another dear soul to latch onto in the days ahead, after I left Miz Waller's protection.

I also wondered if Captain Harper would take an unaccompanied woman in his train. I hoped so! Captain Johnson and his men were leaving the train in Louisville to travel north with their three wagons to trade for furs with the Indian tribes.

Riding on the hard seat next to Miz Waller, my mind just seemed to skitter along to the cadence of Miz Waller's chatter. I listened to her and prayed my prayers, while she talked.

"I'm sorry we ain't traveling later in the summer, Caroline. Then the berries would be ripe, and we could pick all we wanted to eat. See that prickly vine over there, Caroline? Them's blackberries, and that one over there, they's gooseberries. They's bitter right now, not worth the picking. On t'other hand though, it's nice to ride along in the cooler weather without skeeters eating you right up.

"Why, I mind the time when we moved down from the North to Virginny. It were in the dead of summer, the worst time of the year, some people calls 'em dog days.

Hot! So hot, you couldn't even catch your breath, and the bugs jest eatin' you alive, the sweat attracts 'em. I was nursing my middle girl Janie, then. The trials that babe put up with, I'll swan. Her eyes swole shut from all the gnats alightin' on 'em. I worried she'd come up blind, but the good Lord saw us through. I told the Mister, I'd never travel in the dead of summer again, and he kept his pledge to me. He remembered it."

Miz Waller blessed me when she took me under her wing. Both she and Mister Waller cared for me, and saw to my needs. They fed me three meals a day out of their own stores. They would not let me provide any food from my supplies. When I suggested it, she just said, "I'll swan, Caroline, keep your provisions, you're likely to need 'em later on. Sides, you don't eat enough to keep a chick alive."

MIDMORNING, THE WEATHER turned into a trial for us. A fine mist soon blew into a wind-driven deluge, with thunder and lightning striking close by in the woods. The skittish animals sounded and balked. The road turned into a quagmire of mud. The wheels stopped turning, and the wagons came to a complete halt.

Captain told us to sit it out right there in the road. When the rain began, I found my slicker and put it on. I draped my ground cloth over both of our laps, so Miz Waller and I were as dry as possible in the blowing rain. She set the brake, and tied the lines to it, and we moved to the back of the wagon where we got a little relief. Mister Waller rode up, tied his horse to the tailgate of the wagon, and joined us.

Miz Waller reached for the food box, and brought out leftover pone and biscuits for us to munch. Wet and cold, yet I was glad to be out of the worst of the storm.

We sat on the road for the next four hours before the rain moved south, the sun came out, and the water ran off the road. Captain stopped by to check on each wagon. He told us to start out. The going was slow, the animals sloughing through the thick mud, but after another two hours, we reached a likely place to camp for the night.

Once we stopped, my little shadow the pup, went with me to gather as much dry firewood as we could bring in. I found a deadfall of trunks close to camp. Most of it was wet, but I dug underneath to find the driest pieces and took them back.

I grabbed buckets and filled them with water from a swollen creek, then helped Miz Waller begin the campfire and prepare our meal. Mister Waller fed the horses and mules, and milked the cow.

After a while, Miz Waller told me, "Jest sit yourself down, and don't worry your pretty head, Caroline, I'll do the cooking you needn't do a thing. You need your rest after what went on last night and today."

"I am fine, Miz Waller, I am over last night. I just want to help you. It can't be easy driving mules through the mire and mud all day, and then have to cook our supper over a smoky campfire." I still felt obligated to The Wallers.

"Caroline, I come from good strong stock. I've seen and done lots worse than this. I'd always played whatever hand the good Lord dealt me, and I trust in Him to help me get through. Supper will be ready in two shakes of a bobtail!"

True to her word, Miz Waller filled our plates with biscuits, sliced onions, and potatoes, fried with side meat. Everything tasted so good with the flavor of wood smoke. I offered praise to God.

The next morning, while milking Buttercup, I pondered. "*What to do? What do I do?*" I asked aloud, over and over again. I owed the Waller's so much. How could I pay them back for their help?

After breakfast, I sat next to Miz Waller as she drove the mules along the winding trail through the forest. A fine day, since Mother Nature got over her temper tantrum. The sun shone, drying out the white canvas tops and the heavy wagons.

I wondered why folks strived to go west when daily we passed through magnificent country with plenty of water and game, I saw everything that's needed to live right there, and free for the taking.

That gave me an idea, I reached behind me in the wagon and pulled out Mister Waller's musket.

"Miz Waller?" I spoke before I could change my mind. "Could you pull up for a minute? I want to borrow Mister Waller's gun, and see if I can scare up a little meat for the stew pot. I will be right along."

She pulled up the wagon, and I hopped down saddled, and mounted Chocolate, and rode off before anyone could see me, or say a word to stop me. I knew the rules about straying from the trail, or the camp, yet I wanted to find some way to pay back the Wallers for their kindness to me. If I brought in a deer, I knew it would be welcome, as they were getting low on meat.

I glanced around, and it did not seem as if anyone noticed me riding off into the brush. I trotted a good piece before I looked behind me again, and still did not see anyone. Those three ruffians were long gone, and no one else bothered me at the camp.

"Thank you, Jesus," I said as I looked up at the little peek of blue sky and white clouds showing overhead between the canopies of the trees. I sat Chocolate for a few minutes to get my bearings before going forth to scout for deer. The peace and quietness of the forest filled my heart. Many years had passed since I was a lost eleven-year-old in the deep woods.

For over four years, I lived in the city, and once on the road by myself, I traveled and camped with my safety uppermost in my mind. I did not pay particular attention to the beauty of my surroundings.

Now, I took time to praise God, and to ask him to continue to watch over Grandpa, Gramma, my folks, and me. A redbird sang nearby, and brought a smile to my face, a redbird like me, a good sign.

Now perhaps I could fetch a deer. I rode along a small overgrown forest path, and stopped to look for deer sign. It pointed east, back the way we'd traveled. I would go a little farther, and see what I could find. I didn't want the wagon train to get too far ahead of me.

The deer had taken the path earlier that morning. Their spore still looked fresh. I found a shallow stream, and stopped to let Chocolate drink. Still no sign of a deer, yet there were many droppings so I knew deer stopped by here for a drink. I knew I could not travel much further.

The birds sang up a storm, and I noticed many varieties of spring flowers, white flags, moss roses, swamp lilies, woods violets, wild roses. I almost forgot why I came. I got down, pulled an armful of wild daisies, marsh grasses and white flags into a bundle, and stowed them in my saddlebag for Miz Waller. If nothing else, she would have flowers.

I heard a great crashing through the underbrush. I listened hard to determine what could make such a racket. I pulled off the trail and hid behind the huge butt of a hickory tree, all of five feet across. I was sure no one could see me.

The noise grew louder. It sounded like a horse whipped up. I peeked around the tree and blanched.

"Darn!" I said aloud, for on that big horse sat the angry presence of Captain Johnson! I stepped Chocolate from behind the tree and confronted the angry man.

"Why did you follow me?" I said before I received his vehement tongue-lashing.

"Young woman, didn't you get in enough trouble the other night? I should have known better than to allow you to travel with my train. You've acted unreasonable, and irresponsible, for the last time! I halted the train while I went out to bring you in. You put your life, and the lives of everyone else on the train in jeopardy."

"But!" I said, before he rudely interrupted.

"But nothin'! You turn that horse right around, and get back to the train! Now! There's savages in these woods, white men, and Injuns. They wouldn't think twice't about plucking you off that horse and riding off with you." His eyes blazed with anger.

I decided I should mind him before he exploded worse. He didn't know my experience with the woods, and the tribes of Indians who traveled through them. I still needed to keep my identity a secret.

I turned Chocolate and kicked her into a fast trot, the wagon master followed close behind. I felt ashamed. I tried to do a good deed, and look what it got me.

Before long, we reached the main trail. I could see the wagons stalled in the road. The men pacing back and forth jeered at me as soon as I broke through the trees. I did not expect that, I never thought Captain Johnson would halt the train, and ride out to bring me back.

Misery rode my back and tears threatened, as I trotted Chocolate down to the Waller's wagon. I tried hard not to cry in front of those people. I tied Chocolate to the wagon unsaddled her, and picked up the musket and the bouquet of flowers as a peace offering.

The little dog came up and licked my hand, that helped some. Unfortunately, my little adventure off the road put us behind a good hour, so we must make up for lost time.

I knew the men were angry, and they would blame me when they sat down to a late supper. They already saw me as a troublemaker when it was actually the fault of the wagon master. I would've been fine!

After thinking things over for a minute, I finally told myself: *Enough of the bad attitude, Caroline. You need to quiet your spirit and listen to reason. What if you met up with those three varmints from last night, or maybe some Shawnee braves? They wouldn't know you were Cherokee. You do not look like it, anymore.*

After pondering for a few more seconds, I decided yes, I guess I'd better act sensible, and quit going off believing I know everything about everything.

Maybe the wagon master was right, glad I didn't have to find out the hard way. I knew how to bring home game. I trapped and shot game with Grandpa, and small game at the Indian camp. Yet, it's been over five years since I last lived with the tribe. I'd never fetched a deer, yet I knew how, for I watched it done more than once. The wagon master did not know me. He thought me just another fluttery female, all fuss, feathers, and no brain.

I still felt miffed as I climbed up to the wagon seat next to Miz Waller. I handed her the musket, then I offered her the flower bouquet.

"I am sorry, Miz Waller. I didn't mean to cause you any trouble," I said, choking a little on the words. "I wanted to fetch a deer, to repay you in a small way for all your kindnesses."

"Why, will you look at that purty boo-kay you brung me, Caroline. I ain't seed the like in many a year. Thank you kindly! That's right thoughty of you!" She turned the bundle of flowers and grasses around and around, admiring them, and then laid them delicate-like on the wagon seat between us.

"Never you mind, my pretty," she said, winking at me. "We'll jest let Mister Waller tend to the stewpot. Thank you for trying. I shouldn't have let you go, it's my fault, I knew the rules.

"Sides, Caroline, you need not thank me. I like your company here on the wagon. With the Mister riding up front, it gets a mite lonesome

a-driving these mules the daylong.

The good Lord saw fit to bring you here to our wagon train, and I saw fit to help you. That's what Christians do for one another. Now,

Honey, don't fret yourself. No use a pretty, little lass like you going out to do man's work!"

I felt worse for her saying those nice things, not her fault I was headstrong. Tears slid down the side of my nose, I turned away and sniffled a bit until I gained control of myself. I was appalled at my reaction. Why with all I went through in my life, did I cry now, and not before? So hard for me to figure.

The wagon in front of us began to move. Miz Waller grabbed up the reins, laid the whip alongside the lead mule, and yelled, "Kaintucky, here we come!"

"TWO MORE DAYS AND WE'LL arrive at Martin's Station, in Lee County, Virginia," the captain informed us that night after supper. "Lee County was named for Light Horse Harry Lee, the Governor of Virginia from 1791 to 1794, and formed in 1793. Lee was famous for his exploits as a leader of light cavalry during the American Revolutionary War."

Ho hum, I thought the next morning, chafing at the inactivity of riding along on the hard wooden seat, and the bumpy road all day long, and then having to sit and listen to the captain's boring history lessons after supper most nights. Again, I forgot to pad the seat with my quilt. I brought it forward, felt a trifle better.

"Caroline, you're as jumpy as Patty's flea." Miz Waller remarked turning to look at me. "I know you want to be out riding your horse, but its best you jest stay put right here by me for the time being. You don't want the Cap'n to be throwing you off this train. I swan the wagon master is jest looking for an excuse, if you know what I mean."

I felt bad to have caused this good woman so much extra worry. "I know, Miz Waller, but I am not used to sitting all day long on this hard wagon seat. Now I'm sorry I didn't bring my fancy stitching or my knitting."

"Oh? So, you knit, do you?" She turned to me with a pleased look on her face. "Well now, I jest wondered how I would make the Mister some new socks when I have to be about driving this here team all the durn day long. Next time we stop, I'll bring out my needles and yarn for you."

I smiled and nodded my head. "Thank you, Ma'am!" *Another way, and a better way I could help Miz Waller*, I told myself, squeezing my hands together to keep them still.

At our noon stop, Miz Waller gave me her yarn and needles. We traveled on, with me knitting and knitting. We drove uphill, and down dale, alongside streams, and through magnificent forests, beside meadows and right through tiny little rills smack in the middle of the road.

I loved it all, and could not get enough of the big colorful show God put together seemed like just for me. I felt right at home, as if I'd never left, and lived in the big city to become a lady of quality. Yet, I found that with my hands, and mind focused on knitting, I could better enjoy nature to its fullest.

As I knitted, I thought about my life. I'd often heard that whatever we learn wouldn't ever be taken away from us, so it is never wasted, and whatever happened, happened for a reason. Well maybe yes, and maybe no to both of those ideas.

I do not know why I learned all the many graces Aunt Violet taught me. It happened, that's all I knew. I didn't expect ever to marry, particularly not to a rich man. I wanted to spend the rest of my life with my own folks, and Grandpa and Gramma.

I could not see me ever dressing a fine table, and serving tiny buttered cucumber sandwiches. I did not know if I would ever serve high tea with fancy cakes, and tarts, or even low tea with buttered and sugared bread, to my women friends.

I could not think of serving them to Miz Waller, or to my lovely Gramma. They would think me touched. I hid my smile when I played out the scene in my mind. I almost laughed aloud.

So why did God want me to go live with Aunt Violet, and learn all the fanciness if I would never have the occasion to use it?

I remembered all the beautiful dresses, and undergarments I left behind. There were big hats with intricate veiling's, fans, and reticules to match, dresses made with yards of beautiful fabrics, and two-foot-long trains to complement the luxury of the gowns. The older girls wore longer trains, of course.

To what purpose did those young ladies spend their free time? They did not read scripture. Instead, they read the latest serialized penny novels, which they passed along from one girl to another. I thought of those as nonsense.

They also spent most of their free time curling each other's hair and talking about young men. Deciding which one they wanted to escort them to the latest upcoming soiree, picnic, or boating event, and which of the men seemed the most, marriageable, or desirable.

Desirable? I laughed! Most of the young men seemed like boors to me, not a keeper in the lot. Never! Not for anything! I never expected to miss the life I lived in Norfolk!

I wondered how the lives of those young ladies would play out, once they snagged a prosperous husband. Would they enjoy the lifestyle at home, raising children, taking tea with their friends, and doing a little charity work, or would it bore them?

Aunt said our purpose in life was to create a life of quiet repose for the husband striving out in the world of business each day.

It all seemed empty to me. I did not intend to live life as a pretty bauble, and fawn upon my husband. I wanted to work alongside him, wrenching our livelihood from the soil, and raising sons and daughters who would make a good difference in the world.

There was nothing in Aunt Violet's academy to rival what I was seeing now staring upwards at the green canopy of God's Forest while jouncing along on the hard wagon seat with this good woman.

I could not question His will any longer. I needed to obey and praise Him my lifelong, and He would direct my path just fine. I knew I sat right where He wanted me.

As much as I could, I tried to make wagon travel easier for Miz Waller. One afternoon I helped her as she made the supper. Captain Johnson and the men brought in some venison, and divided it between the wagons. I wanted to make my special venison stew, but I would have to wait for a time when we camped overnight, as it takes the day to cook.

I decided a dish of raw wild greens would go well with the fried venison. I watched the road to see if I recognized any of the greens, I would need. They liked the sunny spots best. I got down from the wagon, took my knife and a bucket, and walked alongside the wagon as we traveled. I gathered ramps, a wild onion with a garlic flavor, also sheep and wood sorrel.

Crossing a stream, I found a bucket full of watercress. I loved 'cress and Aunt Violet did not serve it. I made sure the captain rode away off at the front of the train before I followed the trail out into the woods. I wanted to see if I could find wild mushrooms. I found some large morels, as we called them, and a nice patch of mint, and stalks of chickweed, tender and tasty.

A few wild onions grew a little way off the side of the road, lucky I recognized them and found them at all, it was still a mite early in the year for even the greens I picked to be growing.

There were tender dandelion leaves, and I used what I could find of them, but I wished I could find some wild burdock, and poke greens, and many other greens I remembered from home. I found and recognized more than I expected though, as every road grew its own unique variety of greens.

Once we circled the wagons, Miz Waller sliced some potatoes and onions to fry with the venison. When the venison was done, I took a goodly portion of the bacon grease she used to fry in, and poured it over the washed and chopped greens. I added vinegar, salt and pepper, and a mite of sugar to cut the tartness. That was how I learned to make greens when I lived in the Cherokee camp. I hoped the Waller's would like my tasty dish. If they did, I would make it often.

I FELT A KEEN DISAPPOINTMENT when we pulled up at Joseph Martin's Station late one afternoon. I thought we would reach a manned, well-kept fort where we could stock up on our supplies. Instead, the buildings were abandoned and running to ruin. The sat unprotected from the elements for many long years.

Once we circled our wagons, watered, and hobbled the mules, oxen, and horses, we filled our buckets with fresh water for ourselves. The captain stood in the center of the circle and told us,

"We've traveled far enough, every one of us can use a rest, so we'll remain here for a couple of days, wash clothes, relax, hunt, fish, and enjoy ourselves. Tonight, we'll have a campfire in front of the stockade, and we'll all share a meal. Bring whatever you feel like eating. See you then!"

I liked the idea. I spied some good-sized trout in the small creek running alongside the compound. Also, with my limited clothing supply, I needed to wash.

After an early supper, Captain Johnson began our time together with another history lesson on Joseph Martin's Station. I thought we should have been calling him professor rather than captain, as he seemed to enjoy the sound of his own voice. I will admit though he could spin a good yarn, or two, and knew his history.

After lighting his pipe, he balanced himself on a large boulder at the side of the fire. Families gathered around, the young children sat cross-legged at the front, close to the fire. Men stood in the back holding their guns. Women and young girls were in-between sitting on their wooden stools. The young boys were another matter. They ran around the compound, enjoying the fresh air of the early evening, whooping, hollering, and playing Injun.

Captain Johnson cleared his throat, and spat into the fire before beginning. "Martin's Station was an important part of the safety of folks traveling along the Wilderness Road for over twenty years. Here families came for protection from Injun raids." He let that sink in.

"Look 'round you, folks. You'll see the remains of several frontier cabins, outbuildings, and a stockaded fort. At one time, a working blacksmith, a surveyor, and a trading post supplied the outlying farms hereabouts."

"Our grandsire, Old Dan'l Boone, and other frontiersmen with an advanced party of the Transylvania Company first traveled the Wilderness Road. They used old buffalo, and Injun trails in the beginning and later cut a path through the wilderness. The road come up from Richmond, Virginia, in the east, and in the north began at the town of Shenandoah Falls, where the two roads met at Fort Chiswell, in the Shenandoah Valley.

"In 1750, Mister Robert Harper received 125 acres. He established his ferry across the Potomac River about 1761. His ferry made the town a starting point for European, and American settlers moving into the Shenandoah Valley and further west.

"In 1763, the Virginia General Assembly established the town of Shenandoah Falls at Mister Harper's Ferry, later called Harper's Ferry.

"Old Dan'l's road ran southwest from there through the valley, across the Appalachian Mountains, and through the Cumberland Gap into the Kentucky bluegrass region, to the Ohio River.

"In the early years, many travelers fell victim to hostile Injun attacks. Then once Kentucky became a state in 1792, they widened the road to allow the passage of wagons. They hired men to keep up sections of the road, and charged tolls for its use.

"Today, in the 1840's, travel on the Wilderness Road has slacked off some. Most people favor the newer National Road. Yet, there's still those who say the Wilderness Road is the best way to reach Kaintucky!"

To my way of thinking, the captain was long winded. I heard much the same story when I first joined the train and sat with the men at breakfast one morning, before the captain let me know he did not want me there. I laughed!

Many in the company hung on every word he spoke. The women heard this story for the first time, and I knew I'd felt just like them when I first heard the amazing story about our old grandsire, Daniel Boone.

I turned away from the fire, and watched the young'uns play a game of hide and seek.

I saw the three Thomas boys running into one of the abandoned cabins to hide. I heard some pounding, and the eldest boy appeared on the roof through a hole he forced through on top of the building. *Scamp!* I thought.

The second boy drug out an old straw ticking from inside, and took it around to the back where he hid under it.

"All outs in free!" One of the other boys yelled after a few minutes. Young'uns ran from all over. They lined up, and the last one in was it.

"Where's James?" The eldest Thomas boy called out. No one could find James. They looked high and low.

The eldest boy Alfred ran into the cabin and hollered, "James where are you at? All outs in free!"

Right then I heard a bellowing the like of which I'd never heard in my life! "Mama! Mammmma! Help! Mama!"

A small bundle of boy energy flew through the door of the cabin screaming as if he hurt himself! Following close behind him looked like some kind of varmint right on his tail!

I grabbed up a few rocks and ran after the boy. I didn't know what kind of varmint until I saw the shape of its head!

"Skunk! Oh Lord, no!" I cried out. I shied rocks at the skunk, and hit him a couple of good ones before he stopped, looked around, and tottered away as fast as his short legs would take him to the woods.

"Did he get you, James?" His brother Alfred called out.

"Yeah, he got me good," James sobbed.

"Phew!" The other boys yelled, pointing their fingers, and laughing at James.

"James! Alfred! Arthur! Is that you boys making all that racket Their mother called out from the fire.

"Yeah, Ma, that ole skunk done got me!" James called wiping tears from his eyes.

"Oh, lordy! Oh, lordy!" she called, running over to the tree where James sat crying. "Why couldn't you young'uns keep out of trouble? Now what'll I do for clothes for you?"

"Alfred! Take James to the creek and scrub him down! Arthur, you go get James' blanket, then take the shovel and bury his clothes out in the woods."

"Aw, Ma!" the two bigger boys cried in unison. "Then we'll smell like skunk!"

"Now get! All three of you! I don't want to see any of you again 'til you get James all cleaned up. Well, I never!" She said, walking back to the fire.

Captain Johnson continued with his talk despite all the commotion, but his audience shrunk some. The men found the boys' doings more interesting, than what captain went on being long-winded about. The men got up from where they were sat and began a little exploring of their own in the old buildings.

"Hey, what say we crank up the fiddle and have us a dance?" One man said, strumming the strings of his violin, further interrupting the captain.

"Well, why not?" Captain said, "I've jawed long enough for one evening." He got up stretched, and clamped his pipe back in his mouth, as he strode off from the fire to take a walk around the camp.

The couples joined up, bowed and whirled, in the jolly music filled air. I sat off to one side tapping my foot to the music. After a while, I noticed a man stood in front of me with his hands outstretched. "Miss Ashbill? Care to dance?" I looked up in surprise to see Captain Johnson standing there smiling down at me.

"Shall we see if we can do justice to this music? Though it ain't the equal to the orchestra at your Aunt Ashley's last soirée," he replied, chuckling at my confusion. "Bet you didn't know I recognized you at her house, young lady?"

"I hoped you didn't, sir! I surely hoped you didn't!" I felt my face burn in embarrassment.

"Why you would want to give up the life Miz Ashley prepared for you, to trade it for the wilderness, I'll never know," he said with a laugh, leading me where the others were dancing.

He fooled me, I thought, curtsying to the captain, and glancing around at the other dancers. I felt embarrassed by his attention, singling me out, but I held my head high, determined to show them I was a true lady of quality and one who knew my way around a dance floor, or even this hard-packed earth!

He returned me to my seat after the dance, yet I knew the gossip would abound with me at the center as long as I stayed with the train. I could already see the catty tongues wagging.

I sat down next to Miz Waller, and told her I wanted to turn in, and make an early start.

"You jest go right along, my pretty. I'll be following you, before too long!" Then she whispered, "Don't worry about them biddies Caroline, they's jest jealous of a young pretty little thing like you!"

MORNING CAME EARLY, and I awakened to the lowing of the Waller's cow, Buttercup. I dressed, took down the bucket, and milked her. A good cow, she lets down her milk, she does not kick, or set up a fuss.

After breakfast, Captain Johnson passed by and told us we'd be staying an extra day as Miz Crawford was having her baby. He asked Miz Waller to help out.

She asked if I could fix some food for the men folks, Mister Waller, Mister Crawford, and the other men whose wives were over there helping.

"I am glad to help," I told her. I wondered if I could catch enough fish to make a good meal for the men.

After breakfast, I saw a comical sight. The three Thomas young'uns marched in a line toward the woods. Alfred, the eldest, led off wearing his pa's trousers, which looked about three sizes too big for him. Arthur followed behind, with britches two sizes too big for him. Little James looked the most comical, the tops of his britches rode right under his armpits, with the bottoms rolled up about four turns. All three of the boys wore rope tied around their waists to keep their trousers from falling.

I could see James tried hard not to cry, embarrassed by the strong odor he carried. Alfred must have failed in getting the skunk smell off James. The older boys were keeping their distance from him. Other boys trailed behind the three, jeering, laughing, and pointing fingers at them.

I went behind the three, and ran off the hecklers. Then I called out to the boys as they headed toward the creek,

"Hey, let's have a fishing contest. I caught some nice fish this morning, but I need a mess more, so I can make dinner for the men."

"What's the prize?" Alfred asked me.

"Yeah, what's the prize?" Arthur parroted his big brother.

James only stood there hanging his head.

"Wait jest a minute," I told them, running back to the wagon. I found a few interesting things I kept in a leather pouch. I dumped them out, and found three small coins, a seashell rock, a pine knot shaped like a squirrel, and best of all, an obsidian arrowhead. Those should do it!

The boys ran back to their wagon, got their line and hooks, and met me at the creek. We cut poles, and stretched ourselves along the edge of the creek. I went to the big rock where I'd fished the day before. We tried for a while with no success, and then James pulled out a big bass.

We all ran over to him, and admired his fish. Then we all began pulling fish out of the creek. When we got seventeen, I called a halt. Everyone brought their fish over to the rock, and compared our catch.

"What a good haul," I told the boys. "It looked like Alfred caught the most fish, and Arthur the most unusual fish, a long eel with teeth. James caught the only catfish, and I hooked the smallest fish, an eight-inch perch. Now, who will help me clean our catch?"

"What about our prize?" James asked. "Who won?"

"Yeah, who won?" the other boys asked.

"Why, you all won." I told them with a smile.

I dug in my pocket, and pulled out the three coins. "How's that?" I said, holding out the coins to the boys. "Hurrah!" they said in unison.

"And how about this as well?" I handed the pine knot squirrel to James, the seashell rock to Arthur, and the obsidian arrowhead to Alfred.

"Oh boy! Oh boy!" James said jumping up and down in excitement.

With the boys' help, I cleaned the fish, made a big fire, put water on to boil, seasoned, and fried the fish in batches in Miz Waller's heavy black skillet. I added coffee to the furiously boiling water in the large pot, mixed biscuits, and baked them in the makeshift metal oven set at the edge of the fire.

I heard a weak cry, and watched the men running toward the Crawford wagon. "It's a girl! I got me a baby girl!" Mister Crawford told everyone in excitement.

Once the food was ready, I walked over, and invited him and the other men to eat. "Bring your cups and plates," I called out to them.

The smell of fried fish, coffee, and biscuits browned to perfection lined the men up to my fire. I filled each plate quite full, saving the rest to take over to Miz Crawford's wagon for the women.

There, I peeked at the sweet baby face of little Virginia May Crawford, named for the month of May, and the state of Virginia, where she was born. She had a good set of lungs, and a lot of bright red hair standing straight up in the air.

Chapter 14

<u>GRANDPA</u>

After breakfast the next morning, the captain called the company together. "We'll stay in camp another day, I want you men to break up into groups, some of you hunt for meat, and the rest of you fish the Holston River. If we get enough meat and fish, it might last us a while, then we won't have to stop to hunt.

You women can smoke the fish, and cook, or smoke the meat. Fish don't take long to smoke, and it lasts. Always favored smoked fish, it's mighty tasty. If you know how to make jerked meat or bannock, make it!"

Captain's bossy today, I thought, listening to him. I could fish too. I found the small stream full of many kinds of fish.

Instead, I thought I would take some time off, though my conscience gave me a twinge. I saw enough men going out after meat, and I needed time alone.

I picked up my revolver and skinning knife, grabbed Chocolate's reins, and walked her downstream a long way to the south. The little pup followed me. She nuzzled my hand for attention. I petted her and made sure she followed.

Once there, I took off my boots and stockings, hiked up my skirts, and tucked them into the waistband of my dress. Then, I rolled up the bottoms of my pantalettes. Barefooted and barelegged, I stepped into the cold water and tugged on Chocolate's reins, she seemed willing enough.

Once in the stream, she snatched the reins from my hand and lay down in the cold water. She rolled over and back again, having a good time. I pulled out a small sack of soft soap, and began to scrub her coat; dirt, dust, and muddy water ran off in rivulets.

I called the pup to me, and brought her into the water, too. I doubt she'd ever had a bath in her life. At first, she fought me, then she too enjoyed it. I soaped and rinsed her fur.

Good no one could see us here, for it was unladylike for me, but I enjoyed being improper once in a while. As the muddy water ran off the animals, I thought a lot of muddiness ran right out of my spirit. Both Chocolate, and the pup ran out of the water with me, clean and refreshed.

We walked back and forth in front of the stream. The water ran down Chocolate's coat, and the warm breeze blew through her mane. I dried her more with some cloth sacking. I roughed up her coat and smoothed it down again until the sun dried it to a shimmery, dark brown color.

The little pup shook herself hard, and ran in the sun drying herself. Then she ran up to me, barked and barked, alerting me to trouble. I picked up my revolver, and jumped to hear a man's voice coming from behind the trees.

"There you be Gal, lady over to the camp said I'd find you down here. Ever since I got Violet's telegram saying you, and her horse run off with a wagon train, I been searching for you all along this here Wilderness Trail.

"If I didn't find you here, I would've headed back to Roanoke, then on down to Norfolk, north to Rappahannock, and on to Fort Chiswell in the valley. Didn't know how much longer I'd have to travel!

"I'm plumb glad to see this wagon train pulled up at Martin's Station. It's a likely spot, close to the river, with the stream jest a stone's throw from camp."

I turned, and stood there open-mouthed looking at my grandpa. All at once, I launched myself into his arms the way I always had as a child.

"Whoa, Gal! Whoa now!" He said, stepping back from me. "You're a mite too old for these little girl shenanigans anymore. Besides," he said looking at me. "You're all growed up now, Caroline.

When did that happen? You're 'most tall as me." He shook his head and grinned.

"Grandpa! Grandpa! Oh Grandpa!" I said, laying aside the revolver and wrapping my arms even tighter around him. He held me close, despite my wet clothing. Tears ran down my cheeks.

Too long! Too long! Over four and a half years since he left me with Aunt Violet.

"I'm glad I found you, Child, I'd been packin' to ride to Violet's to fetch you home. Instead, I got word you'd run off. I figured you'd gone lookin' for your folks. That's not good, you stealing Violet's horse and all," he said with a thunderous look in his eyes.

"Yes, I ran away, but as you can see, the horse is well, and I left payment for the mare and saddle.

"Since you're here, Grandpa, you can join the wagon train, and we can go find Ma and Pa together. Maybe you could help the men hunt for meat.

"I am staying with a nice family, but they are leaving the wagon train soon, and heading up the Ohio River to Northern Kentucky. With you here, I won't be alone anymore," I chattered on and on.

"No, we can't, Caroline! You got to return home with me now, Gal. You're jest chasing the wind. I tried to find your folks a while back, and it's useless. They could be hither or yon. There were many trails west during the removal, and we can't search every town or camp for them. It would take years.

"But Grandpa," I said, sinking down to the ground. "Gramma wrote that you heard from them, and you knew where they lived. I want Ma and Pa and my brothers. They are my family. I have been away from them for too long. I want us to be a family again."

My tears turned into sobs. I hid my head in my arms, and couldn't stop crying. The grief welled up within me, six years of not understanding why they took my folks away. Why I hid in the cellar, and went away to live in the mountains with my tribe. Most important, why did I have to travel to Virginia? Why did Grandpa abandon me with a stranger, though he called her his sister?

I endured over four years of slights and insults from the young ladies at the academy, and yes, from Aunt Violet, too. She knew my heritage and she could never quite accept me.

Then there were the six years of separation from my folks, and six years away from Grandpa, and Gramma! I sobbed and sobbed. He sat down alongside of me put his arm around me, and patted my shoulder.

"You been through a lot, Honey, but it was for the best. You're educated now, and no one can ever take your education away from you. You grew up a fine strong young woman. You are a woman the Lord in his goodness has loved and protected, for me and for your Gramma.

"There's another thing I want to tell you, Honey. Your Gramma needs you now. When you left, the heart about tore right out of her. Yet she made the best of it. She's like that, you know. She jumped right in alongside me, and helped your people. You know she lost your folks too, and she's bore that great loss for many years. You were the last of our family, and she let you go away for your own protection."

"Grandpa, if Gramma missed me so much, why did she only write me one letter in four years?"

"She thought it best if you could forget the lot of us, and make yourself a fine marriage, and have a stable life.

"Now Honey, your Gramma's ailing, and took to her bed. I promised her I'd try to find you and bring you home.

" Last year she caught a fever helping our friends at church, she finally shook it off. But it come back again a few months ago. Susan Cole, our closest neighbor, come to help your Gramma while I rode out to find you."

I could not believe my precious Gramma was ailing. I still carried the letter she sent to me in Virginia, tucked away in my parfleche. She told me to stay in Virginia and marry well. I thought she did not want me. From what Grandpa said, it sounded like Gramma gave me up for my own good.

Ma! I want you, Ma! I screamed inside my head! *Pa! My strong father, I need you! This is too hard! I cannot do this by myself anymore. I want to lay eyes on my brothers too. I would swear an oath on my Bible, I would never tease them again, if only the good Lord would fetch them to me, right now! I want my family!*

"Grandpa, when I joined the train, I convinced myself I would find them. I trusted that God would not keep me from my family any longer! I knew He would answer my prayers. I went on faith! How can I turn back now, when I'm so close to Kentucky? I know I would find them in Kentucky."

"It weren't meant to be Child," Grandpa said with tears in his blue eyes. There's a verse in the Bible, Proverbs 19:21, it more or less says you can make your plans, but the Lord's purposes will prevail."

I choked up all over again, seeing his tears. More tears slipped down my cheeks in a torrent of grief, a hard grief that I'd never dealt with during the six years since the removal.

What to do, what should I do? I agreed with Grandpa. The verse made sense to me, but I wanted my ma, pa, and my family.

"You've got to come home with me, Child! I won't hear no from you, I don't want somethin' to happen to you, too.

"It's safe to return now. The tribe took the oath of allegiance to the federal government. After the death of one of their chiefs, they finally come around to it. The government allowed the Eastern Cherokee to remain in their homeland, and our tribe joined them. There aren't many left, only about eight hundred, but they've come out of hiding. The soldiers have left Tennessee, you can return home now, too. No one will try to harm you any longer."

"Yes, Grandpa," I finally nodded. A warm feeling came over me, the burden I carried for so long disappeared. In its place, I felt a strong love for these two wonderful people, Grandpa, and Gramma. They have always been a special part of my life. I was going home, not to Ma, Pa, and my brothers, but just as good. I was going home to Grandpa, and Gramma! God has blessed me!

We walked back to the camp hand in hand. The little pup ran in circles around us, barking, and barking. Chocolate walked alongside me, too. She knew she looked pretty. She trotted along and tossed her head and tail. I laughed to see her.

Before we reached the Waller's wagon, Captain Johnson trudged up to us. He looked belligerent, an expression he wore on his face much of the time for as long as I knew him.

"Grandpa," I said, "this is Captain Johnson. He leads the wagon train. Captain, this is my grandpa, Reverend Hiram Amos Frost, he rode here to take me home," I introduced the two men.

"Well, well, nice to meet you, Reverend Frost." The captain thrust his hand out to Grandpa.

"Good to meet you too, Cap'n," Grandpa told the man. "Thank you for looking out for my favorite granddaughter," he said with a chuckle.

"No problem at all sir," the captain said, looking right at me. "Why, it's my pleasure to have such a lovely, good-hearted young woman on my train. She's been no trouble at all!"

After hearing this, I almost lost my composure. No problem? He told a bald-faced lie. He'd wanted to strangle me most every day. I didn't tell Grandpa guess it would be my secret.

"Why, we'll be sorry to see her go, sir. She's a competent young woman, and a great help to Mister and Miz Waller. I know Miz Waller dotes on Miss Ashbill's company, a great deal.

"Miss Ashbill always pitched in and helped out whenever anyone needed her. Why, she even went out to fetch a deer for the

Waller's stew pot one afternoon. I'm sure she'd have brought one in too, but I saw some Indian sign, and thought it better to go after her before she got herself into trouble."

Grandpa raised his eyebrows at me, and I felt myself coloring up. "You went out to fetch a deer, Caroline? Is that what you learned at Violet's Academy?" He roared with laughter.

I stammered out part of an answer. "Yes Grandpa, I mean, no Grandpa Aunt Violet didn't teach me to fetch a deer. But I wanted to pay the Wallers somehow, for all their help," I ended, lamely, thoroughly embarrassed.

"Sorry you have to go, Sir," Cap'n said again. "I'd hoped to have another dance with your granddaughter at our next gathering." His face filled with a big grin.

That did it! I wanted to throttle him. He teased me, and tried to embarrass me in front of Grandpa, the despicable man! Ugh!

"Come on, Grandpa," I rudely pulled him over toward the wagon. "I want you to meet the Wallers, and I need to get packed if we're going home."

"Yes of course, Caroline. Good to meet you, Cap'n," he said as I pulled him along. Grandpa decided we would spend the night in camp and then leave early in the morning.

When I arose the next day, I looked for him, but couldn't find him, or his horse.

"Well!" I said aloud, thoroughly miffed. I realized then it would give me time to milk Buttercup, and say a few goodbyes. Maybe then, Grandpa would be back from wherever he rode off to.

We had almost finished eating the breakfast Miz Waller made for us, when Grandpa walked in leading his horse. He carried a nice-sized deer roped to his saddle. He dropped the deer by the fire, and gave me the reins of his horse to hold. The little pup barked at him, and then went over to sniff at the deer carcass.

"Mister and Mrs. Waller," he said, walking over to the couple. "Thank you for all the good care you gave my granddaughter, Caroline. Without you, I don't know what would have become of her. She's a mite flighty, and high-strung at times, and once she gets a notion in her head, she acts on it. I could see right away you're caring people, and I hope you could use this deer."

"Well, that's quite somethin' Reverend Frost. We surely could use the meat. We're much obliged, Sir," Miz Waller said, rising from the log where she sat.

"As far as Miss Caroline being flighty, and getting a notion in her head, I think she done right, leaving that brute of a husband. Any man who would beat a woman is jest like Satan in my book, Sir!"

"Caroline?" Grandpa said turning toward me. "You ran away from your husband, did you? Well, well, well!" He chuckled, and turned his back on the Wallers. I watched as he tried hard not to break out laughing at my expense! He even wiped his eyes. Then he turned back around and apologized, saying something flew in his eye.

I ran off with my apron over my head in shame, glad we were leaving. I did not know how I could ever face anyone again, and now Grandpa thought I had spun a web of deceit.

"Don't pay Caroline no mind, Reverend Frost, I expect she's jest broke up about leaving," Miz Waller said. "I am too, if you must know, Reverend Frost. I become right fond of that pretty little thing. Don't hardly know how I'll get along without her." She wiped her face with her apron, then stopped, and collected the tin breakfast dishes.

"I think we'll be gettin' along down the road. We have a far piece to ride today," I heard Grandpa say as he left the fire to walk over to the wagon.

I packed my belongings, saddled Chocolate, and laid the filled saddlebags on her withers. My sack and the other bundles I hung from the saddle horn, or tied to the saddle. Then I strapped my pistol and skinning knife to my waist. As I began to mount Chocolate, the people gathered to tell us goodbye.

I didn't expect any goodbyes, yet they were all there, and each family brought us a gift of food. I knew many of them didn't have it to spare, and they wouldn't find any trading posts on the frontier.

Grandpa smiled, and graciously thanked everyone. "Your kindness makes a great difference for us. My wife's ailin' and I plan for us to get right along. Now we won't have to stop and hunt as often." He filled his saddlebags, and another bag with food, and gave me a share to carry.

I confess, I about broke down crying. Their generosity touched my heart. I went around shaking hands, and I held baby, Virginia May Crawford one more time. I planted a kiss on her forehead and gave her back to her mama.

Little James Thomas ran up to me. "Thanks for the good time fishing. Do you have to go, Miz Ashbill? We had a swell time with you!"

"I have to go home with my grandpa, James, but I won't ever forget you and your brothers. Yes! The fishing was great fun!"

He nodded at me and said, "We brought you something." He thrust a package in my hand. "Remember that old skunk? Well, Alfred and Arthur dug it out of its nest. They fixed that ole skunk, all right. We saved its tail for you, so you won't forget us. Don't worry, we doused it good in vinegar, and it's only a bit ripe with the skunk smell."

"Oh, James!" I said and gave the little lad a hug. Then I gingerly held out my gift to Grandpa.

When I wrapped my arms around Miz Waller, the tears ran down my face. I sniveled my way into Chocolate's saddle. She thrust the little pup into my arms, and told me to take her along as her gift to me. I held the pup in front of my saddle, but she soon wiggled to get down.

My eyes smarted and I could not see the road through the tears as we trotted our way out of camp toward Cumberland Gap. I waved and waved until I could not see the camp anymore. The pup trotted beside Chocolate as if she truly became my own dog.

Once out of sight of our friends, we rode up to the captain, sitting his horse by the side of the road. "Could I have a minute with your granddaughter, Sir?" he asked, tipping his hat to me.

"Sure thing, but we need to get down the road," Grandpa winked at me, and slowly rode on ahead.

"I wanted you to know, Miss Caroline Ashbill, I deemed it a pleasure to have met you, and to have you in my wagon train. I admit I didn't think so at first, but you're quite a gal. If I was a good ten years younger, I might even consider thinking about you in a more serious manner."

"What?" Was all I could get out! Now I heard it all!

"You are a very lovely young woman who'll grace the home of a lucky man, someday." He leaned over from his horse, and tried to kiss me right on the mouth.

Horror filled, I drew my weapon and leveled it at the man. As he backed away, I picked up the reins, said giddy-up to Chocolate, and rode on out of there before he could get any more ideas, or fill my head with more of his fluff. I didn't look back once.

PART TWO

TENNESSEE

1844

Chapter 15
<u>CHANGES</u>

WE LEFT THE WAGON TRAIN at the beginning of June 1844. It took us three weeks of hard riding to reach home in the hills of middle Tennessee. I remembered our trip well. It still brought tears to my eyes when I thought about the loveliness of the late spring countryside where we rode.

Being with Grandpa made me realize just how much God had blessed me. It reminded me of how I loved and missed him when I was away in Virginia. I vowed I would never separate from Grandpa again.

We trotted our horses through our hometown early one morning, before the merchants began their day. I slowed Chocolate to a walk, while Grandpa rode on ahead. He pulled up to wait for me. I had dreamt about our town for many years, this town where I lived as a child. I looked at each small building without understanding.

There flashed through my memory the city of Norfolk, where I lived in Virginia, a large and vibrant city. Then I thought about Roanoke, where I joined the wagon train. That city was four times the size of the town where I now sat my horse.

Everything seemed different from what I remembered. When did the town change into a small, dusty village? I thought it was much bigger! I rode past the school where I learned my ABs. Yet, it was only one room. I didn't remember that.

The mercantile where I shopped with Ma sat on the left side of the street, next to the millinery. The newspaper office, the bank and the attorney's offices, were across the street. Further down, I saw the blacksmith shop where Pa took our horses for shoeing, and to have his implements repaired. The buildings were all small, old, and rundown.

"Come along, Honey, your Gramma's waitin' for us," Grandpa said riding up where I sat bemused, and not understanding.

I nodded, and set my eyes on the road ahead. "Guess it'll take me sometime, Grandpa. Everything looks different!"

We rode the three miles to our farm, which sat at the edge of the piney woods. When we reached the farmyard, I sat a-looking and a-seeing with my 16-year-old eyes. Six years away, I'd changed, but the sleepy, dusty little town likely remained the same. But what about the farm?

So small, I thought, when we rode into the farmstead. *What happened? Did it shrink?* Was my first thought.

I felt disloyal as I stared at the rustic cabin with the wide, wraparound porch. A small breeze swayed the homemade rockers back and forth next to the front door.

I saw the undersized barn, with the corral in front where the two plow horses sauntered along the fence. A chicken coop sat next to the barn, with the hog sty farther back behind it. I could see other outbuildings off behind the house.

Take your time Honey, he told me. I'm going on ahead and see how your Gramma fares. You come along in a few minutes.

I nodded to Grandpa, and looked over the farm. The fields were growing well. Grandpa had plowed and planted before he went chasing across the country to find me. I turned and looked where I remembered Sugar Creek flowed along behind the oak tree . . . my tree, which sheltered us during the removal.

My tears fell as I slipped down from Chocolate's saddle, ground hitched her, and told my dog Nellie Belle to stay. I rushed to the gently flowing creek. I stood on top of the rock that I remembered as massive. It must have shrunk along with everything else. I peered into the water. and saw the brown trout still swam there. One wiggled a little maybe saying hi to me, and then swam off to wherever trout swam off to, and I felt better!

I climbed up the ridge and stood there as I used to as a small girl. I turned and saw the house in the distance. Home! It looked the same as my memories of living there with Grandpa and Gramma.

God's peace filled me, as I climbed down, picked up my skirts, and ran over to Chocolate. Nellie Belle trotted to meet me, jumped up and licked my hand. I named her for Miz Waller, a wonderful lady who I would never forget.

Grandpa had pulled up in front of the house, while I played at my memories. He had tied his horse to the front porch, then went inside to check on Gramma. I should be there with him instead of remembering. I tied Chocolate next to Grandpa's horse and ran inside.

At once, the familiar odors assailed me, cooking smells, but also the faint smell of lavender water Gramma favored. The house looked unkempt, not at all like my gramma. She believed in keeping the house tidy and clean. She held to the old saying, "cleanliness is next to godliness." Now I believed Gramma was ill. She would never allow the house to gather dust.

"Gramma! Gramma! I'm home now, Gramma," I called out. "Where are you, Gramma? It's Caroline! I'm home at last!"

"Hush, Child! Your Gramma's resting Grandpa told me walking out of their room. "We need to be quiet. She's still not herself."

"I am sorry, Grandpa. I did not mean to bother Gramma, I just wanted to see her."

"Come this way, Child. You can see her for yourself, but realize your Gramma's ill and needs her rest, so she can get better."

I stood in the doorway to Gramma's room. It hurt to see my beautiful Gramma, so small and shrunk inside herself. Her long gray hair hung lank, and limp around her face. She lay covered with a bright and cheerful crazy quilt up to her chin. She shivered a little from time to time. What happened to her?

I saw some movement in the dark little room, Gramma's friend, Susan Cole, sat rocking by the side of the bed. She looked up and nodded to me.

Our hound Thumper lay on the floor at the foot of the bed. He opened one eye, looked at me, and went right back to sleep!

Even Thumper does not know me, I thought. The tears began running down my cheeks. I wiped them away, nodded to Grandpa, then went outside.

I noticed Gramma's vegetable garden wasn't doing well, and the lavender, that she had planted all across the front of the house was about dried up. Her lilac bushes also needed a good watering, same with the new leaves of the flower bulbs, they lay flat on the ground. Sad, I thought, Gramma thought the world of her garden, her flowers and herbs. I must do something to restore them for her.

I unloaded the supplies from the horses, led them to the barn, unsaddled, and rubbed them down. I gave them each a measure of grain. They had earned it after our long journey.

I sank to my knees and prayed to God. I asked Him to cleanse me of my selfishness in wanting Gramma to recognize me, and welcome me home. Above all, I asked Him to make Gramma well again. I asked Him to love and support me, as I cared for her, for I decided in my heart I would take care of her. Then I asked God to cast His grace on Gramma and Grandpa, and help them through this illness.

BEDFORD COUNTY, JUNE 28, 1844 2 a.m.

I went to bed, and couldn't sleep, so, I decided to begin writing a journal of my time at home with Grandpa and Grandma. I just checked on Gramma. She seemed the same. She hardly moved, and barely breathed. I don't think she's in any pain.

Sure, wish Aunt Violet had taught me nursing skills, rather than how to catch a rich husband. I have never been around anyone ill, or anyone old and ill. I prayed the Holy Spirit would guide me with Gramma's care.

Gramma's friends helped me during the day. That way, I could rest a little from my nightly care giving. It also gave me time to cook meals, and water and tend to Gramma's garden, herbs and flowers.

WE'D BEEN HOME TWO weeks, now. I helped Gramma daily, and I decided if I could heal her, I would not lose her. I was with her at night, and some during the day. I drew on the memory of the things I cooked at Aunt Violet's, seeking to strengthen her, so she could fight off this illness.

I made hearty meat teas from venison infused with herbs, puddings from milk, and many eggs. I brewed herb teas to stimulate her constitution, and dishes to tempt her appetite. She never woke, so I spooned the food into her. After a week, her cheeks took on a rosier bloom, but she still did not awaken very often.

Grandpa came to me one morning and said, "Caroline, your Gramma has one foot in heaven. Do you want to deprive her of her heavenly reward? Don't you know if Jesus wanted your Gramma healed, he would do it without all the fancy food you're making in the kitchen? I could use some stick to my ribs, meat and vegetables, Honey. I have the farm to tend to!"

I did not mean to cry. I tried hard to save Gramma, yet I'd never thought of Grandpa's needs when I prepared the pretty dishes. I saw then, that if God wanted Gramma home, He would take her. If He wanted her healed, He could do it without my help. The tears coursed down my cheeks, but I felt more peaceful.

Grandpa reached over and gave me a hug, and said, "You're doing fine, Honey!"

As I tended Gramma, she seemed to grow worse. I took extra good care of her garden plot, the lavender bed, and the other plants, wanting with all my heart for her to see them restored, and beautiful again once she was well.

GRAMMA DID NOT LIVE to see her gardens restored. Three months after we arrived home, she went to be with God. She never recovered. She came into the world in Virginia in 1779, and died in Tennessee, in 1844, making her 65 years old. I endured such a hard wrenching hurt, to lose first my family, and then my gramma.

Guilt set in. If I'd stayed with Aunt Violet, and not run away, likely Gramma would still be alive if we had come home to care for her a few weeks sooner. I told that to Grandpa, and he pooh-poohed the idea.

"Caroline," he said, "this thing with your Gramma's been coming on for several years. It's not your fault. If truth be told, I'm glad you're home, I've missed you, Child!" So maybe it was good I ran away, yet I would never know for sure.

Grandpa conducted Gramma's funeral service on September 23, 1844. Folks traveled from as far south as Franklin County to bid her goodbye. Everyone loved Gramma.

I helped Susan Cole prepare her body. We dressed her in a fine, black silk dress I found in the chiffonier. We laid her out in the aromatic, cedar wood coffin handmade by a neighbor. Many friends arrived, and sat with us through the evening for Gramma's wake.

I lined her coffin, with a quilt for padding, and then Gramma's favorite silken spread that she brought with her from Virginia when she married Grandpa.

She'd kept it nice in her trunk. She would take it out from time to time, stroke its silken texture, and look out the window into the distance. I did not know what she thought or remembered, but I knew the memories made her sad. After a while, she would wrap it and put it away again. I knew she set great store by it, so it was fitting to bury it with her.

The morning of Gramma's service, I filled her coffin with dried lavender from the flower bed, that grew in front of the house. It was fitting for her to be surrounded by the fragrant herb she favored above all others.

Since the fall weather was warm with a comforting breeze, the neighbor men set up tables under the trees near the house, where we would eat after Gramma's services.

The women filled long tables with every type of good food imaginable. They brought six kinds of meat, and many different kinds of vegetables. Kettles of stew, potato dishes, hominy, liver mush, and cornmeal mush. I saw a table piled high with at least fifteen loaves of bread, as well as biscuits, cornbread, and corn pone.

They brought butter, preserves, jams, and jellies, and a variety of pickles, kraut, and red cabbage. The desserts caught my eye, blackberry dumplings, sweet biscuits, buttered jam bread, rolled sugared bread, puddings fruit pies, fried pies, donuts, even a one-layer cake with brown sugar and honey frosting, sprinkled with pecans.

I saw buttermilk in abundance, sweet milk, apple cider, water, and coffee. A few of the men ducked away by the side of the house with a jug, guess they could not leave the spirits alone even at a funeral.

I'd never seen so much food in one place, except one time at Aunt Violet's home, when she held an open house and invited the young ladies, the young gentlemen, their families and friends.

A lady walked up next to me carrying a large pan of apple cobbler. I looked up, and saw Sarah Louise Burke, a girl I remembered from the school we both attended, as small girls.

Sarah Louise had changed very little except that she now wore her shiny, light brown hair piled high on top of her head, and her full-length dress reached the ground as was fitting, since she was past sixteen years of age. Her golden-brown eyes, held a look of welcome and happiness to see me. She was still the friendliest girl I had ever met. She always wore a smile on her sweet face.

Sarah Louise placed her dessert on the table, then walked back to stand with her family. When I glanced there, she waved and smiled at me, a blessing in the midst of my huge grief.

As I watched, some people from my tribe walked out from the woods. They stood a good distance away from the assemblage. There were about 15 or 20 of them. I waved, and a few girls my age waved back. That lite a spark of joy in my heart. I felt at peace to see them there honoring the memory of Gramma.

I heard that many of the tribe had walked back home from the reservation in the west. Now they once again lived in God's Country which they called the Great Smoky Mountains of North Carolina.

Many years ago, Grandpa told me of the promises in Isaiah 51:11.

"Therefore, the redeemed of the Lord shall return, and come with singing unto Zion, and everlasting joy shall be upon their head: they shall obtain gladness and joy, sorrow, and mourning shall flee away."

I always believed, and prayed those promises for our tribe. Now perhaps some of that had come true for them. I wished I could go and greet them, but it wasn't seemly. Maybe one day, I could travel east to visit. I still remembered my friend Lily, nightly in my prayers. I asked Jesus when we would be together again?

The gratitude of the assembled people touched my heart. I only recently learned that Gramma spent her life helping others. In return they brought gifts of food to show their love and thanks for the help she gave them through the years. I knew she traveled away from home from time to time, but I did not know how much she helped our friends and neighbors.

As the men carried Gramma's coffin out to the stream by the oak tree, we gathered around her gravesite and Grandpa told us her story:

"My beautiful wife, Mary Polly Dillingham Frost, born in Norfolk, the Commonwealth of Virginia on August 23, 1779, is 65 years and one month old. Polly grew up in a stately home. Her father, a legislator, entertained many dignitaries and statesmen.

"Polly and I met as young children, at the church where our families worshipped. I am the same age, and we grew up together.

"I studied at the university. There I met some of our Cherokee neighbors who also pursued their educations. They were Christian young men, and from them, I learned about this place here, and the need to bring the word of God to the Cherokee.

"Soon after college, where I became a preacher of the gospel of Our Lord and Savior Jesus Christ, I returned to Norfolk and pursued delicate little Polly, and asked her to become my wife.

"Without hesitating, she turned her back on everyone she held dear, and her gracious and comfortable home, to travel with me here to Tennessee where we began our ministry. Polly never saw her people again to this day.

"I'm humbled to think my beautiful lady, with hair the color of the sun, and a heart filled with the goodness of gold, would turn her back on her comfortable life to wed me and live in a simple cabin in the woods, so I could preach the word of God.

"And that's not all by a long shot. Polly ministered by my side throughout her life, often traveling with me to the homes of the Cherokee people, helping them, teaching them the word of God, and the practical arts of life.

"A year after we arrived here, God Blessed us with our lovely baby girl, with Polly's golden curls, and eyes like the cornflowers lining our roads in these parts, our Elizabeth Anne.

"Polly showed patience and courage throughout her long illness. She did not fear death, instead she welcomed it as her due. She looked forward to meeting her Lord and Savior Jesus, and now she has joined Jesus and the family who went on before her.

"I declare today, Mary Polly Dillingham Frost, dwells at the hearthstone of the Lord, free of pain and sorrow, rejoicing and singing praises to God and His Son Jesus Christ.

"As it says in Psalm 116:15, *Precious in the sight of the Lord is the death of his saints.'* Jesus brought Polly to himself, and told her, 'Well done, Mary Polly Dillingham Frost, you are my good and faithful servant!'

Now, let us pray!"

After the service, I stayed at the gravesite as the men lowered Gramma into her grave. My heart broke within me, but I could only say Amen and Amen to the message Grandpa gave us.

I knew Gramma walked the golden streets leading to the throne of God. She received her crowns of glory and righteousness, and threw them to the feet of Jesus as an offering, while she bowed down, and worshipped him. Her illnesses gone, her youth and her beauty restored. She became as lovely as a bride on her wedding day.

Yet, knowing this did little to ease the lonesome feeling that lived deep inside me. I wanted Gramma back.

I wanted her to wrap her arms around me, and ease me down to her lap, and cover me with my quilt, even though I was now a great grown girl.

I joined Grandpa in greeting and welcoming the folks who came here to honor Gramma. They all shared a good word, or a story about Gramma and how her love and care made a difference in their lives.

I met young'uns Gramma helped birth, and widows and widowers whose loved one's Gramma helped ease onto the road to heaven. There were many who survived the pox, and fevers all because of the herb's Gramma steeped for them to drink. They blessed me with their stories, and I felt fortunate to meet these folks. They made me proud of that wonderful woman, my gramma.

After the last of the folks left for their own homes, and we brought in the remains of the food, I realized I missed our hound Thumper.

For weeks, he would lie in Gramma's room, as close to her bed as he could get. She would reach down, and scratch his head and he would lick her hand. In the years while I lived in Virginia, and during the times Grandpa traveled, Thumper became Gramma's dog, they relied on one another.

I believe Thumper left the morning after Gramma' s death. I wasn't sure, maybe he went off somewhere to mourn. When he didn't come back, I began to feel bad for the times I called him an "old bag of fleas." Thumper always acted like a knot-headed dog, but I loved him, and he was the last link to my life and home with Ma and Pa.

Thumper limped home a few nights later torn up, dragging a hind leg, his ear tore about in two, and claw marks all down one side of him. He must have fought something much bigger than himself.

I cleaned and sewed his wounds, nursed and nursed him. I shed tears over him. I wanted him to live with every fiber of my being. A few days later, he died during the night. I cried hard, I prayed over him, asked God to heal him. I told him what a good dog he'd always been. I loved him, and yet I could not save him.

Losing Thumper hurt our little girl dog, Nellie Belle, I brought her back home with us from the wagon train.

Nellie mourned Thumper just like Grandpa and I mourned gramma and Thumper, too. Nellie and Thumper lived as special friends. We buried him near the oak, right next to Gramma.

I dragged Nellie Belle home after we buried Thumper. She'd stretched herself out on top of his grave. She howled and whined, but I couldn't lose her, too. I was so ready for all the sadness to leave. I wanted no more grief in my life. There'd been enough to last my life long!

BEFORE I KNEW IT, SPRING arrived and with it, the blessed sunshine and warmth we missed through the long winter. Daily, I worked in the gardens, the herbs were growing well, the lavender bloomed, and tried to take over the flower bed. I cut mint and bergamot to add to our tea pot for dinner. I enjoyed growing medicinal herbs, my tribe always used them for a variety of ailments. Once ripe, I would dry the herbs and store them.

I weeded my vegetables a good deal on one long day. The plants seemed healthy and strong. The tomatoes did not do much until the rain we had in July. Now the plants were three foot tall, filled with yellow blossoms, and growing taller each day.

I enjoyed the satisfaction I received from gardening, and loved feeling the warm soil on my hands. God worked with me helping grow the food we needed to keep us fed through the long winter.

Grandpa's crops flourished, and after we finished our spell of spring and summer chores, life settled down some. Since he had more time on his hands, grandpa started remembering gramma, and missing her, again. In two more months, it would be a year since she passed. I knew gramma was on his mind. He would come looking for me and ask what I called, "the do you remember game."

Like one morning right after breakfast when he should have been riding around the fields checking on the crops, he sought me and started talking.

"One time," he said, "when your gramma and me first moved here to Tennessee, we lived in our new cabin less than two months, and I was the new preacher at my first church.

"A family jest moved to town, and I invited them to visit our church, and they said they would come. Therefore, on Saturday I told your Gramma, I wanted to bring the family home for dinner after services.

"Polly liked the idea. She enjoyed getting to know new folks and said she would make them a fine meal. She went outdoors to find the old rooster someone gave us as a welcome gift.

"Now, that old rooster was mean and cantankerous as they come, he made your gramma a mite afraid. She decided she couldn't abide him any longer, and wanted him gone. She knew the rooster might be tough and stringy, but if she boiled him long enough, he'd make a fine stew for these new church folks.

"As I told you before, Caroline, your gramma came to me finely bred, and raised in the upper reaches of society," he said, going on with his story. "Before she wed me, she never set foot inside a kitchen to cook a meal in her entire life. The first month of our marriage, I suffered through some mighty burnt dinners, but I knew she prepared them with her love scattered throughout, so I ate 'em, and never let on.

"Well, one day, stubborn little thing I knew her to be, she went out to the chopping block, grabbed up the stringy old fellow and readied to cut off his head.

I think she would have too, except the rooster flapped his wings quick like, and jumped clean out of her hand. He flew down behind the chopping block, and began pecking at something hiding there. A big old timber rattler reared right up, and hissed at the old rooster.

Your gramma never knew it was there. The old fellow warned her, and likely saved your gramma's life.

"I don't know where your gramma got her spunk, Caroline. I told you her ma raised her delicate-like to be a lady. She took one look at that old rattler, raised her ax, and cut his head clean off. Then she lifted its body on the handle of her axe, and carried him over to the hitching post in front of the house where she draped him. She surprised me when I got home, that she did!

"Your gramma made up to that fellow the rooster, and you know it got to where she would walk around the farmyard with him perched proudly on her shoulder, that's how close they come to each other.

She cried herself to sleep one night when I discovered a coyote got to him. There wasn't nothing left of him but a pile of feet and feathers. I still see his mark on our flock today. There's some young roosters out there in the henhouse who have the same coloring, and the same proud strut jest like that old cock of the walk."

I liked the times when Grandpa played the memory game with me, but I was usually in the midst of cleaning, churning, or trying to make up my mind what to cook.

As the anniversary of Gramma's death drew near, Grandpa stopped talking to me. He just wanted to spend time on the front porch in the rocker staring at the hills in the distance with his Bible on his knees. He rested his folded hands, on top of the Bible, so maybe he was talking to the Lord. I didn't know.

For a few days right after her death, I thought Grandpa wanted to join Gramma, but I was glad to say we got through that time.

His recent lack of interest in life concerned me. So, one day I took him aside, and told him straight up, "Grandpa, you're all I have left, if you leave, what will become of me? I want Gramma too, and I want Ma, Pa, Hiram, Earl, and old Thumper, but I don't count on ever seeing any of them again this side of heaven.

"I'll always miss Gramma, but I know she's fine, happy, and contented there with God, Jesus, and the Holy Spirit. We'll be with her again before too long, Grandpa, we need to just bide our time."

I guess my little speech set him to thinking, because an hour later, he got up from his chair, pulled on his coat, and went outside to do the chores Then he began weeding and cultivating the corn crop, again. God gave us a miracle, and I praised Him for it!

DURING THE LAST WEEK of February, 1845 the weather warmed, but it could still get cold. I yearned for the warm spring days to come and stay. *Enough of this long winter*, I thought.

A few weeks later, the blessed warmth of spring stayed with us, and made the days run along quick like. I rose from bed early in the morning, made breakfast, got a few chores done, fixed and ate our dinner, then it seemed like suppertime came soon after, and bedtime before I knew it.

Grandpa rode in close to supper one afternoon during the third week of March. "There's four new families moving in, Caroline. They's all related," he, told me, getting down from his new, young mare, Dorcas.

"I saw 'em from the church when they pulled in. They come in a wagon train from out east in North Carolina.

"I went over, met 'em, and talked to 'em. Their family liked the lay of the land here in Bedford County. They pulled up stakes to try their hand at farming more acreage than they owned back east. The family bought southeast of town, close along the Duck River. I invited them to church and offered to help them settle in.

"Andrew Sutherland, the father, and his wife Elizabeth led the train in the first wagon. The oldest son, Hammond, his wife, Lucinda, and their family of three little girls, rode in the second wagon.

Next came, the second son William, with his wife, and three sons. The biggest old hound dog I think I'd ever seen traveled in their wagon. In the fourth wagon rode the youngest of the men James, his wife, and a young son. The last son, Wiley, a single young man, rode a wild, black stallion, and led a pack mule. They're a fine-lookin' bunch of people, Caroline," he continued as we walked to the barn together.

"Andrew Sutherland bespeaks his Scots ancestry with coal black hair, piercing black eyes, and a slight burr to his speech, but he didn't say if he'd come from Scotland.

"Elizabeth Sutherland, his wife, is fair, light-skinned, and blue eyed. One son resembles the father, and two resemble their mother. I surmised the family, or likely their ancestors, once hailed from Sutherland County, in Scotland.

"Two of the men work in the timber trade, a good trade, Caroline. Since its March, they come early to get a crop in the ground, won't take 'em long with five men working together. If the spring rains hold off a mite, the families' homes will go up in nothing flat. In the meantime, they'd live in their wagons."

Grandpa seemed perkier and more voluble than I'd seen him in quite a while. He loved folks, and he loved to meet new people in our community. I liked to watch him get excited. I thanked God the new family brought out a spark in Grandpa. He enjoyed placing folks' heritage. He liked to notice and compare their similarities and differences. His vivid descriptions got my mind whirling trying to picture the lot of them.

"Sounds fine Grandpa, I would be happy to meet them. Tell me when you plan to visit, and I'll make up some food baskets for you to take along.

I can send some fresh-baked bread, and maybe a pie or two. It's hard to bake over a campfire. I have some preserved vegetables, and I'm sure a hasty pudding would be welcome. They traveled a long way from North Carolina!"

Three days later Grandpa, hitched Dorcas to the buggy, and I piled my baskets of food in the seat next to him. No, I didn't go, Grandpa thought it would be better for me to visit later, once they settled in.

When he returned in the evening, he told me the family built most of two sides of the main cabin and will be soon finished, and ready to roof. They'd add a chimney later, in the fall.

Soon, three of the men would start the plowing and planting. While, the other two finished the cabin. Once they got the crops planted, they'd build three more cabins. The women cleared out a space for a big garden, and seemed ready to plant.

Sorry, Grandpa did not take me, I could have helped them with the cooking and planting their garden, but then I thought about my own big garden I needed to plant, and the house and animals to care for since Grandpa often visited his congregation. Maybe I could meet these good folks, later in the year, when things were not so busy.

GRANDPA ENJOYED GOOD days, like when the Sutherland family moved over next to the Duck River. He went to visit and took the food baskets I prepared for them. He stopped by to say hello a time or two, but that was all that came of it. He never took me along, and they didn't come to visit our church, or visit our home to become acquainted. Too busy settling into their new homes, I guessed.

Grandpa stayed busy about the farm, weeding and cultivating the corn. He showed me a letter from Aunt Violet, that a neighbor had brought him from town last week. She wrote every few months, and included a bank draft for Grandpa's ministry with the Cherokee and the church.

Grandpa said I could read the letter, but more importantly, he asked me to take the draft to the bank, and deposit it in his account.

I was excited to read Aunt Violet's letter, I always hoped to hear news from the Academy, where I lived for over four years.

My Dear Amos,

I take pen in hand today to send you greetings, I trust you remain sound and healthy as you continue with your farm, and the ministry that took you away from all that you held dear in Norfolk, Virginia.

I am well, and the academy is excellently fulfilling the tenets of educating young women to embrace their future callings as the wives of professional, or successful men of business and commerce.

Today, I am pleased to convey that three of the young ladies are on the road to proper matrimony. Against my better judgement, Miss Saunders also requested that I inform you, for Miss Ashbill, that she would soon wed Dr. Thomas Shaeffer, a renowned physician associate of her father, Dr. Saunders.

I have enclosed a bank draft for your ministry, and trust that God will keep you in his capable hands, as you minister to the heathen Indians.

Affectionately,
Lady Violet Ashley

AFTER OUR NOON DINNER, I decided to drive to town to deposit the bank draft for grandpa. I harnessed Chocolate to the buggy, and dressed myself carefully wearing the new green frock, I made last week from material I found in gramma's trunk. I carefully followed a dress pattern from Godey's Ladies Book, and felt pleased, that the dress fit me well, and appeared in the height of fashion.

I knew I looked attractive, until I tried on my old straw bonnet with the sagging ribbons and flowers. I must freshen it with new trimmings to match the dress.

I smiled, and decided I would visit Anna's Millinery Shop after going to the bank and leave the mercantile for last.

As I drove Chocolate along the old road to town, this beautiful day, bright sunshine lent new life to my heart, and warmth to my spirit. The sky filled with cotton-like clouds, and I liked to imagine what I saw in the different cloud shapes riding across the sky before me, flowers, animals and maybe even an angel. I laughed aloud at my silliness.

I waved as I passed farmers cultivating their fields, and they waved back. I slowed Chocolate, and enjoyed watching the neighbor's children as they splashed and dove into a roadside pond. *I remembered some of those days*, I thought. *Yet, I missed out on most of my childhood, because of the removal.*

Once I arrived in town, I parked the buggy in front of the bank and deposited the bank draft. Anna's Millinery Shop beckoned to me across the street, and I gladly went inside.

Almost at once, I heard the bell on the door ring. I turned and saw my friend Sarah Louise Burke rush in. She ran up to me excitement filling her pretty face.

Wonderful to see her, we were long overdue for a visit. We saw each other for a few minutes each Sunday at church, but we never had time for more than a quick hello, Sunday dinner preparations, always summoned each of us after services.

"Caroline," she gushed, "you would never guess what happened. I have met a young man. He visited our farm with his pa three days ago. While our fathers' talked business together, I observed the young man walking around the farm, looking at the crops, and the horses.

"When I saw him through the window, I remembered I had forgotten to take a pan of feed out to our chickens, and guess what? When I did, he walked over to speak to me.

Caroline, such a fine-looking man, very tall, with dark red hair. He told me he farms with his Pa on 350-acres in North Bedford County.

He said his name was Richard Mott, and he was 22 years old last December. After we spoke together for a while, he asked if he could come and call on me, again. Of course, I said, yes!"

Together, we walked through the store, discussing Sarah Louise's good news, chatting much more than we shopped.

We paused several times to try on tempting bonnets, and laughed at our reflections in the mirror.

Miz Anna displayed her bonnet creations in every nook and cranny of the store. It would have taken us an afternoon to try them all.

I gathered some summery flower stems, as well as lace and ribbons to brighten my bonnet.

Sarah Louise nodded her approval before saying, "Caroline, I must go now. Mother sent me to the store for baking supplies, and made me promise not to dawdle.

When I saw you come in, I just had to tell you, my news!" She gave me a brilliant smile, a quick hug, then ran out the door and down the boardwalk to the mercantile.

It was fun seeing Sarah Louise, and hearing her good news, just wish she could have stayed longer.

"Thank you, Miz Anna," I said, while paying for the flowery accents. "You have a lovely shop I will be in again."

"Yes, please come, Miss Ashbill. I will have more bonnets on display next week." She smiled and waved good bye, as I opened the door.

Chapter 16
JULY 1845: THE FIRE!

Grandpa farmed, tended to the chores, and ministered to his church, but he still did not take much interest in life. I was thankful he did as much as he could. I tempted his appetite with hearty meals, but he stirred the food around on his plate, and told me he wasn't much hungry.

When I was busy fixing my own plate, or fetching more bread or coffee, he snuck food off his plate to Nellie Belle, sitting at his feet under the table. Scolding him did no good. I often wondered if it was my cooking. Grandpa's blue overalls were getting a mite loose in the waist, not something I wanted to see. I did not want to take them in, like I did with his preaching clothes. Sometimes, I felt I did not know this nice old man who I cared for. He was just not like my grandpa anymore.

20th of July, 1845, Grandpa brought good news home from his church. A congregation asked him to preach at their tent revival in the next town over. I hadn't seen him this lively in months, and I praised God to see the change in him. The old glory light showed in his eyes again. He always used to wear this beautiful glow whenever he preached or shared Jesus with folks. I believed he lost the glow when he lost Gramma.

On Tuesday, Grandpa saddled his horse right after breakfast. He rode over to the town to watch them set up the big tent for the revival. Wished I could have gone along too, but I knew in my heart he wanted to go by himself.

He rode back in time for dinner. "Caroline," he said, once we sat down at the table. "The revival tent will hold 360 people with plenty of standing room in the back. They placed three rows of benches side by side, twelve benches in each row, and each bench will seat ten people.

They made a big altar at the front and center of the tent with chairs down each side for the church dignitaries. They expected the whole county to show up," he said, grinning in excitement.

I knew everybody looked forward to revival. It excited folks and lifted them out of their day-to-day sameness. They filled the revival tents full to overflowing and welcomed everyone, saint and sinner, to come and meet with God.

The people clapped, and sang one song after another. They responded to the preaching, with loud "Amens," joined one another in prayer, and greatly rejoiced with those who walked forward to the altar to receive Christ as their Lord and Savior, and that was just the first day. Revival often lasted five days.

"Caroline," Grandpa said after dinner. "I'm of a mind to take the buggy. You could ride along if you want to, Honey."

"You couldn't keep me away if you tried," I told him. I loved it when my grandpa preached hellfire and brimstone to the townsfolk. I always sat in the front row and followed along in my Bible while he preached.

I planned to fix an early supper for us, so he could get back to town in time to prepare. For most of the afternoon, Grandpa looked over his preaching clothes, blackened his boots, and reread his sermons.

At dawn, I had put bread to rise, and baked it in the afternoon. For supper, I pulled out rabbit from what I stewed for our noon dinner, piled it on the hot, sliced buttered bread, and served fresh berries, I picked the day before, mounded with clotted cream. After supper, I quickly dressed and climbed into the buggy with Grandpa.

WE REACHED THE REVIVAL grounds a little before 5:30 p.m. The sun was still up, and we'd have plenty of light for the next few hours. People gathered close to their wagons, preparing supper, and visiting back and forth with others parked close to them. A pack of youngsters and their dogs, ran around the tent grounds in excitement, shouting gleefully and making mischief.

A large group of people stood outside the revival tent, talking, laughing, and waiting to enter the tent, and grab the best seats. I could see their excitement. There was a festival feel in the air and I praised God to see this.

As we drove up, a huge smile covered Grandpa's face. He called out a welcome to the people, parked the buggy, climbed down, and shook hands with many of them before entering the tent to pray. A small portable organ played began playing hymns inside the tent before the service.

I waited outside, and offered my hand in welcome to many of the people. They seemed happy to see me. I waved to some of my friends, Jean and Betty among them. They joined others their age and went inside to find seats.

I hoped to see Sarah Louise it had been too long between visits. We were both busy at home with one thing or another.

A group of loutish young men called out snide remarks, and jostled each other under a massive chestnut tree across the road. A few tried to give me the eye, but I ignored them, rabble-rousers every one of them. I knew, because I went to school with a few of them when I was small.

The bunch of rowdies across the road let go with a yell that would have challenge my Cherokee folk, as a big fancy painted wagon pulled in next to an even bigger sycamore tree, down a piece.

Sitting on the front seat of the wagon, a drab little man held the reins in his hands. Next to him, fine as you please, sat a woman who wore more war paint than anyone in our tribe would ever have thought acceptable.

She dressed in a short, bright-red dress made of silk and satin cut indecently low on the neck. There were no sleeves on the dress, only tiny red puffs of fabric on her shoulders. Two deep ruffles around the bottom of the dress flipped up as she stood, and allowed her lower limbs to show.

The woman saluted the young men, then climbed down from the wagon seat, and sashayed around to the back. Some of our women averted their eyes from her obvious charms, but a few of the men couldn't get enough of looking at her.

Shocking, I thought as I watched her flounce off. *Oh! No! I hoped she wouldn't come to the meeting in such a dress. What would the folks here think?* Then I remembered, *Jesus loved the sinner and the saint. He visited and dined with the Pharisees and tax collectors, so I should not judge.*

Suddenly, the back of the wagon burst open, and out waltzed six more women flaunting their charms! They stood in a line of seven, eyeing and gesturing to the menfolk on our side of the road.

The women stuck lit torches into the ground, and hung lit lanterns from the side of the wagon. One of them brought out a fiddle and began playing, another strummed a banjo, and loud dance music filled the air.

Some younger men went over and asked the women to dance and soon there were five couples spinning gaily in front of the wagon while the music went on faster and faster.

Oh, Grandpa, what will we do? I thought. It looked like the revival had some competition with those women right across the road.

My fists clenched tightly inside my lace mitts, I felt helpless, and knew I could do nothing. I felt someone come up next to me and put their arm around me. I looked up and there was Sarah Louise Burke.

"Don't worry sweetheart," she said giving me a big hug, "Jesus will find a way." I nodded and smiled, so glad to have her with me through this terrible time.

We watched as men and boys from both sides of the road began swarming around those women, and cutting in on the dancers. I saw some men pass around jugs they'd retrieved from their wagons. The beat of the music egged them on to join the fun.

Wives and mothers turned, and looked indignantly at their own men who stood beside them. They turned their backs on the brazen women, and quickly made for the tent with their men folks in tow.

Before things could get out of hand, the little man climbed to the seat of the wagon. He held bottles of an elixir in each hand. The music stopped, and the man began his spiel.

"Welcome! Welcome folks! I am Doctor Fletcher and I am here tonight to give you the fountain of youth! Here! Take a bottle! My precious elixir will cure every ache and pain known to man, or woman!

You sip a tad of the elixir every morning first thing. Before you know it, you'll feel like a youngster, again. I know you'll never regret making a little investment in my powerful elixir. Ha! Ha! Ha!"

As soon as he began his speech, many of the men turned their backs, and began talking to those women again. The little man got mad! He jumped up and down and began shouting!

"You men don't know what I've got here! If you did, you'd forget those women, and line up to buy the fountain of youth. I have it in this here bottle! RIGHT HERE! RIGHT NOW!"

The loud music began again. It urged the menfolk to stay, and forget about the tent revival. I shook my head, and offered a silent prayer for Jesus to stop Satan in his tracks.

The call to worship sounded, Sarah Louise gave me another hug, and told me we needed to visit soon. I watched as she joined her family and walked into the tent for the services

Women went boldly across the road to claim their menfolk, and turned them into the tent. A smaller group of men ignored the call, and kept talking to the painted women.

As I entered the tent, a rowdy new song began outside. Shaking my head, I offered another silent prayer to Jesus.

I stood in the biggest tent I had ever seen in my life. I found a place in the front row just a few seats away from Grandpa. People continued walking inside. They filled the row next to me, slowly trickled in to fill all the rows to the back. They were a happy and noisy crowd.

Grandpa sat in a chair next to the altar with his Bible open on his knees, his eyes closed, and his hands clasped in prayer. I was glad he didn't know what went on across the road.

The revival opened with a long-winded word of prayer from Elder Collins of the Methodist church in our town. I peeked at those seated around me through half-closed eyes. After a while, I saw many a hand covering mouths in wide yawns. Next, we sang songs, one after another. I loved worshipping God by singing his praises.

When Grandpa rose to begin preaching, we heard big shouts from outside. Someone ran into the tent and yelled,

"Fire! That fancy wagon across the road's on fire. They need help!" I rushed outside with the throng of people to see the wagon lit up with huge flames. The fire spread rapidly from a lantern hanging on the side of the wagon. It quickly engulfed the canvas top and sides.

A woman inside the wagon began to scream! Men ran to the back of the wagon One man tried to get inside to help, but the flames drove him out.

The woman's shrill screams sounded louder. The fire must have found her. I don't know why she didn't get out through the front over the wagon seat.

Explosions went off one after another. The elixir must be pure alcohol to explode that way, someone said! The fire continued to spread, it reached the trees, and grass around the wagon. The terror-filled screams of the horses were awful to hear, they bucked and reared, trying to get away. Some men unhitched the poor beasts from in front of the wagon, led them away, to salved their burns.

A bucket brigade formed, but it couldn't keep up with the spreading flames. The fire leaped up high, following the branches of trees canopied over the road.

It began to reach other wagons where they had parked close to the tent, and began licking at one wagon, and then another.

Men rushed over to pull on the harnesses of horses, and moved the wagons out of danger.

Many, beat at the flames with their coats, wet gunnysacks, and anything else they could find, before the fire reached the revival tent.

I couldn't do much more than stand there wringing my hands in horror. Then I spied Grandpa running across the road. I saw him leap inside the front of the burning wagon.

"Oh, my Jesus," I prayed aloud. "Help Grandpa! Keep him safe! Protect him from burning up. I need Grandpa, Lord Jesus. You took Gramma. Don't take Grandpa from me! He's all I got!"

As if God heard my pleas, Grandpa jumped back down from the wagon box holding a smoldering bundle to his chest. Others took the load from him, and led him away

The wagon burst anew into bigger and brighter flames. The explosions continued. With the canvas gone, the wagon staves silhouetted sharply against the night sky. The paint on the box of the wagon curled, and the wood glowed like embers. The fancy women stood nearby, sobbing and sobbing.

I ran where Grandpa sat, holding his hands out in front of him, his clothes singed black, and he smelled of smoke. He grimaced as a doctor greased and wrapped the burns on his hands and face. I couldn't touch him, not wanting to make it worse. He saw the tears trailing down my cheeks. and gave me a big wink!

"Whoso stoppeth his ears at the cry of the poor, he shall cry himself, but shall not be heard Proverbs 21:13," he quoted, looking right at me.

"Thank you, Lord Jesus!" I prayed aloud. "He's all right! He'll be fine! You saved his life!" I knew that wink. It was Grandpa's practice to have a scripture ready for any situation. The scripture heartened me and gave me courage.

Grandpa saved the woman's life, he heard her frightened screams, and ran to help when no one else dared try. They told me the doctors treated her in a house in town. She suffered many burns. I prayed when she recovered, she would come to know the light of true repentance and salvation. If I knew my grandpa, he would visit her, and see to it. He would never let go of her, until she changed her wicked ways, and accepted our Lord Jesus Christ as her Savior.

AFTER THE FIRE, OUR lives settled down some. No, Grandpa did not preach at the revival. Everyone agreed his heroic example of Christianity in saving the woman's life uplifted the congregation, and many people went forth to receive Christ as their Savior.

Grandpa seemed renewed and peaceful. He went to his church, preached, and continued to visit the sick of the congregation, yet he wore a glow about him these days.

He still loved to study in his old Bible, and wrote out his sermons. He read me bits and pieces of them and I realized one day that I was getting a Christian education, a great blessing.

I could read and write but I did not know the scriptures like Grandpa. Many parts of the Bible were hard for me to understand. He often sat with me, and explained until I understood the verses.

Summer arrived and quickly went. Our harvest was plentiful both in the fields, and in my garden. I preserved much of the food I grew for our winter meals. When I visited the cellar under the floor of the cabin, the well-filled shelves gave me a deep sense of satisfaction. I thanked God and looked forward to what the New Year would bring!

OCTOBER 2, 1845. I wrote in my journal.

Summer's over, it gave me a melancholy feeling to say that. Yet, the end of harvest was also the time for fun get-togethers like taffy pulls and husking bees. We also went to singing parties, and enjoyed fresh-made apple cider, freshly popped corn, cracked walnuts, and pecans, to snack on.

I attended one husking bee after another with Sarah Louise, Jean, and Betty. At the 2nd one, Sarah Louise found the red ear of corn, signifying she would be next to find a husband. We laughed and laughed, especially since Sarah Louise was also the first one of us to have a young man visiting her.

I glanced over at Sarah Louise, and noticed she looked a trifle uncomfortable. "Are you embarrassed about finding the red ear?" I asked.

Betty and Jean lit up in excitement, and waited to hear her answer. Then they pointed their fingers, and begin laughing. "Sarah Louise," Jean asked. "Are you keeping something from us?"

With that Sarah Louise turned a deeper shade of red, and shook her head in confusion.

"Well?" We all said in unison.

"Ok! Ok! I didn't want to say anything, but last month, Richard Mott asked me to marry him next year, and I said yes!"

We were incredulous, and sat there with our mouths open.

"Wait, I have other news, I want to share with you," Sarah Louise said, "The Bedford County school officials asked me to teach at Country School #4, near your farm, Caroline. The teacher needed to take a leave of absence. I begin teaching in November!"

Chapter 17
<u>April, 1846</u>

God blessed us with a mild winter, which quickly turned into an early spring. Sarah Louise's school would soon close for the year, the children were needed at home to help plow and plant the crops.

What a blessing to have had Sarah Louise just a few miles away from here for five months. I rode Chocolate to the school every chance I could, and helped her teach the children in the one room school.

What fun! They gave Sarah Louise six books to teach from: the King James Bible, Pilgrim's Progress, and a set of four graded McGuffey readers. She taught other classes from her own experience.

In particular, I loved the times when I could tell the class stories. The girls enjoyed hearing about the Academy, how we were taught manners, decorum, how to walk, speak, dress, and become young ladies of quality.

The boys enjoyed stories of my wagon train travel, hunting, fishing, riding Chocolate, and the history of the Cumberland Gap.

I would miss helping at the school, visiting with Sarah Louise, and eating our dinners together at her desk at noon. Her teaching job was only temporary, and the previous teacher was returning in the fall.

Yet, now I had my garden to keep me busy. Grandpa plowed the large plot, and I planted a few days ago. After I sowed the seeds, I spent a great deal of time praying over them. Weeding and watering, would come later.

Once Grandpa finished plowing our fields, men from town rode out to help him plant our many acres of corn. "I could help plant corn, Grandpa." I told him the first day.

"No, Caroline, Grandpa, said, "You are busy enough keeping up to the house, and herbs, and the garden."

With my garden planted, and spring chores behind me, I noticed I was still growing. My skirts were almost above my boot tops. I didn't expect to grow at eighteen years old. I'd must lengthen my skirts another three inches. I hoped I won't have to do that again.

Lately, I can look down on the bald patch in the middle of Grandpa's head. How did that happen, Grandpa was 5' 7" inches tall? I am now a great, grown girl, 3 inches taller than Grandpa, my arms and legs are long and lanky, big feet too, the bane of my existence.

One day, when I fished in the creek for our dinner, I chanced to see my reflection in Sugar Creek. I put my hand up and discovered I now have a great nose coming straight out of my face. I did not expect to have a big nose. I cried a little at the thought.

Once I got used to the idea, I delved up the courage to take Gramma's precious piece of looking glass outside to see my reflection.

I would never forget what I saw. My pa's face looked right back at me. I stood a full five minutes mouth agape, just a-looking and a-seeing.

At the academy when I stood in front of the mirror wearing the white ball gown, with my hair all done up pretty-like, I was beautiful. What happened? I shivered, I never thought I would look like Pa. As a little britches, everyone said how much I resembled Ma. I believed that would stay true.

THE 28th day of June 1846, Grandpa rode off to North Carolina, to visit the Cherokee tribe. He would be gone for about six weeks. There, he would meet with the Cherokee council, conduct church services, and pray God's blessings on the tribe.

He pulled a packhorse laden with the many bags and parcels, I prepared for his comfort on the trail, as well as supplies, provisions, and necessities to help the tribe.

I watched as he trotted out on his young horse Dorcas. He turned one time to tip his hat to me. I waved until he disappeared over the hill.

For the first few days after Grandpa left, I experienced hot grief riding my back. It seemed like the gall and wormwood spoken of in the Bible.

I did my chores, and cared for the animals, but also gave in to my grief, and sometimes lay on the bed bawling my eyes out.

To give up Grandpa even for six weeks, hurt me more than I could bear. I'd already lost Gramma, my folks, my brothers, and old Thumper.

The last time I stayed alone by myself, I had run away from Aunt Violet, and road Chocolate to Roanoke to meet the wagon train . I detested being alone.

The third day self-pity rose around me, I finally took hold of myself in the afternoon, and forced myself to wash my face, re-braid my hair, and dress myself. I started a stew for my supper, took care of the house chores, and walked to the barn to care for the animals, still wanting to blubber.

Nellie Belle, trailed along nuzzling my hand in sympathy. I dropped to the ground, held Nellie to me, and sobbed some more. I received a good tongue licking from her, wiped my face on my sleeve, then somehow, I felt better.

The next morning, I awoke to beautiful mild weather. After breakfast, I cared for the critters, and finished the chores in the barn.

I noticed the sweet smell of summer on the land, it urged me to don my buckskin shirt and leggings, and stuff my hair up into the top of Grandpa's old hat, rather than stop and braid it.

I grabbed Grandpa's squirrel gun and a leather pouch, then followed the path behind our cabin leading into the piney woods to look for meat for the frying pan, and herbs and flower roots to plant in front of the house. I was thankful Aunt Violet could not see me now.

Nellie wanted to go too, but she's a nuisance, and she would scare off the game. I tied her to a tree in the shade, with a pail of water nearby. As I walked along, I could hear her yipping and yowling a mile off into the woods. I knew she would eventually fall asleep, and wait until I came back to rescue her.

As I trod deeper into the woods, a gentle breeze began blowing the grasses at my feet. I could hear the sighing of the pines, and the rattle of the leaves of the cottonwood and sycamore trees. The colorful birds sang their precious melodies, and the bugs and butterflies scampered before me as I walked.

Now and then, I could hear the ringing of an axe against the bole of a tree. I thought nothing of it. Many folks came to the woods to chop trees for their firewood.

I loved being in God's woods. The smell of the furry pines, and the comforting boles of the huge trees made me feel more secure inside. The birdsong lifted my spirits like nothing else on this old earth.

Squirrels chattered, and magpies answered back. Wildflowers nodded to each other in the soft breeze. They were all a delight to me.

As I walked along, I recited praises to God:

Make a joyful noise to the Lord all you lands. Serve the Lord with gladness and come before his presence with a song. Enter His gates with thanksgiving and into his courts with praise. Be thankful unto him and bless His name. For the Lord is gracious his mercy is everlasting, and his truth endureth to all generations. Psalm 100

My dinner hung from the belt at my waist, next to my skinning knife. The sun climbed in the sky, and peeped down at me through the boughs of the trees. I found a downed trunk, sat down and rested. Close by a pretty little brook chuckled merrily as it ran along the trail.

Near the brook, I found white flag rhizomes, they resembled iris, wild bergamot for tea, wild onions, fresh mint, feverfew for illness and witch hazel bark to make antiseptic. They all fit nicely in the leather pouch I carried.

I set the gun against the bole of a sweet gum tree, slaked my thirst with the fresh water of the brook, then took up my dinner of pone and fat back meat. I enjoyed watching the beauty around me while I ate. Once again, I heard the ring of an axe. It seemed much closer.

Oh well, I thought. *If I'm quiet, no one would ever find me here.*

After I finished eating, my eyes closed in drowsiness. I stretched out, relaxed and happy in the middle of a ray of sunshine with the hat over my eyes. I must have dozed, but soon I heard the cheerful whistle of a satisfied man coming along the path in my direction. I was confident the branches of the nearby trees would shield me, and he would go right on by without noticing me, or being the wiser.

He would not have found me except for the huge lop-eared, hound dog leading the way before him. The oversized beast pounced right on my stomach, leaving me breathless, wide-awake, and trying to get hold of my weapon. I drew my skinning knife, prepared to whack at the creature, when the call of a captivating baritone voice made me stay my hand.

"Off! Angus! Can't you see this fella's trying to catch himself some sleep? Sorry there fella, Angus don't mean you any harm. He's mostly all play!"

I reared to my feet, hat falling to the ground, leaving the curling masses of my red hair tumbling all down my back. I looked up into the clearest blue eyes I'd ever seen on God's earth! A young man, a good four inches taller than me, stood close by. His long, unbound hair, shone bright blond in the sun which shifted through the trees! He wore a slouch hat pushed to the back of his head, and a wide grin split his face in two when he saw me.

He laughed aloud and said, "Whooee! I never expected to see anything like you out in these deep woods!"

I felt a hot red flush begin on my cheeks and travel to the tips of my ears. He'd caught me lollygagging in the woods like a ninny, dressed immodestly like a boy, and sleeping away the day. Why, anyone could have come up and grabbed me. That man might try it yet. I clutched my knife tight in my right hand.

"Hold off, sir," I said, showing him my skinning knife, "just back away, and restrain your brute! I know how to handle a knife."

The young man pulled his head back, and roared with more loud laughter. That took me aback. He laughed at me after I threatened him! I didn't like that one bit!

"Why do you laugh?" I demanded, waving my knife.

"Now there, missy," he replied. "I didn't expect to find a fair maiden asleep in these woods. Why, that's sure the luck of the Irish, as I seemed to have heard tell about. Yet, Irish I am not, but pure Scots," he said with a chuckle, and a twinkle in his devilish blue eyes.

Filled with anger, I picked up the hat, slammed it on my head, tied the pouch of herbs, and food bag to my belt, put my nose in the air, and lit out of there fast. I carried my knife in my right hand and the squirrel gun over my left shoulder. I wanted to put as much distance between the man and me as possible. I knew I startled him with my sudden departure, but soon I could hear feet pounding along behind me. I needed to keep my wits intact. It was a good three or four miles from home, and I knew I was in a terrible pickle.

I wondered if I could evade him by going down the ridge, through the bramble, and come out close to the stream. If I forded the stream, I'd be a good mile closer to home. It might work. Maybe he didn't know these woods.

The next thing I knew, I lay flat on the ground with my face pushed hard in the dirt. That huge beast of a dog sat down on my backside. I gasped for breath, and tried to roll away to get out from under that foul dog.

"Angus!" The young man ran up and swatted at the dog with his hat. "Get off Angus! Get off, now!"

The dog, tongue lolling, looked over at his master, yet he wouldn't mind. He just sat there. I wiggled and squirmed but couldn't get away. I reached up and slugged the brute in the side, but then he growled. I didn't know what to do. I wished hard I had brought along our hound, at least she could have distracted this one, so I could get away.

"Jest lie still missy, while I pull Angus off. You shouldn't have lit out like that. They trained Angus to pull down running game. Glad you ain't hurt any!"

"Get him off me!" I screamed frantically. I wanted to get as far away from that smelly brute, and his vile master, as I could go. I wanted to go home, hide under the covers of my bed, and lick my wounded pride.

He took me unaware, and I was self-sufficient. I told Grandpa I could take care of myself. Yet, the first week he's gone, I got myself in such a heap of misery, I didn't know if I could come out of it with my honor.

Sweet Jesus! I prayed. Help me, Jesus! Keep me safe!

The big dog moved away from me, snapping and slathering, barking, and growling. He didn't like his master pulling him away from his game.

The man slapped the dog across the nose, and scolded him. He made the dog sit at his feet, and then glared at him before turning to me.

He reached down a hand, and hauled me up. Once again, I faced that tall young man, with his shining thatch of bright gold hair shimmering in the sunlight. My hand felt hot where he clasped it. Mute, I could not even sputter.

"Sorry missy," he apologized sheepishly, as he reached out to brush dust off my nose.

I reared back. "Keep your hands off me!" I retorted. I reached down, grabbed my knife, the gun, and the hat. I took one more look at him, then hitched up my belt, and walked off for home, trotting after a little while. I could feel his eyes following me. When I reached the jog in the road, I turned a little.

How rude! He stood there watching me from a long way off! He held his hand high in a goodbye wave!

Whew! I thought. *Thank you, Jesus! I praise you for keeping me safe from the hands of that Philistine Scotsman. What would Grandpa say if he'd come home to find me ravished? Never again would I venture off the farm alone. I would starve first!*

Then the thought struck me. *No! He would not keep me from hunting in the woods. I would go out as much as I pleased, but I decided to always keep the gun and my knife handy.*

I jogged on and after a while reached the edge of the forest, there I spied a nest of squirrels. I brought up my gun. At least I would not return home empty-handed.

"THAT MAN!" WAS HOW I thought of him, rude, forward, full of himself. Not courtly, the way Aunt Violet taught me to expect a young gentleman to act toward a lady of good breeding.

Then my conscience smote me. *You resembled a wild boy, he did not know you were a young lady, or even a girl. He sounded like one lad greeting another.*

"Yet, when he knew I was a girl, he did not change his tune," I answered aloud.

"Perhaps, I took him by surprise, yet didn't his mama bring him up to treat women, as ladies, even ones dressed like me? He was not courteous! Imagine him whistling at me and going 'Whooee!' NO! He did not treat me right, even though I wasn't dressed like a lady."

My conscience continued to nip at me while I pulled tight the strings of my second-best bonnet. I brushed at the front of my pretty dress, the blue dimity that I brought home from Aunt Violet's Academy. I'd spent the last five days lengthening the hem and letting out the side seams. I smoothed imaginary wrinkles with my hand, glad I could wear it again.

"I will not think about That Man. I will put him right out of my mind," I told Nellie Belle while we walked out to the barn together.

"I better get to town for those supplies, and see if Grandpa sent a letter. You stay here, and guard the place while I am gone." I reached down and scratched her behind the ears.

I hitched Chocolate to the buggy, and enjoyed the three-mile drive to town on this warm summer day, putting both That Man and the incident out of my mind.

The town seemed busy for a pleasant day in July. Many people out and about, going hither and yon. I thought folks would have been at home doing chores. Instead, like me they took advantage of the nice weather to shop and tend to their business.

The general store, the millinery, and the blacksmith shop seemed to have attracted the most customers. I saw a few people going into the bank and the lawyer's office.

I parked the wagon on Main Street, took out my basket, and paused in front of Anna's Millinery Shop to see the latest summer hats displayed in the window. Mister Smither's store was a few steps further down the boardwalk.

A loud rush of hoof beats struck a quick tattoo on the dirt of the street. There were loud whoops and hollers, followed by whistles and catcalls, as a large group of rowdies galloped through town.

Wastrels, I thought as I continued to the door of the store. Something compelled me to turn, and there in the midst of them, I glimpsed someone who looked a mite familiar.

With a flourish, a wild black stallion pulled up to an abrupt halt, spraying dust and pebbles over the boardwalk at my feet. Against my will, my eyes locked with those of That Man from the woods. I felt my cheeks redden. Against my will, my hand went up to cover my mouth.

He swept the slouch hat from his head and made an elaborate bow from the back of his prancing horse. "I would have recognized that red hair anywhere," he said looking me up and down, giving me a wink and a wide grin.

Beside myself with embarrassment and horror, I turned and fled through the doorway of the store, angry and insulted. His loud raucous laughter followed me as he whipped up his horse to catch the pack of men charging down the street.

"Are you all right, Miss Ashbill?" Miz Smithers asked as I neared the counter. "I can't imagine why the sheriff allows those ruffians to ride through the town like they owned it!" She walked over to the front window and watched them as they rode away. She sniffed twice and returned to her counter.

I murmured something to her about being fine, but I wasted my time in the store, and forgot what I came for Grandpa's letter of course, but what else?

A cursing girl I was not, if so, I would have done a lot of it right then. Angry, yet I must allow no one in the store to see it! Grandpa was an important man in the town and I must uphold his reputation.

That ruffian stopped to speak to me on a public street, as if I were a common trollop. What if the people of the town saw me talking to the wastrel?

Several matronly types in the store gave me knowing glances. There's the preacher's granddaughter conversing with one of that rabble, they seemed to say nodding to each other.

After a long while, I made my selections and escaped from the store to the buggy. I turned Chocolate off on to a side road, not wanting to meet any curious town folk, or That Man, again. Where could I go to get away from the likes of that fella?

JULY 10, 1846, I wrote in my journal:

I was thankful for this quiet week. I tried to keep to myself, no sense in taking risks. I stayed busy at home, not venturing from the farm even to hunt. I made myself simple meals, pone and fatback one day, porridge the next, and a kettle of flavorful soup lasted me three days, for supper.

I ventured out as far as Sugar Creek and fished. I caught twelve large ones. I salted, smoked, and dried the fish. I would make fish stews, and chowders, flaked it would add substance to the simple dishes I prepared with fresh herbs and greens that I gathered in my herb garden, and close along the stream. I enjoyed not having to fix big meals as I did for Grandpa.

Today, a neighbor, brought our mail. I asked him in for a cup of coffee, he thanked me, but said he wanted to work the corn then get right back home. Nice of him to come and help.

I LAID DOWN MY PEN and went to the window to see what Nellie Belle barked about, so long and loud. I reached for the gun and walked out to the front porch, seeing nothing at first. Then down along the road, I could almost make out a sizable black horse tethered under a tree.

Nellie Belle ran back and barked closer to the house near the cottonwood. I saw the sleeve of a blue shirt sticking out from behind the tree.

I grinned to myself, checked the rifle, brought it up to my eye and shot. A big chunk of wood flew off the branch hanging over that arm, making it pull right back.

Birds flew out from the tree, and squirrels complained. I watched that polecat skedaddling from tree to tree, zigzagging out of my range.

I reloaded the rifle then followed, and sent another shot over his head. He grabbed reins jumped into the saddle, and galloped away down the road as if the hounds of hell were after him!

That wild black horse, and the awful man were familiar to me now. He had spied on me long enough. Word must have got out that Grandpa traveled again, and I lived here alone. I scared him off this time and decided to be more careful in case he returned.

I patted Nellie Belle, and praised her. Happy she's a good watchdog. I also praised God that Grandpa took me out behind the barn for hours, and hours to practice with the shotgun, musket, and handgun until I could hit what I aimed at most every time.

JULY 26, 1846, I WROTE near the top of the page of my journal.

Many weeks passed since I last wrote down my thoughts. I still looked for Grandpa's return from North Carolina. God blessed us with good neighbors, and church members who stopped by to check on me, and helped us with the farm. They knew the importance of Grandpa's work with the Cherokee. I could not do the farming alone, and I did not know how we would survive without their help. The fields were beautiful. Nicely cultivated, and without a weed in sight. Won't be long until harvest was upon us.

The middle of July, my garden began to show promise of a bountiful harvest. I picked my first tomato, and runner beans, squash, carrots, green onions, beets, lettuce, peppers, and cucumbers. I thanked God they would continue producing until the first frost.

In the fall, I would harvest melons, pumpkins, turnips, potatoes, onions and apples from our trees. I had a lot of work ahead for me to dry, and preserve the food for winter.

When I was a girl, I helped Gramma with the harvest. When I lived with my tribe in the mountains, I learned, smoking, preserving, drying food, making bannock, identifying, preparing, and harvesting wild herbs and natural foods.

I learned my culinary skills as a result of helping Cook in the kitchen at the academy in Virginia. Cook taught me to prepare nourishing meals, as well as fine foods appropriate for entertaining.

That Man seemed to have left me alone. I hoped that held true. Yet, the 20th of July, I saw someone that looked like him ride by the house.

Nellie's been barking a lot the last few days. One time it was a man riding a brown horse, he took his time riding by, seemed to pause, and look at the house. He looked a little familiar to me, and that made me nervous.

The next day, I talked turkey to myself to calm down. I decided to quit looking for trouble, and it would not find me. Perhaps I was flattering myself that the fella would come to spy on me. Farfetched to think a man would find interest in a woman with a face like that of my Pa, a handsome man. yet, it made me laugh to think of his look on the face of me, a woman!

AUGUST 2, 1846, I WROTE: *Grandpa's home! I sang it through the day as I worked in the house. He rode in, and went right to work in the fields, harvest was almost upon us.*

I felt better, I hadn't realized how much strain I felt alone at home with just Nellie for company. Grandpa would not have left me alone, if he thought it dangerous. I did not tell him that fella spied on our house, about once a week since the day I encountered him in town. Now, I won't have to worry anymore.

However, one morning at the end of the week, when I opened the door to throw slops out to the chickens. I glanced toward the fields, and saw Grandpa wave and stop his work as That Man rode up.

I recognized that big black stallion right away. Nellie did too, she ran out, and began barking. He dismounted with the reins in his hand, leaned on the fence, and stood there visiting a long while. Finally, Grandpa smiled, clapped the fella on the shoulder, and shook his hand good-bye. That day, I watched the man until he rode out of sight. I won't deny, he sits his horse well, but that's neither here nor there! Nellie chased him down the road, and come running back to me with a big doggy grin on her face.

As I prepared our dinner, I couldn't stop thinking about Grandpa's encounter with That man. Curiosity pricked my spirit some, yet Grandpa was a well-known man in our community, and the preacher at the Baptist church, so it would have been natural for That Man to stop, and say howdy.

Yet, why did he ride way over here? The fella might be a logger, I heard him chopping trees, when I encountered him in the woods. Don't loggers have to work for a living? Well, I decided I would wait and see if Grandpa said anything about his visitor when he came in to dinner. I would just keep quiet and not say a word.

WE ARE AT THE BEGINNING of October, and at the end of harvest. I only have a few pumpkins left ripening in the garden. I liked the colors they turned once the cool weather set in good. Our days were still warm, with the evenings cool and often crisp. Autumn's coming soon.

Every Sunday, I enjoyed going to church where Grandpa preached loud enough to wake the dead. I loved it when he thumped the pulpit to awaken the congregation. They didn't get away with much when my grandpa preached.

I always sat on the front bench following along in my Bible. One Sunday about three weeks ago, I heard a stir in the congregation, and everybody turned around to see who had walked in.

I turned too, and spied a young man come down the center aisle, hat in hand, hair shining in the sunlight that streamed through the open windows. My mouth opened in surprise.

That Man I encountered in the woods walked swiftly down the aisle, coming right toward me. I thought he was through antagonizing me. I hadn't seen him in a few weeks, and enjoyed the peace. I hoped he'd find somewhere else to sit rather than right next to me.

Grandpa nodded, and stopped preaching long enough to welcome him. He called him Wiley. Then he waited until the man sat down two benches right behind me before resuming the message.

I glanced at the pew next to mine where my friend Sarah Louise sat with her folks. She gave me a wink, looked behind me at That Man and then covered her mouth to keep from laughing.

I nodded to her ruefully, and shook my head. I felt sorry he came to church that morning, which was not Christian. I wanted nothing more to do with the man.

After that, I could not concentrate on Grandpa's sermon. Chills went up my neck knowing that fella sat there in his seat, staring at me. I began to get my dander up. What a pickle! I resolved to concentrate on Jesus, God, and Grandpa, and not think about That Man.

Before long, Grandpa wound it up, prayed, and we sang the final hymn. The congregation shook hands with Grandpa, and then with me at the door. That Man was the last one through the line. Darn! I thought he would have snuck off through the other door, but I guessed not.

I decided to do my best to make Aunt Violet proud of me. I would extend my hand, look him right in the eye without flinching, and say, "Good day to you sir," then turn and walk out to the buggy, but that didn't happen.

Grandpa seemed glad to see him. He shook That Man's hand and then began to introduce me.

"Caroline, this is Wiley Sutherland, I don't believe you've met. Wiley and his family moved to the Duck River south of town a year ago last spring. Wiley, this is my Granddaughter, Caroline Ashbill."

Again, That Man's big hand enclosed mine. Warmth radiated between our clasped fingers. I shook his hand then fast took mine away, feeling befuddled. I babbled something, but what? When I chanced to look up, a smile broke across his face, and his eyes danced with mirth! He was laughing at me, again!

I clutched my Bible with all my strength, willing the unwelcome feeling to go away from my hand and arm. I would allow no liberties from That Man, who it turned out belonged to the new family in town. I remembered now, Grandpa singing their praises last year.

"Miss Ashbill, and I met in town a few months back," Wiley Sutherland said, still grinning at me.

"Well, that's jest fine son, it's good to see you here at church today. Do you have any plans for Sunday dinner?"

Grandpa didn't help me at all. He invited the skunk home for dinner. I should have told Grandpa about That Man spying on me while he traveled to North Carolina.

Glad I had fried some chicken during breakfast that morning, so fixings would not take much time. I always made extra on Sundays, as Grandpa enjoyed inviting people home after church.

With the chicken, I made runner beans, and had an apple pie that I made the day before from our own apples. I only needed to slice the fresh-baked bread, and a few of the late tomatoes.

Again, things didn't go as I planned! Grandpa, with the light of challenge in his eyes, quizzed That Man, Wiley Sutherland, throughout dinner about the state of things in North Carolina, where he and his family once lived.

Grandpa told him he'd recently returned from visiting the Cherokee people there. Most of the tribe had moved to the western part of North Carolina after the soldiers left Tennessee.

It turned out Mister Sutherland knew some of the same folks we knew. His family had stopped to winter in the Smoky Mountains before coming into Bedford County last year. He said he met Hawk, and Long Path, when they were out felling trees in the forest. The people were getting along, and they felt fortunate to be in God's country, as our people always called the Smoky Mountains.

After dinner, he stayed and hunkered down on the porch steps. Then Nellie Belle trotted up to the porch from the woods. She sniffed at the man, then began barking frantically and refused to stop.

"Enough of that Caroline, take her out and lock her in the barn," Grandpa ordered me.

I wondered if Nellie remembered him from the times he came sneaking around, spying on us. Nellie and I thought alike as far as That Man went.

When I returned, Grandpa read to us from Psalms, and then from the book of John. Grandpa quizzed him about his relationship to our Lord Jesus Christ.

Mister Sutherland told Grandpa he was a born-again Christian, and read his Bible regular like. He seemed to want Grandpa to believe it. Yet, time will tell all.

I kept my knitting with me. I wanted to keep my mind busy, and away from watching that polecat. Why did he idle away the day with us instead of being with his family, or out with his wild friends? I doubted the story of him being a Christian.

Just when I thought I would have to rustle up another meal for him, he rose, thanked me for the fine dinner, and thanked Grandpa for the conversation and Bible reading. He held the reins in his hand, mounted the black horse, and rode off with a wave of his hand.

I breathed an audible sigh of relief, Grandpa turned and grinned at me.

"What's so funny, Grandpa?"

"You!" He said with a chuckle.

"Me?" I squeaked.

"Yes, you," he laughed again. "Your first beau and you don't know how to make the man feel at home. Maybe you didn't get that far in your education with Violet."

"My first what? Where did you get that idea?" I sputtered. "That polecat's the last man on God's green earth I would want for a beau!"

"Well now, you could do a lot worse, Caroline," he said "bout time you looked around for a nice man to mate up with. I won't live forever, you know!"

OOOOHHHH! To think Grandpa defected, and joined the camp of the enemy! He must approve of That Man to be my husband. What happened to his loyalty to me?

"Sides," he continued. "Wiley told me he admires you. He asked my permission to come courtin'."

"Who does he think he is?" I fumed, "coming around here and sweet-talking you, Grandpa. No! I will not have that polecat around here anymore. If he comes again, I will stay in my room and you can deal with him!"

Grandpa laughed long, and loud as if he knew a lot more than me, and I did not like that one bit.

Chapter 18
LITTLE SPITFIRE

"Little Spitfire," is what Grandpa called me anymore. I have a right to my own opinion, and I'm old enough to pick my own friend or beau, as Grandpa called him. We were at loggerheads. I refused to see That Man, and I did not want to tell Grandpa why.

That Man as I continued to call him, stayed away from our home and the church. The next Sunday, I dressed carefully and felt hot as cinders thinking he would stride up the aisle, seat himself behind me, stare at me, and render me so nervous, likely I could not concentrate on Grandpa's sermon.

When he did not show up, maybe I was a little disappointed. I relished the chance to put that smart-aleck man in his place again, but I did not have the opportunity.

After the next three Sundays went by without seeing That Man, I began to relax. He told Grandpa he wanted to court me, but he hadn't come by the house. Did Grandpa misunderstand him? Maybe I scared him off. I sure hoped so!

Then what about me? He never said a word about any courting going on. I should have a say in the matter. Every time I thought about him, I got mad all over again! "Imagine the nerve of That Man!"

THE FIRST PART OF NOVEMBER, Grandpa finished turning over the land to fallow until spring, and took care of the hog butchering, so now he could rest and just take care of daily chores.

That Man rode up to our front door one day right after supper. Nellie Belle set to barking as soon as the man turned into our gate. No one got past her without alerting us to company. She never let up until Grandpa answered the door, and brought the polecat right into the house.

There he stood just like I remembered him, blond hair lighting up the room, eyes just as blue as the sky. He was taller than I remembered, a good head higher than me with his boots on. I was too tall for a girl, yet I needed to look up to meet his sardonic grin!

He walked in the door hat in hand, and with a small bunch of flowers for me. Where did he come by flowers? It was November, for goodness sake! I invited him in to sit, Grandpa joined us and they started talking politics.

They began by rehashing the defeat of President John Tyler to James K. Polk last year. I took no interest in their conversation, glad to see President Tyler defeated.

I remembered the turmoil in the academy when two months after they elected William Henry Harrison president, he died of pneumonia, leaving the presidency to John Tyler.

When Aunt Violet heard the news, she took to her bed with a bad case of the vapors for most of one week. She had embraced Harrison for president, arranged elaborate teas, and an evening at the theatre to raise funds for his campaign. When he died, she mourned his loss and refused to accept Tyler as her president.

Aunt Violet grieved sorely for the man, turned the classes over to the older girls who laughed, winked eyes at each other, then educated us on the latest penny novelettes. They also taught us popular songs, and unladylike dance steps.

After the first day, I took my Bible, knitting and fish pole, out to the stream, and made myself useful. The other girls seemed glad to have me and my devout attitude elsewhere.

Next Grandpa, and That Man discussed the political maneuverings between the United States and Britain over the Oregon Territory, it brought me out of my reverie a bit. They talked of fighting a war with Britain over the annexation of the territory. The slogan '54-40 or fight' became the rallying cry throughout our country, 54-40 were the coordinates of the border between Oregon and Alaska.

President Polk went into negotiations with Russia and Britain. He believed the United States held legitimate entitlement to Oregon. Talk of the threat of another war did not catch my fancy either. War was not my cup of tea, so I knitted away and daydreamed not wanting to hear That Man's political opinions on any subject.

After a while, they began talking about a wagon train which left Tennessee for the Oregon territory last spring. My ears perked up. John Gantt, a former army captain, squired the wagon train, the first of its kind. He led 1,000 people to Fort Hall for $1.00 per person.

Once at Fort Hall, the soldiers there, told the settlers to abandon their wagons, and go on by pack mule. A man staying at the fort named Marcus Whitman disagreed. He had traveled the trails many times, and volunteered to lead the wagons on to Oregon.

He said, in such a large wagon train, the men could build whatever road improvements they needed to accomplish the journey to Oregon with their wagons.

I stopped knitting and glanced at That Man. His face glowed with enthusiasm as he told his story.

"Good timber country, there. I'd heard a man could make a fine living logging in Oregon," he said, looking over at me. "I'm tempted to join a wagon train myself, and travel out west to Oregon." He paused, finally running out of words.

I refused to meet his eye, and thought, *fine with me, he can join a wagon train to Oregon anytime he has a mind to.*

Again, I took up my knitting. I knitted and listened to Grandpa's reply to That Man.

"Well Wiley sounds like quite a story, but are you serious about leaving all you hold dear in Bedford County, Tennessee to chase smoke across the plains to the northwest?" Grandpa chuckled a bit before reaching down to the fire to grab a hot twig to re-light his pipe.

I looked over at That Man, and saw his face turn bright red.

"Naw sir jest making conversation," he said backing down. "But it captured my imagination for a bit when I first heard about it."

His story captured my imagination too. I thought about my own wagon train adventures traveling from Virginia toward Kentucky a few years ago.

I still wished I went on to search for my folks, but I realized now I would never have traded my last month's here at home with gramma for all the wagon train travel in the world. Yes, I was familiar with wagon travel, but my precious gramma came first in my life.

So, would That Man want to leave his own dear ones behind and head west to start a new life? I guess time would tell.

Cap'n Johnson had contracted to lead the train I traveled with to Louisville, Kentucky, and would turn it over to Cap'n Harper in July of that year.

Harper contracted to lead the wagons on to Independence, Missouri to winter, and planned to head west the following spring. I wondered if they had traveled through Fort Hall, or in another direction.

I still thought about the friends I made, and the experiences we enjoyed together traveling the Wilderness Road. I wondered what happened to them. I hoped they made it safely to their destinations.

The men sat comfortably in front of the fire. After a while, I noticed That Man looking over at me, trying to catch my eye. I ignored him and concentrated on my knitting, not wanting to be drawn into conversation.

Grandpa cleared his throat a time or two, then That Man caught the hint and got up from his chair, "Would you like to go for a walk with me, Miss Ashbill?"

"A walk in the cold night wind?" I said shaking my head. Then Grandpa let out a big harrumph, and cleared his throat again.

I put down my knitting, reached for a shawl on the peg by the door, and went out with him, wishing I'd brought my skinning knife with me. Once outside, he caught me by surprise when he apologized.

"Miss Ashbill," he said, after hesitating several times. "I think we got started off wrong and I am here to ask you to forgive me."

His apology took me aback, and made me think some. What was he up to now?

"I've been away for the last month. I traveled east to the Smokies, where I've been logging with a crew of men for a while. We'll float the logs south in the spring, and sell them to a sawmill."

"Oh?" I said, not wanting him to think I noticed his being gone.

"Yes," he said. "I'm nearing 24 years old, getting on in years. I'm thinking of setting up a house of my own, and wanted to earn some money."

Again, I only answered him. "Oh?" I didn't care if he thought me a ninny or not.

"Miss Ashbill, Miss Caroline . . . it's like this. I've admired you ever since we met up in the woods last spring. I'm sorry to bring up a sore subject, but I jest wanted you to know I'm apologizing for everything that went on that day, and I'd like to come and visit you."

"Hmmm!" I answered. Hard to believe the fool of a man would want to come and court me. First, he was not what I wanted. I waited for Christian man, not one who professed Christianity and then ran through the town with rabble-rousers.

Then, I thought, *why me, with my wild red hair, my big nose, and big feet, what's wrong with the critter? Can't he do any better? Yet, he said he was close to 24 years old, maybe he had sat on the shelf long enough.*

"Why, Miss Ashbill . . . Miss Caroline? I think you're the most beautiful young woman I've ever laid eyes on, and I think we would make a fine team."

That caught my attention. *Me? Beautiful? Were those bright blue eyes of his blind?*

"Yes, you are quite a young woman. I like your spunk, your spirit, and your self-sufficiency. I would be proud to have you by my side. In time I would like to ask you to marry me, Miss Caroline?"

Enough of his fluff! I hauled off and struck him right on the chin, knocking him flat on his back. I picked up my skirts and ran for the house, barring the door afterward. Grandpa ran from his room to see what happened.

"That varmint almost asked me to marry him," I told Grandpa.

"And what did you say, Caroline?" He said, a wide grin spreading across his face.

"I knocked him flat on his back, Grandpa. Imagine a man funning me that way!"

He threw back his head and laughed long and loud. I took myself off to bed in a huff, and lay awake a long while contemplating my life, and contemplating the nerve of That Man.

My life didn't improve much after that. Grandpa kept bringing up the fact that he wanted me married up to That Man! I don't know the man, and I thoroughly disliked him. So why would I want to marry him?

When small, I always hoped I would marry someone from our tribe. I admired the Cherokee men with their strong profiles, the rich color to their skin, raven hair, and dark eyes.

Yet, there was something to say about hair the color of sunshine, and eyes like the sky. I don't know what to think about my marrying a Scotsman.

IT WAS SUNDAY AGAIN before I knew it. I would long remember that day because everything finally came to a head with That Man. I dressed in my navy-blue serge suit dress with the white piping, I loved that dress and wore it often. Today, I complimented the suit with a new ruffled bonnet with ribbons that I tied under my chin.

When Grandpa saw me in my dress, he just stared at me and could not say anything for a minute. "You look just like your mother, Honey," he wiped his eyes and blew his nose, before sitting back down at the table.

I knew I was nothing like Ma. I looked like Pa, only with auburn hair and green eyes. Pa's hair was black and he had blazing blue eyes.

We rode to church in the wagon, and arrived before anyone else to give Grandpa time to pray. I went in with him that day, and knelt right down beside him in front of the cross and spoke a lot to Jesus.

I told him about That Man, and how I didn't trust him, any farther than a stone tossed into a pond would float. I told him about how That Man snuck up to our farmhouse with Grandpa away from home, and how I shot the gun to run him off. And how the man rode the countryside with rowdies when he professed to be a Christian man.

"Is That Man the one you have in mind for me to marry, Lord Jesus? Or do you want me to go search out someone from my tribe? That would entail another journey either out to the west, where my folks went, or back to the Smoky Mountains.

Why should I be in such a hurry to leave Grandpa, and start a home of my own? I am only 18 years old. Please, Jesus think about this, and give me an answer in your time. I will bide until I hear from you."

I remembered a Bible verse from Proverbs. I did not know if God sent it or not.

"Trust in the Lord with all thine heart, and lean not unto thine own understanding. In all thy ways acknowledge Him, and He shall direct thy path, Proverbs: 3:5-6."

I rose from my knees, refreshed, and ready to worship. I turned my cares over to God, and I would try to trust Him. I also promised not to fret. After all, Jesus knows what's best for me!

AS THE PEOPLE WALKED into the church, they filled all the pews from the front to the back. Once they settled themselves, Grandpa nodded to the organist and announced the opening hymn.

And Can It Be?

And can it be that I should gain

An interest in the Savior's blood?

Died He for me, who caused His pain

For me, who Him to death pursued?

Amazing love! How can it be,

That Thou, my God, shouldst die for me?

Amazing love! How can it be,

That Thou, my God, shouldst die for me?

From Acts 16:25, Charles Wesley, 1738

Grandpa asked the congregation to turn in their Bibles to the passage of Acts 16:25-34. The people quieted and leafed through their Bibles to the right scriptures as he told the story of the great miracle from God:

"Paul and Silas lost favor in the city of Philippi. The multitudes rose up against them, ripped off their clothes, and beat them. They cast them into prison and charged the jailer to keep them safely locked up. The jailer took them into the inner prison, and secured their feet fast in the stocks.

"At about midnight Paul and Silas prayed and sang praises to God, and the prisoners heard them. Of a sudden, there was a great

253

earthquake. The foundations of the prison shook, the doors of the cells opened, and everyone's bands came loose.

"The keeper of the prison awakened. He saw the cell doors opened, and he drew his sword to kill himself. Paul called out in a loud voice, 'Do yourself no harm for we are all here!' The jailer called for a light and ran in trembling. He fell down before Paul and Silas, brought them out from the cell and said, 'Sirs, what must I do to be saved?'

"And they said to him, 'Believe on the Lord Jesus Christ, and thou shalt be saved, thou and thy house.' Then they spoke the word of the Lord to him.

"The jailer took them to his house, washed their wounds, and fed them meat. They baptized the jailer and his family straight away. They rejoiced, for the jailer believed in God, along with everyone in his house."

After the scripture reading, Grandpa opened with prayer and then started in preaching:

"Believe on the Lord Jesus Christ and thou shalt be saved!" He thundered to the congregation.

"What is Salvation? Can anyone tell me?" He pointed to several people. "Salvation is the work of God's grace. It is through His unmerited grace, that God bestows salvation on us. In other words, he gives us grace even though we don't deserve it.

"And jest how does a person receive salvation, you might ask? Again, I say to you, 'Believe on the Lord Jesus Christ, and thou shalt be saved!'

"We all sin! In the history of the world, only one perfect sinless individual ever lived, our Lord Jesus Christ.

"To receive the salvation Jesus offers, and an eternal relationship with God, we must first confess our sins, be sorry for our sins, and vow to sin no more.

"Then we must believe in, and accept Jesus as our Lord and Savior. No matter how bad our sins, God will forgive us of our wrong doings. He throws the memory of our sins into the deepest sea.

"Christ died on the cross for our sins. Romans 5:8 says, 'God demonstrated his love for us in that while we were yet sinners, Christ died for us.' God placed all the sins of mankind squarely on Jesus's shoulders as he hung there nailed to the cross. He bore all sins, from the first sins of Adam and Eve, understand?

"The kicker is we must confess those sins, all of the past sins, the sins we commit today, and the sins we have yet to commit.

"Even though Jesus died for all our sins, we must still confess those sins to God. We must turn away from sin, then He will grant us His redeeming grace.

"Jesus is God, or he could not have borne the terrible weight of so much sin. He who was without sin became sin to save us. His death was a living sacrifice for us.

"If you turn away from God, there's no chance you'll be saved! Instead, turn your back on sin, and turn to Jesus. Confess your sins, or you'll suffer God's eternal judgment in Hades, forever.

"Jesus said, 'I am the way, the truth, and the life! No one comes to Father God except by me!' Believe It! It's true! Embrace it and hide this important knowledge in your hearts!

"As the song we jest got through singing says, 'Amazing love! How can it be, that Thou, my God shouldst die for me?' Above all, 'Believe on the Lord Jesus Christ and thou shalt be saved!'"

Grandpa announced the closing hymn. As we stood to sing, my mind lingered on his message. I knew I was a Christian. I knew someday I would go to heaven.

I was sorry That Man hadn't come to church today. If he had heard Grandpa's message, maybe he would turn to Jesus. I prayed that Grandpa would share the message of salvation with That Man and his family.

I'd never before prayed for anyone's salvation. I vowed to pray the scriptures that Grandpa gave us today for the Sutherland family, and see if the Lord would grant my request for their salvation.

I thought of a verse in Matthew that Grandpa was fond of quoting.

"Let your light so shine before men that they may see your good works, and they will glorify your Father in heaven."

Maybe I should just set a good example for him, rather than judge him. I prayed God would lead me in the coming days.

I brought myself up short. The hymn was over and Grandpa said the closing prayer of benediction. I bowed my head, and thanked Jesus for these thoughts about reaching out to people, and letting my light shine. If God wanted me to tell That Man and his family about Himself, I decided He would give me the opportunity.

In the meantime, I would shine my light and bide my time. I would never marry up with any man unless he knew Jesus as their Lord and Savior. I refused to become unequally yoked, no matter how pretty his blue eyes.

I picked up my gloves, my Bible, and my shawl and prepared to walk to the back of the church and greet the people with Grandpa.

Chapter 19
THE SUTHERLAND FAMILY

As the last family shook our hands, and said goodbye, Grandpa closed the church door, and took my arm leading me outside to the wagon yard.

We heard a horse and wagon coming along the road. As it got closer, lo and behold, we saw That Man driving a buggy pulled by his big black horse. The horse fought the harness, it seemed as if he wasn't used to pulling a buggy. I hid my smile when I saw the horse fighting and kicking at the traces as That Man sought to pull up near our wagon.

"Good morning, Preacher Frost," he said, stepping down from the buggy and wrapping the reins around the hitching post. "How are you and Miss Ashbill on such a fine Sunday morning?" He said with a smile, doffing his hat in my direction.

"Good morning to you, too, Wiley. Missed you at services," Grandpa said, mounting the wagon. He seemed anxious to get home to his Sunday dinner.

"I'd planned to come to services today, Preacher Frost, but my cantankerous horse gave me such a hard time harnessing him to the buggy,

I thought we'd better take our time getting here. I'd like to invite Miss Ashbill to take Sunday dinner with me, and my family at our home by the Duck River. Ma puts on a fine spread."

I stood there shaking my head at Grandpa. "I couldn't think of going with you Mister Sutherland, I have Grandpa's dinner to see to," I answered for him feeling flustered, and upset! Imagine him inviting me to his home, and on such short notice!

"Well, why ever not, Caroline?" Grandpa said, sounding exasperated with me, as he climbed back down from the wagon seat. "I'm an old bachelor, and I can see to my own victuals. I know you have something simmering in the stew pot that I could dish up myself."

"But Grandpa," I beseeched him, not wanting to go anywhere with That Man. I didn't trust him, and couldn't understand why Grandpa fobbed me off on him.

"Oh, go along with you, Child. Do you good to get away, see new things, and meet new folks, have some fun for a change. You'll bring her home afore dark then, won't you, Wiley?" Grandpa added, fixing him with a stern glance.

"Yes sir! I will sir! Preacher Frost, sir! She'll be home long before dark. Thank you for allowing her to come with me," he told Grandpa, while piercing me with an intense gaze, a smirk forming in his eyes, at my discomfiture.

I put my Bible in the wagon with Grandpa, and then marched over to That Man's buggy. Thankfully, I had strapped on my skinning knife that morning. After the encounter with this varmint out in the woods, I vowed never to leave the house without it. He would not take unfair advantage of me again!

He helped me into the buggy seat, walked around to his side, and climbed in. Immediately I wanted back down. I wished the man had brought a wagon, rather than a buggy. We sat too close. My sleeve touched his arm every time he moved the reins. He giddy-upped, and we were off. His ornery horse prancing and prancing, until at last, he settled down to a fast clip.

Then I remembered the idea of telling the man about Jesus. I cringed when I thought of that. Coward, I told myself, and yes, I admitted I was. I would leave it in the Lord's hands for a while and see what developed.

Caroline, I seemed to hear in my head, *I arranged this meeting, so you could put the matter to rest with Wiley Sutherland.*

"Yes Lord, I will do what I can," I murmured.

I enjoyed watching for birds, and critters along the pleasant wooded road, determined not to start a conversation. Guilt nagged me. I needn't have worried though. He seemed like a talker.

"Boy, Gal, you sure took me by surprise last week. I never saw that punch comin'." He reached up, and felt of his chin a little, looking for some sympathy from me.

I ignored him.

"I don't know what made you haul off and slug me. You're lucky I came to see you again."

I just huffed at him.

"What's the matter with you? I told you I wanted to ask you to be my wife, and all I ever get from you is silence."

I glanced at him, noting the screwed-up expression on his face. "If you must know, I consider your behavior entirely unacceptable," I finally told him. "Setting your hound on me in the woods, running through the town with ruffians, and spying on me when you knew Grandpa traveled away from home. But you will never get the best of me," I added with satisfaction.

He stopped the buggy up under the hanging boughs of a big tree. He turned so he could face me. "I'm not out to get the best of you. I love you Gal, and I want to marry you. I've never seen the likes of you! A wildcat you are right now, but I believe you'll settle down in time. I think we match up plenty good enough to last. I know we'd make a good marriage!"

"Are you a Christian?" I challenged him. "Do you know Jesus as your Lord and Savior? I will never be unequally yoked with any man.

Then, I will ask you one more thing, are you Cherokee?" I said, getting angrier with him by the minute. Imagine him saying I would settle down in time! I would not settle down for any man, let alone him!

"You know, I'm not Cherokee. I'm full-blooded Scot," he replied with a puzzled look on his handsome face. "As far as being a

Christian. Yes! Ma brought all of us up in the church. I don't know why you ask."

"Well, I am waiting for a Christian, Cherokee man to marry. You don't act like a Christian man. Now let's get on to your home. I am sure your mother has dinner waiting for us!"

"You're right there, Gal. Ma don't like us to keep her waiting. We'll talk about this again, later." He whipped up his horse, we tore down the road as if we there was a critter at our tail. In a few minutes, we reached a fork in the road where he turned right, drove another half-mile, then we were there.

When I saw their place, it looked almost like a compound, fenced all around with a gate that he got down to open. In the distance, I saw plowed fields stretching back away from the barn, and several outbuildings. They had lived here such a short time. They must be a family of hard workers.

A double cabin with a wide wraparound porch stood front and center overlooking the Duck River. On either side of the main cabin, two large, single cabins stood strong and well built. One more cabin sat across from the others close to a wooded area, next to a big cottonwood tree.

Those must be the homes of the brothers, and their families. They were all here together, living and working the same land. No wonder they accomplished so much with five men in the family.

Wiley stopped the buggy inside the front gate, and pointed with his whip. "The big cabin in the center is Ma and Pa's home, and the smaller one over close to the cottonwood tree is where my brother James, his wife Lillian, and their son Jamie live.

"The cabin with the lean-to on the side is where my big brother William and his wife Jenny live. I call him Bear. They have three young'uns all boys.

"The cabin on the other side of Pa's, with all the bushes in the front, is the home of my oldest brother Hammond, and his wife

Lucinda. They have three of the purtiest little ladies you'll ever want to lay eyes on. Lucinda gave the girls flower names."

"And where is your cabin?" I asked, though not really interested in his answer.

"I ain't home much. When I am, I bunk with Pa and Ma."

Something big loped along in the distance. It ran right for us. I saw it was the nasty hound that attacked me in the woods. I reached in and pulled out my knife for just in case.

A big grin filled the face of That Man. "What 'ya got there, Miss Ashbill?"

"I am ready for your brute if he causes me trouble," I replied with spirit.

"You won't need that I told you he's friendly."

"I do not believe you," I answered back.

The hound launched himself at the buggy, and ended up in Wiley's lap. He licked his face a few times before Wiley heaved him over the side. "Down, Angus! Dern dog jest don't know when to quit."

Then he trotted around to my side of the buggy, I waved my knife and scooted toward Wiley. I did not know which was worse, the man or his hound. The dog put his front paws on my side of the buggy and sniffed me. He leaned over and began to lick my hand.

"See Miss Ashbill, Angus likes you. He remembers you from that time in the woods. Don't worry, he won't hurt you!"

"Let's get on, Mister Sutherland," I said, putting away my knife. "I want nothing to do with your hound!"

"Whatever you say, Miss Ashbill!" He slapped the reins, and the horse began walking again. We pulled up at the side entrance of the main cabin. A woman opened the door, doffed her apron, and put up a hand to pat the neat coil of braided blond hair at the nape of her neck. A welcoming smile filled her lovely face.

The hound ran to her, and sat panting and drooling at her feet. She turned a caring look on him. "Go on with you, Angus, we can play later. We have company, now!"

The dog calmed down at a word and a touch from the lovely lady.

Then a shock went through me upon seeing her up close, for there stood my ma. She seemed a great deal like my own ma, yet perhaps a few years older. Tears pricked my eyes. I brushed them away before anyone could see. I allowed Wiley to help me down from the buggy. I could not take my eyes from the lady standing there on the porch, a smile lighting her vivid blue eyes, Wiley's eyes.

Upon further inspection though, Ma did not have the fine lines and wrinkles around her eyes, or the laugh lines surrounding her mouth. Yet, Ma may have aged too. I had not seen her in many years. Still, I loved this woman on sight.

God, I said in a silent prayer, *are you trying to tell me something? Are you telling me I have misjudged this man standing here by my side? Should I feel guilty for the way I have treated him?* I would reserve judgment. Many a villain hailed from a wonderful mother, or so I always heard.

In the meantime, I would try to become acquainted with this beautiful woman who reminded me so much of my own cherished mother. Maybe we could become friends, whether I gave in to her son, and his plans for me, or not.

I followed her inside the tidy cabin, and caught a whiff of roasted meat. The elegant table set with fine China caught my attention. The grace and refinement shown seemed more in tune with where I lived in Norfolk, Virginia, than this area of the wilderness. For me? I wondered. I certainly hope not.

"Wiley," she said, turning to the man by my side. "Please call your pa and the family to dinner."

"We don't intend to overwhelm you all at once, Miss Ashbill," she said, turning to me. "You will meet Wiley's father, brothers, and their families. The men expect me to serve dinner as our family custom every Sunday after meeting, when we can all be together."

It relieved me to hear they attended services, and ate together as a family every week at this elegant table.

Hammond, the eldest, resembled Wiley with blond hair and blue eyes. William took after their Pa, a large man with black hair and eyes. Brown haired, and green eyed, James the youngest, seemed smaller than his older brothers, yet no less handsome.

Two of the wives came in next, along with their six children, pretty women! They sat the children at a table of their own. The children were a special delight for me. Mrs. Sutherland told me James's wife Lillian stayed at their cabin with a teething baby.

The men filled the large space of the cabin, and took seats at the long table. Mrs. Sutherland invited me to sit next to Wiley. I felt strange and shy, as the only woman at the table with all those big men surrounding me. Mister Sutherland prayed the blessing, every bit as nice as my own Grandpa would.

The women helped their mother-in-law with the generous meal. They served the men first, then me, and the children last.

Once Mrs. Sutherland sat, I relaxed a little, and began to enjoy the delicious meal, and the lively conversation. The men talked about weather, farming, and politics. No one spoke to me, and I was grateful. The two daughters-in-law joined us, sitting next to their husbands after they served the large platters of food.

I saw at once that the Sutherlands were a happy family. The men spoke kindly to their wives and parents. They all seemed compatible with each other. A niggling thought began at the back of my mind. Could I have been wrong about this young man? I glanced sideways at his handsome face, and almost jumped when I noticed him watching me.

"Well, what do you think?" He leaned over and whispered, a broad smile on his face. "Am I such an ogre? Has seein' me here with my family made a difference in what you think of me?"

I felt myself color up, embarrassed to have him come out with something like that at his family table. I did not answer him. I would have to think about that, and ask God what he wanted me to do before I admitted, That Man, Wiley Sutherland was right!

DINNER OVER, THE MEN went out to the back porch to smoke their pipes. The young women took over the kitchen, washed the dishes, and put away the leftover food.

Mrs. Sutherland invited me to the front porch to sit, and wait for the men to finish smoking. I went, eager to find out more about her and the family.

"May I call you Caroline, Miss Ashbill?" She asked sitting down in the woven seat of a handmade rocker on the front porch.

"Yes, Mrs. Sutherland, please do," I replied, taking the seat next to hers. The men had built the house on a bluff facing the river, and overlooked a wide expanse of forest, colorfully painted in the gold and scarlet of autumn.

The view amazed me. I had not noticed how high we climbed when we drove in. The breathtaking view from the porch stretched off in the distance to the west, where I saw many small, quaint homes interspersed along the higher slopes overlooking the Duck River. It seemed like heaven to me.

Below, the river flowed wide and sluggish. I saw here and there swiftly flowing eddies embellished with the wild beauty of colorful fall leaves.

"What a beautiful home you have here, Mrs. Sutherland," I whispered, feeling reverent in the presence of God's creation.

"Yes, God has blessed us, Andrew heard from a man he met about the beauty of the Tennessee hills, and asked us to move. I loved North Carolina, we lived in the eastern part of the state near the sea. We were settled and happy with everything we desired there, but Andrew would go west and explore. I admit I do like it here. I miss the sound of the sea, but we have such a beautiful view of the river.

"The men take a boat out whenever they have a chance, the fish are abundant and easily caught. We also have a trout stream running through the back of our land, the young boys like to fish there, so I still have my water. I must confess, that we are spoiled with fresh trout for breakfast on many of our mornings."

"The grandchildren have more land to run on, and each of the little boys now has an animal of his own to raise. Where we lived in North Carolina, we owned much less land, but lived in larger homes. I guess we gave up something, and in return, received something equal in satisfaction."

"Please tell me about yourself, Caroline. Wiley said you are a princess. I have wanted to meet you for a while, and I must admit you are everything he said, and more. What a beautiful girl you are with your auburn hair and your unusual green eyes."

My breath caught in embarrassment. How could she say I was beautiful? I saw the truth with my own eyes, when I looked into Gramma's mirror.

Yet somehow, I believed this lovely lady. Perhaps I did not see myself the way others saw me. That was something else I would puzzle out later.

"I do not know as I am a princess, Ma'am," I said with a laugh. "For one thing, I do not resemble one. Yes, my pa was a member of the Cherokee tribal council. He was very tall, and strong, with black hair and blue eyes, not full-blooded, yet I did not know enough to ask him about his family when I lived with him and Ma. Seemed like my head was too full of playing, fishing, and enjoying my life, rather than the serious things about the history of my family.

"Ma, I know her family history well, for I live with her father, my Grandfather Hiram Amos Frost. I believe you've met him, he's the preacher at the Baptist Church in Bedford County."

"Yes, I know your grandfather," Elizabeth Sutherland said. "He is a fine man. He visited here with us many times, and asked us to join him at his services. We go to meeting down the road a little way, just a small house of worship, but we feel the power and spirit of the Lord there."

"I'm glad you have found a church," I said. "It is very important."

"And your mother, she asked?

"Ma was like no one I'd ever met. She's of medium height and blond, with the kindest look in her blue eyes. She smiled all the time, and sang with her work. I can still hear her singing in my mind." My eyes teared up, but I determined not to cry before Mrs. Sutherland.

"Where are your folks, Caroline?" she asked.

"The government took them away in the removal many years ago," I told her the truth. "They left me behind when I spent the night with my grand folks." I paused a second and then rushed on. "I hope you don't mind my saying so, Ma'am, you are very much like my own ma and that makes me feel better."

"Why Caroline, what a sweet thing to say. I am so sorry about the loss of your family. I imagine it must be very difficult for you."

"Not so bad for me now. I've accepted their loss, but Gramma died last year, and Grandpa and I are living alone together, now."

Mrs. Sutherland picked up a basket sitting next to her chair, took out several squares of fabric, and began stitching. "Do you quilt, Caroline?"

"I have not quilted, Ma'am, but I can sew, knit, and crochet."

"Would you like to help me sew?" She asked, holding out the three squares to show me. "This is my favorite pattern, called Barn

Raising. I favor it. It seems to fit with this beautiful Tennessee landscape. I have also made quilts of the Birds in the Air, and Chimney Sweep patterns. They make up into beautiful quilts. Just sew the squares together along the edges.

"I work on these squares every chance I can. I have one unmarried son, seven grandchildren, and a new little one coming soon to William and Jenny. I am making nine wedding quilts, it is never too early to begin," she said with a laugh.

I took the squares from her, and began stitching with slow careful stitches, relieved to have something to do with my hands. I hoped my stitches were small enough for her approval.

"I like the colors, and the pattern is unusual," I said, hoping she would not watch me as I sewed. She glanced over at my work, and for a few seconds, I thought they weren't good enough.

"You stitch beautifully, Caroline, your stitches are small and even," she said with a smile.

"Thank you, Ma'am," I said, relieved that I pleased her with my stitching of the squares.

I heard a commotion coming from around the side of the house. Three young boys rushed to the front yard, followed closely behind by three pretty little girls. I watched these beautiful children at the dinner table, of course. Yet, here they were taking on their own personalities rather than sitting quiet under the watchful eyes of their mothers.

"Gram?" The first little girl ran up to Mrs. Sutherland. "Can we please have another piece of cake? We's all hungry."

"Hungry already, Lavender?" She said with a broad smile. "Come here, Honey. All of you come here. I want you to meet Uncle Wiley's friend, Miss Ashbill." Three little girls in stair-step order stood in front of us, followed by the three boys.

"Caroline, these are six of our grandchildren. God has blessed us to have so many, and have them live here on the farm with us. These little girls are my three flowers. They belong to Hammond and his wife, Lucinda.

Here we have Lavender Sophia Sutherland, whom we call Vender, next is Amaryllis Victoria Sutherland whom we call Rilla, and Larkspur Susanna Sutherland, we call her Lark.

Each of the beautiful little girls walked forward, and bobbed me a curtsy as Mrs. Sutherland called her name. They looked to be about nine, seven, and five years old. They were beautiful blond little girls, two with big blue eyes, and the youngest with green eyes.

"You haven't met their little brother David. He should be up from his nap soon, he is two-and-a-half years old." We also have wee Jamie who is at home teething.

The little girls sat down on the edge of the porch, and looked at the three boys standing in front of their grandmother, pushing, and tugging at one another.

"These are my grandsons, Miss Ashbill, William, and Jenny's boys. Here is Alric Douglas Sutherland. He carries his Pa's middle name, Douglas. We call him Ric. He is ten years old. I fear he will be bigger than his pa. Next is Monroe Jefferson Sutherland, eight years old. We call him Jeff. He carries the names of two of our presidents. Then, this little imp with the frog inside his shirt is William Young Sutherland, named for his Pa, William, and my Maiden name is Young. He is six years old the youngest of William's boys. Our coming grandchild, we call Afterthought. Jenny promises to name the child Alexander or Alexandra when it arrives in a few weeks."

The boys were as dark as the girls were fair. They were all a delight. I wished I could stay, play with them, take them fishing, and tell them stories. I last played with children when I helped Sarah Louise at her school last winter.

A moment later, the mothers came to call the children home. I hoped at another time I could visit, and become acquainted with these beautiful young women.

"Caroline, I am sorry you missed meeting James' wife, Lillian, and their little boy, Jamie. We will introduce you the next time you visit!

Come girls, sit with us, we are getting acquainted with Miss Ashbill," Elizabeth Sutherland invited her two daughters-in-law.

"We'd like to Ma, but you don't need all these children in your way." William's brown-haired wife, Jenny, spoke up with a smile. "We must get them home they have chores to do!"

The two women placed completed quilt squares into a second basket next to Mrs. Sutherland, and took out piles of single squares to work on at their homes.

"Miss Ashbill, we make the quilts as a family project. Glad you can help," Jenny said with a smile, reaching out to shake my hand in greeting.

"Yes, it's good of you to help, Miss Ashbill," Hammond's wife Lucinda said, as she brushed a wisp of blond hair from the face of the little boy she carried. "Miss Ashbill, meet our son, David."

"What a beautiful child," I said, rising from my seat to become acquainted with the woman and her wonderful little boy, blond and blue-eyed like two of his sisters.

So precious, I thought. *Just like a cherub!* "I am very glad to meet you and your beautiful families," I said, returning to my seat.

"We don't want to go home, Ma, we're hungry and Gram said there's more cake," Ric interrupted me rudely.

"Now Alric, get yourself on home. There's chores for you to attend to, you ate cake at dinner." Jenny gave her oldest a pat on the seat of his pants to get him started.

We heard footsteps coming from around the side of the house. Wiley walked over to us with a glad light in his blue eyes. He mounted the steps, and took a chair to the side of mine.

"Don't leave girls," he called out to the departing women as they walked away with the seven children in tow. "Stay! Let's talk for a while, I don't get to visit with you much anymore!"

"You would if you were ever home, Wiley." Jenny turned around, laughing. Her boys raced each other back to the house. "I have many things to get ready for tomorrow. Good to meet you, Miss Ashbill. Come again soon," she called.

Lucinda shifted David to her left arm, and then offered her hand to me.

"A pleasure to meet you, Miss Ashbill. I know we will become very good friends. Please visit often!" She said with a warm smile.

I watched Vender and Rilla begin skipping, and running through the fallen leaves. Lark ran after them, then ran back to take hold of her mama's hand.

"Well, I'm glad to see you and Ma are gettin' along," Wiley said, winking at me. "Sorry to say, but are you about ready to go, Miss Ashbill?" He asked, crinkles of laughter standing out in his face as he teased me. "I promised your grandpa you'd be home before dark and it gets dark earlier these days."

"Why yes I am, Mister Sutherland," I said, turning to smile at his mother. I pulled the shawl around my shoulders, and handed the quilt squares back to her. I extended my hand to her as I rose from the chair.

"Thank you for a wonderful dinner, Ma'am. I don't know when I have enjoyed a more pleasant day."

"Thank you for coming, Caroline," Mrs. Sutherland said, smiling. "We enjoyed having you here very much. We hope you will come see us again soon." She stood, and clasped both of my hands in her own.

"Would you like to finish these squares at your home, Caroline? Here take these along, as well." She gave me a small basket full. "You can give the finished squares to Wiley for me, or return them the next time you come to visit," she said with a twinkle in her eye.

"And you, young man, see that Miss Ashbill gets right home and no lollygagging, you hear me? We don't want her grandfather worrying about her the first time she comes to visit us."

"Yes, Ma!" Wiley said, reaching down, and giving his mother a kiss on the cheek. He leaned in and whispered, "Thanks, Ma!"

My face flamed hot as I thought of the implications of his whispered message. I walked to the buggy with Wiley, and prayed I made a good impression on his family. I waved goodbye to Mrs. Sutherland as we drove away from the house. Peace filled me for the first time in a long while, I said a prayer of thanksgiving to God for this wonderful day!

Chapter 20
<u>**THE HARVEST MOON DANCE**</u>

The next few weeks were quiet, and gave me time to think while I cooked, washed clothes, cleaned the house, spun, knitted, and sewed upon the quilt squares for Mrs. Sutherland.

Grandpa seemed happier now, he rode out most every day to take care of his little flock of people. He loved folks, enjoyed visiting them, and talking to them about Jesus.

I felt better, too. The only difference was maybe my attitude about That Man, who I now thought of as Wiley, hard for me to accept that I might have been wrong about him. He belonged to respectable people. His ma said they go to church as a family. Maybe he was a born-again Christian, as he said. I would reserve judgment, I have yet to see him toting a Bible to services.

Wiley did not come to see us at church on Sundays anymore, and I didn't look for him. He rode by every few days, either in the afternoon or in the evenings to talk to Grandpa. They discussed politics, the plight of the Cherokee, crops, timbering, hunting, slaughtering hogs, and other things in which men are interested. Far as I knew, they did not discuss the Word of God.

To me, he paid very little attention. I sat and listened, tended to my knitting, spun at the wheel, or sewed on the quilt squares. He gave me an idea of what he thought, and felt about several things. I guess, I was getting to know the man, a little.

He asked me to walk out to his horse with him a time or two. I just stood by, watched him mount the big black beast, doff his hat to me, and ride out, nothing else.

He rode in to visit us again, on Monday. Before he left, he said, "Caroline, there's a Harvest Moon dance in town this Saturday night, I'll come by for you."

He took me by surprise, so I didn't answer him right away.

The last time I danced, I wore beaded lace, and white tulle at the birthday ball the evening before I left Aunt Violet's many years ago. Now, I would not know what to wear.

Grandpa answered for me. "Of course she'll go with you Wiley."

"Fine! See you Saturday night," he said tipping his hat to me as he went out the door.

THE NEXT MORNING, I was in a quandary about the dance. Should I go? What would I wear? There were my spring cottons, but they were too lightweight for the November weather.

The blue serge suit dress I brought with me from Norfolk would do, I wore it Sundays. But I had nothing frilly or fancy, except my too fancy, too ornate, green silk ball gown.

Then I remembered the trunk that Grandpa saved from our house after the soldiers took my folks away. I had never opened it to look inside, not wanting to dredge up memories of my ma.

I climbed up to the loft, and found the dusty trunk, left alone at the back of the room, these many years. The lock was undone, so I sat down in front of it, opened the lid, and smelled lavender.

The fragrance filled the loft room. Ma grew lavender, and put away her clothes in it, I remembered that now. My eyes teared up a little as I pulled out the top tray, and there in the center was Ma's hair brooch. Ma wore it all the time. She made it with braided locks of hair from her grandpa, and grandma, who were my gramma's folks.

Next to the brooch, Ma's jet earrings, set in gold, winked at me in the soft light, and there were one or two other trinkets. Under the jewelry, were winter mittens, scarves, and little packages of braided hair from Ma's three children, our baby dresses, and other keepsakes filled out the rest of the spaces in the tray. I set the black earrings aside to try.

Under the tray, I found many fine dresses made of linen and silk. Ma's ceremonial robes came next, then my pa's ceremonial turban, and his feathered cape.

Finally, close to the bottom, I found what must have been Ma's wedding dress, light blue silk shot through with delicate lace ruching, belled sleeves, and a wide skirt. I also found her petticoats in silk and satin. Then, her satin slippers, a parasol, and a carefully wrapped bouquet of dried flowers. Lastly, I found a few mementos from their lives together.

Such a treasure trove of precious memories stored away in the loft above my head. Tears streamed down my cheeks, as I reverently replaced everything, except for one lovely, beaded shawl, a lace collar, a colorful silk fan, and the gold and jet earrings. I took those things downstairs to try with my blue serge suit, and see if they would complement my dress for the dance.

I could not bring myself to wear any of my ma's lovely dresses. Besides, when I held up one of the dresses, I saw it was too small. I didn't know I was bigger than Ma. Maybe someday I could alter some of her petticoats to go with my ball gown if I ever decided to wear it again.

Not having a large mirror presented me with a problem, but I laid the dress down on the bed, unbuttoned the top few buttons, tucked the plain collar inside, and tacked it to stay. Next, I draped the lace collar around the opening, and sighed with relief as it fit close enough, and I secured it.

The collar came down into a V where it would rest at the base of my throat. I fastened the gold brooch I brought home with me from Norfolk at the center, my first occasion to wear the brooch, and yes, it did add to my costume.

The shawl I dipped in cold water, and hung it close to the fireplace to dry, and remove the wrinkles. Its creamy color would look well with the dark blue of my dress. The beads winked at me in the lantern light.

Shoes were a problem. Since I owned no elegant slippers, I blackened my shoes with ashes from the fireplace, and rubbed them until they shone. They would have to do. I knew my feet were too big to fit into Ma's delicate slippers.

I rubbed the earrings until they sparkled, and tried them in my ears. I took up Gramma's piece of looking glass, and admired the effect. Yes, the earrings, and the golden brooch completed my costume.

I wished for the necklace of crystals I last wore at Aunt Violet's the night I ran away. I had left it behind along with many other pretty things I could use now. Wishful thinking, I realized. I must put all of that behind me, and keep it there.

SATURDAY AFTER SUPPER, I dressed with care. I did not have any ornamentation for my hair, so I brought in a few sprigs of holly from down slope of the cabin. I piled my curls on the top of my head, as they taught me at Aunt Violet's school. I secured them with pins, buried a few of the green leaves and red berries in some of the curls. They gave me a holiday look.

When I came from the bedroom, Grandpa dozed in his chair in front of the fire. He jerked awake when I spoke to him, pushed himself up out of his chair, and stared at me for a full minute before breaking into a smile.

"You are the picture of your dear mother, Caroline," he said, brushing away a tear.

"No, I'm not, Grandpa," I said a little disgruntled. "I've told you before that I look like Pa, and that's not pretty," I felt my mouth pull down in a pout.

"Maybe a little at that, Child, but still your mother all over again." He reached out and gave me a hug.

We heard a noise in front of the cabin that set Nellie Belle barking. "Must be Wiley," Grandpa said, going to the door.

Wiley looked more resplendent than I ever remembered seeing him. When he removed his black slouch hat, and held it in his hand, I noticed his slicked down hair, clubbed back, and scented with pomander, and his close-shaved cheeks.

He wore fawn-colored trousers stuffed into his high polished, black boots, a dark red brocade weskit rode around his middle, and he topped it with a fine, black wool jacket, which complimented his black silk necktie. The gun belt strapped around his waist surprised me. Was he expecting trouble tonight? I wondered.

Looking up at my handsome escort put me in mind of others from my past, such as short and portly Abbot Parmenter, who had pressed hard for a suit with me, or nice steady and boring Wilfred Addison. I ran away from the likes of those young men. Now, I would continue to wait and see if God gave me a future with this handsome man.

Aunt Violet was wrong when she said men did not want a wild girl as their wife. Wiley saw me at my wildest and worst, and he still came to visit me. I laughed to think of that!

I excused myself, and walked to my room. I almost forgot my skinning knife. I placed it carefully in its sheath, and pinned it in the pocket of my cloak. I was not taking any chances either.

A huge harvest moon rode low in the sky, and brightened the road in front of us as we traveled to town in the buggy. Late for a harvest moon, I thought, but welcome. The full red moon lifted my spirits and filled me with excitement.

The last time I danced, was my last evening at Aunt Violet's Academy for Young Ladies of Genteel Quality. Of course, I did not count the one dance I had with Captain Johnson during my time with the wagon train.

At the gala, I remembered my racing heart, and the happiness I felt as I heard the orchestra begin playing the first waltz. I floated down the stairs in my white beaded-lace ball gown, knowing I was dressed like a princess, yet at the same time, nervous and excited, by the plans I had made for that evening to gallop west on the little horse Chocolate, join the wagon train, and leave Virginia behind to go search for my folks.

Was it only two and a half years ago? Seemed like a century, yet when I turned to look at the handsome young man sitting next to me, I thought for a minute maybe it was worth it, but then again, we would see!

Before I knew it, we were on the outskirts of town without incident. Wiley passed the new livery stable, and pulled up close to the large barn where they held tonight's dance.

As we walked to the barn, I admired the decorations on the exterior of the barn: a scarecrow, hay bales, corn stalks, and pumpkins both large and small.

Inside, bales of hay for seating snugged the walls around the interior of the large barn. The food and drink tables neatly draped in white cloths, were embellished with autumn leaves, gourds, and small pumpkins, arranged at the center of each table. Long strings of dried ears of corn decorated the edges of the platform where the musicians played their hearts out.

As we stood at the entrance, I swayed to the music of the fiddles and watched the whirling figures of the dancers in a reel.

I noticed speculative glances shift our way as girls danced by in the arms of their stalwart escorts. They glanced not at me, but at Wiley. Bold looks!

Hmmm, I thought. *Do they see him as handsome? Do they see him as desirable? I wondered, I knew he was a good-looking critter, but I never thought other women would react that way to him. If so, why was he still single? That would give me something else to ponder.*

At the close of the song, we moved away from the door. Wiley took my cloak from me. Alarmed, I remembered my skinning knife went with the cloak. I prayed I would not need it. I'd be surprised if did, but I always liked to keep it close. I kept the fan, my reticule, and the beaded shawl with me.

Wiley walked with me to the refreshment table for apple cider, before we sat down along the wall to watch, and wait for the next reel.

"Did I tell you how beautiful you look tonight, Caroline?" He asked, taking hold of my hand, and leaning close to whisper to me.

The music began again, and a young man came over and asked me to dance.

I demurred, I hoped with politeness. I did not understand Wiley's reaction.

"Get along with you! Can't you see she's taken?" He answered the man rudely.

I turned to look at him, amazed to see his dander up, jealous. Something else for me to think on.

During the evening, I danced with Wiley, and against his wishes, with everyone else who asked me. As I danced, I saw him sitting on a hay bale next to the wall, sulking. What was the matter with the man? He should dance with the other ladies, wasn't that why we were here?

Later, at the food table, I tried to jolly him out of his black mood. "What is the matter, Wiley? We came here to have a good time."

"Good time," he spat, "seeing you here in the arms of all those other men!"

"That's nothing," I answered him back, surprised by his attitude. "Why should you mind? I have known most of them my whole life."

Just then, Judge Miller came by to claim me for the next dance. I glanced over at Wiley, he sulked again. Judge Miller was my grandpa's age. I guess Wiley expected me to dance every dance with him, but why should he expect that?

I danced the remainder of the evening with Wiley. As the band began playing a waltz, I saw my friend, Sarah Louise, and her fine, red-haired, young man swing past us. She looked over at Wiley, winked at me, and made the OK sign with her hand.

I laughed out loud, and Wiley did not know why I was laughing, which made me laugh even more.

Before long, the evening ended, and we were on our way out the door to the buggy. A drunken lout blocked our path.

"Hey Sutherland, what 'ya doing with that squaw, huh?" He said with a leering grin on his unshaven face. "Save her for me when you get through with her! Ha! Ha! Ha!"

Wiley hauled off and slugged him right in the mouth knocking him down, and most likely breaking a few of the man's teeth.

I got still, then began to cry. Wiley fought with the man who insulted me! What if Wiley got hurt? It was my fault! I started bawling and could not stop.

He pushed aside the brute, took my arm, and steered me out the door, huge tears continued running down my cheeks, and my nose began streaming. I tried to fumble for the hanky inside my reticule, with no success, so I wiped my nose on the shawl.

"Come along, Caroline. I'm taking you home. Don't cry, Caroline," he said rushing me toward the buggy.

His noticing my tears made me mad, so I cried harder. "I'm not crying," I retorted.

"Well then, I don't know what you'd call it," he said gruffly. Away we trotted in the buggy down the pike toward home. I sniffled into the shawl, horrified at myself.

Wiley stayed silent for a long while, then he pulled over onto the side of the lane near the crossroads, and said, "Come here, Hon." He pulled me into his arms. "I'm sorry you saw that. He deserved what he got. He had no right saying those things about you."

"That's not why I'm crying," I sniffled. "I'm used to being called names. I thought he hurt you!" I confessed.

"Hurt me? Him? Naw!" Then he said in an awestruck voice. "I didn't think you cared, Caroline? You never acted like it."

I nodded against his shoulder.

"Well now, guess it's good that happened. Well worth some sore knuckles, to find out you cared about me," he said, pulling up my chin.

The next thing I knew he gave me a soft kiss. What a nice thing to happen. No fella ever kissed me like that, except the dance master when he kissed my hand, and Captain Johnson when he tried to kiss me to say goodbye, but I stopped him, those didn't count.

Wiley's kiss was the most pleasant thing I'd ever experienced, it filled me with happiness. Maybe I liked him. Maybe I was wrong about him, but darn it as far as I knew he was still a polecat.

I was getting in over my head. I pulled away from his arms, and to my side of the buggy. "We better head for home now, Wiley, it's getting late."

WINTER CAME IN COLD, and blustery with very few warm days, and enough cold to cause us to wish for spring.

I looked forward to Christmas, and even knitted Wiley a pair of fine dress socks from fingering wool.

A few days before Christmas, Grandpa left after breakfast to visit someone from his church, who was ill.

I brought Nellie Belle inside to warm up. She lay on a rug in front of the fireplace.

Right after dinner, I heard the jingle of a harness, and then the sound of big feet stamping mud from their boots on the front porch.

Nellie Belle began barking, and would not stop. I dragged her to the back door, and put her outside.

Then, I grabbed up the rifle, opened the door to the porch, and there stood Wiley getting ready to knock. I brought him quickly into the house before Nellie could run around the front to annoy him.

"Hello Wiley, so good to see you, come right inside and warm up. Grandpa isn't here he rode out to visit someone from his church."

"Good to see you too, Caroline. It'll feel good to sit by the fire for a bit, cold day," he said unnecessarily.

I took his hat, and sheepskin-lined coat from him, and laid them in the next room, I snuck my gift to him in the front pocket of his coat. He sat at the kitchen table, and leaned over to hold his hands out to the warmth of the fireplace.

I sat down with him, filled our coffee cups, and passed him a plate of my fresh bread, buttered, sugared, and cinnamon sprinkled. He quickly drank his coffee, took a few bites of the sweet bread, then he handed me a Christmas gift, wrapped nicely, and tied with a fancy ribbon.

"It's like this, Caroline," he said without any pleasantries, even though we had missed seeing each other for the last few weeks.

"I'm going away for a while, there's the trees I helped cut last fall, and the men I work for want 'em floated south. We'll make rafts out of the trees, and once the rivers flood with the spring rains we'll float the rafts south to sawmills in Georgia and Alabama.

"Then, since I'm already there, I want to make a trip of it, and go for a look-see one more time before I settle down."

"That's fine, Wiley. I will be here when you get back," I told him. I knew I needed time to myself to get used to these new feelings roiling around inside of me whenever I came within spitting distance of the man.

I refilled his cup, and opened his gift. I found a finely made lace handkerchief, as well as a hand-drawn portrait of himself, framed in a carved, birch-wood frame.

It touched my heart, that he brought me nice gifts, and more so, that he wanted me to remember what he looked like.

The picture was a good black-and-white pencil portrait. He stood in his working clothes, and boots with his hat tilted at a jaunty angle, he had added a fancy sash around his waist maybe to dress up a bit. I do not know where he found such a good artist, the picture was a fine rendition of Wiley.

"Thank you for thinking of me, with such nice gifts, Wiley, you are very considerate!" I hope you can stay for a while I have a lot to tell you, and I have a basket of quilt squares for your mother.

"Can't visit today, Caroline, got to get back and pack up my gear. I'll take the squares though Ma would like that."

He held my hand for a few minutes, patted me on the shoulder a few times, finished his coffee in a big gulp, then donned the coat and hat I handed him.

I wished him a Happy Christmas, as he mounted his big black horse, and galloped away, he lifted his hand to me in a wave, but no goodbye kiss.

Oh well, guess the man was eager to get on with his travels, I thought with a smile. I placed the portrait on the mantle of the fireplace where I could see it each day.

I smoothed the folds of the lace handkerchief, it was lovely, and as finely made as the ones I always carried when I lived at Aunt Violet's Academy. I held it to my cheek for a minute, and decided I would put it away to use for good.

Chapter 21
<u>WILEY</u>

The bright spot of the season was the Christmas Sing, held the 20th of December at our church. Sarah Louise, Betty and Jean worked with me to help the children practice their hymn. We met with the children a few times the week before the 20th.

Sarah Louise played the organ, while Betty directed the children's singing, and Jean kept them in line and on task.

Since I enjoyed no fine arts talents, I took my usual place in the audience where I felt most comfortable. I clapped loudly each time they finished their rendition.

The night of the 20th, the children sang Charles Wesley's song, "Hark! The Herald Angels Sing." They looked like angels themselves, dressed in white sheets with fashioned halos around the tops of their heads! After they sang, the church rafters shook with the thunderous applause from the audience.

The children beamed their joy, skipped over to join their parents, and watched as others from the church performed.

Betty and Jean together took turns reciting a Christmas poem about the Christ Child. There were other songs, recitations of poems, or bible verses, and a quartet sang a favorite hymn accompanied by Sarah Louise playing the portable organ.

Afterwards, I helped serve refreshments, and visited with many of our friends and neighbors. As they left, the people shook hands wishing each other a Happy Christmas. They all expressed thanks to Grandpa for having the Christmas Sing.

Christmas morning, Grandpa outdid himself preaching from the book of St. Luke, chapter 2. We celebrated Communion, rejoiced, praised, and thanked God for the wonder and majesty of the birth of our Lord and Savior Jesus Christ, the Redeemer of the world. We shook hands as we left, feeling blessed, joy filled, and touched by the Christmas Spirit.

The Saturday after Christmas, Grandpa presided at the wedding of my friend Sarah Louise to her tall, red-haired, Irish gentleman, Richard Stanley Mott. Sarah Louise was luminous with joy.

I laughed when I remembered Sarah Louise had found the red ear of corn at the harvest husking-bee last year. Then, I truly believed she would become the next bride among our friends, and today she had fulfilled that dream. She was a beautiful bride.

I made her a bouquet to carry over her bible, as she walked down the aisle on the arm of her father. A sheaf of baby pine cones was attached to a small delicate fir bough, accented with holly berries, mistletoe, ribbons and lace. It added charm to her elegant, forest green, wool costume, and the exquisite bonnet created for her by Anna, of Anna's Millinery Shop.

I cried huge tears of joy for Sarah Louise, but I was sad, too. I was losing my best friend, again. Yet, my tears couldn't compete with the tears and sobs of Betty and Jean. I nudged them with my elbows to be quiet. I don't blame them they've known Sarah Louise longer. I am glad they will still have each other.

Sarah Louise would move away from us with Richard to the Mott family farm in the northern part of Bedford County. True, she might drive into town on occasion, but I knew it wouldn't be the same, anymore.

After the wedding, Sarah Louise's mother and grandmother, served honey cakes and apple cider in the back of the church to family and friends of the wedded couple.

Later, Grandpa winked at me, laughed and said, "You're next Honey!"

"We'll see, Grandpa, we'll see about that!" Was all I said.

FEBRUARY 15TH, A TERRIBLE ice storm hit Bedford County. The Floyd family sent word that Minnie Floyd wanted Grandpa to pray with her before she passed. I made sure Grandpa bundled up well. I heated a few rocks that I wrapped in a quilt, and tied them around his middle to keep him warm on the long ride.

He did not come home for dinner, or supper. With him gone all day in the cold, I fretted, fumed and talked aloud to myself as I paced up and down in front of the fireplace.

"I should not have let him go out in the storm," I told myself again and again! Then I decided it was time to pray. I realized I should have prayed for Grandpa from the time he left, until he came home again. Guilt smote me, but I vowed to pray hard now.

I had meat stew simmering in a big pot on the hook in the fireplace. I added a bit more water, and stirred the stew one more time. I didn't want it to burn. Once Grandpa came home, he would be hungry.

About an hour later, Nellie Belle set to barking long and loud. I grabbed up the rifle, and went to the door. I saw a wagon coming down our road with Thaddaeus Taylor driving, and Jim Clark sitting right next to him with Grandpa's horse Dorcas tied to the back of the wagon.

They pulled up in front of the house, and jumped down. "We've got Amos, Miss Ashbill," Jim hollered to me.

"On our way home from town, we found him lying in the road, must have fell from his horse. He's cold and wet to the skin. The horse took off, and we come up to her on the way here."

I put away the rifle, added another log to the fire, set a kettle of water to boiling, started a new pot of coffee, and set Grandpa's nightshirt to warm near the fire.

Together they brought Grandpa inside. I pulled back the covers of his bed, and laid some old sheets and blankets in place. I knew Grandpa was probably full of ice and mud, and about half frozen.

They laid him down, and helped me remove his boots and his wet clothing. I brought warm water, and cleaned off most of the dirt.

The men helped me get him into the night shirt, I wrapped him in two thick quilts, and put heated rocks into the bed to keep him warm. Then I spooned cups of hot broth from the stew, and hot tea into him before he finally quit shaking, rolled over and began snoring.

Thaddaeus Taylor came in from outside, he said he had covered their team with blankets against the cold, and took Dorcas to the barn, rubbed her down, and gave her water, and a bate of oats.

I talked the men into sitting for a few minutes at the table. I filled the coffee cups, and set fresh bread and butter on the table for them. Then I dished up plates of the meat and vegetable stew that I had saved for Grandpa. I knew they likely had missed their own suppers. I brought over a sweet bread for dessert, and I refilled their coffee cups several times each.

"I appreciate you both," I said with tears in my eyes. "Thank you isn't enough to say. You both saved Grandpa's life!"

"God saved Amos's life," Jim said. "We were late coming home from town. If we weren't delayed, we'd never have found him. We don't know how much longer Amos could have lived laying out there in the ice and the cold. No thanks needed, Miss Ashbill."

"Thank you for the good victuals," Thaddaeus told me with a big smile. "We need to be on our way now, our families won't know what had become of us. We'll keep Amos in our prayers."

The next day, Grandpa came down with chills, fever, and the ague. I wanted to send for the doctor, but he said, "No!"

I spent a lot of time pouring hot tea and broth into him. He fought me about it.

"Jest let me be, Caroline! I've lived through worse over the years!"

I looked through my supply of herbs, and found feverfrew, vinegar leaf, chamomile to relax him, and the cone flowers I used to brew the cold remedy echinacea. I would dose Grandpa as long as he let me.

I'd never seen Grandpa so sick. Scared I would lose him, I kept up nursing him, and praying down on my knees next to the fireplace at night before bed, and during the day while I did my chores. I prayed without ceasing, until I heard a slight ease in his breathing, and saw the bright-red flush of fever leave his cheeks.

Outside, we were cold soaked. I don't remember this much rain, sleet, ice and snow every few days. Hard for me to get out to the barn to care for the animals, yet I still attended to them even on the coldest days, while Grandpa now sat hunched over his Bible by the fire.

On warmer days, he left the house to help me take care of the stock. Mostly, I'd taken over the chores each morning and evening. I didn't mind a bit, but I knew it was hard for Grandpa to see me don my old work clothes and boots, and go out to the barn in the worst weather, while he continued to sit.

Grandpa had sent along word to his congregation that he cancelled services until the weather warmed up. Now and then, when the sun came out for a bit, Grandpa would hitch up the buggy, and ride to town for the mail and a newspaper. Yet, that was about all he did. The trips to town seemed to sap whatever strength he'd built up.

I bit my tongue more than once. I wanted to scold him for overdoing. It took him three days to regain the strength he lost driving to town and back. Blessed that no one called for him to minister to them. I believe he needed ministering himself.

MARCH CAME IN COLD and windy. It stayed windy for most of the month. We felt closed in a mite. I wanted to get back outside and garden. It seemed like spring would never arrive.

One day, I walked the house from top to bottom. I do not think I had ever looked this closely at the house. I'd always accepted that it belonged to Gramma and Grandpa, and I only lived here. I wondered what Grandpa would say if I made a few changes. Would he even notice?

I looked through the yardage I knew Gramma kept wrapped up tight on a shelf in the attic. Gramma, always particular, wanted her fabrics to stay nice, and away from mice and other critters.

I opened several packages. One large piece of calico, like many other pieces, caught my eye. It made me feel better looking at it. This one, a bright cornflower blue with yellow flowers sprinkled all over, seemed familiar to me somehow. There was a large amount of it in the bundle.

A smaller, wrapped package sat next to the other pieces. I brought it down and broke it loose from its bindings. Out spilled a pretty little dress made of the same bright blue cloth that I had just found. A stained gray pinafore lay beneath it, and then I noticed two hanks of braided hair in a bright, burnished red color, wrapped in linen.

I had to sit down. I sprawled right there on the dusty attic floor, and began remembering the day that I turned ten years old, and spent the night with Gramma and Grandpa as a special treat.

The morning Gramma gave me this birthday dress and pinafore. She said I was growing so fast it was hard keepin' up to me with new dresses.

She asked me to put it on, then she brushed out my braided hair. It went every which way but she tamed my curls with water and a stiff brush. I remembered feeling like a princess.

Gramma made me wear the gray pinafore over the dress to keep it nice. Then she told me to bring in a load of kindling wood, but I did not mind her. I ran down to the clear waters of the creek, which flowed behind the old oak tree, to see how pretty I looked.

I climbed up high on the big rock, and as I looked at my reflection in the water, I heard gunshots and shouting. I turned and saw in the distance Cherokee people sobbing their way down the road, wiping tears from their cheeks.

Soldiers on horseback force-marched my family, and all our friends and neighbors, away from me. It seemed like everyone I knew and loved was out there on the road leaving me behind.

I shouted loudly, tears running down my cheeks, "Ma! Ma! Don't leave me! Take me, too!"

Gramma caught me, and pulled me down to the wet, muddy ground under the huge oak tree. The low-growing branches covered us and kept us safe.

Later, she slipped me into the house, and the dark cellar for safety. A few weeks later, she cut off my braids, dressed me in some of my brother Hiram's clothes, and friends from the remains of our tribe took me away to the mountains where they sheltered me.

A tragic, bittersweet time, and especially hard for me. Seeing my dress and braids brought it all back. I sobbed out my memories of that terrible day. I'd only worn that pretty dress one time. I soiled the dress and the gray pinafore when we hid under the tree. It looked like Gramma tried to wash out the stains, but I could still see them.

Re-wrapping the dress and the braids, I placed them back on the shelf. I needed to put that time behind me, crying would never bring back Gramma or my folks.

I carried the roll of fabric downstairs, and the next day, I held the bright blue material up to the windows in the kitchen, and front room, and planned its use. Gramma seemed closer to me somehow.

Curtains, I decided, would brighten up our home, and there might even be enough for a tablecloth and napkins. Napkins? Where did that come from? Of course, from my upbringing with Aunt Violet, I smiled.

What's wrong with making a few napkins to use the next time Grandpa invited company home from church? He would most likely snort, and call them fripperies, but I knew he used them growing up in Norfolk, Virginia.

I grinned to myself, imagining what a new brightness our home would have once I made a few things. Likely, I would live here the rest of my life, if I had anything to say about it, so why not?

Grandpa came in from the barn a few days later, grumpy for him. "I'm not sure how we'll plant crops unless it warms up, Caroline," he said, huffing and puffing as he walked into the front room.

"I hate the thought of going out to hitch up the horses to the plow, its jest too durned muddy. Give me a cup of coffee Child, my back aches something fierce. I think I'll jest sit here by the fire for a spell, can't plow, and I finished the chores, for now."

I brought him his coffee, settled a quilt around his shoulders, and handed him his Bible. He looked up, winked at me, then opened his Bible to read. I knew Grandpa still felt a mite weak, though he would never admit it. It was not like him to make excuses when he had work to do, no matter what the weather.

THE NEXT FEW DAYS WERE a little warmer. The wind didn't blow as hard, and the frost disappeared by the time we woke in the mornings. Grandpa began talking more about farming. His last trip to town, he heard talk about some folks wanting to plant their land in hemp, a new crop for this region. He wanted to try it on a bit of ground to the south of the house to see how it would grow. If the hemp grew well, he could sell it to the rope factory. I praised God when I heard him planning again.

April the first, put a smile on my face. In a few weeks, I would celebrate my 19th birthday. The spring days were sunny, and filled with birdsong, trees and flowers burst forth with fragrant blooms, and I felt filled with life myself.

I finished my sewing, and the old house looked fresh with the bright curtains at the windows. A new tablecloth covered the scarred oak table, and I put away six napkins to use for good.

I still had enough material to make cushions for Grandpa's rocker, and the other chair sitting next to the hearth. I loved what I made with Gramma's material. It seemed to me like she was right here with me.

The next day, I entertained my first company in many months. Wiley's mother, Mrs. Sutherland, came for a short visit in the early afternoon. I felt blessed to see this kind lady, it made me glad I had brightened the house with my sewing.

My nerves set in for a minute though, as she came unannounced. I knew, *if she'd first written a note that she planned to visit, I would have cleaned and prepared for a week in advance, then dressed myself in a sweeping, green silk creation, and presided over high tea in my own dining room, which Grandpa needed to build for me, someday.* I wanted to laugh aloud at the fantasy I wove in my mind. Then my training took over.

Yes, I realized as I greeted her. I would enjoy entertaining Mrs. Sutherland and I could entertain as a young lady of quality, even in the kitchen of our small house. I said a prayer to Jesus, thanking him for Aunt Violet's teaching of the niceties of life.

I tried my best to walk with grace, use good manners, and see to the needs of my guest. I took her hat and wrap, and seated her at my pretty table, glad I had picked a fresh bouquet of white flags, lavender, lilac, and marsh grasses for the table this morning.

I used Gramma's favorite white plates and cups, with the yellow roses and green leaves. I set a basket of just baked sweet bread, fresh butter, and cream on the table in front of us, and I poured the coffee with care into the delicate cups.

She remarked on my bouquet, and the tablecloth and napkins. Her praise lit a little bubble of joy in my heart. Her visit reminded me of the lessons I'd learned with Aunt Violet. She shook out one of my new napkins and laid it on her lap.

Many times, I had thought about Mrs. Sutherland since the previous fall when Wiley had invited me to dinner at their home. We did not return. He always seemed to be off somewhere, or doing something.

Mrs. Sutherland still looked the same to me, tall and stately. She wore her blond hair back into a soft chignon at the nape of her neck. She gave me a charming smile that held a look of warmth in her bright blue eyes. Eyes much like Wiley's, I realized anew. A beautiful woman in her own right, yet she still resembled my own dear mother, I decided again.

"Thank you for preparing such a delicious repast for me, I shall enjoy it very much, Caroline. I am sorry to say I had forgotten how very beautiful you are my dear. I asked Wiley to bring you for another visit, but then he would travel. He said he wanted to see the south again. That boy of mine has an itchy foot, I fear." She took a sip of the coffee and then smiled at me, looking a little apologetic.

"Again, I am sorry Caroline," she finally said, looking nervous. She settled herself, and took another sip of coffee before plunging in.

"I hope you will not mind, but I am getting behind in my quilting and thought perhaps you could help me once again. I brought a basket of quilt squares. If it is inconvenient, I can take the squares back home with me. I have a very special quilt I need to complete soon."

"Thank you, Mrs. Sutherland. You are very kind to ask for my help with your quilt. I enjoy sewing the squares, they round out my evenings," I said, while looking through all the bright bits of cloth filling the basket she gave me.

"You do a fine job Caroline. I am ashamed to say, I should have stopped by with the squares long before this, but with Wiley away we have more work about the place.

I help too, I endeavor to keep Mister Sutherland fit and healthy while he readies the ground to sow our crops.

"Yet, I am glad Wiley travels, his work gave him a good opportunity to visit some new places. Once he settles down, he may not have many more chances to visit and experience this big country of ours.

"I received a letter from him the other day," she continued. "He finished his work in the timber camp to the south. He might be on his way home before long. That could not happen soon enough for his Pa . . . and for me," she said, laughing.

"And how is your grandfather, Caroline? I heard he became ill during the winter."

"Yes Ma'am, Grandpa came down with the ague, his chills and fever raged for over ten days, leaving him weak. He refused to slow down until his body convinced him to rest, I feared losing him. I am thankful he feels better, now but it took him a long time to recover.

"He's working in the fields today and he left with a smile on his face. A few weeks ago, he despaired of ever getting to plow. The fields were thick mud after so many days of rain. Now, it seemed like spring has arrived, a big relief for both of us."

"You are right, Caroline. Mister Sutherland fretted and fretted. After a few days of that, our son William sat him down, and together they planned the spring plowing and sowing. That did a lot to relieve Andrew's mind.

"Once William got Andrew to accept the fact of the weather, they played a few rousing games of chess, and ended by taking their guns and the dog on a hunt. They brought home a fine buck. We welcomed the meat we have many mouths to feed in our compound."

"Our other sons, Hammond and James, worked jobs in town this winter, so much of the time, it was just William and Andrew on the land with the families living close around us.

"Today has been very pleasant Caroline, but I should return home and prepare Andrew's supper. He will be in from the fields soon, and expects to find a hot meal on the table."

"I wish you could stay a little longer, Ma'am. I have enjoyed visiting with you. Please let me wrap up the rest of the sweetbread to take to Mister Sutherland for his supper."

"Why thank you for your kindness, Caroline. This is delicious, and Mister Sutherland likes a little something sweet with his coffee. I won't stay, but I promise to return again before long. Please visit us too. Perhaps Wiley will bring you when he returns."

I stood in the doorway waving good bye, and watched until her buggy drove out of sight along the lane leading to the pike.

What a pleasant and enjoyable visit, I thought. *And yes, she still reminded me of Ma.*

Somehow, I wondered if her eyes deceived her. I knew I was not beautiful. I saw the truth myself in Gramma's mirror. And today I wore my housedress and work apron, rather than an elaborate costume as I wore at the academy when I made high tea for the young ladies. I felt embarrassed at my appearance, but she made me feel pretty. I loved Mrs. Sutherland!

The next day after our noon dinner, I washed and put away the dishes, pulled out a spade from the barn, and dug a little in the garden. I slowed my digging after a while, and thought again about my visit with Mrs. Sutherland.

She didn't tell me for whom she made the quilt, and I forgot to ask. It seemed like it would take a lot of work to finish. No wonder she asked me to help. She'd told me last fall she planned to make eight wedding quilts. She mentioned Wiley wanting to settle down.

Perhaps he planned to build a cabin of his own, he would need a quilt then.

I straightened and looked over my garden patch. It was much bigger this year, I marveled as I paced it off and thought of where I wanted to plant my vegetables. It made me excited to think of planting again. My preserved food lasted us through the winter. Now, I could replenish our stores, and have even more for Grandpa to take to folks who could use it.

ONE SUNNY MORNING THE second week of April, I stood at the table kneading biscuits for our noon dinner. I heard a lot of barking and carrying on from Nellie Belle out toward the road. Her barking became frantic and came closer and closer to the house. I looked outside, and did not see anything, so grabbed the rifle and checked the load. It was up to me to defend our home while Grandpa worked in the fields.

Nellie's barking continued, on and on, then abruptly stopped. I feared the worse until she appeared at the door with the biggest bone, I'd ever seen filling her mouth. I watched from the door as a black horse rode along the lane.

Oh! No! I said, putting the rifle down on the table. I quickly took off my old work apron, pulled on my new green one, washed my face and hands, and patted at the braids pulled into a coronet on top of my head, no time for anything more.

I returned to the door as Wiley pulled up his great black horse, and pointed to the dog. "I think I finally made friends with your hound, Caroline," he said, laughing.

I laughed too, thinking, *and there he sat as if I had just dreamt him home.* A jolt of memory rushed through me, as I remembered the dream lad I once saw by the stream in the woods when I was small, and the handsome blond, blue-eyed dance master who I would never forget.

It seemed like God ordained, or maybe planned for me to care for handsome, blond, blue eyed young men, like the handsome one sitting there on his wild black stallion.

Wiley, more handsome than I remembered, his blue eyes filled with the joy of homecoming. A dark blond beard covered his cheeks, and a bright, blond mustache rode along his upper lip. He looked rugged, strong, and fit.

Yet, I saw he wore a tight bandage across his chest, and his left arm rested in a sling. I caught my breath, wondering how he'd hurt himself. Of course, I wouldn't ask. He would tell me if he wanted to.

"Good morning," he said, dismounting, as if it was only a few days since we last set eyes on one another, instead of the better part of four months.

"Morning, Wiley! How are you? Would you like to come in? I could warm the coffee for you."

"I don't mind if I do," he said with a grin on his handsome, roguish face. "Is that all the greeting I get?" He wrapped the horse's reins around the porch railing, grabbed his saddle bags, and followed me inside.

He glanced around the room, and looked puzzled for a minute. "Looks different in here somehow," he said, pulling out a chair to sit at the table. I laughed aloud, and he did not know why. It just confirmed to me what I already knew, menfolk did not notice the niceties of life.

"And what do you have here, Miss Ashbill?" He said, pointing to the rifle lying on the table. Deeply embarrassed, my face flushed as I rehung the rifle over the fireplace.

He sat, and he talked while I warmed the coffee. "I helped float a huge raft of cut timber down the river to southern Georgia. It was an exciting trip. The river was deep, swollen from all the rains, there were two of us to each raft. One used a sweep to steer the raft, and the other stood with a long pole, to push us off from running into half submerged snags.

"Once we arrived, they paid me off, and I rode southeast, through Alabama, Mississippi, and Florida. I hired on to cut timber in four or five different camps.

"I saw towns, I'd only heard about, and stopped for a few days in each one to look around. I crossed a lot of rivers, and enjoyed seeing the ocean again. You know we used to live close to the sea in North Carolina, kind of miss it.

"Found this on a beach in Florida. It looked pretty, and reminded me of you. He pulled out a large, white and pink sea shell from his saddle bag, and gave it to me

I couldn't say anything. It was heavy, and glistened with layers of colors. I traced the whorls, swirls, and spires of white and pink around the shell, and up to the elaborately carved spiral top.

"Turn it over Caroline it's pretty inside."

I held my breath again, as I turned to see more pink swirling loveliness, and an exquisite soft pink coloring within the large outer lip of the shell.

"Do you like it?"

"Oh Wiley! Yes! I can never thank you enough for this wonderful gift, I will keep it forever!"

"I thought you'd like it, Caroline. I believe they call it a conch shell! If you hold it to your ear, you can hear the ocean!"

"It is beautiful, I have always wanted a seashell. It reminds me of my time at the ocean with Grandpa when I was 11 and a half. We spent four wonderful days there. I always regretted not bringing back any sea shells. But Grandpa packed us up, and began to ride off without me because, I refused to leave!"

"Guess I should have brought you more. But I didn't know. I left for Georgia right after that. Rode straight through, and signed a contract to work for a few weeks in a camp there before coming back home.

One day when I was working, my ax struck the tree it glanced off the trunk, and the axe buried itself up to the hilt in a nearby branch, tearing it off sharp-like, and cut my chest and arm. Not bad though, only a few stitches, and it's healing up pretty well. That's why I come home early, couldn't work anymore for a while."

I placed the beautiful seashell on the fireplace mantle next to Wiley's portrait where I could see it.

"Glad you are home." I replied, filling his cup with coffee.

I returned to stand by the bowl to finish kneading the biscuit dough for our dinner, relief coursed through my body. I couldn't stop eyeing the bandage, and the sling. It seemed to me like a fair-sized bandage for just a few stitches. I wondered how badly he'd hurt himself, just like him to pass it off as nothing.

I did not want him to see my deep concern, so I just kept kneading and over kneading the pile of dough. I knew they would be the driest and hardest biscuits I had ever made.

"The least you can say is you missed me, Caroline, or that you're sorry I got hurt." He grinned, reaching over to still my hands.

"There's something I want to say to you, Gal," he said, getting up from his chair and coming around the table.

Well here, it comes, I thought, *back to the old marrying question. This time, I believed I was ready for it.*

The spirit inside me lit up a little at the thought! I hoped my smile offered him a mite of encouragement.

"Caroline, all the while I traveled, I thought about you and me, and the kind of life I wanted us to have. I want to build us a cabin in the family compound. You'd like living there with Ma and the family," he said, making me look him in the eye.

"Now, don't say a word, Gal, just let me finish. I love you! I want to marry you! I want to do it as fast as we can. We've wasted enough time. I want you to be my wife, and that's that! So, what do you say? Caroline?"

I paused a second, then nodded. "All right, Wiley!" I said, in a quiet voice, feeling shy, and not wanting to meet his eye. Then, I came to myself.

"But you need to talk to Grandpa about it before you get too far ahead of yourself, Wiley John Sutherland. "If he says we can go ahead and marry, I would need time to get ready, and I must tell you something else."

I paused, looking down at the dough sitting there in the pan, beginning to rise a little. I wanted to knead the dough again, to stall before the rest of my say. Yet, it seemed like Wiley knew, for he kept ahold of my hand, not letting me go.

I glanced up at him and then plunged ahead. "Yes, I would enjoy living close to your family, but I'm not leaving Grandpa! If you marry me, you'll live here with us. He needs care. He won't say so, and he won't admit to it, but he does."

My little speech seemed to set him back some. First, I guess he thought he would have to cajole me into marrying him, maybe that was why he told me the good plans he made for us.

He said nothing right away, just looked at me as if he wasn't sure he heard me right. He frowned, his eyes scrunched up, and then a smile broke across his face.

While he'd been away, I'd thought and prayed about everything for a long spell. The fact, Cherokee or not, God sent me a good man. He earned a fine living timbering. He seemed like a hard worker, and he could help Grandpa on the farm. I liked his family, and I loved his mother almost as much as I loved my own ma.

I finally admitted it, though it took me a long while. I loved the man, more than I ever thought I could love another human being, more than my folks and Grandpa, even though I'd known them longer.

All these good things, wrapped up together finally decided me about taking on a husband. Yet, I wanted to stay here in my home. The home I yearned to come back to for so many years, and Grandpa needed me to take care of him, so I prayed.

I believe God answered my prayer about Wiley. He gave me a hope and a future, as it says in the book of Jeremiah, in the Bible.

Wiley, bent down, and kissed me again like he did last fall. My spirit lifted and soared. Then, I wrapped my arms around the waist of that big galoot, and gave him a kiss of my own!

"Whooee," he hollered, holding me in his arms. "We've sealed it! Get yourself ready as fast as you can, Honey, we're having us a wedding!"

Don't miss out!

Visit the website below and you can sign up to receive emails whenever Linda Rynell Kristof publishes a new book. There's no charge and no obligation.

https://books2read.com/r/B-A-WLOSC-JELGF

About the Author

Linda grew up near the Pacific Ocean. Her natural curiosity and spirit of adventure led to her active, spontaneous lifestyle, while extensive world travel fed her fascination for historical and biblical research.

A great love of God, family, and friends, and an affinity for reading and writing have uniquely shaped Linda as an author and writer of Christian historical fiction. Cherokee: Left Behind is the culmination of Linda's study of the travesty known as "The Trail of Tears."

Linda and her husband Steven currently live in the country, close to a charming town that closely resembles "Mayberry." They have two grown children and five grandchildren, who delight up their lives.